MW00884422

THE FINE ART OF
LOSING CONTROL
ASHLEY SHEPHERD

THE FINE ART OF LOSING CONTROL

ASHLEY SHEPHERD

Cover art: Jasmina Jovanovic

For my mother

Sorry this isn't the bodice-ripping historic romance with wayward dukes impersonating pirates that you requested.

1

When the plane starts to shake, Daphne makes sure to document her final moments with a selfie. She has the same chronic fear of being forgotten that I imagine all narcissistic social media stars have. If this is it, she's not going down without a tweet. Peace sign in hand and dog filter on face, she sends one last message to her 4,981,943 followers: #crashlanding.

I have the opposite of whatever the chronic fear of being forgotten is. I want to be deleted. I want to be swallowed by a black hole. I want to disappear into an endless abyss. Unlike Daphne, I'm less inclined to upload my impending death onto the internet. My boobs are already floating around there. Death seems dull in comparison. Besides, how am I supposed to sum up this moment in 240 characters or less? My mother doesn't even know I'm going to New Zealand. An explanation warrants more than a few acronyms and emojis.

I decide this is a blessing. I no longer need to worry about the *Foundations of Western Art* class I failed or my roommate hating me. My ex-boyfriend sending a naked picture of me to his debate team? Don't need to worry about that either. My mom and stepdad starting a family? Definitely don't need to worry about that. I'll be replaced in no time. Sure, Mom might be sad for a while, but the new baby will mend her broken heart. She'll have her perfect little family while I'm nothing but a misplaced memory.

I especially don't need to worry about not meeting my father. Because, really, he never wanted to meet me at all. Now I'll have the opportunity to haunt him. I hope he scares easily. I hope I make him cry.

But when the captain comes over the speakers and reassures everyone that we'll be okay, I decide I have the worst luck ever. I failed my *Foundations of Western Art* class. My roommate hates me. My ex-boyfriend sent a naked picture of me to his entire debate team. My mom's having a baby. I'm in New Zealand. And I'm going to find my father.

Holy shit.

2

The Christchurch Airport is so loud that I can barely hear the woman over the intercom telling people to stay calm. I'm not surprised that an emergency landing has shaken everyone's nerves. Looking death that closely in the eyes was enough to scare the life right back into us.

Well, *most* of us.

Some fellow passengers are put off by the sudden delay.

Myself included.

Had we stayed on track, the flight was supposed to land in Queenstown at seven, but the torrential downpours and high winds led to our turbulent landing in Christchurch before sunrise. Before we got off the plane, the pilot and stewardesses vowed to get us to our destination as soon as possible. But their words held little promise to the tour group of crotchety seniors who, like me, didn't fare well with change. They were shouting about complimentary vouchers before the seatbelt signs were turned off.

I consider taking a seat and waiting patiently like the flight attendants instructed us to do for all of two seconds.

I'm in panic mode, shaking with rage, fear, and doubt. This is not part of the plan.

"You don't understand," I tell the woman—Sefina, her name tag read—who has been listening very patiently and probably does understand, but can't do much because of the weather. "I'm not supposed to be here."

"Yes, ma'am, I know that," she says for the third time. "None of us are supposed to be here. We'll get to Queenstown as soon as the rain lets up."

"But I need to be there *now*! I'm meeting my father tomorrow. For the first time. *Ever*. I need to get a hotel. I need to take a shower. I need to rehearse the speech I wrote during my finals week. It's very long winded and a little irrational, but it sums up nineteen years of abandonment issues beautifully."

"Ma'am—"

"He had the *nerve* to come to *my* school under the *guise* of a *scholarship* offer. Who does that? I don't want anything from him, let alone his money! Where was he when I was born? Where was he when I got stung by a bee and almost died? Where was he when I graduated high school? I'll tell you where he was! He was *here* not being a father."

"Ma'am—"

"And I should have said this to him a month ago. I should have said this to him when he was in LA setting up a scholarship in my name for a college degree that I'm probably not good enough to get, but I didn't—*I couldn't*. Because he never showed up. The art department had an exhibit honoring him and he didn't show up. Who does that? Who flies across the world to give their estranged daughter a scholarship and then blows off the people who flew him there? How selfish can one person be?"

"I'm sorry, ma'am—"

"But I'm not letting him off that easily! Nope! Not me!

Hell hath no fury like Willa Loveridge scorned! Because you know what? Everything else in my life has gone wrong! I'm really bad at college. My ex-boyfriend is the biggest asshole in the world. My roommate locks me out of our room every weekend. My mom's having a baby. I mean, come on! Most people don't walk out of parent-teacher night with a date, and they definitely don't end up married. So I deserve for one thing to go right in my life. And this is that one thing."

"Willa—"

"I need to get to Queenstown and I need to yell at my father, so I can get back on a plane and fly to LA before I miss another class," I say, suddenly very aware that the whole terminal has gone quiet and is listening to my hysterical rant. "I failed last semester. The professor hates me. He'll fail me again if I'm not there."

I'm not sure who I'm trying to fool. This isn't me. The scene I wrote played out much better in front of a mirror. This girl—this character I created in the middle of the airport—is a figment of my imagination.

I want to shrivel up and hide.

Why did I say all of that?

In front of everyone?

I follow the rules. I'm practical. I analyze and overanalyze. I don't have a rebellious bone in my body. I'm the girl who shows up fifteen minutes early to a final exam that's not mandatory. I'm *that* girl—the one who reminds the professor we had homework. I can barely keep it together at a university that's across the country from my home. How did I expect to keep it together on a completely different continent?

"Willa, I can assure you that if you just take a seat, we'll get you to Queenstown as soon as the rain stops," Sefina says calmly.

Her words do nothing to reassure me, but I still trudge back to my seat. I think about connecting my phone to the airport's wifi to see if my mother has realized I'm gone, but I don't bother. As far as she's concerned, when I left JFK on January 9th, my final destination was LAX. I responded to her text when I landed. She knew I'd be busy with school. She won't expect to hear from me until the weekend. With her new bundle of joy on the way, she has probably long forgotten about her *other* child.

Daphne falls into the chair next to me, a grin swallowing up her face. She looks at me as if I'm the more fascinating of the two of us. She's the internet star with hair that fades from gray to white to seafoam blue in waves of curls. Like the weather, she seems to be unpredictable.

She's originally from South Africa and on her gap year, information I learned as soon as she boarded my connecting flight in Auckland. I also learned—rather quickly—that she was unbelievably chatty. She spent the entire flight complaining about her—now ex—boyfriend and the blisters she had on her feet. She claimed to be a free spirit and wasn't about to be tamed by a boy with wandering eyes (and hands), who had a penchant for wearing socks with sandals.

Most girls my age would be dying to be in my position. Daphne Purcell is kind of a big deal. But I don't buy into the whole internet star phenomenon. To me, she's just the girl I met an hour ago, who took up the whole armrest, ate my bag of mini pretzels, and talked way too much.

"You look like you could use a drink," she says. "Or a Xanax. Maybe both."

"That's not safe," I tell her. But she's not wrong. I could really, *really* use a Xanax right now. I'm half-tempted to dig through my backpack, but I know I need to stay alert. Xanax makes me sleepy.

"Is safety really your main concern right now?"

"Considering we almost died? Yes."

Daphne hums, that mischievous grin still tugging at her lips. She seems like the type who always finds a way to get herself into trouble.

"Considering you're a twitch away from a manic episode, I suggest you take me up on my offer. I have an entire pharmacy in bag. Pick your poison. Your palms will thank me."

I shake my head and look down at my hands. Crescent moons are bruised into my palms. It's a nervous habit I've had for as long as I can remember. Maybe she's right. Maybe I am going to have an episode. Smaller mishaps have set me off before. A rescheduled test. Someone sitting at my desk. When the grocery store was out of my favorite almond milk. Those all pale in comparison to a diverted flight. If there has ever been a time for an episode, it's now.

"I'm just going to sit here and wait for the weather to clear," I tell her. "I'll get to Queenstown eventually and then I'll go home."

"I know Hollywood's calling after that award winning performance, but did you really just fly, like, thirty hours just to fly back?"

"I mean, the plan was just to find my father, so yeah," I say. "Besides, this was probably a bad idea. I think it's best I leave as soon as possible."

"I find that my bad ideas generally end up being my best ideas."

"Generally, my bad ideas are just bad."

"Of course they are with that kind of attitude! You've got to own them, Willa!"

I shrink down in my seat and hope that with enough maneuvering I'll disappear into the hood of my sweatshirt. Hopefully, Daphne will forget I'm here and I can spend the next few hours perfecting the scenario I have running through my head.

"Are you really just going to sit here and wait for the rain to tell you when you can leave?"

"All the airports are closed," I say. "I really don't have a choice."

"Of course you do." She smiles. "Come with me."

"Where?"

"To Queenstown."

"How?"

She shrugs before standing up, tossing the straps of her backpack over her shoulders. "I don't know. We'll figure it out."

She makes it sound so simple, as if changing plans is as easy as snapping her fingers. It's not. If it was, there wouldn't be a terminal full of passengers angry over a little rain.

"C'mon, Willa. If I were you, I'd be running all the way to Queenstown to tell my dad to piss off."

I sigh. "I'm sorry, but I can't."

"Alright, then I guess this is goodbye."

"I guess so," I say. "It was nice meeting you, Daphne."

"Likewise, Willa," she says. "I hope everything works out for you."

I don't know Daphne very well—or at all, really—but there's something about her that makes my stomach flop. Not in the gushy heart-eyes way it does when I watch a romcom, or when I see a display case of cheesecake, but in a desperately envious kind of way. She has a taste for adventure. Not a single care in the world. Nothing gets in her way.

I want to be like that.

In fact, my therapist told me time and time again to be

more like that. I mean, not in those exact words, but she told me that I need to get out of my comfort zone.

"Attention passengers of Flight 292 with service from Auckland to Queenstown, due to the inclement weather, all flights will be grounded until tomorrow morning. Your safety is our number one priority and we will work to get you to your destination as soon as the weather clears."

No.

No.

No.

We can't be stuck here until tomorrow. Where will I sleep? What about my toothbrush? I need to floss and change my underwear. There has to be another way. This can't be the only option.

And then I see her—a glimpse of her ocean-blue hair stirring up a hurricane-like wave. Daphne's the eye of the storm and I should get as far away from her as possible.

So, naturally, I follow her through customs despite all the red flags going off in my head. If she can find a way to get me to Queenstown tonight, I have to trust her.

I don't know what to tell the agent checking my passport when she asks why I'm here, so I force a smile and mumble something about my gap year as she stamps the page. I barely have it tucked into my backpack when I see Daphne dash towards the exit, leaving me panting as I chase after her.

I have no idea what I'm getting myself into, but I'll probably regret it.

Christchurch is damp and drizzly with howling winds that nearly have me stumbling into the street. It smells strongly of grass and soil and rain, raw and earthy in a way it never does in Brooklyn. When it storms in the city, it just magnifies the stench of sewage. It's also warm, but not overwhelmingly so. I can already feel my hair reacting to the humidity of the southern hemisphere's summer. Coupled with my oily skin and the zit that appeared mid-flight, it's obvious that New Zealand and I aren't off to a great start.

I almost lose Daphne when she darts over to the car rental kiosk. She squeezes through a group of tourists waiting in line and they glare when she hits one with her massive backpack. I wonder if she knows I'm following her and if this is her attempt to lead me astray. I'm not sure who she thinks she's dealing with. I was a Girl Scout when I was younger. I earned my trailblazing badge. I had the best sense of direction in my troop, which means I know the moves she's going to make before she even thinks about making them.

She takes a right and then disappears around a corner where an attendant is showing a family to their rental. Everyone seems friendly in a way they aren't back home. I'm pretty sure I remember being in that same position with my mother and stepfather and the rental place told us to find it ourselves.

I briefly wonder if Daphne plans to steal a car. I'm confident that I can talk her out of jumping off a bridge (something she talked about endlessly on the plane), but vehicular theft is out of my realm. I talk a good game, but definitely not good enough to convince the police not to arrest her.

And me.

Because I'd be an accessory.

I'd go to jail too.

How do I explain that to my mom?

"Why are you following me?" Daphne has her hands looped around the straps of her backpack and she's looking at me with one eyebrow cocked, a smirk lingering on her lips.

"I'm… not?"

Daphne laughs and takes a step closer to me. "You've been on me since customs."

"No, I haven't," I try.

"Willa," she laughs again. "You're like six feet tall. You're kind of hard to miss."

I frown. "I'm five-ten!"

"Which is still hard to miss." She shrugs and licks her lips, still waiting for an answer to her first question. "So why are you following me?"

I sigh. I'm not sure why I'm playing dumb.

"I need to get to Queenstown," I say. "And you said you were going bungee jumping, and I think that's dangerous."

She sputters out a laugh. The look she's shooting me suggests she thinks *I'm* the crazy one. "Well, yeah," she says. "There's always a bit of concern, but that's why they make you sign a waiver."

I'm cautious by nature. In fact, it's kind of obvious that getting on a plane to fly across the world is the most un-Willa-like thing I've ever done. The wildest I get is not bringing a sweater to the movie theater.

"You're really willing to sign your life away?" I ask.

She shrugs. "What's life without a little risk?"

"A life worth living?"

Daphne sighs and adjusts her straps once more. "C'mon, Willa, you flew to New Zealand!"

"I didn't come to jump off a bridge, that's for sure! And I definitely didn't come to die!"

"Well, neither did I!" she laughs. "What a boring vlog that would be."

"Of course. Can't forget about those likes."

"You're catching on fast." She grins. "The video of me

breaking my arm on a zipline in Costa Rica has over seven million views and almost a million likes."

I blink. Why did I ever think this was a good idea? She seems to have a death wish and I'm not sure I can stand by idly while she dabbles in her so-called adventures. I just want to get to Queenstown in one piece.

"Anyway," she says and nudges her head towards the airport exit. "I have to find a ride. You're more than welcome to come if you'd like."

"What do you mean you have to find a ride?"

She lifts her other brow. "I mean, I have to find a ride? How else would I get to Queenstown? I'm not about to walk. It's on the other end of the island."

"You're going to find a ride… with a stranger?"

"Well, not a sketchy looking one."

That goes against everything I was taught as a child. Does she not have parents to teach her those rules? A friendly dinosaur? A cast of hand puppets? Anyone?

"What's with you people from the States? You're all skeptics."

"I'm not a skeptic!"

She narrows her eyes. "You're not the first American to look at me like I've gone mental."

"I just think getting into a car with someone you don't know in a country you've never been to could potentially be very dangerous."

Daphne smirks and turns around, her hair whirling in the wind like foaming waves against the shore. "Says the girl who's following a person she very well doesn't know."

She walks away and I'm not sure if I should continue to follow her. The logical side of me says to go back to the terminal, but the foolish side doesn't want the rain to dictate when I can get to my father.

Get out of your comfort zone, Willa!

My feet are moving before I have a chance to stop them.

"It's all about trust, Willa," she says as if she knew I was going to follow. "Trust the people, but most of all, trust your gut. You'll know a bad situation when you get into one. Remove yourself from it. Move on. It's pretty simple."

"I don't think it's always that simple, Daphne."

"Hasn't failed me yet," she says, approaching a cross-walk. I'm surprised she looks both ways before crossing. "It's life, Willa. You need to have a little faith."

"And what if I don't have any?"

She glances at me over her shoulder, that mischievous smile on her lips. Her eyes are so bright and alive that I have to wonder how one person could have so much life in her.

"Then we'll have to find you some," she tells me.

Somewhere deep inside of me, I want to be like Daphne. I want her carefree spirit and her thrill for life. I want to be reckless and take chances and be brave.

There's also a small part of me that wants to make sure she doesn't get herself killed.

So when she approaches the side of the road and sticks her thumb out as cars pass by, all I can do is swallow down the knot in my throat.

"*Live a little, Willa,*" I tell myself. "*What do you have to lose?*"

3

THE VAN HITS a bump in the road and the peanuts I ate ten hours ago crawl back up my throat. I'm not very familiar with cults, but I'm pretty sure Daphne has gotten us mixed up with one. All she manages is a smile and a small shrug when I glare over at her. Her half-hearted attempt at comfort does little to reassure me. I'm still convinced we're going to die, which will be the third worst thing to happen to me today.

The first was meeting Daphne.

And the second was leaving my suitcase at the airport.

It didn't take us long to get picked up. I had my reservations when it was an old musty van that pulled over. I watched the news. I read the papers. Every red flag that had been implanted in my brain since I was a child went up as soon as *Truth* rolled down his window and *invited* us on his *journey*. I wanted to run straight back to the airport, but Daphne already accepted his very *gracious* offer and was climbing in through the back before I could stop her.

Now I'm recounting every move I learned in the self-defense class I was required to take my sophomore year of high school. If I need to, I can get Truth in a headlock or severely injure his reproductive organs in five seconds flat.

I sincerely hope it won't come to that, because I would probably cry.

I sit back and rest my head against the purple and yellow paisley print fabric that hangs along the interior of the van, taking a long and slow breath. Truth is diffusing essential oils from a contraption tapped to the dashboard. The entire van reeks of a mix of lavender, jasmine, and ylang ylang. It's supposed to be relaxing, but it leaves me with a headache and an unsettled stomach. Couple that with how uncomfortable I am from the pillow I'm sitting on, the drive is unbearable.

I have a lot of questions. Daphne doesn't share my concerns, seemingly more interested in the granola bar she's eating than why a man is driving a van full of women and children to God knows where. No one's talking. They have their faces buried in hand-bound books. Bibles? Maybe? Upon further investigation, I see the faded *Truth & Happiness* etched into the leather covers. Is this some sort of underground congregation? A denomination of something much bigger than this van? Or is it something completely new? The beginning of something more? Whatever it is, I don't buy it and I definitely don't trust it. I'm sure that Truth was just as generous and inviting to these other women before he brainwashed them into joining him on this crusade.

But the joke's on him because I'm not easily persuaded by men anymore.

"Would you like a gummy bear?" I look over at the little girl sandwiched into the small space to my left. She has mousy brown hair and a smile that seems so genuinely pure and naive to the circumstances. She can't be older than eight. "They're vegan and made of organic strawberries and beet juice."

"Um… no thank you?"

"Suit yourself," she says and pops one into her mouth. "They're delicious *and* nutritious."

"I'll take one," Daphne says from my other side, leaning over to offer the girl a smile. Once she has three of the delicious *and* nutritious vegan gummy bears in her hand, she lowers her voice to me. "When you realize how expensive it is to eat, you'll start taking advantage of the free stuff."

"I'll buy you a gourmet meal if we get out of here alive." I hiss back, my voice only loud enough for her to hear.

The entire situation has all the fixings for a network TV movie. Eight women, four children, two misfits, and one dodgy van… the script practically writes itself. There will be nightly specials. A tell-all book. Exclusive interviews with my mother, who will be so stunned to find out that her first born—who was intelligent enough to get into a top university in California—joined a cult that promised to help her find peace and happiness and all the truth about life and love and the universe. She'll briefly wonder where she went wrong, but then she'll look down at the chubby-cheeked drool monster on her lap and forget all about her bastard daughter, who was dumb enough to listen to a South African with a death wish.

"Can I ask you something?" I say quietly, looking down at the girl.

"Sure?"

"How did you end up here?"

"My mum met Truth at the park near our old house," she whispers. "He used to sleep under the slide with the squirrels."

"Oh," I say because I don't know how else to respond.

"We tried to bring one on the ferry over, but they confiscated him. I'm still sad about it," she says, popping another gummy bear into her mouth. "Truth said we'll find another one, but I don't think he'll be the same."

"Right…"

The good news—because there has to be a silver lining somewhere—is that Daphne doesn't waste a moment before she brings out her camera. She makes sure to get the perfect angle to record what could very well be the only evidence police have when the inevitable search for our bodies begins.

"Hey, guys," she whispers. "Sorry, it's been a while! The internet connection in Fiji was awful and I wasn't in Australia long enough to get anything up! Hopefully I can get this posted soon, but hiiiii! I'm in New Zealand! I made a new friend! She's afraid of her own shadow, but we're working on it! We're headed to Queenstown. I mean…" She pauses and looks over at the girl next to me. "We're going to Queenstown, right?"

"We're going to Timaru."

"Oh," she says with a shrug. "I have no idea where that is, but hopefully it's fun! Talk to you soon!" She puckers her lips and blows a kiss before ending the recording.

I blink at her. Mostly because I have no idea what she's doing, but also because she has no idea *where* we're going.

"What? It's the 21st century! Have you never witnessed someone vlogging before?"

"No, I—"

"Everything wrong with this world is manufactured into that device," Truth says from the driver's seat, glancing back at us in the rearview.

"Sorry?" Daphne's face puckers like the gummy she ate was sour.

"This society is so dependent on technology and being in the know," he explains. "Do you ever wonder what it would feel like to be completely disconnected? To just be in-tune with Mother Earth?"

"I'm plenty in tune with Mother Earth," Daphne replies. "I'm also in-tune with what the lead singer of my favorite band ate for dinner! The internet is beautiful and sushi is delicious."

"They've made you believe that," he tells her. "They've made you become a slave to the media! You're controlled by billion dollar corporations who see you as nothing more than a pawn to manipulate into buying into their greed! They're turning your beautiful mind into mush."

On a *very* small scale, I see his point. We are far too dependent on technology and social media. It's not just about airing our own dirty laundry; it's also about sticking our noses into others. My mother couldn't wait to post a photo of her sonogram, adding a few quirky emojis and a "*Coming May 2019*" caption. She got over a hundred likes in fifteen minutes. She went on and on about how excited everyone was for *our* newest addition.

But on a much larger scale, I think Truth is a complete and total wacko.

"He's right, y'know?" the woman sitting across from us says. She mentioned her name was Celia or Cecilia. I can't remember which. "Truth can save you and *the truth* will set you free."

"I don't need saving," Daphne says pointedly.

"Everyone needs saving," Truth replies. "When we get to Timaru, we can have a ritual cleansing ceremony. We'll destroy all traces of technology and give your souls back to Mother Earth and then pray for forgiveness. It'll be your rebirth."

"We've all had them," Celia/Cecilia adds. "It's so liberating."

"We can teach you the readings of *Truth & Happiness* and the way of life."

Daphne, who seemed to be up for anything just a few hours ago, looks over at me with fear in her eyes.

"*Finally*," I think. She's coming to her senses.

"I'm a pretty open-minded person," she whispers into my ear, "but we're getting the hell away from these people as soon as possible."

"Do ritual cleansing ceremonies not meet your criteria for adventure?" I ask.

She glares at me as the van hits another bump, jostling our shoulders together. We spend the next three hours trying to drown out the sounds of their religious chants and their desperate attempts at converting us. They're wasting their energy. Daphne and I are beyond help. And *Truth & Happiness* is not going to set us free.

It's dark and dreary when we pull up to a farm. As Truth haggles the price of soybean biofuel with a burly man with a farmer's tan and two full sleeves of tattoos, Daphne and I make a run for it. With our backpacks and rain soaked clothes, we're a sight to be seen, but we keep running despite the calls for us to come back. I'm pretty sure I forgot to zip my bag back up and things are spilling out behind me, but all the truth and happiness in the world isn't enough for me to look back.

"Well, that was fun." Daphne is struggling to catch her breath, letting out a wheezy cough as she looks over at me. She's all adrenaline with a touch of fear. She never stops smiling.

"I'm sorry?" I stammer, bewildered by her entire outlook on life. "You thought that was fun? Were you not just telling me—I don't know, two hours ago—that we had to figure out a way to get rid of them?"

"Yeah, but it was still fun." She shrugs, tugging on the straps of her backpack. "It's all part of the adventure, Willa."

"I don't want an adventure! I want to get to Queenstown!"

Daphne lets out an exasperated sigh and she stops on the side of the road to look at me. "I thought we established that you need to chill."

"That was before I was almost cleansed into a cult!"

"You can't let one little wrong turn scare you."

"It's been nothing but wrong turns since we landed! And if you recall, we almost died in an airplane. Bad things happen in threes! We're already up to two!"

"You can't live your life in fear, Willa," she tells me, shaking her head as she starts walking. "Honestly, if I've learned anything in the past few years, it's that you've got to live with no regrets. Do you know all the fun I *wouldn't* have had if I stopped to let myself be scared? You've just got to do it! Rip the band aid off! Seize the moment! *Live*!"

"Your version of living comes with an extremely high chance of *dying*."

She smiles at me. "I'm still breathing, aren't I?"

"Barely."

"C'mon, channel all those raging daddy issues into something productive! Preferably something that makes you a little less uptight."

Everything inside of me is screaming not to follow her, but I don't have many choices—at least, not until we reach civilization. I'll find a phone or get an internet connection.

I have enough money in my account to get a bus ticket. I'll be fine. That's what I have to keep telling myself.

I still can't shake the feeling in my stomach, a bundle of nerves growing with each step. New Zealand is as much a part of my story as New York—a prologue of sorts. It's where my mom lived. Where my parents met. Where my story began. I thought I'd feel the same way I did after I stepped off the runway at JFK after the semester from hell—I thought this would feel like I was coming home. But New Zealand is as foreign to me as my father is.

This was my mother's past. New York was her future.

She told me once that I was the only souvenir she needed. I liked the sound of it at the time, but now I wonder if those words held any truth. I'm a memento from her past. A keepsake. A novelty that wore off as soon as she saw into her future. With her present having all the makings of a romantic comedy, I wouldn't be surprised if she sells off our memories at a sidewalk sale to make room for her new life—her new baby. She doesn't need me anymore. I'm just a reminder of a place she left behind.

I wondered for a long time if my father thought of me that way too—if I was just some dusty reminder of a mistake he made at eighteen. I wondered if he thought of me at all. If he ever picked up the phone. Or if he ever put postage on a letter. I wondered if I crossed his mind at all. I came to terms with the fact that I didn't. That I was nothing to him. That I was just unwanted and unplanned. A mistake.

But now… now I don't know. Who drops an eighty-five thousand dollar scholarship on a mistake? Who flies across the world to do it in person? Who doesn't have the guts to stick around long enough to face that *mistake*? To answer her question? Her *one* question.

Why?

Why now?

Why not nineteen years ago?

Why not when he let my mother move me across the world?

Why?

"So," Daphne starts, a few drops of rain splattering across her cheeks as she glances up at me under the hood of her jacket. "Does the fact that you're still following me mean you're still up for the adventure?"

"No," I say, reaching behind my shoulder to secure the zip on my backpack. "It means I need to find a wifi signal."

"Come on, Willa! I got us this far! I can get us to Queenstown. You just have to trust me."

"I don't know you," I scoff. "I definitely don't trust you."

"Okay, fair enough," she says with a nod. "I'd tell you to google me, but we're a bit restricted right now, and my Wikipedia page says I have a foot fetish, which is a fucking lie, so! My name is Daphne. I was born in Johannesburg, but moved to England when I was ten. My mother is Nigerian and my father is Welsh. I have a younger sister and two older brothers. I'm twenty! I'm an Aries! I've broken seven bones, including two toes! Not a huge fan of bananas. I'm terrified of hermit crabs. I know it seems silly, but I was traumatized as a child. Older brothers *suck*. Oh, I love a good green curry! And I have a massive sweet tooth! I've never seen *Grease*. It's been, like, twenty years and I'm still upset Rachel got off the plane. I don't drink coffee. I've got a scar on my bum from a ski accident in Switzerland. I think I'm hilarious and despite being virtually tone-deaf, I think I have the voice of an angel."

Daphne says so much at once—without stopping for a breath—that my head is spinning by the time she finishes. What planet did she come from?

"That's about all you need to know." She grins. "What about you? Your mum got knocked up, yeah? Your boyfriend's an asshole? You're looking for your dad? What's your favorite color? Cup half-full or half-empty? Do you have any allergies? Where were you when you found out One Direction was taking a break?"

"Uh…" I swallow and figure she isn't going to let up until I answer. "Yes. Yes. I was going to. Yellow. Half-empty. Bees. I don't know?"

"How do you not know?" she gasps. "Everyone knows! I was sitting in an airport in Guadalajara. I was *devastated*."

She goes on to tell me just how devastated as we navigate ourselves down the long road that leads into a town. Aside from a few wayward cows, there isn't much scenery. Everything is brown from the southern hemisphere's summer sun. At least the miles and miles of fields will benefit from the rain. God knows my hair won't.

The sun is still hidden underneath a blanket of gray clouds when we enter the city center. *Timaru*, the welcome sign reads. With the added scent of salt in the air, I notice that life is breathed back into the landscape. Everything is greener and in bloom, a massive contrast from the snow-filled streets I left back home.

Daphne decides it's time for me to make good on the gourmet meal I offered her in the van. For a rainy Sunday afternoon, the high street is buzzing and we quickly realize we won't be getting anything much more gourmet than a small cafe. The menu posted outside is limited, but they boast free wifi. That alone is enough for us to pull open the door.

The Noisy Fox is bustling, nearly filled to the brim with customers, who are all busy chatting as baristas call off names and numbers of the orders that line the bar. Daphne manages to snag a seat in the corner by the window, which leaves me with the daunting task of ordering our meals. Something about being lost in a foreign country suppresses my appetite, but I still request a flat white and a bowl of muesli with toasted macadamia nuts. Daphne wants a burger, as rare as they'll make it, to get the bad taste of *Truth* out of her mouth.

"Good news," Daphne says after I put our tray on the table. "Queenstown is only, like, four hours away. I told you I'd get us there."

"I'll believe it when I see it," I say as I sit down.

Daphne wastes no time shoving her phone in my face, my nose leaving a smudge on her screen. I'm crosseyed and snarling when I grab it out of her hand to examine the map. The blue line that zigzags down the east coast and then across the island to the west confirms what Daphne said. Queenstown is four hours and one minute away. My stomach bottoms out.

"I think you owe me an apology," she decides, shoving her burger into her mouth.

"I think you owe me the common decency of chewing with your mouth closed." I stir a packet of sugar into my coffee and then another and then another. "You're British. Where are your manners?"

"Must have left them with my crown at the palace," she scoffs. "What kind of Americanized version of England do you think I live in? I'm not weekending in Windsor with Meghan and Harry. I'm vomiting two-for-one pints into bins in Hackney wearing last night's makeup and no shoes."

I blink. "I can't believe the internet thinks that sort of ideology warrants four million followers."

"The camera's not always rolling, Willa," she says. "But I do pride myself on being open and honest and unapologetically me. I'm not trying to be a role model. I just want to have fun and be Daphne."

"But don't you have a sense of responsibility to these people?"

She shrugs. "I'm not their parent. That's who should be having a conversation with them. If you can't educate your own children, don't expect me to. I'm not gonna hold your hand through life. I'm gonna tell you how it is."

"Right." I take a sip of coffee. "What about the kids who don't have a parent they can talk to?"

Daphne sighs, her elbows smacking against the table. "You're killing my buzz."

"You have a buzz?"

"You're vastly underestimating what a good burger can do to a woman."

I spoon some muesli into my mouth. I could push the conversion. I could make another point—that kids don't always tell their parents what's on the internet and that trust and communication aren't always there, but I don't. Daphne exhausts me. I'm reconsidering ever wanting to be like her. I would need a permanent caffeine drip. Plus, my guilt complex would never let me live with Daphne's lack of conscience. The only thing we have in common is our non role model status.

I have naked pictures.

Daphne is perpetually drunk.

We're a parent's worst nightmare.

"So your dad." Daphne drags a fry through a glob on mayonnaise and pops it in her mouth like it's not the most disgusting thing ever. "What's up with him? He's loaded, right? You said he gave you a scholarship. Is he an artist, or something? Didn't you mention an exhibit? Or did I misunderstand your award winning performance?"

I roll my eyes. "The details aren't really important."

"Of course they are," she says. "The details are the most important part of the story. The details *are* the story."

"I'm more of an ending fan."

"An ending isn't satisfying without the nitty-gritty and the happily-ever-after."

"Not everyone *gets* a happily-ever-after."

"What kind of depressing shit are you reading? Life's too short for disappointing endings. That's why I don't read books written by men."

"What?"

"They're generally disappointing," she says. "And pretentious."

"Men or the books?"

"Both."

I hum.

Maybe we have more in common than I thought.

"So who's your dad?"

I sigh. "Benji Atkins."

His name leaves a sour taste in my mouth, but Daphne's eyes light up like I just told her she won a million dollars. I don't tell many people who he is, but I figure this would be the reaction I'd get.

Yes, my father is Benji Atkins. Yes, *that* Benji Atkins. The elusive hermit of a painter whose works sell for seven figures. Yes, *the* Benji Atkins. The quiet yet disgruntled photographer who sued a major film production company —and won—for using one of his prints in a movie that starred an actor he didn't like. Yes, *that* Benji Atkins is my father. He has battled movie studio executives and filthy rich lawyers and art critics, yet he couldn't be bothered to introduce himself to his daughter before dropping a pocketful of cash on her education.

That's my father.

I'm the luckiest!

"Wait. Seriously?" Daphne practically throws herself over the table, her eyes sparkling with wonder. "Benji Atkins is your dad?"

"It's not something I like to think about."

"He's, like, a big deal, Willa!"

"More like a big disappointment," I say, slumping into my seat. "And honestly, I just want to tell him that so I can leave and go back to school. I'll beg my professor not to fail me again, cross my fingers my roommate didn't burn all my things, and get on with my life."

"And what? You'll just pretend like this didn't happen?"

I shrug. "I'm pretty good at that."

"So what are you going to tell your mum?"

"Nothing," I say, spooning more muesli into my mouth. "I'm pretty good at that too."

"Willa—"

"She's too busy with her little love goblin and dorky husband to care where I am or what I'm doing."

"That's a lie."

"It's really not."

I pull out my laptop from my bag, hoping that will stop the endless string of questions and the impending lecture. I need to check my email and find a bus to Queenstown before Daphne gets another crazy idea.

But when I open my inbox and see that daunting red circle with a bold twenty-four stamped on it, it takes everything in me not to close it out.

From: **Oscar Mendez** (AHIS 120-02: Expectations)
From: **Kiwi Air** (Feedback on your flight!)
From: **Lyla Flores** (Stop ignoring my texts! Stay at mine tonight!)
From: **Oscar Mendez** (AHIS 120-02: Class Material)
From: **Oscar Mendez** (AHIS 120-02: Course Syllabus)

From: **Delia Sprigs** (Saturday nights too)
From: **Delia Sprigs** (You can't stay in the room Thursday nights)
From: **Mason Stueck** (Baby Im sorry xx)

And right there at the top is an email from the last person I want to hear from.

From: **Ana Loveridge-Herrera** (Nursery ideas! Moving your room? xoxo)

We live in a three bedroom townhouse in Brooklyn. It isn't anything luxurious, but it's nice and easily affordable for two people living off the salaries of a private school biology teacher and a partner at a publicity firm. Considering our third bedroom is a joint office for my mom and stepfather, I'm not sure where my room is moving to. Mom probably bought a tent to pitch on the front stoop. I wonder who's going to break the news to the stray cat who usually sleeps there.

I don't bother opening the email. I send it straight to the trash along with all the messages from my professor, my roommate, and my ex. I keep the Kiwi Air one in hopes that filling out the survey will get me some sort of voucher.

Not that I have a home to fly back to, so it doesn't really matter.

And I keep the one from Lyla, my only friend at school and the girl I sit next to in group therapy.

"I can't believe your dad is Benji Atkins." Daphne is smiling and shaking her head in bemusement when I look up at her, the remains of a french fry on her lips. "I went to one of his pop-up galleries in London. He wasn't there, of course, but it was that voyeur exhibit with all those nude photos taken through keyholes, which, like sounds really violating, but it was a shoot, so y'know, it was consented. Still, beautifully creepy."

I cringe.

Naked pictures—consensual or not—are a touchy subject for me. I want the conversation dropped before I end up hyperventilating in the bathroom again. War flashbacks flood my head from when I got a call from a high school friend telling me her brother had seen a *scandalous* picture of me. I'm clenching my fists just thinking about it.

"Will you at least let me tell him how talented he is before you tear into him?"

"Daphne!"

"What? This is gonna be my only chance to talk to him! And if you get to him first, you're gonna completely ruin the mood and—oh, well, I mean, I guess I could always comfort him."

"Daphne!"

"What? He's a total dilf, Willa."

"*Daphne!* That's disgusting."

"I could be your new stepmom."

While I choke on my coffee, Daphne plans her wedding to my estranged father.

* * *

Getting to Queenstown is easier said than done. By the time we figure out how to catch the bus, we miss it, which leaves me stuck in Timaru with Daphne, who has an unquenched thirst for adventure.

"The guy at the cafe said there's a river just north of here that's great for rafting," she tells me as we walk down the street. The crowds have died down since getting dark, leaving Daphne and I alone on the sidewalks with nothing but the streetlights to guide the way. "But I don't have proper equipment for night rafting."

"Sounds dangerous."

"That's the best part." She grins.

I don't humor her with a response. Instead, I keep dragging my feet along the cobbled streets. I need to get to Queenstown. One way or another, I'm going to be at that gallery opening. I did not fly around the world and almost get abducted into a cult to not meet the man who's the reason I'm here in the first place.

"It's the eleventh of January, right?" Daphne asks me, looking down at her phone.

"Yeah, why?"

"Just trying to figure how long I have until I need to be in Auckland," she says. "My mates won't be there until the first of February, so I have plenty of time to explore before then."

Of course she sounds optimistic about that. I'd be freaking out if I had to spend three weeks alone in a foreign country. I'm freaking out just spending *hours* alone in a foreign country.

"Where are they now?"

"Oh, who knows," she laughs. "Probably just getting into Sydney, I think. Everyone was keen on a bit of surfing. We were supposed to stay there a week before we headed up to Brisbane and then eventually here. We're all meant to be going to the Rhythm & Sound Festival on the first of February."

"And you just decided to come a little early?"

Daphne shrugs, which I notice she does a lot. She's so carefree that I can see it turning into a problem. "I found out Xavier shagged this girl he met in Thailand and I was just done being around him. It's not the first time I've up and left them. I get edgy. I like to do my own thing."

"I've noticed."

I also notice that she doesn't worry, which I seem to do too much of. It's already dark and our options are limited. I'm starting to think Daphne has us walking in circles.

"Are you sure there aren't any hotels around here?"

She shrugs again. "I'm not really big on hotels. I don't mind a hostel, but hotels are just so… confining."

"Yeah, they also offer you shelter and running water and sometimes a continental breakfast."

"I went two weeks without showering once," she tells me. "Baby wipes were a godsend."

I can't remember a time when I went two days without showering. I cringe so hard at the thought that Daphne bursts into a fit of giggles.

"Oh, Jesus, Willa. We really need to loosen you up. There's a pub down the way. I'll buy you a pint."

"No, thank you," I say tightly. "I don't have time. I need to get to Queenstown. I need to find a hotel and take a shower and rehearse my speech."

"Babe, you'd be lucky to get to Queenstown tomorrow."

I groan, my shoulders slumping in defeat. I'm *exhausted*. There isn't a bone in my body that doesn't ache. And I'm pretty sure I have a blister the size of this entire island on the back on my foot. All I want is for something to go right. I deserve that after the day I've had.

"I could always find us a ride—"

"No."

"Oh, c'mon—"

"*No!*" I stress. "We've already been over this. I'm taking a bus or a taxi or a *shuttle*. I'd even take a horse and carriage! I'm done with all of your *bright* ideas."

She sighs wistfully, the wind breezing through her

turquoise hair. "Alright, then this is where we say goodbye."

"What?" I panic. "You're not going to come with me?"

"Me and my bright ideas have a lot of ground to cover," she says. "I'm not going to waste time searching for a way out of here. Sounds silly to me."

"But… where are you going to go?"

She shrugs. "Don't know. I'll figure something out. I always do."

She takes off with not much more than a wave and I'm frozen in my spot outside of a brightly lit ATM vestibule. Where am I supposed to go from here? My phone doesn't work. I have no idea where the nearest hotel is. I have directions to the bus station, but that's not going to be much help tonight. I've been stranded in the middle of Timaru by the girl who got me into this mess in the first place.

I chase after her, which seems to be a theme in this chapter of my life. She doesn't stop or slow down despite my calls. I watch her disappear around a corner with all of her airy whimsy. She's going to get herself killed. And probably me too.

Which is why I'm not surprised that I find her heading straight for another van when I turn the corner. Tonight her poison of choice comes in the form of an old, beat up, rusted camper van that doesn't look like it will start, let alone get her to where she's going. It's chipped and tattered and the missing pieces of dingy white paint gives it a polka-dotted pattern that definitely wasn't in the original design. With one windshield wiper and a window made of duct tape, it's an accident waiting to happen. I see her life flash before my eyes.

"Daphne," I say when I finally catch up to her, grabbing her arm before she can head towards the two guys sitting outside of it. "You can't get into a van with people you don't know. Do you not remember the cult? Did you not learn your lesson? Do you want to become a news headline?"

"Willa, relax." She deadpans back to me. "I've already been a news headline, and how dangerous can they be? One has a guitar and the other is reading a map. *Upside down.*"

"It's probably a trap."

"They both look genuinely confused."

"Maybe that's part of the act!"

"Maybe you're just crazy," she laughs. "Stop worrying about me."

The problem is that I can't. I'll be worrying about her the whole way to Queenstown and then the whole day I'm there. She'll to do something stupid if she doesn't have someone there to stop her.

Still, she moves towards the two guys with the same ease she did earlier with Truth. She's far too trusting. That worries me the most.

"Hey, I'm Daphne," she says sweetly, batting her eyes at the boys.

The one with the guitar glances up through the frames of his glasses, a chord strumming off his fingers as he smiles crookedly at her. He has his back against a wall, and his lanky legs sprawled along the sidewalk. He has a mop of messily coiffed blonde hair that goes brown at the roots and his flannel shirt is in desperate need of ironing. His friend is much more put together in his neatly pressed white tee and black pants.

"I'm Ollie," he says, squinting up at us. "And this is Toshiro—*Ow*!"

Ollie frowns and rubs the spot on his arm where Toshiro hit him, glaring at his friend. Daphne and I watch as Toshiro quickly scribbles something onto the top corner of the map before he shoves it back at Ollie.

"This is *Tosh*," Ollie corrects himself. "It sounds *cooler*. But I think Toshiro is pretty cool too, mate!"

Tosh rolls his eyes and looks back down at the map.

"Where are you two headed?" Daphne asks.

"Not really sure," Ollie says, strumming quietly at his guitar. "Auckland eventually. I'm meeting my mates at the Rhythm & Sound Festival and Tosh is meeting up with his boyfriend. They've never met. It's quite cute, honestly."

Tosh glares over at Ollie, writing something new on a blank corner.

"Hey!" Ollie frowns. "I'm not a twat! That's rude! Do your fans know you've got such a fowl vocabulary?"

"Fans?" Daphne asks.

"He's an actor," Ollie explains.

Daphne looks puzzled for a moment, but then a lightbulb goes off and her eyes bug out of her head. "Oh my god! I saw your billboard in Tokyo! What the hell are you doing here?"

"It's a long story," Ollie answers for him.

"Longer than him wanting to meet his boyfriend?" I ask.

"Much longer."

Daphne coughs. "I've got the time if you've got the space."

Ollie lifts a brow, seemingly curious about her proposition, and sets his guitar against the wall. "You want to come with us?"

"I've got nowhere else to be," she tells him. "I'm meeting my friends at Rhythm & Sound too."

"We don't really have a plan," he says. "We're just sort of going with the flow."

"Those are my favorite kind of plans."

Ollie looks over at me with that soft smile that's all too charming, but I'm not Daphne. I don't trust him.

"What about you?"

"Oh, this is Willa," Daphne answers for me. "She made an awful mistake by following me and is now waiting for a bus to get to Queenstown because she's ragingly boring and lacks adventure."

"That's a shame," Ollie says.

"That's what I said."

This time it's me rolling my eyes as Ollie stands up. He's barely taller than me and has a softness to him that Daphne is buying into. She's putty in his hands, which is probably part of his act. I've seen *To Catch A Predator*. I know how their minds work. Camp outside of a van. Bring out the guitar. Girls just *love* a musician. Find an unsuspecting one. Smile. Flirt. Play her favorite song. Get her in the van. Dispose of the body. Daphne will be a textbook case.

"Well, we're not really sure of a direction," Ollie says and nudges his head to the van. "We're just sort of driving, but you're more than welcome to join us."

Daphne accepts the invitation by tossing her backpack into the back of their van, her grin going wry as she looks at me. "Be sure to watch my vlogs!"

"Daphne—"

"And thanks for lunch!" she says, jumping into the back as Ollie hops into the driver's seat. Tosh opens the passenger's side and gets in. "Oh, and give your dad my number!"

I feel the nerves in my stomach grow tighter as I catch Daphne's stare for what I think is the last time. This is typical. I've known her for fourteen hours, and I can already confirm that *this* is typical. She gets the two of us into this mess, and then abandons me when it's convenient for her.

If I wasn't angry before, I definitely am now. I *refuse* to let her leave me.

She needs me just as much as I need her. She just doesn't know it yet.

"Fuck it," I say and now I'm jumping into the back of the van too. "We're going to Queenstown."

"Someone's bossy," Ollie says.

"Just drive," I say and settle in next to Daphne, who already has her camera out.

"Hey, guys!" she says to the lens. "You'll never guess what happened to me today! #storytime! I almost joined a cult!"

4

Ollie has this awful habit of playing his guitar along to every song on the radio, which is why I'm surprised when he insists that Tosh change the station as soon as a song by The Filthy Doorknobs comes on. No one ever turns off The Filthy Doorknobs. They're a staple as far as road trip sing-alongs go.

Not that I've participated in many road trip sing-alongs.

But I watch a lot of movies.

Regardless, the novelty of Ollie's serenades wear off as soon as they start. He makes sure to keep all of us awake the entire drive to Queenstown.

Our nine hour journey—because we *had* to pull over to rest—doesn't go without an icebreaker. It's bad enough in a classroom setting, but it's much worse in a small group of people in a cramped camper van. My only saving grace—and Tosh's too—is that Daphne and Ollie both like to talk, so I'm left to pick at the frayed stitching of the cushion I'm sitting on as I try not to die of boredom and exhaustion.

Ollie's from Glasgow. I don't know where in Scotland

that is, but he made a lovely little diagram of the United Kingdom just in case we ever need a reference or don't have access to a map or the internet. He has a large family that consists of a mother, a grandmother, three aunts, five sisters, and ten cousins, all of whom are female. He doesn't mind being the only boy—he added with a charming little chuckle—because he's pretty sure he's the favorite. Like Daphne, he's on his gap year and trying to wade through the throes of being a young adult with the whole world in front of him. He likes peanut butter cups and sour gummies and pineapple on his pizza. He drinks too much coffee, calls soccer *football,* and missed one day of secondary school and is now rendered useless in *maths*. He also sleeps with his socks on, which is a complete and total blasphemy and also information that I don't care to know.

He met Tosh at an airport in Jakarta when he was looking for his connecting flight to Auckland. Tosh seemed a little lost and confused, so he helped him out. Ollie's final destination had always been Queenstown, but the bad weather had also grounded their flights. They met up amidst all the chaos and confusion and Ollie invited him along on his little road trip. The rest is history.

Or, well, the rest is heavily detailed in a notebook they exchanged and what he told us was the abridged version. I'm *so* thankful.

By the time he turns to me with his lopsided smile, I'm not in the mood for his game of twenty questions.

"What about you, Boss Lady?" He grins and offers me a strum of his guitar. "Tell us about yourself."

"There's not much to know," I tell him.

"I don't think that's true."

"Because it's not," Daphne answers for me. "She's got, like, a soap opera for a life. Mum's knocked up with step-dad's kid, which doesn't seem like that big of a deal to me, but *Dramatics* over there basically thinks her life is over. And get this—her dad? The reason she's here? Yeah, he's Benji Atkins."

"Wait." Ollie pauses to look at me. "Like the artist?"

"Yeah!" Daphne says. "Like are we even a little surprised he spawned this weirdo?"

"It's probably the least surprising thing ever." he laughs.

"Right? She's got as much chill as the fiery flames of hell. She's ragingly uptight. And she could probably stand a drink or two." She pauses for a moment as if to think. "And probably a good shag."

Ollie finds Daphne's overview of my life so amusing that his face goes red from laughing. I don't find it nearly as funny, but he still puts her words to the tune of the song on the radio and sings about my lack of chill at the top of his lungs. For the next three exits, I contemplate throwing myself out the duct tape-lined window.

I'm tired and cranky with a massive headache when Tosh pulls into a parking spot in the visitor's center just outside of Queenstown. When I finally get to step outside —after sitting for far too long with Ollie's knobby knees knocking against mine—I stretch so hard that I can feel it from my fingers all the way down to the tips of my toes. I almost feel human again. All I need now is a shower, some sleep, an intravenous drip of caffeine, and I'll be good to go. Where? I'm not sure, but at least I'll feel more alive than I do right now.

"Look at all of them," Daphne squeals once we're inside, her eyes doubling in size when she sees all pamphlets advertising the attractions Queenstown has to offer. "Bungee jumping! Skydiving! Canyon swinging! Flyboarding!"

"Have you lost your mind?" I ask through a yawn.

"Honestly, Willa, we're gonna have a problem if you don't loosen the reins."

"We're going to have a really big problem if you get yourself killed."

"There's probably a bigger likelihood that I'll get hit by a bus than there is for my bungee cord snapping."

"Is that a chance you're willing to take?"

She thinks for a moment and eventually shrugs. "Fuck yeah!"

I groan and walk away before she gives me an even bigger headache.

There's plenty of things to keep me distracted. The visitor's center is full of novelty items to purchase, but I don't think anyone back home will want a keychain or a t-shirt. Mom would probably burn them both as she rants and raves about *why* I would even *think* to come here.

New Zealand—more specifically, the life she left here—is a topic we never discuss. There are a few things I did know that were found out through childhood snooping. We moved apartments a lot when I was younger. There was an endless supply of boxes to go through. The ones she kept all her secrets hidden in just happened to look like the ones I packed all my dolls in. That's where I found a book of my father's sketches.

Ollie is hopelessly flirting with a woman behind a station near the maps. She looks at least ten years older than him, but she's eating up all of his charismatic charm. All he has to do is bat his lashy blue eyes and she melts into a puddle of goo. If only she knew he sleeps with socks on and likes pineapple on his pizza.

"Thank you, Sheila," he tells her with a smile. "You've been so helpful."

She fumbles over her words and I try not to roll my eyes as I stand by the keychain display and watch them with my arms crossed. I've met plenty of Ollies in my short stint at college. In the dorms, their motives were as transparent as their glass bottles of cheap beer. I knew exactly what they were after when they knocked on someone's door at two-thirty in the morning with a sudden desire for help with homework they'd been ignoring all semester. I'm just not sure what provoked Ollie. I'm fairly certain he doesn't want to sleep with this woman.

"What's that look for?" He frowns at me, but still lifts a curious brow.

"Just admiring you in your natural habitat," I tell him, adopting one of Daphne's careless shrugs as I grab an assortment of maps. I don't trust these three to find their way out of a paper bag. "I'm surprised you didn't break out your guitar and serenade her."

Ollie's face scrunches. He seems genuinely confused as he glances back at Sheila to confirm what I'm talking about. "She was helping me find somewhere for us to stay for the night."

"Did she invite you to hers?"

"No, but she gave me directions and a voucher for a youth hostel," he explains.

"You worked really hard for it. You must be proud of yourself."

"What are you on about?"

"You were flirting with her."

"What?" He chokes out a laugh. "I was not flirting with her."

"Yes, you were," I scoff. "Honestly, at least own it."

"Are you…" He looks back one more time to make sure we're talking about the same thing. "She said I reminded her of her brother. He's gone off to Perth for university. I was just… giving her a bit of attention? She said she's been lonely since he left. Not many people come in here asking for help. She just wanted someone to talk to."

I shrink back slightly. My face warms to a shade of red that comes along with complete and total embarrassment.

"Do you always jump to conclusions?" he asks. "More importantly: do you always have such high opinions of people you've just met?"

I swallow my words, unable to force anything out before Ollie walks outside to find Daphne and Tosh. I may have failed *Foundations of Western Art*, but I passed *How to Make a Situation Go From Bad to Worse* with flying colors.

* * *

The Mountain View Youth Hostel is nestled right in the heart of Queenstown between a bike rental shop and a liquor store, which has bad news written all over it. I don't have time to dwell on just how terrible of an idea it is because when we walk in, an enthusiastic receptionist at the front desk immediately starts boasting on and on about the facilities and all of the amenities they have to offer.

Luggage storage!

For the luggage I don't have!

Internet access!

To ignore more emails!

Private ensuites!

So I can cry without interruption!

Balconies!

Perfect for flinging myself off of.

I'm sold. It's perfect. I want all of it. Who cares about drunks riding bikes? Not me! I want a wifi password and a shower.

So when I shove my debit card at the girl and she simply giggles and twirls her hair and tells us that it's peak season and most rooms have been booked months in advance, I almost start crying.

But Daphne steps in with all of her whimsy and charm and social media megastar status and she manages to get us a room. And when my card declines and I *actually* start crying, Daphne swoops in and saves the day again. I have 4,981,943 reasons to thank her.

Until I climb three flights of stairs with a very heavy backpack only to find the room she got us only has three beds.

It's an easy fix—at least that's what she tells me. She takes it upon herself to decide that we'll share the full bed while Tosh and Ollie take the bunks. My issue with the sleeping arrangements has more to do with wanting some time to myself. I want to be alone. I'm more than just physically exhausted; I'm mentally drained too. I need to recharge, a few hours of quiet to figure out a plan for the gallery opening, away from the group I'm somehow a part of. I have a monologue to refine and lines to rehearse. I don't want to do that in front of an audience. Not again.

"Look at that view!" Ollie gasps and drops his backpack and guitar case to the floor, one much gentler than the other.

It is a nice view, I'll give him that. Beyond the balcony of our room, we can see the rolling hills of the mountains in the distance, a billow of fog disguising the peaks. I lived in the city my whole life. The only rendezvous with nature I've had were with Central Park and that can't compete with this. They're not even on the same level.

"It's beautiful and all," Daphne starts, "but I'd much rather be one with it than stare at it."

I watch her set her backpack on a chair and then she unzips it. She digs around the bag, eventually pulling out a white t-shirt. She gives it a quick sniff and then shrugs before she takes off the shirt she's wearing. Her lack of modesty is alarming.

"Daphne!"

"What?" She furrows her brow. "Tosh is gay and Ollie is being a gentleman."

I catch Ollie out of the corner of my eye. He's making himself busy with his guitar case and is unconcerned with the fact that Daphne is standing in the middle of the room wearing a lime green bra.

"Honestly, Willa, I'm buying you a drink tonight," she says, flattening the new shirt over her torso.

"I don't need a drink. I need some sleep."

"Do you plan on wasting the day away in bed?"

"Do you not?"

Daphne laughs—a full belly one—as she crosses the strap of her purse over her shoulders. "Of course not! I've been cooped up in a car for far too long."

"You also haven't slept in, like, twenty-four hours."

She shrugs and offers a smile. "I'm good! I need to film something for my vlog!"

Without another word, I watch her disappear out of our room. I don't have the energy to follow her, but Tosh is out the door as quickly as she is. I convince myself that he's going to keep an eye on her.

Ollie hasn't made any moves to leave the room, which may unsettle me more than Daphne and her taste for adventure. After our conversation at the visitor's center, I want to be around him as little as possible.

I'm embarrassed. I don't typically act that way. If anything, I'm more inclined to give people the benefit of the doubt. I try not to judge. I always considered myself a good person.

But if these last twenty-four hours have taught me anything, it's that I don't know who I am anymore. I'm making rash decisions. I'm not thinking things through. That's not normal behavior from the girl who once wasted fifty minutes of her biology final trying to decide between B or C. *On the first question.*

"You're not going out?" I ask, avoiding eye contact as I unzip my backpack.

"No," he says and I can feel him glancing back at me. "I need to get some sleep. I'll probably head out in a few hours."

I try not to pay him any attention. Instead, I grab my emergency pair of underwear and a t-shirt. I dig past a usb cable, a protein bar, and an EpiPen in search for my pill box.

It's not there.

No.

No.

No.

I wouldn't forget that, and I definitely wouldn't put it in my suitcase. I made a list. I cross-checked everything. I know I put it in there.

I silently count down from ten and try not to panic.

"Willa?"

I swallow. "So I don't have to worry about you tuning your guitar while I try to sleep?"

"Uh… no."

"Good," I say tightly, clutching my things to my chest. When I finally turn to look at him, he's crouching on the floor by his guitar case, looking up at me with a furrowed brow, like I've just been teleported here from another planet. "I'm going to take a shower."

"Okay," he says, looking away from me. "Have fun."

"I will."

What?

More importantly: *why?*

If there was ever a reason to smash my head against a wall, this is it.

Thankfully, I forget about our exchange as soon as I step into the shower. I forgot what hot water can do for the soul. And even if it's just for the moment, I take solace in watching all my troubles wash away as I scrub off the layers of dirt, grime, and *Truth* that cling to my skin. I let myself forget about my mom and my father and the fact that my house is no longer my home. I know this is just a temporary fix, but even if it's just for a few minutes, I'm going to let myself be a nineteen-year-old without a care in the world. I owe it to myself.

When I'm finished, I walk back into the room with sleep on my mind. Ollie is curled into the bottom bunk, his gangly limbs tangled together in order for him to fit on the small bed. I feel bad for all of five seconds. By the time my head hits the pillow, I'm out.

* * *

My carefree way of living lasts as long as I imagined it would, which is an hour into my nap. I had a dream that my mother moved to the suburbs without telling me. I'm not sure what's more terrifying: the thought of being abandoned by the only family I have or the thought of her living in a house with a white picket fence. The latter definitely rattles me the most. Thinking about my mother becoming a suburbanite that runs the PTA and hosts bake sales and coordinates matching outfits of pastel polos and khaki pants is traumatizing.

I've never gotten out of bed faster.

The upstairs lounge of the hostel is empty. I take up shop at a table by the window. The view is distracting. I catch myself slipping into a daydream of warm summer air that smells of pine needles and sunblock and musky-wooded forests. I'm Daphne—carefree and fearless. I take the world by storm—one adventure at a time. I rock climb and bungee jump and swim with sharks and kiss strangers. Everyone wants to be me.

I'm exhausted.

I need another nap and twelve shots of espresso.

Seven hours stand between me and telling off my father. I don't have time to go on adventures with the dreamed-up version of myself. I need to focus. My first order of business is to check why my card was declined. I'm not exactly rolling in funds, but I definitely have enough to book a night in a hostel. Thankfully, I don't have to search further than my email inbox.

From: **Tribeca National Bank** (Fraudulent Activity)

Awesome.

My purchase at the cafe in Timaru was what caused my card to get flagged. Removing it requires a trip into a branch, which is pretty much impossible at the moment. I could call my mom, but that means having to explain that the purchase wasn't fraudulent and, surprise, I actually am in New Zealand.

Shit.

That bowl of muesli definitely wasn't worth this headache.

And even though my money issue is all I want to think about, I can't. On my list of priorities, it's not at the top. My speech is my focus. It needs to be perfect. And it needs to make him cry.

And then I'll get a vile of his tears and sell it on the internet, and all my problems will be solved.

Except life's not that easy and luck has never been on

my side. It's going to take a lot more than wishful thinking for this to go remotely well. First drafts, second drafts, and third drafts aside, how am I supposed to make it through a speech—an encounter—with the man I spent my whole life resenting?

My mother didn't talk about him much, only fleeting answers to questions I asked as a child. She was quick to tell me that families came in all shapes and sizes. Some were big. Some were small. And size doesn't affect the quality of love. But, if anything, I was a persistent child and an even more persistent young adult, so once I grasped the concept of the internet, the search engine left me with limitless access to my father.

Which, funnily enough, was pretty limited.

Benji Atkins is a world renowned artist who has never done a single interview. Or spoke at a single engagement. His short stint at college left him with a handful of friends, but they're as tight-lipped as he is. I'm sure he probably threatened them into silence. Along with his family. I bet he hands out nondisclosure agreements like they're candy.

Before I can let the anger rage on, a white paper cup is held out in the empty space in front of me. *Boss Lady* is scribbled at the top in black ink. Next to it is a haphazardly drawn smiley face that looks like it had a stroke. I follow the calloused fingers wrapped around it all the way up the semi-sunburnt arm until I eventually land on Ollie's face. He was gone when I woke up from my nap. I didn't expect to see him back so soon.

"Daphne said you drink it with milk and a shit ton of sugar," he chuckles softly and pulls out a chair to take a seat.

"You didn't have to," I tell him, but that doesn't stop me from taking the cup and chugging it like caffeine is my only life source. "Where was the lovely Daphne?"

"Found her haggling some poor bloke for discounted bungee tickets."

I groan and consider dropping my head to the table, but I fear it'll worsen my headache. "And you didn't stop her?"

"I don't think she likes to be stopped," he replies, sipping his own coffee. "I also really want to go jumping, so if she can get a good price, I'm gonna take it."

I blink at him. "I think you're both crazy."

"And I think you have control issues."

My whole body tenses. "You don't even know me."

His face lights up. The sun flooding in from the window hits his eyes in a manner that sends the flecks of gold glowing. He looks smug as hell. And I know exactly why.

"I shouldn't have made that comment at the visitor's center," I finally say.

"No, you shouldn't have."

"It was rude of me."

"Yes, it was."

I narrow my eyes, annoyed with the smile pulling at his lips. "I'm trying to apologize."

"I know." He grins. "And I can see how much it's killing you to admit that you were wrong about me."

"It's not *killing* me."

"It's definitely bothering you," he muses. "I reckon you're a girl who gets off on being right."

"Who's the one making assumptions now?" I glare at him.

He laughs into his cup of coffee, nodding his head to me. "Touché."

I shoot him one last hooded glare before burying my face back into my computer. My fourth draft deserves my full attention.

"So your dad is Benji Atkins?" Ollie asks.

"Unfortunately."

"Does he know you're here?"

"Nope."

"Does he know you exist?"

"Yep."

"Ouch," he says after another sip of coffee. "World famous artist is a shitty father? Who would have guessed?"

"Spoken like someone who has a world famous artist for a father."

Ollie scoffs and his eyes shift to the window and then back to me. "So your mum's cool with this? I mean, New Zealand is an awfully long way from…"

"New York," I tell him. "And no, she doesn't know. She would kill me if she knew I was here. That's why I left from Los Angeles, where I go to school."

Ollie lets out a slow whistle as he sits back in his chair. Judging by the tight look on his face, he thinks this is as good of an idea as I once thought. "Sounds like it could be messy."

I shrug. "She's kind of busy tending to her fetal goblin, so I doubt she even knows I'm gone."

"Fetal goblin?" he laughs. "Willa, you're mental. It's a baby."

"No, it's an accident," I snap. "My mom used to go on and on about how she never wanted another kid because of how miserable she was when she was pregnant with me."

"People can change their minds. You live. You learn. You grow up."

My lip twitches and I glare at him over my laptop.

"Don't give me that look," he laughs. "You must know how ridiculous you sound."

"I don't recall asking for your opinion."

"Just trying to instill some sanity into you," he replies with a shrug. "Your mum hasn't forgotten about you. You should call her."

"So she can scream at me over the phone and demand I come home? As if I even have a place to go home to! She wants to make my room into a nursery! She wants me to sleep outside with the stray cats!"

My little outburst sends Ollie reeling with laughter while my cheeks burn so red that I think I might heave over from heatstroke.

Get a grip, Willa!

"Are we sure Daphne's the crazy one?"

"I'm not crazy," I said quietly. "I'm just looking out for myself."

"I think you're looking for excuses," he replies, sitting back in his chair. "But what do I know?"

"Exactly," I say tightly. "You don't know anything."

* * *

MY FATHER'S POP-UP GALLERY? YEAH, IT'S AT A BARBER shop. I'm terrified I'm going to walk in and see various pieces of art made of old hair clippings—giant sculptures of a muse's pubic hair, old wax removal sheets, beard trimmings strategically placed on canvas. And the worst part—because it does get worse—is that some weirdo is going to pay millions for it.

"Seriously, Willa, can't you call Daddy up and get us some VIP treatment?"

I turn to Daphne. "Please don't call him *Daddy*."

"I think we should leave it up to him to decide that."

I roll my eyes and bring my attention back to the line in front of me. As far as I can see, there's no beginning in sight. And we got here early. Or, well, I got here early.

Everyone else said I was being ridiculous to come three hours before it opened. Normally, I'd relish in being right. Rub it right in their faces. But when you have no clothes, you can't bite the hands that clothe you. I'm wearing Ollie's jeans belted with a shoelace, a striped crop-top from Daphne, and a cardigan from Tosh. Basically, I look like I just stumbled out of an indie bookstore in Brooklyn. All I need now is a hemp milk latte and a Bukowski complex.

"I gotta hand it to you, Willa," Daphne says. "I thought it would take much longer for you to get into Ollie's trousers."

I don't get a chance to respond.

"Now's definitely not the time, Daphne," Ollie says.

"Alright, but let me know when it is a good time because I have jokes for days."

It's easy to ignore Daphne when all I can focus on is the knot in my stomach. I'm nauseous. I might throw up, which would be a shame because the girl in front of me has a very cute purse.

And if I have to throw up on anyone, it should be my father.

Make some art out of that!

"Line's moving." Ollie nudges me forward. We take ten steps and then ten more and soon we're next to be let in.

"How does my lipstick look?" Daphne asks.

"Looks like lipstick." Ollie shrugs

"Ugh, don't be such a guy," she says. "I need to make a good impression."

"It's probably not the time to try to chat up Willa's dad." Ollie replies.

"You and your timing," she says. "Sometimes you just have to grab the day by its balls."

"Please don't ever use that analogy again," I say.

"What? It's not like I said I'm going to grab your dad by the—"

"FOUR MORE!" a security guard screams.

My stomach bottoms out, but before I have the chance to run, Ollie pushes me into the building.

It's now or never, Willa.

The wave of relief comes when I realize there are no sculptures made of pubes or beard clippings arranged into faces. Instead, I see eight workstations with their mirrors replaced with gold-framed canvases. The photos are black and white—before and after pictures of men and women in tent cities. They're getting haircuts. They're smiling. And laughing. Each photo comes with a caption—a name, an age, a story, a memory. It's a conversation about humanity.

"Wow," Daphne gasps. "He truly knows how to capture a moment."

I'm stunned silent. I knew tonight was going to get heavy, but I didn't expect it to be because of the artwork. And as I move further down the row, I feel it more. Not their pain, but their happiness—how they're choosing not to be victims of circumstance.

I'm not going to cry.

I'm not going to cry.

I'm not going to cry.

"Excuse me." I stop a man in a business suit. He's overdressed, so I assume he's more than just a spectator. "I'm looking for Benji Atkins."

"So is everyone else," he laughs. "Benji isn't here tonight, but I'm his curator, so I can answer any questions you have about the pieces, and if you're looking to purchase, all proceeds go directly to charity."

No.

No.

No.

This is not happening.

"It's his pop-up."

The man laughs. "Benji only attends openings if he has a good reason."

"I'm a good reason!"

"And you are?"

"Willa," I whisper. "I'm his—I'm no one."

"Sorry, Willa, but it's probably for the best," he says. "Benji isn't one to interact with fans."

Fan.

He thinks I'm a *fan*.

"Let me know if I can help you with anything else."

Yeah, you can call Benji up and tell him to get his entitled ass down here, so I can scream at him for continuing to be a raging disappointment.

But I don't say that. I bite my tongue. And I walk away.

I shouldn't be disappointed. I mean, this is the man that blew off a speaking engagement at my university. Of course he's not going to show up here. I shouldn't have expected him to.

"He's not here."

Tosh, Daphne, and Ollie all turn when they hear me.

"I'm sorry, Willa," Ollie says.

Tosh has nothing to write on, so he hugs me instead.

"We can keep looking for him," Daphne says. "This country isn't that big."

"Feels like a waste of time."

"Well, drink on it," she says.

"Drink on it?" I ask. "I don't think that's the saying."

"It's the saying when we're going to the pub!"

Because that's exactly where I want to go right now.

* * *

The Laughing Pig is the last place I expect to end up tonight. It's a pub just down the road from the barber shop and Daphne's been invited there by a group she met while exploring the city. It's a recipe for disaster and, hygienically speaking, food poisoning. I'm reaching for hand sanitizer before I get through the door.

Aesthetically speaking, it smells like stale beer and vomit. The posters that hug the walls are faded and weathered by decades. A shrine to idols of the 80s leads us down a long hallway—Monday Morning Booze, Lemon Fizz, and The Filthy Doorknobs. And if I had to guess, I'd say the floors haven't been washed since any of them had a hit single.

"Don't touch anything," I whisper, clutching the strap of my purse to my chest. "You don't know what's lurking around here."

Ollie glances back at me with a quizzical smile. "I slept by a dumpster in an alley when I was in Budapest. This place is like the *Four Seasons.*"

I cringe at the thought.

"You're from New York," he laughs. "The subway is a haven for God knows what. I think you're safe here."

I'm not naive. I know what goes down in the subway. It's why I carry hand sanitizer and don't spend my time recreationally drinking down there. It's an accident waiting to happen. Sort of like this *place.*

The atmosphere doesn't do much to stop people from coming. The small space is filled to the brim with customers demanding attention. I figure it has something to do with the fact that they advertise dollar pints.

"What are you drinking?" Ollie screams over the noise that fills the bar. What should be a simple answer completely bewilders me.

"I don't drink."

But after the night I had, I should probably start.

"You don't drink?"

"No."

"Is it a religious thing?"

"No, it's just a Willa thing," I say, hoping that's enough for him to drop it. I don't want to get into it now. Or ever, really. But I know from experience that it's never as simple as saying no. Everyone wants an explanation. And I hate that I always have to defend my choices.

"*C'mon, Willa,*" Mason said to me once. "*Stop being such a killjoy.*"

That was the first and last time I drank. I lost more than just my inhibitions that night.

"So what's your poison?"Ollie asks, nudging his head towards the bar.

"Diet Coke."

Ollie finds that amusing for some unknown reason and laughs the entire time it takes him to get the bartender's attention. He orders a pint for himself and then turns to Tosh, who slips him a piece of paper. He orders him a gin and tonic and then he orders mine.

"Try this out for size," he says and hands me a glass garnished with a lime.

I take a sip. It's flat and syrupy, but it'll do.

"Everything you hoped it would be?" he asks.

"Gotta love that aspartame. " I lift my glass to him and set off to find Daphne.

It's not much of a treasure hunt. She's sort of always there even when she's not. Her personality could swallow this whole planet like a black hole.

She stumbles over to us once she breaks through the crowd, seemingly three drinks in and sloshed out of her mind.

"Friends!" she squeals and flings her arms around me

with so much force that I stagger back and spill my entire drink. "Oops!"

"God, Daphne, how much have you had?"

She shrugs. "Dunno! Come meet my new mates! They'll cheer you up!"

She doesn't give us an option to protest, her hand—clammy with sweat—is gripped around my own, tugging me over to a table of people.

"Friends," she says, motioning to Tosh, Ollie, and me, "meet my new friends—Amir, Calla, Javier, and Cody! We're going jumping tomorrow!"

"You're going to bungee jump with a hangover?"

"I've never had a hangover in my life," Daphne says and downs the rest of her drink just for show. "I'm like a miracle! Or like… a robot! I'm a robot!"

Her manic fit of giggles is enough for my eyes to double in size. It isn't that I haven't been in this sort of situation before, it's that Drunk Daphne terrifies me more than Sober Daphne does. She already has enough courage. She doesn't need any of the liquid kind.

I'm the only one who's thinking logically. Her new friends are cheering her on as she downs another shot and Ollie is quietly amused with the whole situation as he slides into their booth to start a conversation with Amir, who might be wearing the entire country's supply of hair gel. Tosh and I slide in after him. I already know I have little in common with them, which leaves me twiddling my thumbs as I count down the minutes until it's suitable for me to leave.

"We broke into this abandoned hospital last night," Amir says candidly. "Javi read about it online, so we figured we're here, right? So why not go? Let me tell you… it was haunted as fuck! And they were not happy to see us. Pretty sure I'm going to die of supernatural causes. There was this high pitched scream when we were down by the morgue and—fuck, mate—we ran for it! Never moved that fast in my life."

Leave it to Daphne to get mixed up with a bunch of vandals.

"That's sick, mate! I would have pissed myself."

Leave it to Ollie to enjoy their company.

"Wait till you hear about the time in Thailand when we had to borrow a boat—"

"Do you mean steal?" I ask, my eyes narrowing to Amir.

"No, he said borrow," Ollie replies with a lopsided smile. "Clean your ears out, Boss Lady."

I roll my eyes as Amir starts his story about *borrowing* a boat, which suspiciously sounds like they stole it. They only returned it when they got caught by the coast guard and were forced to. In his defense—as quoted by Amir himself—they were going to leave cash at the kiosk when they got back. I don't believe him, but Ollie nods like he does.

I'm starting to think Ollie is putting on an act. Or, maybe, he's just seriously deranged. How can he like everyone? From a lonely visitor's center worker to a group of reckless kids on their gap year, Ollie finds something positive in everyone. Maybe he's the robot. That's the only reasonable explanation.

And if he for one second thinks I'm going to start breaking into abandoned hospitals and stealing boats, he has another thing coming.

My one lingering hope for humanity comes in the form of a square napkin Tosh pushes towards me. "*I think all that gel in his hair is affecting his brain.*"

I fight a smile as I glance over at Tosh. He's grinning back.

"*That's the only logical reason for wanting to disrupt a bunch of spirits,*" I write.

He laughs. "*And for stealing a boat. Daphne must already be forming ideas.*"

I groan and shoot him a pained look. "*We're all doomed if that's the case.*"

"What are you two gossiping about?" Ollie whispers, trying to sneak a glimpse at our note. I quickly place my hand over it and frown at him.

"It's private."

"Yeah, alright," he muses. "You lot of little gossips."

"We're not gossiping."

For extra emphasis, Tosh slides a new napkin over to Ollie. "*We are not gossiping.*"

"You're both shit liars," he says, taking a sip of his drink. "Didn't we just talk about you not jumping to conclusions?"

"They stole a boat," I hiss, just loud enough for him to hear.

"They *borrowed* a boat," Ollie corrects me. "And if you were listening, they also mentioned volunteering at an orphanage in Romania."

I slink back in my seat, ignoring the grin that never seems to leave his lips. He has some nerve to tell me that I get off on being right. Because he sure looks satisfied when *he's* right.

5

As it turns out, Daphne isn't safe from the dreaded hangover, thus confirming that she isn't a robot and is, in fact, an average human being like the rest of us. With half of her body thrown over the table we're crowded around, Tosh has to continually move his plate in order to save his egg yolks from strands of Daphne's turquoise hair.

"It feels like someone's jackhammering my brain," she groans.

"That's what mixing liquor will do to you," I hum, bringing my mug to my lips. I sigh at the warmth of cinnamon and sugar on my tongue.

"Shut up, Willa," she mumbles. "You only live once."

"I'm sure you wish you were dead right now."

That comment is enough for her to push herself from the table, throwing a nasty glare my way as Ollie pushes her breakfast burrito back into the space in front of her.

"Actually," she says, taking a bite, a string of melted cheese dangling from her bottom lip. "I'm quite happy to be alive!"

I roll my eyes and dig my spoon into my oatmeal,

reflecting back on how last night she was a little too happy to be alive. She was so wasted by the time we left the bar that Tosh had to throw her over his shoulder and carry her back to the hostel. She made sure to giggle the entire walk, screaming about how she was flying and how everyone could definitely see her underwear. I was happy that she passed out as soon as she was dropped on the bed. I wasn't happy that she spooned me the entire night, her face buried into my neck, her drool pooling in my hair. I learned quickly that life with Daphne wasn't glamorous. I also learned that Tosh snored—so loudly that it kept me up most of the night.

"What time did we agree to meet everyone?" Daphne asks after downing a gulp of orange juice.

"Half twelve," Ollie answers. "Which is in twenty minutes, so we really need to get going."

"Relax," she mumbles, shoving her burrito back into her mouth. "We have plenty of time."

"Not really," I add. "It takes six hours to digest food. Do you really want to jump off a bridge on a full stomach?"

"I have a stomach of steel."

"Is that why you were getting sick into a waste bin this morning?" Ollie chuckles.

"You both suck," she decides.

"I'm just saying." He shrugs, breaking off a piece of his toast. "There's a reason I went for a light breakfast."

"There's a reason I got into a van with you," Daphne starts, "and it's not because I wanted a dad. I've already got a Willa—"

"Hey!"

She ignores me. "It's because you're cute and quirky and I thought you'd be fun to be around."

"You think I'm cute?" Ollie grins. "And quirky? No

one's ever called me quirky before. Is it my hair? Or my guitar?"

"It's because you remind me of my gran."

"Oh." He frowns

"Sorry, love."

I laugh quietly to myself, my smile hidden by my coffee mug. Ollie doesn't look too impressed that I find amusement at his expense. He snarls across the table at me and I merely shrug in response before I turn my attention to my phone and the seven email notifications that I've been avoiding.

From: **Delia Sprigs** (are you gone for good?)
From: **Lyla Flores** (Missed you at group today!)
From: **Oscar Mendez** (AHIS 120-02: Room Change)
From: **Mason Stueck** (Call me!)
From: **CSU Student Accounts** (Your Tuition Summary)
From: **Ana Loveridge-Herrera** (Baby names? Too soon? So excited!!)
From: **Tribeca National Bank** (Your Account Statement is Ready)

I lock my phone without opening a single one. A headache is already setting in. I want to forget about everything that's happening back home. I'm too angry to care about anything other than the disappointment raging inside of me. I flew across the world to see my father. I wrote four drafts of a speech. And for what? Him to decide not to show up at his own gallery opening?

I stab at the oatmeal Tosh bought me and pretend Benji is the tiny raisin I squashed.

Take that, you dried up grape!

"Alright," Daphne says, sitting back in her chair. She

lets a groan slip out of her mouth before she continues. "Let's get this show on the road."

Tosh smiles and scribbles something onto a napkin, pushing it over to her.

"*You don't sound very enthused for someone about to jump off a bridge*," she reads and then narrows her eyes. "Whose side are you on, Tosh?"

He smiles sheepishly as Daphne pushes her chair back and walks out of the cafe.

* * *

ON MY LONG LIST OF FEARS, HEIGHTS HAS NEVER BEEN ONE of them. I do fine on airplanes. I have no issues with roller-coasters. Nosebleed seats at concerts aren't so bad. But standing on an expanse bridge with a river of water 150 feet below? I'm lightheaded.

What are they thinking?

"You're both going to die," I croak, my eyes bugging out as I look over at Daphne and Ollie.

"Enough with the *D* word," Daphne says, nearly throwing herself over the ledge to get a better view. "It's *gorgeous*."

"I'm glad you think so," I say, "because it's about to be your grave."

"I think it's about time you started to live a little," Daphne decides. "Because this adventure is going to be very boring for you if you don't."

Jokes on her because I'm going to book the first flight out of here as soon as I can figure out how to pay for it!

Despite having fleeting thoughts about wanting to be more like Daphne, I don't think I can commit to her thrill-seeking ways. I worry too much. I overthink every step I take, rationalizing all the consequences in my head.

Coming to New Zealand was a figurative leap of faith. I'm not about to take a literal one. Especially not after everything with Benji came crashing down. I have terrible luck.

Tosh is the only one who shares my sentiments. I like him the best.

"Let's do this!" Amir claps his hands and then rubs them together. His hair is so gelled up that I'm pretty sure it won't move for the next century.

Let's not.

My stomach feels sick and I'm not even jumping.

"You sure you don't want to come?" Daphne asks, eyeing me with her devilish smirk. "Might knock the life into you."

"Or out of me," I scoff. "I'm good."

She shrugs and grabs Ollie's hand, wrinkling her nose at him before she tugs him along the bridge. He's stumbling behind her, but looks just as excited as she does.

"They're insane," I say when it's just me and Tosh.

He instantly pulls out a notepad and pen from his back pocket. He scribbles something and then shoves it at me.

"*Maybe we're just cowards.*" I narrow my eyes to him. "Who's side are you on?"

He offers me a dimpled smile—one that I roll my eyes at. They are insane. *Certifiably.* To put their lives in the hands of a bungee cord? That's crazy. *They're* crazy. That's the only reasonable explanation. And trust me, I know crazy.

Tosh nudges me with his notebook, startling me out of my thoughts. I knock my elbow against the rail of the bridge and my heart drops into my stomach, the fear of falling consuming me. It makes him laugh.

"*You think too much,*" I read and then sigh. "I know. We all have our bad habits."

He smiles and writes something else.

"*I bite my nails*," I laugh. "Paint them and you'll quit that real fast."

Tosh laughs again before sitting down on the floor of the bridge. I'm hesitant to follow, afraid that I'll somehow manage to fall between the narrow rods of the railing. But with a deep breath, I slide to the ground next to him.

In the brochure it says that jumpers have to listen to a twenty minute safety lecture that's mandated by law. With the size of the group, I know we'll be here a while. If there was wifi, I'd use this time to figure out how to make money fast, but all I have to keep me occupied is Tosh's notebook.

"Tell me about yourself," I say. "You're an actor? Have I seen you in anything?"

Tosh swallows before picking up his pen with his left hand and jots some words onto the paper.

"*I am, but you would have to watch a lot of Korean dramas to recognize me*," I read, a smile cracking my lips. "Does that mean you're, like, super famous? Would I make a lot of money if I exploited these handwritten notes on the internet?"

"*Maybe*," Tosh writes.

"I won't," I assure him. "Unless I have to bail Daphne out of jail, which seems likely at this point."

"*You are a good friend*," he tells me.

"That might be a stretch," I say. "I barely know her."

"*It doesn't matter how long you've been friends.*"

I guess that's true. Friends I had since kindergarten dropped me the second I dropped Mason. Time really has nothing to do with friendship.

Still, I'm doing a pretty bad job at this whole friend thing. Daphne's ready to jump off a bridge. I won't be winning a *Friend of the Year* award anytime soon.

"Can I ask you a question?" I turn to Tosh and he nods. "Why aren't you comfortable speaking?"

He takes in a slow breath and starts writing.

"*I did an interview in London and the host commented whenever I said something the wrong way. The audience would laugh every time she corrected me. She even told viewers they would add subtitles,*" I read. "I'm so sorry, Tosh. She's a terrible person for doing that to you."

He smiles.

"Your English is great," I tell him. "You don't have to be afraid to speak around us. We would never make fun of you."

He nods and writes a quick *thank you*.

I glance over to where everyone will be jumping and my stomach sinks again. "I don't even have their parents' phone numbers. How are we supposed to contact them if something goes wrong?"

He laughs. I don't know why. It's a genuine concern I have. Their parents deserve to know about their children's untimely death.

Tosh nudges the notebook at me. "*Are you going to keep looking for your dad?*"

I can hear Daphne in the back of my head telling me that I came here for a reason. And she's right. It pains me to admit it, but she is. I can't run home scared. Mostly because I don't have a home to run back to. I came here to meet Benji Atkins. It would be a waste of time and money to give up now.

It's the shrill screams echoing through the canyon that eventually brings me and Tosh to our feet. When I see the body dangling off the bungee cord, my heart plummets into the river below.

"Good God," I swallow, my eyes locked on the person —Amir, I think—as they raise him back up to the platform. He's screaming and shouting, pumping his fists in the air as if taking the plunge has given him a new lease on life. I feel like I just lost ten years of mine.

Daphne's up next. Her unmistakably blue hair gives her away. I hold my breath as she turns her back to me, her heels teetering on the edge. I want to scream and cry and demand she get herself away from that ledge. But I can't.

Because after I blink, she's gone—fearlessly free-falling through the air with all the grace and dignity of a natural disaster. Nothing gets in her way and nothing survives in her wake. Daphne's the storm and there's a seventy percent chance someone's going to get swept away with the rubble.

* * *

After all is said and done, it's Ollie who's dry heaving into the street. Tosh tries to offer a helping hand by patting his back, but it's safe to say that Ollie is out of commission for the rest of the day. Daphne has eagerly taken the keys to the van, much to Ollie's dismay.

Before she starts the engine, I watch my life flash before my eyes.

It flashes again when she backs into a curb and again when she takes out a row of trash cans.

Somewhere between Ollie spewing on the side of the road and Daphne jumping into the driver's seat, she decides that we should take an excursion out to Milford Sound with Amir and friends. It's a New Zealand must-see and Daphne's so excited that there's no talking her out of it, which is how we find ourselves in a department store a few miles outside of Queenstown. Because, after all, a night in Milford Sound means we need equipment.

It also means I need clothes.

"We should be good with one tent," Daphne says as

she tosses one into the cart. "The van will sleep two comfortably, so we'll just rotate."

"I hate to break it to you, but I don't have one outdoorsy bone in my body. I wouldn't even know how to pitch a tent."

"You really need to get out of the city," she scoffs. "What kind of move is New York to Los Angeles? They're practically the same place."

"It's always 70 degrees in L.A.," I tell her. "Unless it's 105, but I'm usually back east when it's that hot."

"Still," she reasons, tossing four sleeping bags in with the tent. "You just traded one soul-sucking city for another. There must have been a better option."

"Hawaii," I laugh. "But the humidity would have been awful on my hair."

Hollywood was never my dream. I have no desire to try my hand at acting or singing. And while I have the height down, I don't have the coordination or the looks for modeling. When it all boiled down, Los Angeles was on the opposite side of the country and I needed to detach myself from the bubble I grew up in. New York was my mother's dream. It wasn't mine.

"Well, you're here now and we're going to make the most of it," she says. "We need to get you some clothes. Are those shoes comfortable? Do you have a bathing suit in your backpack? You're so pale. You'll need sunblock too —*SPF 1000*."

Daphne spends the next thirty minutes moonlighting as a reality show fashion expert. I'm suddenly her project. She doesn't listen to anything I say, only questioning my shoe size and giggling at the small size I need for a bathing suit top. Once she has an idea in her head, there's no changing it. I'm not sure whether I want to laugh or cry at the flimsy bikini she picks out for me. She smiles devilishly as she holds up the pink top as if she's trying to entice me into showing off my lack of goods. I have no interest in catching someone's eye. I have even less interest in this whole camping ordeal.

We live in the 21st century.

Camping seems ragingly archaic.

"You can keep my phone for collateral," I tell her when we get to the register. "I promise I'll pay you back. I'm keeping a list of everything."

"I'm not worried about it, Willa," she laughs. "I've got the cash to burn. Last week I got five thousand quid for making a sixty second advert for teeth whitener."

Damn, that almost makes me want to sell my soul to social media.

Almost.

Back in the van, Ollie's moaning and groaning on the small couch in the back. His guitar is resting on his chest and he's sucking on a peppermint to settle his stomach as he sings along sullenly to a song on the radio, a rather emo version of a dance hit from the 80s. I have an instant headache.

"You boys ready?" Daphne asks, hopping into the driver's seat.

"Only if you drive a bit more cautiously," Ollie says between lyrics. "I didn't get the insurance and you nearly took out a guardrail. My stomach is also in my throat and my head is spinning."

"Stop exaggerating."

"I wish I was."

I take a seat on the couch opposite of Ollie while Tosh holes up in the passenger's seat. If Daphne's GPS is right —*it's not*—we'll be in Milford Sound in three hours. After I cross check my maps with directions I found online, I decide it's going to take us closer to four. That gives me plenty of time to figure out my next step.

Well, at least, that plan sounds good in theory.

I barely get through the first bullet on my list—search the deep depths of the internet for any new information on Benji—when Ollie starts strumming haphazardly on his guitar and bellowing at the top of his lungs. I press down on my keyboard so hard that I almost break the J.

"I think you're being very dramatic." I glance at him as I set my laptop onto the cushion next to me. "Did you take acting classes back home?"

"I've got five sisters," he says. "I never needed drama lessons."

"As a woman, I can confidently say we don't act like this when we don't feel well."

"But you're bloody savages when someone nicks your lip gloss."

"Do you know how expensive lip gloss is?" Daphne's eyes flash to the rearview. "Because—let me tell you, mate—it's bloody pricey! And if some bird has the *audacity* to steal mine, you bet your arse I'm gonna be a savage! Besides, I'd put a tenner on you being right pissed if someone stole your bloody guitar."

"I'm not that attached." Ollie shrugs.

"Then stop playing it before I throw it out the window." I say.

The look of fear hidden behind Ollie's glasses is enough to assume my point has been made.

But then he starts strumming again. I bite my tongue before I can scream.

"You're driving me crazy."

"That's the point, babe."

"Don't call me that."

"Alright, sweetheart."

Because nothing else gets my point across, I whip a granola bar at him.

But after he dodges it, he continues to strum.

And for reasons unknown to me, I crack the *smallest* smile.

* * *

Milford Sound looks like what I imagine bungee jumping feels like. There's an instant rush, a gasp of air, and a sudden outbreak of goose bumps running down my arms. It's freeing, awe inspiring, and completely breathtaking. The sound of Ollie gagging into a trash can doesn't even phase me.

The sun is beaming through a cluster of marshmallow clouds, reflecting onto the lake as if some sort of god is shining a light through the gates above. It feels ominous. As if these are my final moments and I can't think of a better way to go. From the high-peaked mountains dusted with lush green trees to the crystal clear water that is eerily still, Milford Sound is everything I never realized I needed to see.

Very few places make me feel at peace. I've learned to appreciate the quiet of an empty library the same way I appreciate a deserted cafeteria on a holiday weekend. But it's the roof of my dorm where I feel most at home. The only thing that can rival Los Angeles traffic is that of New York City. It sounds like the only place I've ever known. And, in a way, it's like a security blanket. When Delia kicks me out of our room, at least I have somewhere familiar to go.

But I feel different here. I feel a sort of peace I've never felt before. I feel like I'm home. Like I belong. Like this is where I was always meant to be.

"I think I'm dying," Ollie says after he stumbles over to us.

"Quit complaining," Daphne hushes him. "You knocked your equilibrium out of whack. You'll be fine in the morning."

"The world is spinning and I'm *dying*," he insists.

"You're not dying," I say. "But you are ruining the moment."

"I'm glad everyone cares that I left my bloody stomach in a river in Queenstown."

"You knew what you were getting yourself into. You signed a waiver," I remind him.

"Yeah, I signed away my right to sue them! Not the rights to my internal organs!"

I roll my eyes. "I'm finding it hard to sympathize with someone whose rights to their internal organs aren't regularly up for debate."

"I think you just find it hard to sympathize in general." He snarls.

That's not completely true. I sympathize just fine with waitresses who deal with shitty customers, professors who teach students who don't want to learn, and bus drivers who never get thanked. But a boy who willingly flung himself off a bridge? I have no compassion and even less patience.

Tosh nudges me, breaking my train of thought with a piece of paper. "*We must start driving back to the campsite soon. These roads are quite tricky.*"

I nod and we all pile back into the van and drive to the campground.

Camping near Milford Sound is definitely not glamping at Coachella, but Rolling Creek has some impressive views and a small waterfront. There isn't much else besides some picnic tables and—*thankfully*

—bathrooms.

Javi and Cody are putting the finishing touches on a tent when we pull into the spot next to them. I cringe immediately at the empty glass bottles carelessly tossed on the ground, and I have flashbacks to the nights I had to walk back to my dorm. Frat boys have no problem spotting a pretty girl half a mile down the road and whistling unwarrantedly at them, but that trash barrel directly in front of them? It might as well not be there.

I sigh heavily once my feet touch the ground and I toss two bottles into a recycling bin with enough force to get the twos boys' attention.

"I was going to do that," Cody says with a half-hearted smile.

"Yeah," I scoff. "Sure."

Daphne bumps my shoulder when she gets out of the van, sending me a narrowed glare that I shrug off.

"Can you lighten up? This is meant to be fun."

"They have no respect for the environment."

"They said they were going to pick up," she says. "It wouldn't kill you to have faith in people."

I bite my lips together and cross my arms, resisting the urge to say something I might regret.

"Your face is going to get stuck that way," Ollie chimes into my ear.

"Someone's feeling better."

"Not really, but I can't stay away from your sunny personality," he says.

"Some might call you a glutton for punishment."

"I like to think I'm just a nice guy."

"From my experience, anyone who classifies themselves as a nice guy, is probably not a nice guy."

"Someone broke your heart, didn't they?"

I scoff and walk away. Ollie doesn't need to know the

torrid tale of my relationship with Mason. There's only so much judgement I can handle. I had to deactivate all of my social media when word got around. You can only be called a slut so many times before it starts to wear on you. I shouldn't have taken the pictures. It's my fault. I don't need my entire graduating class reminding me.

I sneak back into the van when no one's looking. I have no desire to watch Cody and Daphne shotgun beers, and there's no need for me to watch Tosh and Ollie attempt to set up a tent. Instead, I take advantage of the wifi and start my search.

Daphne wants me to loosen up, but I can't forget about why I'm here. This isn't my gap year. I'm not drunk off newfound freedom. I'm not in the market to be carefree and reckless. I want to tear my father a new one.

So far I've found reviews from showcases he did in college. There's a few pictures of him with fellow students —James Tua and Arthur Wang—and they looked comfortable enough to be friends. Even if they're not close now, they still knew him then.

I'm searching their names when a plastic cup is set down in the holder next to me. I glance at it before looking up to find Ollie sitting across from me.

"Diet Coke," he says, taking a sip from a bottle of water.

"Thanks," I mumble, looking back at my computer screen. "You're not drinking?"

"I've spent the whole day sick and nauseous. I'd rather not spend tomorrow hungover."

"That's smart," I tell him. I'm mostly happy that I won't have to deal with his moaning and groaning.

"I'm sorry about earlier," he says. "I shouldn't have made that comment."

"It's whatever."

"No, it's not whatever. I'm so—"

"Willa!" Daphne stumbles up to the van with enough force to leave it shaking as she leans in, demanding Ollie and I give her our attention. "Can you grab my camera from my purse? I need to vlog."

"You're hammered," Ollie says, lifting a brow.

"So? I'm bloody hilarious when I'm plonkered! That's some quality content!"

Any other night, I would have sided with Ollie. Those activities probably shouldn't end up on the internet. Y'know, speaking as someone who's lived the repercussions of such activities… But I have work to do and I need to do it in peace.

I pull Daphne's purse onto my lap and rummage through a few receipts, cap-less pens, a granola bar, and a handful of lip balms before my fingers slide over the cool metal of her camera. I have it in my hand when I see the orange bottle, Daphne's full name written on the label along with a whole list of side effects. It's a prescription for Oxycodone.

There are two more bottles—Xanax and Ambien.

"Willa?"

"Right," I swallow and look over at Daphne, handing her the camera. "Here you go."

I'm not nosey, but part of me wants to go back into her purse after she hurries off to film whatever shenanigans she's getting up to, but Ollie's sitting across from me and I can't. What Daphne is doing with painkillers, anxiety medication, and sleeping pills will be a question I'll have to get the answer to later.

"Who are James Tua and Arthur Wang?"

"Benji's friends from college.

"What are you going to do? Knock on their doors and ask them if they've spoken to him lately?"

I shrug. “I mean, maybe.”

“Have you considered just asking your mum?”

“That’s not really an option.”

“So you’re going to wing it?”

“I’m not winging it,” I say, waving my notebook at him. “I have a plan.”

“Would you like me to list all the flaws in that plan?”

“No, not really.”

“Okay,” he laughs. “So where are you going to start?”

I shrug again. “I don’t know. Probably with James.”

“And where does he live?”

I looked down at the piece of paper, my messy writing scrawled across the top line, barely legible. “Makarora.”

6

THE COFFEE I'm drinking has the taste and texture of mud, but I choke it down because I have no other choice. I got next to no sleep at the campsite. After losing a coin toss, I was stuck in the tent while Tosh and Ollie slept like babies in the van. Daphne was up and down and in and out every hour on the hour, but my lack of sleep wasn't all her fault. My body was adjusting to life without regularly scheduled medication—an adjustment that was meant to happen over a gradual period of time. I was already feeling the withdrawal symptoms from stopping so abruptly. High on that list was restless sleep and headaches. So when the sun went up, so did I. Daphne barely got a chance to say goodbye to her new friends before I dragged her into the van. We woke the boys up and then started our drive to Makarora.

James Tua owns the Makarora River Adventure, a small company that runs jet boat excursions. The video on his website suggests it's right up Daphne's alley, so I conveniently left out that information when I told her where we're going. From what little information I found, he's thirty-six and divorced. He uses a lot of emojis and too many puns and his hairline is receding, but he seems like a decent person who might know where my father is.

We're just outside of Queenstown when we stop for gas. Daphne has a sudden epiphany about an underwater camera, which means we're stuck in god-knows-where until she finds one. That's why I'm drinking virtual sludge on the ground outside of the gas station, burning my thighs against the pavement so I can bum wifi off the motel next door.

"This coffee is shit," Ollie mumbles, putting his paper cup down. "Like literal shit. Someone took a shit in a cup and I bought it."

I stop mid sip to cringe. I lose whatever taste I've acquired for my drink and push the cup as far away as possible. His words make my stomach churn. So does the *Boss Lady* written on the side of my cup.

"You should take up writing," I mutter. "Your analogies are very vivid and poetic."

"You think?" He looks so hopeful—like an actual ray of sunshine—and for a moment, I feel bad about what I say next.

"No! You're disgusting! I'm going to throw up on you! Thanks for that."

"Is that any way to talk to the bloke who bought you a cup of shit?"

I side-eye him. But all he manages to do is smile, and for a brief second, my lips betray me and start to smile back. I put a stop to that *real* quick, and instead I consider wrapping my hands around his neck. Unfortunately, I need to keep him alive. He may get on my last nerve, but he drives better than Tosh and Daphne. He's useful for *something*—something other than getting under my skin.

And maybe, just maybe, I find him a *little* funny.

But I'd rather drink the entire pot of this coffee than admit that.

A flood of new emails pop into my inbox when I hear the familiar ring of a video call. At first, I think it's coming from my computer, and sheer panic washes over me. My mother is notorious for calling at inconvenient times, like when I'm in class or when I'm hiding under the sheets while Delia is hooking up with her flavor of the week. I'm not prepared to explain why I'm sitting outside of a gas station in New Zealand drinking the world's *literal* shittiest cup of coffee.

But thankfully, the call is coming from Ollie's computer.

"Ollie Bear!" someone squeals. "Mum! He's answered! Get Gran and Auntie!"

"Hey, Frey," Ollie chuckles, scratching the top of his head. I glance over just in time to watch a hoard of blondes crowd into the frame. "The whole lot's there!"

"Oh, Ollie! My boy," another voice cries. It's a rosy cheeked woman who has eyes that match Ollie's—his mother, I assume. "For heaven's sake, Freya, make the bloody screen bigger! I can't see him!"

Ollie simply laughs at the commotion. "Where's Aggie?"

"It's half ten in the evening, you nutter," Freya says. "She's eight! She's sleeping."

"Wake her up." He frowns. "She's my favorite."

"Oi!" another snaps. "See if I let you bum off in my flat the next time you're in London, you little wanker!"

"Holly! Watch your mouth!" his mother shouts. "You weren't raised in a pub."

"Might as well have been," Ollie chimes. "She does love a drink."

"Oh, you two! Would you stop it," their mother laughs. "Where are you, love?"

"New Zealand," he says and turns his computer to me. Suddenly I'm faced with a group of seven very eager looking women. "This is Willa! Say hi to my family, Willa!"

I swallow. "Hi?"

"Oliver, she's a proper fitty! Are you nice to her?"

He whips the screen back around and glares. "Of course I'm nice to her, Emma! Ask if she's nice to me."

When he turns the computer back to me, my cheeks go twelve shades of red.

"Are you being nice to my baby brother?" Holly asks. "Because you don't have to be! Hit him upside the head if he's being a complete prat."

"Oi!" Ollie snaps and turns the screen to him. "I've been nothing but a gentlemen! Tell them, Willa!"

When the screen is back on me, I shrug. "If I see his guitar one more time, I'm going to smash it over his head."

"Oh, that bloody thing." His mother grimaces. "Do us all a favor! Please!"

"Honestly, Ollie," another says. "Are you trying to annoy your way into her knickers?"

"Eva!" Ollie snaps and a blush rises up his neck. "She's got a boyfriend!"

I do?

"Well," Emma says, leaning over Freya's chair, "don't go falling in love with her, Oliver. I'd hate to hear the songs you'd sing about a broken heart."

"I'm hanging up," Ollie groans. "If you don't hear from me again, it's because I've drowned myself in a sea of embarrassment."

"He's so dramatic! Someone get him a BAFTA," is the last thing Eva gets in before Ollie ends the call.

He snaps his laptop shut and pushes it away as if it's

infected with something contagious. He's still blushing. It's kind of endearing.

"You have a big family," I say because I'm not sure how else to fill the silence.

"I do." He nods.

"Your sisters—they're funny."

"Yeah, they like to take the piss out of me," he says. "Also like to kick the piss out of me. A right bunch of savages they are."

"You must have done something to provoke them."

"Why is it automatically my fault?"

"Just a hunch," I laugh. "What about your dad?"

Ollie pauses and licks his lips, diverting his stare away from me. He looks across the street at the motel and stares as if the weathered sign advertising their name is some sort of work of art, leaving him completely silent and in awe. Eventually he shrugs.

"Dunno," he says. "He left after Aggie was born."

He leaves it at that and I decide it's best not to press the subject. I return my attention back to my computer and the three tabs I have open—Makarora River Adventure, my email, and a web search of all of Daphne's medications. I'm too nervous to continue my research on the latter with Ollie so close and with Daphne and Tosh due back soon, so I click on my email and sigh.

From: **Oscar Mendez** (AHIS 120-02: Research Project)
From: **The Coffee Corner** (Latte Art Class! Earn Bonus Points!)
From: **Ana Loveridge-Herrera** (Paint swatches!!!! More nursery ideas!!!)
From: **Mason Stueck** (Babe, talk to me!)
From: **Trenton Smith** (SOC 102-01: Race and Class in Los Angeles OPEN)

From: **Vincent Herrera** (HELP! Mom's going baby CRAZY!)

I mimic Ollie and push my computer away like the infectious disease it is.

* * *

Makarora River Adventure is a ghost town. The only soul in sight is the woman in the ticket booth, who is chapters deep in a book. She doesn't look up when we approach her.

I expected more. After all, it's summer in New Zealand. With all the ads and videos I found while scouring the internet, I assumed this was a bustling business. It's not. It's on its last legs. The signs are fading. The boat anchored to the dock is rusting. Even the kiosk could use some updating.

"This place is a dump," I say.

"Don't go judging a book by its cover, love," Ollie says and wraps his arm around my shoulders, giving me a firm shake. "Could be a hidden treasure."

"Enough with the pet names."

"Whatever you say, darling."

I shrug his arm off and surge forward, startlingly the woman in the booth when I slap my hands against the warm metal counter. "Good afternoon!"

"Yes, hello!" she stammers, shutting her book and sliding it to the side. "How may I help you? Do you need directions?"

"Oh… um, no?" I say. "We want to know when the next boat ride is."

"You do?"

I blink and step back to look at the sign, making sure

we're at the right place. We are.

"Yes," I say more firmly—more confidently. "We would like four tickets."

She's so flustered by the request that she knocks her book off her side of the counter, bumbling onto her feet. Is this an unusual request? Business is slow today, but is it like this every day? Is there a reason no one wants to take a jet boat ride offered by Makarora River Adventure? Did I miss something in my searches? Some giant red flag? A review that was liked by thousands of people that all agreed that a jet boat ride here is the worst decision *ever*? Are we going to die? Is that why I didn't find anything? Are all their bodies decomposing in the river?

I clench my fists.

And count down from ten.

"Willa," Daphne nudges me, sending me stumbling into the counter. By the time I come to my senses, I notice everyone has set down their cards. "Stop looking so terrified. It's a boat ride!"

"It's a *speedboat*! We could di—"

"It's highly unlikely," she cuts me off. "Now strap on your bloody life jacket and put on your big girl knickers! This is going to be *fun*."

I want to tell her just how *not fun* this is going to be, but before I can get the words out, the cashier shouts something over her shoulder.

"Jamie! You've got some customers!"

James Tau is exactly what I was expecting.

And what I was expecting was a man with an impressive beard. It was his most notable feature in all of his promotional pictures.

"Nice beard, mate," is Ollie's brilliant opener.

James laughs, running his hand over it. It's long and

thick and peppered gray. "Yeah, I didn't like it at first, but it grew on me."

Daphne and Ollie crack up. Tosh doesn't understand. And the woman in the kiosk rolls her eyes.

"Oh, Jamie."

"C'mon, Mum, I'm funny."

"Funny, yes, that's the word," she mumbles and buries her face in her book.

"You can follow me down to the dock," James says, nudging his head to the water.

He says it so calmly—as if we aren't walking down the platform of our death—that I almost believe that it's safe. But then I see the danger warnings posted along the harbor and they're enough to make my hands clammy. It's not that I have a fear of water. I've been out to see the Statue of Liberty on countless field trips. I've taken water taxis. I've been on a dinner cruise. But none of those trips required a life vest and all the warning signs—if there were any—were practically mythical. No one has ever died on a dinner cruise.

Well, at least not to my limited knowledge.

But even if someone has died, they more likely choked than drowned, and if they did drown, there was probably alcohol involved.

"So are you all on your gap year?"

Ollie opens his mouth to answer, but Daphne quickly cuts him off. The wild glint in her eyes suggests I'm not going to like what she has to say.

"Actually," she starts, so confident and cool, "we belong to this research group that all of our universities chartered and funded, and we're going to different schools around the world to gage the access to sexual education students have."

"Oh, wow, that must be interesting," James replies.

I'm happy he doesn't see my face turn five shades redder, or the grin Ollie can't conceal.

"It's been really eye opening," Daphne explains. "And also really scary. We live in an age where teenage pregnancy is the norm and yet these kids still have no access to birth control or contraception or even a safe place to ask questions. How can we expect kids to know the dangers of unprotected sex if we're not educating them? It's more than knowing how to put on a condom. They need to learn the emotional effects too. I've spoken to so many women who've had to raise children on their own, and other men and women who've had damaging experiences. And if we can do something to help combat that, I think we need to. Sex isn't something taboo and we definitely shouldn't be shamed for it."

James has one brow raised when we stop at the boat, which is bobbing in the water and is most definitely a rusted death-trap. He smiles and nods, somehow completely sold on Daphne's fabricated story.

"That's some very important work you're doing," he says, placing one foot on the ledge of the boat to still it. "I wish I had something like that when I was a kid."

"Most adults we speak to say the same thing," she says. "We just did a panel at the University of Queenstown."

"Really? That's where I went to university."

"You don't say!" she smiles.

I sigh in relief when James steps into the boat to do some last minute preparations. I'm thankful for a moment to glare daggers into Daphne's soul.

"What?" she whispers through a smile.

"You know what!"

"That was brilliant," she says quietly. "We've just established a lead into his educational history."

"All we've established is that you're a pathological liar."

She shrugs. "I studied drama in college."

"Well, the classes paid off."

Daphne sticks her tongue out and then wriggles her nose. James is calling everyone aboard before I get a chance to push her off the dock.

"Willa should get the front," Daphne suggests as she follows Tosh into the second row.

"What?" I panic. I have my sights set on a seat that's safely in the middle.

"The front's always the best," James adds.

"Oh, no—"

"In ya go, lovey."

Ollie pushes me forward and I have no chance to protest. He takes the seat next to me, blocking me in with no way to escape. I want to kill him.

"Alright, strap in!"

The moment James hears that final seatbelt click, he taxis away from the dock. I don't have a moment to admire how blue the water is or even gaze up at the mountains that are sprouted with fresh green leaves. Once he's safely in the middle of the river, he floors the gas pedal, and I say a silent goodbye to my stomach that's now buoying by the dock.

My need for speed doesn't stretch further than a subway car. I get anxious when it pulls away from the station before I get the chance to grab ahold of something, so imagine how I feel when I'm being throttled to my death in a boat that probably isn't up to code. I instinctively grab onto the first thing I can get my hands on.

The force keeps my back glued to the seat and with each sharp turn, I feel the beginning effects of whiplash. Unlike what the ad said, there is nothing enjoyable about this. I can't breathe. My eyes won't stay open. And I'm pretty sure I'm going to throw up. How am I supposed to appreciate the "lush scenery of the Makarora River Valley" when I can't even see it?

I want a refund.

And some ginger ale and crackers.

After what feels like hours—years, even—the boat finally slows and approaches the dock.

Land.

Sweet, sweet, beautiful land!

"Holy shit," I gasp.

"You think you can get your nails out of my thigh now?" Ollie asks. "I think you pinched about twelve nerves."

I look down at my hand and blush when I see the grip I have on him.

"Sorry."

"You should be," he laughs. "I bruise easily. You probably left a mark."

I did.

The crescent moon scars mirror the ones on my palms.

James climbs over us and secures the boat to the dock. Once it's still enough, Ollie gets out first. I'm unsteady on my feet, but he offers me a hand and takes the brunt of my weight when I stumble into him.

"Look who's off balance now," he chuckles. "See if I show you any compassion."

I don't give him the satisfaction of a response. My head's all jumbled, but I can't let that get in the way of why I came here. I have questions I need answered.

"So you went to the University of Queenstown?" Daphne asks James once she's on the dock.

"From what I remember, I was there," he laughs. "Drank a little to much most days. Memory's a bit foggy."

"While we were down there, we went to a Benji Atkins exhibit. He's a Queenstown alum too."

"I think he dropped out before he got alum status."

"Did you know him?"

"Yeah, we took some art courses together. He was a cool guy. Fucking weird, but in a cool way. Didn't talk a lot, but I'm not surprised by his success. The guy's got passion."

Just not enough passion to be a father.

"Do you still talk to him?"

"Haven't seen him in about seventeen years," he laughs. "Last I heard he was living up in Auckland, but you didn't hear that from me."

Perfect.

Another dead end.

* * *

IT'S BOTTOMLESS FRIES AND DOLLAR PINTS AT *THE STICKY Cricket*, a pub across the street from where our van is parked. It's also open mic night, which Ollie is taking full advantage of. To show her support, Daphne bootlegged some merch, taking a marker to her t-shirt and writing *I ❤ Ollie Dunbar* big enough for the whole bar to see. I, however, am one Oasis cover away from smashing his guitar over his head.

"I'm telling you guys, he's gonna be a mega star."

At first I think Daphne's talking to me and I'm ready to choke on my Diet Coke. Ollie the mega star? In what dream world?

But then I notice her camera. She's vlogging to her millions of subscribers. For someone who has that sort of platform, I don't understand why she's leading them on. Giving Ollie an audience will just give him more incentive to play and that won't be good for anyone.

Especially me.

I have a perpetual headache whenever he's around.

Which is always.

"Stop lying to them, Daphne," I mumble, shoveling another handful of fries into my mouth.

She rolls her eyes. "Ignore, Willa. She's going through some things. #daddyissues! #mummyissuestoo! But she always has hand sanitizer and gum, so we keep her around. We're actually going on a little adventure trying to find her father! He's kind of famous, so I can't tell you who he is."

I tune out the rest of her speech. Instead, I find entertainment in dragging fries through ketchup. I'm trying not to think about the horrible outcome of today.

I know my search for Benji isn't going to be easy. Finding him on the first, well I guess second, try is the kind of luck I don't have. There's still a chance Arthur might know where he is, but what if he doesn't? What if I cross them both off my list? What if I go back to square one? What if this is just one giant bad idea?

"Can you at least try to smile?"

I frown. "I don't have to smile if I don't want to. There's no law that states I must be happy at all times."

"You're not happy any of the time. Don't you ever want to let go?"

"No, not really." Letting go sounds absolutely terrifying.

"Willa, you're going to live a very sad and miserable life if you don't learn to lighten up. Life's too short to be angry all the time."

"I think I have a right to be upset after today."

"Yeah, you do," she says as she takes a sip of her beer. "But you can't fester in it. So he doesn't know where your dad is. Move on to the next person! Don't dwell on what you can't change."

I stare at her with gritted teeth, watching her down the

rest of her drink before she smiles tightly at me and gets out of her seat. I watch her walk over to the stage where Ollie is finishing a song. She climbs up with no hesitations. He welcomes her with a grin.

I reach for my drink and Tosh takes this opportunity to slide me a note written on a napkin.

"*She is right*," I read. "Who's side are you on?"

He holds up one finger and then scribbles something else.

"*There are no sides. I want you to be happy*," I sigh, frowning at him. "I will be happy once I find Benji."

He grabs the napkin again.

"*You must be happy with yourself first*," I read and lift a brow. "Are you trying to get philosophical on me, Tosh?"

He laughs and goes to grab the napkin, but there's a loud tap that rings through the speakers. We both look over to the stage and see Daphne with the mic in her hand.

"I would like to dedicate this song to my new friend, Willa Loveridge," she says, winking at me. "I'm pretty sure it was written about her. It's called *Bitch*."

My jaw hits the floor when Ollie strums the first note. She's unbelievable. Not in the sense that she's *unbelievably* good—she's virtually tone deaf—but she's unbelievable in the sense that she's doing this to get a rise out of me. And I'm just stubborn enough to not give her a reaction. I sit there with my stone-cold bitch face, not showing an ounce of emotion. I even ignore the fact that Ollie is smiling so wide that his cheeks have lifted his glasses.

This isn't funny.

Not even a little bit.

In all honesty, it's rude.

And I'm going to think twice the next time we stop at a dodgy gas station and she needs hand sanitizer.

I finish off the rest of my drink by the time she hits the

final chorus. I'm so distracted by the plate of fries that I don't notice she got off the stage until she plops herself down in my lap.

I'm so not in the mood to be serenaded.

"You're ridiculous," I shout.

But Daphne doesn't care. She throws her whole self into it (and over me), singing so passionately out of tune that everyone in the pub is blocking their ears. But she's so happy and so confident. Everything I wish I could be.

And stupid, stubborn me caves in and smiles.

7

SHORTLY AFTER OLLIE gets us lost, I come to an unfortunate realization.

"I need a gas station," I say tightly. "Right now."

Ollie scoffs, digging his hand into the bag of chips he has resting between his legs. "Sure, let me just build one for you."

"I'm not kidding, Ollie," I snap and twist my legs together. "You need to turn around."

"I'm not turning around," he says, chewing and swallowing. "This is a shortcut."

"No, it's not! You're not some suave local who can just hop, skip, and jump around the backwoods of *fucking* New Zealand! You were supposed to stay straight and now we're going the wrong way and I need a gas station. There's one two miles down the road in the right direction."

"I'm telling you—"

"No, I'm telling you that I just got my period and I need a gas station right now."

"I—what? How do you even know? You're just… I

don't know..." He waves his hands around briefly before grabbing the wheel again. "*Sitting there.*"

"I mean, it's something that I've been getting for seven years, so I kind of just know." I roll my eyes. "You have, like, twelve sisters. Why does this surprise you? And I'm sure if I told any one of them that you were arguing with me over it, they would assault you with a tampon, which I very well might do if you don't *turn around.*"

Ollie's face goes still, his greasy and salty lips sealed tightly together. He pulls a u-turn that nearly flips the van over. I would have a few words of constructive criticism for him if he wasn't doing what I want.

"Fucking hell!" Daphne cries from the back. The loud thump must have been her and Tosh falling off the bed they've been sleeping on for the past two hours. "Ollie, what's the matter with you? Have you gone mental?"

"Willa's got her period," he announces, which earns him an instant glare from me. "We've got to get her to a gas station before she assaults me with a tampon."

"Kinky," Daphne says.

I slink down in my seat and cross my arms and legs, trying to remind myself that this whole trip is worth it.

Our quest to find Benji is taking us to the Marlborough region, which is a nine hour drive from Makarora. From what little info I found about Arthur Wang, he works at the local hospital and came in third in a half-marathon in 2013. His social media is private, so all I could see was his profile picture, which was of him facing a sunset. It won't be much help in the spectrum of identifying him, but I appreciate his aesthetic.

I have us on a strict schedule—right down to every rest stop and bathroom break. We'll get into Spring Creek at four o'clock and park at the campsite I found. It's right on the river with access to great fishing—an activity I hope will keep everyone busy while I go to the hospital. After the riverboat adventure, I figure it's best to meet Arthur alone.

I didn't, however, plan for a very unexpected monthly visitor. Doesn't she know we also have a schedule? One I require her to strictly abide by?

Between dealing with her and Ollie's passion for going off the beaten path, we're behind schedule.

And no one seems to be as upset as I am.

"*Did they stop for snacks?*"

I glance back in time to watch Daphne read the words off a slip of paper, and without hesitating, she peeks her head into the front cabin. She frowns at Ollie's greasy fingers and crumby lips, but not for the same reason I do.

Does he not know how to use a napkin? Surely his mother taught him better.

"You made a snack stop without us?" Daphne gasps.

"You were sleeping." Ollie shrugs. "Willa has us on a tight schedule. I wasn't about to miss our ten-thirty window because you two lazy sods wouldn't wake up."

"Did you even try?" She swats at the back of his head, causing him to duck and swerve. My stomach launches into my throat.

"Oi! You mad woman! I'm driving! Yes, we tried to wake you, but you both sleep like you're dead! And if it wasn't for Tosh's snoring, I would have thought he was!"

"Well," Daphne huffs. "Now we have no choice but to stop."

"*Obviously*." Ollie rolls his eyes. "Willa has lady troubles."

This time it's me backhanding him in the chest.

"Will you two cut it out!?" he cries. "I bruise like a peach!"

"Honestly, Ollie, you're one of a kind." Daphne says.

"My gran tells me that all the time."

Daphne laughs before retreating back to her bed, leaving me alone in the front to deal with Ollie, who has returned to blissfully drumming his fingers on the steering wheel and humming along to the song on the radio.

"Can you drive any faster?"

"Not without breaking some sort of traffic law."

"You'll pull a probably *very* illegal u-turn, but you won't drive a few miles above the speed limit?"

"Considering I don't know what the speed limit is, no, I'm not going to drive any faster. In case you haven't noticed, I'm not exactly swimming in funds to pay a speeding ticket."

"I'm sure that guitar of yours is worth a few bucks."

He glares at me through his sunglasses.

"Just hurry up," I tell him, dropping my head to the back of my seat. "And stop drumming your fingers. I have a splitting headache."

"Your boyfriend must be the happiest bloke around."

My stomach churns, not because of the excruciating cramps I feel—no, those feel like kitten tickles in comparison—but because of the disgusting feeling Mason leaves me with. I'm about to correct Ollie—to tell him that I must have made my ex so happy that he just had to share my naked photos with all of his friends, but I never get the chance.

The van comes to a chugging stop.

"What's happening?" I ask, sitting up as I look over at Ollie, whose mouth is hanging open, completely dumbstruck.. His sunglasses slide down the bridge of his nose, his stare set on the gauges.

"I think we're out of gas."

"What do you mean you *think*? We either are or we aren't!"

"Okay, we're definitely out of gas."

"You were supposed to fill up before we left Makarora."

"I got distracted by the crisps! They were buy one get one!"

I dig my fingernails into my palms to stop myself from screaming.

Breathe.

Count down from ten.

"*This* is why I need to do everything myself," I say as Ollie veers the van to the side of the road.

"The gas station is like half a mile up the road," he says.

I don't bother responding. Instead, I undo my seatbelt and fight with the lock on the door until I finally get it open, and stumble onto the pavement.

"Get back in the car, Willa," Ollie says after he gets out, slamming his door shut. "It'll take me ten minutes to run there and back."

"Please," I snap. "You'll probably forget why you're there and come back with three more bags of chips and twelve candy bars. I'll go."

"You're being ridiculous."

"Ridiculous is forgetting to fill up the van."

"It was a mistake," he says as he grabs his guitar out of the back. "I didn't do it on purpose. It was an accident. Do you think I like listening to you berate me?"

"Yes," Daphne answers, dimples forming in her cheeks. She has her camera out and she's recording us. "You two sound like my parents before the divorce. Just—y'know—without all the cheating, lawyers, and threatening to take the kids away. #williefight!"

"What the hell is a #willie?" I ask, completely confused.

"Your ship name," Daphne explains. "Willa plus Ollie! Willie! My viewers want you to shag."

"Brilliant," Ollie says with an exasperated sigh. "I'm leaving now."

"There you go sounding like my dad again," Daphne laughs. "We're coming with you. Isn't that right, Tosh?"

Tosh nods and hands me his notebook.

"*Snacks!*"

While I'm typically amused with Tosh's notes, all I can manage is a groan. A scenic walking tour of New Zealand was not in the plans for today. It's hot. I'm cramping. And we have places to be.

Still, I have no choice but to follow Ollie. He may have issues with not driving fast, but he walks like some sort of olympic sprinter on a mission for gold.

I can't complain about that.

* * *

THE BATHROOM IS OUT OF SOAP AND PAPER TOWELS, WHICH leaves me cringing as I dry my hands with balled-up toilet paper. I slather on sanitizer and then use the fabric of my shirt to open the door. The bright sun causes a tickle in my nose that leads me to sneeze.

"Bless you."

I jump at the sound of Ollie's voice. He's leaning his shoulder against the garage of the attached auto repair shop, his sunglasses shielding his eyes from the blazing sun as he pops candy into his mouth. His guitar is slung around his back.

"You're going to get cavities," I tell him. "And do you have separation anxiety, or something? Do you really think someone's going to steal your guitar?"

"A thank you would be nice."

"For what?"

"For blessing your blisteringly cold soul," he hums. "And for waiting for you."

"I didn't ask you to."

"Yeah, well, I'm a gentleman."

"That's debatable."

Ollie sighs and pushes himself off the wall, his sneakers dragging along the dusty pavement. I almost follow him all the way out to the main street, but when I catch a glimpse of *him* out of the corner of my eye, I grab Ollie's hand and yank him back into the alley. He looks puzzled for a second, and then that infamous grin swallows up his face.

"If you wanted to hold my hand, all you had to do was ask."

I glare at him, ignoring the comment as I peek my head out just enough to survey the scene that's unfolding.

"Are you gonna explain why you're holding me hostage? Because if I'm being honest, it smells like shit and exhaust fumes over here. I might be sick."

"It's Truth."

"What is? The fact that I'm going to puke? I know?"

I sigh. "No, you idiot. It's *Truth*! From the cult Daphne almost married us into!"

Ollie cocks a brow and leans around me to get a better look. "Do you two make it a habit of getting into vans with strange men? Have you not watched *To Catch a Predator*?"

"It wasn't my idea!" I snap lowly. "If you haven't noticed, Daphne has a death wish!"

The look on Ollie's face suggests he's waging whether or not he agrees with me. Eventually he shrugs and reluctantly nods, admitting defeat.

I glance around the corner once more and watch as Truth barters over a tire with the mechanic. He's holding seven ears of corn and has two watermelons by his feet.

I'm not sure what planet that translates into a method of payment, but I figure that this is our best chance to escape without another run-in with recruitment.

"Let's go," I say quietly. "Act cool."

"As if I know how to act any other way."

I don't have time to roll my eyes, so I duck my head and we walk as calmly and cooly as we can around the building and out of sight of all things *Truth & Happiness.*

"Not gonna lie," Ollie says once we're in the clear, "an encounter with a cult would have been a cool story to tell."

I deadpan. "Did you get the gas?"

"Tosh and Daphne brought it back to the van."

"Why didn't you go with them?"

"Because I was being a gentleman, remember?"

This time I let my eyes roll freely, which makes Ollie laugh that full belly laugh that would be endearing if it wasn't a thousand degrees and I didn't want to strangle him. I try to think of cooling thoughts, like snow and ice and everything nice, but it doesn't help the fact that I'm in literal hell and sweating like a pig.

"Hey, Willa?"

"What, Ollie?"

"You're still holding my hand."

I'm horrified when I glance down and see our fingers intertwined. I untangle them as fast as I can. I shiver as his calloused hand leaves mine. Gross *and* sweaty. I gag.

"That look of disgust in your eyes," he laughs. "You really know how to make a guy feel special."

"I don't want you to feel any kind of way."

"No, you just want to hold my hand."

I have the luxury of listening to him sing and strum along to a cleverly titled Beatles song the entire walk back to the van. I contemplate jumping in front of a speeding motorcyclist, but decide it would be rude of me to take him down with me. So I suffer as Ollie belts out lyrics on a continuous loop. I'm pretty sure he finds amusement in my misery.

Little does he know, I'm formulating a list of all the ways I can murder him with his guitar. I get up to thirty by the time we reach the van. I could add one more to the list, but when I see another van parked behind ours and spot Daphne leaning against the side, I forget what I was thinking about.

"No," I say quietly.

"I think Daphne may have already said yes," Ollie laughs.

Daphne is busy making eyes at some guy with swooshy black hair, who is filling our tank with gas. He's wearing board shorts and apparently doesn't own a shirt. I frown.

"Your face is going to get stuck that way, love," Ollie whispers into my ear.

"Stop calling me that."

I glare at the back of his head as he walks towards them. He doesn't hesitate introducing himself to Daphne's new group of friends, winning them over with all of his *charisma* and *charm*.

Why didn't I off myself when I had the chance?

"There's our little black cloud!" Daphne croons at me. "She's going to be so excited about this."

My face falls.

Whatever it is, I want to scream no. We have a plan. It's written down and everything. I *taped* it to the dashboard. That practically makes it set in stone. We're going to Spring Creek. We're having Indian for lunch. I'm going to meet Arthur. They're going to fish. It's foolproof. I made sure of it.

I clench my fists.

And count down from ten.

"Niko and his friends are going to Lake Pukaki."

"That's great," I say, faking an enthusiastic smile. "We're going to Spring Creek."

"Well…" Daphne bites her lip.

"You can't come to New Zealand and not visit Lake Pukaki," Niko says. "As someone who has lived there his entire life, it's pretty spectacular."

"We have a schedule," I say. "And we're already behind, so…"

"C'mon, Willa!" Daphne pleads. "It's our adventure too! I really want to see this spectacular lake!"

"You didn't know about this spectacular lake ten minutes ago."

"But I do now!" she cries. "And I want to go! We all do! And you *owe* me. I bought you clothes and I buy your food!"

"Daphne—"

"We took a vote."

"Who? You and Tosh? There are four of us."

"I voted for Ollie." She shrugs. "He always says yes. He's fun! Unlike you."

I bite my tongue to stop myself from screaming.

"We have a plan," I say.

"And it'll still be there tomorrow," Daphne replies much softer this time. "It's just one night, Willa! Loosen up!"

I'm so tired of hearing that, so I sigh in defeat and retreat back to the van, the slamming of my door echoing down the road. I twist the key that's already in the ignition, anticipating the blast of air-conditioning that never comes.

Great.

Everything is falling apart.

* * *

As much as I hate to admit it, Lake Pukaki is kind of spectacular.

Okay, it's *beyond* spectacular.

It's breathtaking.

We've been here for all of twenty minutes and I'm still in awe of the view. The lake is a mystical shade of turquoise that I've never seen before and the scent of pine perfumes the air. The mountainous backdrop makes it the quintessential postcard photo. I almost don't want to take a picture. It's something people need to see for themselves—to experience with their own eyes and all of their senses. I can't capture all of its beauty with one snap of my phone, but I fear that if I don't try, no one will believe a place like this exists.

"What was that?" Daphne grins. "Did you just thank me?"

"You're hearing things," I say.

"Nope, it's written all over your face. You love it here," she says. "And I finally get to say my four favorite words."

"And what exactly are your four favorite words?"

"I told you so."

I groan and tuck my phone into my back pocket, finally tearing my eyes from the view. I almost feel guilty looking at anything else. The lake is so beautiful that it should be the only thing I look at. Even if I never meet my father, at least I have this memory. Because never in my life will I see something as stunning.

When I turn around, I realize just how true that thought is. Niko's ass is hanging out of his shorts as he and his friends help Ollie and Tosh pitch our tent.

Moment sufficiently ruined.

"So what exactly are we supposed to do here?"

Daphne shrugs and walks towards the picnic table set up a few feet from the shore. "We don't always need a plan, Willa. We can grill a little. Swim! I hear there's a party tonight…"

My eyes grow.

"Don't give me that look," she laughs. "It's an annual thing! Niko says it's mental."

"Daphne, you're not going to a party with people you barely know in a place you've never been."

"You would have needed some serious anxiety medication if you were in Thailand with me," she says. "It's all part of the experience. I don't want to look back on my life and regret not taking chances and having fun."

"You can have fun without being reckless."

"But why would you want to?"

I take a deep breath, which is surprisingly calming. The air is so fresh and clean—something I'm not used to—that it clears my head and *almost* relaxes me. I still don't agree with Daphne, but I feel a lot less irritated by her way of thinking.

Relaxation, I learn, is the theme for the day. As I sit at the table with the granola bar and water Tosh bought me at the gas station, I watch Niko pass a joint to Daphne, who takes a quick hit before handing it to Ollie. He inhales a long drag and a dopey smile pulls his lips. When he catches my stare, he holds it out to me, but I decline with a quick headshake. I don't know Niko from a hole in the wall. My mouth is not going anywhere near where his has been.

Tosh takes a seat opposite of me, his notebook and pen clattering onto the table. He's so quiet that I have to wonder what's going through his head. He's an actor.. A quick—and secret—search pulled up a decent amount of movies he's been in, but he doesn't talk about it. Just like he doesn't talk about his boyfriend. It's probably none of my business, but I'm still curious. So I grab his pen and notebook—startling him wide-eyed—and laugh to myself as I scribbled words onto the page.

"*Is your boyfriend excited to see you?*" I write.

Tosh lifts his brow at the question, but doesn't hesitate to steal the pen back. "*It's a surprise. He doesn't know I'm coming.*"

"*Are you nervous?*" I ask.

"*Very,*" he writes. "*We've only spoken online. Meeting is something we've talked about, but neither of us has had the courage to make the first move.*"

"*I think it's very brave and romantic that you're doing this,*" I write. "*He'll be so happy to see you.*"

"*I hope so.*" Tosh frowns. "*My manager was very upset when I told him I was doing this.*"

"*Why?*"

"*I have a big project coming up. It could be my big break in America, but Josh is so important to me.*"

"*Tosh and Josh!*" I practically scream when I write it.

He's glaring at me when I look up, but I don't stop smiling.

"*I'm supposed to be in Los Angeles for negotiations, but I changed my flight when I got to the airport. I keep having to turn my phone off because my manager won't stop calling,*" Tosh writes.

"*Hey, at least if this all goes to hell, we can fly to LA together,*" I write, laughing.

Tosh smiles.

"*But you shouldn't worry. I can't imagine him not being happy to see you. Has he seen your smile? It's brighter than the sun.*"

"What are we doing?"

A shadow casts over the table and I frown the moment I hear Ollie's voice *way* too close to my ear.

"We're having a private conversation that doesn't involve you," I say, slamming the notebook shut.

"That's rude." He frowns. "Don't you know that secrets don't make friends?"

"I'm not in the market for making friends."

"Not with that attitude."

We have a glare off, and as soon as he wrinkles his nose at me, my lips start to flicker into a smile.

How annoying.

"Anyway, we're all going swimming," he says. "I'm taking one for the team and inviting you."

"I'd rather extract my own wisdom teeth."

"Adorable." Ollie says. "Tosh, my man, you coming?"

Tosh looks between the two of us, as if he's a child that has to choose between parents. His cheeks turn red, his eyes trailing from Ollie's to mine. He presses his lips tightly together and stands up, avoiding me completely.

"Really, Tosh?"

He flips open the notebook and writes one last thing before following Ollie to the van.

"*Sorry.*"

* * *

NIKO HAS US WALKING DOWN SOME DUSTY DIRT ROAD TO—what I can only assume—is our death. It's still light enough that I can give a detailed description to the police, but I won't be able to give an accurate location. We take a right at a really big rock. Walk a quarter of a mile—give or take a tenth—and take a left at a sign that specifically states that it's private property.

Yes, officer, we were trespassing, but did you get the part where we were led astray by a guy my friend met on the side of the road? I'm clearly not at fault.

"Why do you have the van keys slotted into your fingers?" Daphne asks. "Who's going to attack you?"

"I don't know. A bear? A coyote? Some gross backpacker who preys on young women!"

"You're in a group of seven people. No one's going to mug you, Willa."

"You don't know that."

"I mean, I do, but you keep living in your strange little world."

I glare at the back of her head as she storms up to the front with Niko, her infectious laugh filling my ears. I wish I could live in ignorant bliss like everyone else. Am I the only one concerned with the fact that we're trespassing? A *felony*? Something we could do hard time for?

The answer is yes.

No one even blinks at the thought and continues to talk over me when I voice concerns.

After what feels like another mile hike up a hill, we finally reach the party, which doesn't look like a party at all. There are acres upon acres of lush green land, and directly in the middle is an abandoned barn that is worn and torn and completely weathered by age. The red paint is chipped. The roof looks ready to collapse. And I've seen enough horror movies to know what happens next.

Panicked, I grab onto the first thing I can find.

"Are we holding hands again?" Ollie asks, grinning at me.

"We're going to die in there," I whisper. "He's going to murder us."

"We're not going to die."

"Said every idiot in a horror movie right before they *died*."

"Willa—"

"I bet his chainsaw is all gassed up out back. I've seen *Criminal Minds*! I know what happens next! He's going to strangle us with pig intestines and—"

"Oh my god, Willa, he's not going to kill us!" Daphne shouts and I suddenly realize how loud I'm talking.

"Yeah, Willa, give me a little more credit," Niko laughs. "I'd like to think I'm much more creative than luring a group of unsuspecting people into an abandoned building."

"Except I'm not unsuspecting. I'm very suspecting."

Niko sighs. "I'm not going to kill you, but you are killing my buzz, so please just relax."

My lips twitch.

"Hey, Willa?"

"What, Ollie?"

"You're still holding my hand."

I untangle our fingers and push him away from him. I pick up my pace until we all reach the barn. I take a deep breath, count down from ten, and try to prepare myself for what's behind the door.

I definitely wasn't expecting the sheer amount of people. Or the lasers. Or the smell. Or the trippy techno music that's somehow contained to this building. I've been to a handful of parties, but none of them were raves.

I did not sign up for this.

Daphne takes off into the crowd before we can make a plan. We need check-in times and a meeting spot and an agreed upon hour to leave. How are we supposed to find each other? My phone doesn't work. Tosh doesn't speak. God knows what trouble Daphne is going to get into. And Ollie, well, maybe it wouldn't be terrible to never see him again.

Everything quickly turns into the mess that I knew it would.

Just sans chainsaws and murder.

But given the choice—with the volume of the music

and the thick stench of sweat—I would rather take my chances with the chainsaw.

It's not that I don't know how to have fun. *I do.* I just know the time and place. I don't procrastinate. I get my things done—y'know after hours of slaved perfection—and *then* I have my fun. My mother instilled these things in me at a very young age.

Mason hated it. He never failed to tell me just how boring I was when I opted to stay in and finish homework instead of spending my Friday night partying on someone's roof.

"*C'mon, baby, have a little fun,*" he would say.

"*It's just one night,*" he would say.

"*Now take one with your top off,*" he would say.

Most of the time he wore me down, guilting me into forgetting about my schoolwork so we could go out or hook-up or do whatever it was that he wanted to do. That was how it was with Mason. He would make me feel bad and then I'd end up doing something I didn't always want to do. It was a never ending cycle of pressure.

But I don't want to think about him.

Not tonight.

Not ever.

I'm done crying over a boy who never mattered.

I take a deep breath and instantly regret it. Between the hundreds of bodies and musty air, I feel like I'm going to be sick. I want this night to be over.

"Hey, what's your name?"

He—whoever *he* is—has his arm around my waist before I have a chance to react. He's shirtless, his hot and sweaty chest pressed to mine, and the grin he's wearing suggests he thinks this sort of behavior is okay.

"Get off of me!" I shout and try to push him away, but

he's six feet of muscle and I have the upper body strength of a gnat.

"What's your name?" he slurs. His drink sloshes over the rim of his cup and spills onto my shirt. "I can't kiss you if I don't know your name."

"I don't have a name, you prick! Let me go!"

"I'm a really nice guy," he says. "I have gum."

"Get off!" I shout again and push against him. He's like a brick wall. He holds me tighter. "Let me go—"

"She shouldn't have to tell you twice, mate."

I never thought there'd be a moment when I'm thankful to see Ollie, but when he steps between us and pushes the guy back, I sigh in relief.

"Piss off," are Ollie's final words to him and he makes sure to watch the guy stumble away before turning back to me. "Are you okay?"

"Yeah," I say. "I'm peachy fucking keen."

If I have to stay in this place a second longer, I'm going to scream or cry or maybe both. I don't care if I have to leave by myself and walk back to the campsite alone. I'll take my chances.

"Where are you going?" Ollie asks as I push through the crowd.

"I need to find Daphne," I tell him. I didn't realize how hard that task would be. Sure, her hair is blue, but with all the different lasers, the lights are reflecting off everything in all the wrong ways. It's making me dizzy.

But I do find her.

Eventually.

She's in the middle of the dance floor, her body flush with Niko's as they sway to the music. She's not wearing a shirt. On any other occasion, I'd be concerned with the fact that she's barely covered by her flimsy lace bra. But when I watch her pop two pills into her mouth and chase them with whatever is in her cup, nothing else matters.

I did not sign up for this.

I did not sign up for this.

I did not sign up for this.

"Daphne!" I shout and yank her arm until she stumbles toward me.

"Jeez, Willa!"

"What did you just take?" I demand, grabbing her jaw between my thumb and index finger to force her attention on me. Her eyes are dilated and hazy. "Was it Oxy?"

"What?" she screams. "Chill! You're killing my vibe!"

"I'm killing your vibe? You're gonna kill yourself! You can't just mix that stuff with alcohol!"

But she doesn't care.

She's already too far gone, swaying off beat to the song, so carefree and alive. It's as if she swallowed up all the energy in the room and personified it. Daphne is the party.

"We need to leave," I say and try to grab her arm, but she pulls it away.

"I'm not leaving," she shouts. "I can't feel my legs! I'm floating."

"Daphne—"

This time it's Ollie grabbing my hand, forcing my attention away from Daphne.

"Willa, you're not her mother," he snaps. "You can't tell her what to do."

"So I'm just supposed to stand around and watch her kill herself?"

"She'll live and she'll learn," he says. "But she has to make mistakes."

"Those are some really risky mistakes you're willing to let her make."

I don't stick around to hear his response. I need to leave. I can't watch Daphne gamble with her life, so I push through the crowd of people until I'm out the door.

The rush of fresh air burns my lungs, but I inhale and inhale and inhale, finding relief in finally being able to breathe. As much as I want to savor the moment, I take off down the hill. I want to get as far away from this place as I can, which means walking entirely too fast. My ankles are going to give out and my legs feel like jelly, but I push through until I pass the No Trespassing sign, and then I finally slow down.

I'm not going to cry.

I refuse to.

I need to keep it together.

I need to think clearly and soldier on.

I'm not going to breakdown, giving in to a bunch of frivolous emotions just because my hormones are out of whack and because I haven't taken my medication.

No, I'm stronger than that.

It's then and there that I decide I'm not going to care anymore. Daphne can do what she wants—throw herself off another bridge, jump off a cliff, swim with the sharks for all I care. I'm going to keep my mouth shut.

From now on, my focus is only on finding Benji.

That's all that matters.

By the time I make my last right turn, my heart slows to a point where it's not pulsing in my ears anymore. And for the first time in my twenty minute walk, I'm able to hear the footsteps behind me, which instantly makes every muscle in my body tense as I grip the key between my fingers tighter.

"I'm a third degree black belt," I say, trying to disguise my shaky voice.

"No, you're not."

Ollie.

I take another deep breath and continue to walk without paying him any attention. We manage to get back to camp without exchanging any words, which I'm grateful for. I have fleeting thoughts of staying up to admire the stillness of the lake, but decide I want to avoid interacting with Ollie at all costs, so I make a b-line for the tent, not bothering to change into my pajamas.

But my hopes of a night alone are short lived. Ollie is unzipping the tent as I slide into one of the sleeping bags, the flashlight on my phone illuminating my glare as I plug my earbuds into my ears. He doesn't say a word. Instead, he quietly slips into the other sleeping bag and lays back against his pillow. I'm reluctant to follow, but I'm also too tired to make a fuss over the situation.

I get as comfortable as I can and close my eyes, preparing to let the music lull me to sleep. But no sooner than it starts does it fade from my right ear.

"What are we listening to?" Ollie asks.

"We aren't listening to anything."

"Sure we are," he says and turns his head just enough for me to catch his smile.

And then, to my surprise, he offers me the peace offering of all peace offerings.

A chocolate bar.

8

"Look guys! Willie finally happened! Aren't they adorable?" Daphne coos. "T owes me twenty quid. I told him they'd shag by the end of the week. Who knew it would be a threesome, though? It's always the unsuspecting ones, isn't it? The ones that are into freaky shit? I guess Willa does know how to loosen up. Who would have thought? Not me, that's for sure! But hey, maybe she just needed to get laid. We should get this trending! #willie2k19! #williethreesome!"

Daphne's voice is haunting my dreams and all I can smell are coconuts.

I consider opening my eyes, but the thin mesh of the tent does little to conceal the sun. It's too early to face something far too bright, so I bury my face further into my pillow and hope I fall back to sleep for a few more hours.

But then I hear it—a shallow half moan half laugh that's gritty and coated with sleep. It's like a shot of caffeine to my system. My eyes snap open.

When I can't see further than the freckle on the back of Ollie's neck, I freeze. When I realize my arm is slung around the cool fabric off his sleeping bag, my stomach twists. And when I catch sight of something scaly out of the corner of my eye, I scream.

"What the—"

"Holy shit! Holy shit! Ollie, what the fuck! Get it off! Get it out! Ollie! Fuck! It's like a dinosaur!"

In retrospect, it probably wasn't a good idea to kick off my sleeping bag. It was a worse idea to stand up. Between Ollie and I—two rather tall humans—we have too many long limbs, which makes flailing around in such a small space a recipe for disaster. The poles loosen from the ground and then the tent collapses on top of us.

"Will you calm down?" Ollie screams. "I don't even know what you're on about!"

"It was *staring* at me! With it's beady little eyes! And scaly little skin! *Oh my god!* I can still feel it! I'm itchy! It's still on me! I know it!"

"Willa, calm down!"

I can't calm down. Not when I can still feel it—when I know it's crawling around here somewhere. I panic, a rush of fear sweeping over me as I thrash around the tent that has caved in. I need to get out and I need to run far, far, *far* away.

But I slip on a sleeping bag and take Ollie down with me, both of us tangled together on the ground.

"Where is it? Oh my god! It's going to crawl on me again!"

"What? Jesus Christ! Was it a spider?"

"A spider?" *As if.* "You think I would react this way to a spider? Really, Oliver?"

He blinks at me, pausing for a moment. He looks confused, but quickly shakes whatever thought he's thinking out of his head.

"I'm still half asleep! Forgive me for being confused!"

"It was a Komodo dragon!"

"It was a Komdo—do you know how *big* Komodo dragons are?"

"Uh, yeah, the size of a brontosaurus!"

Ollie closes his eyes and takes a deep breath. How he can be calm in a moment like this, I'll never know. He gets up and fights with the tent zipper, pulling and tugging until the sun and warm morning air pierce through the opening. He stumbles and trips over the material, but eventually breaks free.

"Fucking hell," he mumbles as I scramble onto my feet. "She's absolutely mad—completely mental. Jesus—Daphne! Were you filming that?"

After I finally muddle through the remains of our tent, I'm completely out of breath and frazzled when I stand up. Daphne's standing in front of Ollie with her camera in hand while the rest of our group watches in pure amusement. My cheeks start to burn.

"Daphne!" I say. "How much did you get?"

"Enough to know that Ollie's the little spoon." She grins. "And enough to know that you're awfully generous with your compliments."

I have no idea what she means until she turns the camera on herself.

"Must have been a good night," she says into the lens. "#itslikeadinosaur."

"Daphne!" Ollie screams. "You better not post that!"

"But you're both so tolerable when you're sleeping," she says. "Besides, the viewers want Willie! I can't deny them that. It's my job. They pay my bills."

"I swear—" Ollie starts to lunge at the camera, but Daphne takes off running before he can get it. "Delete it, Daphne!"

"I can't, I'm sorry," she laughs, stopping at one end of

the picnic table to catch her breath while Ollie stops at the other. "And, Willa? It was a gecko. It was about the size of my index finger. It wasn't going to kill you."

I frown. Did we not see the same thing? Surely I was face-to-face with some *gigantic* prehistoric lizard. It was probably fire breathing and ate girls like me for breakfast. I'm lucky to be alive.

"Daphne, delete it," Ollie repeats. "You can't just film us without our permission!"

"Why are you freaking out? You weren't complaining when your bloody *Wonderwall* cover got five hundred thousand views in twenty-four hours!"

"That's different!"

"Right." She nods. "You weren't having a reptilian threesome in that video."

I scrunch my nose at the thought of having a threesome with anyone let alone Ollie and some sort of cretaceous creature big enough to bite my head off. I need to take twelve showers and scrub my skin just thinking about it.

"Honestly, the video is harmless," Daphne says, tucking her camera into her bra for safe keeping. "It was, like, five minutes of purely innocent cuddling—boringly PG and so very vanilla."

Boringly PG or not, it doesn't change the fact that we woke up in a compromising position. We broke the fourth wall. I have to live the rest of my life knowing I spooned him. I nuzzled my face into his neck. He laughed.

Oh God.

I need to go take those twelve showers right now.

"But now that we're all up," Daphne starts, "we can start the drive to Spring Creek! Niko and his friends are going to drive up too."

"Daphne—"

"Just go with the flow, Willa," she says. "It won't kill you."

It might.

Anything is possible when Daphne takes charge. It doesn't help that she doesn't take anyone else into consideration. Maybe I don't want *another* group of people to know why I'm here.

But I know arguing with her isn't going to get me anywhere, so I shake my head and walk towards the van. If Ollie thinks I'm going to help him pack up that tent, he has another thing coming.

We'd burn it if I had it my way.

* * *

THERE'S ONLY ONE BROWNIE LEFT.

I'm fourth in line at *The Broken Man*, a small cafe just north of Christchurch, and I've developed a nervous twitch watching everyone in our group order. Niko's friend, Ori, has a gluten intolerance, so I don't need to worry about him or their friend, Emere, who must have told us she's vegan about thirty times. My only competitors are Ollie and Tosh, who are taking too long deciding between the offered sandwiches.

We're halfway through our eight hour drive, and before we got to the cafe, I was going stir crazy sitting in the back of the van. Daphne had spent the whole morning complaining about a headache, claiming she was never going to drink again.

I scoff just thinking about it. She'll forget all about this hangover the next time opportunity strikes. What I find most interesting is that the only detail from last night she can recall is the fact that she *may have* hooked up with Niko behind a tree. Our fight may as well have never happened.

But I'm not upset.

Why would I be?

It's not like Daphne ever listens to me.

Everything I say goes in one ear and out the other.

I'm done wasting my breath.

"I'll have the ham and cheese on toast," Ollie says to the cashier, "and the brownie."

And that… that's the moment I realize today is not going to be my day.

And the brownie.

And the brownie.

AND THE BROWNIE.

Being assaulted by a giant lizard pales in comparison to this.

I trudge back to the table with a bowl of creamy broccoli soup and a sad excuse for an oatmeal raisin cookie. I set my tray next to Tosh, taking the seat against the wall. I frown the moment Ollie takes the seat across from me.

Great.

Now I get to watch him eat the brownie.

How considerate of him.

I pull my phone out of my pocket to avoid conversation, connecting to the cafe's wifi. I don't want to check my email, but it's been two days and they're piling up.

From: **Ana Loveridge-Herrera** (Packing up your room!!)
From: **Mason Stueck** (Baby just talk to me I miss you so much)
From: **Lyla Flores** (Willa! You're not responding to my texts!)
From: **Delia Sprigs** (are you gone???)
From: **Bella Karim** (Willa! What the hell?! CALL ME!!)
From: **The Book Warehouse** (20% Coupon! This Weekend only!)

From: **Oscar Mendez** (AHIS 120-02: Research Groups)
From: **Ana Loveridge-Herrera** (Can't sleep! Too Anxious! I think Baby's a)
From: **Ana Loveridge-Herrera** (All this baby wants is ice cream!!)
From: **The Coffee Corner** (Free scone with espresso purchase!)
From: **Mason Stueck** (Can't stop looking at those pictures baby)
From: **Ana Loveridge-Herrera** (Sonogram!!!! Our little baby banana!)
From: **Vincent Herrera** (Mom's lost her mind!)

I groan and leave my inbox without opening a single email. The small red number has grown from a handful to the ever so daunting triple digits. I don't want to deal with them. I don't care that Mason is still getting off to the pictures I sent him, or that Bella is trying to contact me after posting a lovely Facebook status about how *some girls* have no self-respect. None of it matters—not even the fact that Mom is packing up my room. My things are probably already in boxes and in route to the GoodWill on E 23rd Street. I'll be sure to stop in the next time I'm in the city to repurchase some of my shoes.

"Is there a reason you're glaring at my brownie?"

I blink from my thoughts and look up to see Ollie grinning stupidly at me.

"You took the last one," I say.

"Oh, do you want it?"

"No, of course not," I say. "I have an oatmeal raisin cookie. They're the runt of the bunch, aren't they? Always picked over. Always second best. Usually dry and crumbly. I can resonate with that."

"Give yourself some credit, Willa." Daphne tries not to

smile from across the table, but the corners of her lips deceive her. "You're not dry and crumbly. You're sour! Like a lemon bar! Which, funnily enough, is also the last resort."

I scoff. "You flatter me, Daphne."

"It's what I'm here for."

I roll my eyes and spoon some soup into my mouth.

"I really like lemon bars," Ollie says through a bite of his sandwich.

"Why am I not surprised?" Daphne laughs and waggles her brows as if Ollie's love for a pastry is somehow scandalous.

"My gran makes homemade lemon curd," he continues, licking his fingers. "It's spot on."

"Funny that you completely ignored the tray of lemon bars on display," I say, breaking off a piece of crusty bread to dunk in my soup.

"I knew they wouldn't taste like hers, so I didn't bother," he explains. "But you can have my brownie if you really want it."

"I don't."

"Are you sure? Because you've been giving it a very intense look."

"I don't want it."

"C'mon," he insists, nudging the plate forward. "Take it."

"No."

"I want you to have it."

"I want you to stop talking."

"Just take the brownie, Willa."

"I don't want your brownie, Ollie."

"Please, just—"

I finally lose my patience. I grab the brownie and shove it straight into his mouth.

"You couldn't have done that when I had the camera rolling?" Daphne frowns.

I glare at her as I sit back in my chair, so thankful for Ollie's temporary muzzle. Silence should not be taken for granted.

Especially when I'm pretty sure Ollie only talks to hear his own voice.

"Like I was saying," Niko continues, not that I realized he was saying anything at all, "my cousin runs a holiday park up in Picton and she offered us a few cabins for the night if you're up for it."

"Of course—"

I cut Daphne off. "We're going to Spring Creek."

"Picton's, like, twenty minutes north," Niko explains. "It's a really cool port town. You can catch the ferry to Wellington if you're heading to the north island."

"Which we are," Daphne says, eyeing me.

"I already made reservations for us to park in Spring Creek," I reply. "There's a fishing dock."

"There's plenty of fishing in Picton," Niko says.

"Why would I want to fish?"

"You just said—"

"I know what I said, but that doesn't mean *I want* to fish. I was merely stating that there's a fishing dock for anyone who might be interested in such a thing—"

"We would love to go," Ollie says after he finally finishes chewing *the brownie.* He ignores my glare and continues, "it sounds fun and I need to shower."

And just like that, the decision is made.

I slide down in my chair and cross my arms.

I'm brownie-less and annoyed.

* * *

Ollie stops the van in the ambulance bay, and looks over at me with a disapproving stare. I ignore it and undo my seatbelt.

"This is stupid," he says, lifting his sunglasses over his head.

"I know," I agree. "You're parked in a no parking zone. What happens if an ambulance comes and there's an actual emergency? Someone might die because you parked the van here and not in the spot I suggested."

"I think he means you going in alone," Daphne says, placing her chin on the back of my seat. "And I'd have to agree. It's stupid. You should let Ollie go with you."

"Why? So he can come up with another ridiculous story about how we're missionaries trying to educate the world on sexual health?"

She shrugs. "It worked."

I roll my eyes and push the handle on the door. "I'll be fine."

"This guy could be a raging psycho," Daphne says. "He's a forensic pathologist, Willa. He plays with dead people."

"Yeah, he sounds creepy when you put it that way," I say. "He does not *play* with them. He *examines* them."

"When he's on the clock," Daphne says. "God knows what happens when the lights go out."

"You're disgusting," I say, getting out of the car. "I'll call a cab when I'm finished."

"Don't be ridiculous," Ollie says before I can shut the door. "We'll come get you."

"Honestly, I'd rather take a cab."

"I'm offended."

"I really don't care."

"You have no money."

"I'll figure it out."

I stand in the entrance of the emergency room with my arms crossed and my eyes locked with Ollie. I'm not moving until I see the van disappear into the distance. I don't trust them not to park and come in after me. So I wait and wait and wait until Ollie lets out an exasperated sigh and grabs the wheel. He drives away from the hospital with his head shaking, and I wait an extra three minutes to make sure they don't come back.

The hospital smells sickeningly sterile and I gag out of instinct. It's an instant reminder of a dreaded day in third grade. During gym class, I fell after Ahmed Karim whipped a dodgeball at me. I ended up fracturing my wrist, and everyone called me a baby for crying. I was Whiney Willa for the rest of the year. No one passed up an opportunity to point and laugh.

Flash forward ten years, and all those guys that previously made fun of me for crying were sending me unsolicited pictures in hopes that I'd send them some in return.

I didn't.

But one good thing that did come from that trip to the emergency room was that I got the next two days off from school. Mom took off work and we went to the Bronx Zoo and ate hot dogs in Central Park and walked through Shakespeare's Gardens. And we smiled and laughed and stayed up too late. Back then I didn't have to fight for her attention. There was no Vincent. No baby. It was just us. And that was enough for me.

I never realized how lonely memories could be until I was nostalgic for something no one else missed.

I've never been enough for my mother.

She always longed for something more.

Something better.

I take a deep breath.

And count down from ten.

At the elevator, I read through the hospital directory until I find the morgue. Unsurprisingly, it's in the basement and I find myself riding down to the ground floor alone.

A small—and I mean minuscule—part of me wishes Daphne was here. Mostly because I have no idea how I'm going to pull this off. How am I supposed to break the ice with Arthur? I can't even break the ice on the first day of classes. I freeze up. Lose my train of thought. Forget my name. There's a very good chance I'm about to make a fool out of myself.

To say the basement of a hospital is creepy is an understatement. My arms are covered in chills and my hands are in fists—y'know, in case any zombie corpses try to start something with me. I'm prepared to fight them all to death.

"Can I help you?"

I jump at the voice, my feet coming to a screeching halt. I glance into the office that I nearly passed. It's messy, the desk piled high with files and folders, the computer barely visible under a layer of sticky notes. The man sitting in front of it has mad scientist hair, bottle-cap glasses, and spaghetti hanging off his bottom lip.

"I… uh?" I stammer. "I… lost my group?"

"Your group? he laughs. "Are they among the living?"

"Uh… yeah? I mean… my school? Yeah, my group from school! I lost them."

"Did you take a wrong turn over the pacific ocean?"

Shit.

I'm American.

"Oh… I'm studying abroad?" I try. "We're… on a field trip! With the… biology department. I'm Willa."

"I'm Arthur, the forensic pathologist," he says and slurps up the pasta he finally realizes is on his lip, and then he twirls his plastic fork around the container, taking another bite. "We don't usually do tours down here. Students are much more interested in the operating rooms and playing with the children on the pediatric floor. They've got free ice lollies up there. It's a big selling point."

Think, Willa, Think.

I need an excuse to stay down here before Einstein offers to show me back to the elevator, sending me on a one way trip to the children's ward to rejoin a group that doesn't exist.

"I'm actually… very interested in… dead people."

"Same." He nods. "My boyfriend thinks I'm certifiably insane, but I think there's something satisfying about finding the answers, y'know? What happened? Why did this happen? *How* did this happen? I want to be the guy who figures it out."

I smile tightly. "Me too."

"Really?" He lifts a bushy eyebrow. "I rarely find anyone interested in the postmortem side of things."

"Yeah… I like how… quiet it is."

He laughs and tosses his empty container into the trash.

"So where did you go to school for this?"

"University of Queenstown."

"Really?" I say. "I was just down there to see Benji Atkin's art exhibit."

"Really? I went to school with him," he laughs. "I do some photography in my spare time."

"Do you still talk to him?"

He laughs again. "Does anyone really ever talk to Benji? We both donated some pieces to an exhibit at the Honey Hive in Foxton. It was benefiting the bees. Did you know they're really at risk? Anyway, I saw him briefly, but he avoided me at all costs. The only person I saw him talk to was Janey, the woman who owns it."

I'm not remotely surprised.

"Wow, that was kind of rude of him."

He shrugs. "Typical Benji. You learn not to be offended by it."

"Right," I say. "I should probably go find my group."

"It was nice meeting you, Willa."

"Likewise."

* * *

I NEED A LONG HOT SHOWER TO WASH THE SMELL OF DEAD people off of me.

I need a wifi signal or a pay phone even more.

Do pay phones even exist anymore?

I hope so.

The elevator dings and I step through the doors that lead into the emergency room. I have Arthur's phone number in my pocket for any future academic references I might need, a granola bar he offered me since I missed out on all the popsicles on the pediatric floor, and a headache. All I want is to call a cab and take a shower.

I let out a heavy sigh, and try tirelessly to connect my phone to the hospital's wifi.

"C'mon," I say, trying to coax it with a light smack. "Work goddammit! I did not pay six hundred dollars for you not to work!"

"Maybe if you were a little gentler," someone says. "Maybe a bit nicer…"

I stop mid step, my face falling at the familiar voice. I pivot my entire body slowly in the direction of the waiting room and that's where I see Ollie sitting on the floor with his legs crossed. He has a red Lego in his hand and an entire fortress built in front of him that would leave any five-year-old jealous.

"Why are you here?"

"Obviously not for the frozen yogurt," he says. "Can you believe they don't have any? What kind of hospital doesn't have a frozen yogurt machine? It's absolutely rubbish and I'm offended."

"I asked you to leave." I frown. "I *watched* you leave."

"The funny thing about automobiles is that you can turn them around."

"But I told you—"

"I know what you told me," he says. "Doesn't mean we were going to listen."

"We? You're all here?"

"Of course." He shrugs. "Daphne's outside because hospitals make her itchy and Tosh is getting a rash checked out because he's also itchy."

I can't believe I managed to get mixed up with a group of people who completely disrespect my wishes. How rude of them to care!

Ugh, my lips try to smile again.

I set them right back into a frown.

Where they belong.

"We were just worried," Ollie finally says, his face softening.

"Well, I didn't ask you to worry."

"Doesn't mean we're not going to," he laughs. "We're friends, Willa. This is what friends do."

It's such a loaded word.

Friends.

Half the time it's just for convenience—because you're stuck with those people for six hours a day, five days a week. The other half is because of fear—because they could ruin you with one click of a button. So you play the role. You keep your enemies close. You pretend you don't live with the constant fear of them turning on you, or calling you a whore on every social media platform.

But then they do.

And you realize what you've known all along.

The only person you can trust is yourself.

"C'mon, Willa, don't be mad."

My stomach turns at his words. Mason used to feed me that line. Sometimes I can still hear him whispering it into my ear.

"It's whatever, Ollie," I say. "I'll be in the van."

I leave him in the middle of the emergency room, and walk straight through the exit without a second thought. The warm air is a welcomed relief from the bleak feeling my time in the morgue left me with.

"Does that snarl suggest things didn't go well with Arthur?"

Daphne is sitting on a bench with her laptop resting on her thighs, a red mark from the heat visible beneath her shorts. There's a large soda with a rim of condensation next to her. When she looks up at me, I can tell by the wrinkles on her forehead that she's squinting beneath her sunglasses.

"I'll be in the van," I say and begin to cross the parking lot.

"Wait! My video's almost done uploading! I can't leave until the world sees *A Reptilian Threesome*! You're gonna be internet famous!"

I roll my eyes and ignore her, spotting the van a few rows back. I'm not surprised to find it unlocked. Ollie isn't exactly the brightest bulb in the box. He doesn't care about our possessions. Not that there's anything of true value. Thieves would only get away with his guitar, which would be a blessing in disguise.

Why am I complaining?

I curl up on the couch in the back, folding my knees to my chest. My earbuds are shoved into my ears, a clear sign that I don't want to talk to anyone. The music is so loud that I don't hear them come back, only realizing when I feel a dip in the couch. I don't turn my head, or acknowledge who it is.

Well, not until the sound disappears from my left ear.

Ollie is smiling sheepishly next to me.

Now I'm even more determined to ignore him—and everyone—for the entire ride to the campsite.

* * *

The fires are blazing when we get to the campground, a cloud of smoke swirling all the way to the sky. There's an abundance of laughter, which is music to the ears of some, but not me. It makes me sadder—lonelier.

"Smells like summer," Ollie says, hauling his backpack over his shoulder.

It doesn't.

Because summer to me smells like garbage that has been sweltering on the sidewalk for twelve hours. Or the man next to me on the subway who just got out of a spin class and is sticky and sweaty and has the body odor of a wet dog. Or a cab with no air-conditioning and a driver who smells like cigarettes.

Summers in New York City aren't glamourous.

Not unless you belong to a fancy members only club with a rooftop pool.

"Smells like burgers," Daphne says, practically floating over to the grill that Niko is manning. "Oh my god. I'm so hungry. It's been, like, twenty minutes since I last ate."

"The next batch should be done in a few minutes," Niko reassures her.

"Hurry," Daphne says, feigning dramatics. "I might faint."

Niko humors her and laughs, handing her a plastic cup filled with *something* to hold her over.

"There's beer in the cooler," he says, nudging his head.

"I'm actually knackered," Ollie replies. "I'd quite like a shower and a bed."

Niko ruffles around in his pocket and then tosses a key at him, a "12" clearly labeled on the ring. "You three are in cabin twelve."

I frown. "Where's Daphne staying?"

They way he grins is the only answer I need.

"Rest up, Ollie," Daphne says, wrinkling her nose at him. "We have a long day ahead of us!"

"We do," Niko agrees.

"You're coming?!" Daphne's entire face lights up.

He shrugs. "Figured we can get up to some trouble in Wellington."

Trouble.

Great.

I stalk off with Ollie and Tosh in tow, walking up and down a graveled road until we find our cabin. Or *Chalet 12* as the sign reads.

Inside, it's a plain as day cabin. The walls are made of pine wood, and there's a small table tucked into the corner with two plastic lawn chairs on either side of it. We don't have a TV, but we do have bunk beds and a bathroom.

The finer things in life.

"I'm not sleeping near Ollie," I say, throwing my backpack on the top bunk, declaring it mine.

"I'm offended." He frowns.

"I don't care."

Tosh's eyes go wide and he scrambles to find a pen and a piece of paper, quickly scribbling something down before shoving it at Ollie.

"*I don't cuddle*," he reads. "I'm offended! *Again*! And if you want to get technical, it was *Willa* cuddling *me*!"

I snarl. "Put a pillow in the middle. Problem solved."

I let them argue through notes over who gets to shower first, and I kick off my shoes, hiking myself up the flimsy metal ladder. I settle in for the night by unwrapping the granola bar from earlier and connecting my phone to the campsite wifi.

Which has proven to be the biggest mistake of all.

Because right there, at the top of my inbox, is what I've been dreading all along.

From: **Ana Loveridge-Herrera** (Are you seriously in New Zealand? Willa!)
From: **Ana Loveridge-Herrera** (Willa!!)
From: **Ana Loveridge-Herrera** (I'm not kidding Willa! Call me!)
From: **Ana Loveridge-Herrera** (Willa! Answer your phone!)

9

I'm making a break for it.

I don't actually know where I'm making a break to, but I figure my options are endless. Daphne once said Fiji was nice. Thailand has great beaches. The Maldives seem like a good place to hide from the wrath of Ana Loveridge-Herrera, who seems to be quite livid about my little trip.

At least, that's what I assume considering she has sent me over thirty emails in a ten minute span.

(I haven't actually opened any of them.)

Mostly, I'm surprised she managed to pause her baby brain long enough to remember she has another child.

My only goal now is to get far away from my little group of misfit toys before things get any worse. I'll get onto the main road, grab a taxi, and just tell the driver to take my anywhere. Hopefully they'll accept an IOU as payment because my debit card is still flagged and I have no money.

Tosh is snoring so loud that Australia could invade this country and no one on the entire island would hear. For someone who doesn't speak, he knows how to make up for it. I decide to use it to my advantage. It'll mask the creaky floorboards during my escape.

I toss the strap of my backpack over my shoulder, and crawl over to the ladder that leads from my top bunk down to the floor. If I timed it out accordingly—which I did—I could get down, put my shoes on, and be free from this cabin in a matter of seconds.

That, of course, means things would have to go as planned, which they rarely ever did.

The room is so dark that not even a sliver of light coming from the outside lamp posts can cut through it. I consider it an advantage until I put a foot on the ladder, vastly underestimating how slippery metal is when I was wearing socks.

I get down two steps before my weight slips from underneath me. My brief life flashes before my eyes as I float through the air. And as I brace myself for the fall, I feel two hands cinched my waist, which startles me enough to scream.

And then we both hit the ground.

"Holy shit," I screech, flailing around on the floor. "What's your damage?!"

"Most of my body now that I've broken your fall," Ollie groans. "You're welcome, by the way."

"Why are you lurking around in the dark?" I hiss, still failing to get back on my feet. "It's weird! And creepy!"

"A thank you would be nice," he grumbles, his hands feeling around for something on the floor. Probably his glasses. "And I wasn't lurking around! I was sleeping in the bathtub, but I got a stiff neck."

"Why were you sleeping in the bathtub?"

"Because Tosh sounds like a bullhorn and Daphne has the keys to the van. My options were limited."

I roll my eyes, and then out of the kindness of my heart

—and because he looks ragingly pathetic in his desperate search—I pick up his glasses and hand them to him before I stand up. I figure it's best to deal with Ollie the way I always do: by ignoring him. I get my shoes on and head straight for the door, leaving him confused back in the cabin.

Outside, the sun is just starting to rise, casting a pink and purple hue over the sky. I would have stopped to admire the changing colors, but I'm determined to get far away from here. I want to do it fast, which means walking so briskly that my calves begin to burn. Behind me, I can hear Ollie's feet crunching against fallen pine needles.

I'm not surprised, but it's still annoying.

"Where are you going at five-forty in the morning?" he asks, out of breath.

"I'm leaving."

"I know," he says. "*Where* are you going?"

"I don't know."

"What?"

"I'm *leaving*." Do I have to spell it out for him?

"Like *leaving* leaving?"

"Yes, *Oliver*, I'm leaving," I huff. "Goodbye! Adios! It was nice knowing you. I will not miss your dreadful guitar or watching you laugh with your mouth full."

"Hey!" he snaps, finally catching up to me. He grabs my hand—his fingers rough and calloused against mine—and I instinctively pull away. "Why are you leaving?"

"It doesn't matter." I shrug and grab onto the straps of my backpack. "I'm leaving and you can't stop me."

"I know I can't stop you," he says, frowning. "But I'd still like to know why. I'm the one who'll have to tell Daphne and she'll demand an explanation."

"Tell her I was homesick," I say.

I hold his stare long enough to notice his eyes are

flecked with gold. He has bags beneath them, undeniably sleep deprived. He looks exhausted. His rooty blonde hair is tousled in five different directions. He reminds me of an adorable sleepy puppy.

Gross.

I turn away from him, and take three more steps before he grabs my hand.

"The real reason, Willa."

"I don't want to talk about it, Ollie."

"Then at least let me buy you breakfast," he says. "It would be rude of me to send you off without a meal. My mum would have my neck."

"I'm not hungry."

"Then get a coffee."

If I learned anything about Ollie in the past week, it's that he doesn't give up easily, so I know the only way to get rid of him is to wave my white flag and allow him to buy me a coffee.

* * *

The Tackle Box IS DOWN BY THE HARBOR AND IS frequented by many men (and two women) who smell like the bottom of a bait bucket. It's also the only place open at six in the morning, so Ollie and I pile into a booth by a window. Outside doesn't smell any better. It's low tide. I gag each time the wind wafts the smell into the diner. I thought trash day in the city was bad, but this is giving it a run for its money.

"I'm starving," Ollie says, picking up a menu that's sticky from maple syrup.

I cringe.

"I could probably eat three breakfasts," he continues, "maybe four—oh, they've got milkshakes too."

"It's six in the morning," I remind him.

"I know." He looks up from the menu and shoots me a lopsided smile. "It's gonna be a long day. I need to fuel up."

"Right." I glance down at my phone. *The Tackle Box* has wifi. Four new emails. I flip my phone over.

"So," Ollie starts, not bothering to look up from his menu, "are you ready to tell me why you're giving up and leaving, or should we get some coffee in you first? I know you're quite prickly before you get your caffeine."

"You've known me for a week, so don't pretend you're some expert about when I am and am not prone to being *prickly*, you dickhead."

Ollie laughs. "I mean, you're always a bit prickly. Just less so after you've gotten your coffee, Boss Lady"

"You're an asshole."

"An asshole that keeps you caffeinated."

I kick him directly in the shin. His reflexes send his knee into the table, shaking it. He glares at me, but I smile back.

And in an instant, I watch his lips flicker into a grin.

"Are you ready to order?" a waitress asks after stopping at our table.

"Yeah, I'll have the eggs benny with smoked salmon and an order of pancakes with bananas and Nutella," Ollie says unabashedly. "Oh, and a strawberry milkshake."

The waitress nods, seemingly unsurprised by such a large order and turns to me.

"Just coffee."

She finishes scribbling onto her notepad and then leaves us in our little corner. Ollie's taking full advantage of the free wifi while I jump every time my phone buzzes with a new message. Isn't it past my mother's bedtime? She's pregnant, for God's sake! She should be sleeping.

I mean, maybe.

I have no idea what time it is there.

My phone buzzes again and I groan so loud that it catches Ollie's attention, his brow lifting in my direction. I ignore him just like I plan to ignore my suddenly popular inbox, but it dings and buzzes so many times that I have to assess the damage.

From: **Ana Loveridge-Herrera** (Willa! I swear you're so grounded!)
From: **Mason Stueck** (looking real fucking cozy)
From: **Trinity Nichols** (Saw you on YouTube!)
From: **Lyla Flores** (Please call me!)
From: **Mason Stueck** (#willie???)
From: **Mason Stueck** (what the fuck willa)
From: **Andrew Gleason** (Looking good Willa ;))
From: **Ana Loveridge-Herrera** (ANSWER YOUR PHONE)
From: **Ty Hall** (Already in another guy's bed? There's a word for that…)
From: **Delia Sprigs** (get your shit out of the dorm or I'm selling it)
From: **Vincent Herrera** (Please call your mom! We're worried!)
From: **Delia Sprigs** (wtf did you move to New Zealand?)
From: **Bella Karim** (Literally everyone is talking about it!)

"You okay?"

I swallow the lump in my throat and flip my phone over. "Yeah, I'm fine."

"So you're just going to lie to me in our final moments together?" he asks, smiling up at the waitress as she sets down our drinks.

"Why do you even care?"

"Because you're visibly upset." He shrugs. "What kind of person wouldn't care?"

A normal one.

Or, at least, the people I'm usually surrounded by.

"Why are you leaving?" Ollie asks, stirring the mound of whipped cream on top of his glass until it turns the milkshake a paler shade of pink. "And don't try to lie. I'll know if you are."

I take a sip of my coffee after adding a heavy splash of cream and three sugars, savoring the taste. Maybe if I get this over with, I can leave before his breakfast comes.

"Daphne has a very popular YouTube channel," I say.

Ollie quirks a brow. "I know?"

"Word gets around pretty fast when you're a trending topic," I say, glancing down at the table. I push a few stray sugar crystals around with my finger. "My mom knows I'm here."

"So she's making you leave?"

"I'm nineteen. She can't make me do anything," I say. "But she's pretty pissed off, so I figure it's best to go off the radar."

"Where are you gonna go?"

"Dunno." I shrug and take another sip of my coffee. "I hear Australia has a lot of poisonous creatures. Maybe one will off me and solve all my problems. Or maybe I'll take the bus down to Christchurch and take the first flight out. See where that takes me. Maybe I'll stop pretending like I have an adventurous bone in my body and I'll just fly back to LA before my roommate sells all my things for juice cleanses and Soulcycle money."

"And how do you plan on paying for all that when your card doesn't work?"

"I'll figure it out.'

Ollie takes a long sip of his shake before he decides to offer up an opinion I haven't asked for.

"I think you're being stupid."

"I think you have milkshake dribbling down your chin."

He frowns, but still grabs a napkin to wipe his face before he continues. "Just call your mum. Explain the situation to her. I'm sure she'll understand."

"Yeah, I'm pretty sure she'd rather I join Truth on his little journey to happiness than meet my father."

"Then wouldn't you want to stay? Just to piss her off?"

"First you're telling me to explain the situation to her and now you're telling me to stay and piss her off? Do you have any sort of strategy going on right now?"

Ollie shrugs. "The goal is to get you to stay."

"Why?"

"Because you don't strike me as the type of person who gives up easily."

Maybe I want to be that person. Maybe I want to give up. It's not like I'm any closer to finding Benji. I'll call it quits now and cut my losses. I tried. That has to count for something.

"It's not worth it anymore."

"Sure it is," Ollie says as the waitress sets his food down in front of him. He thanks her with a toothy smile. "If it was important enough for you to fly all the way over here, it's still important now."

I'm not about to admit that he's right.

"Just be quiet and eat your twelve breakfasts."

The prospect of pissing my mom off is intriguing. I didn't do a lot of it in high school. While my friends were sneaking into clubs and bars, I played it safe. It wasn't worth getting in trouble over. Mason used to roll his eyes when I said I couldn't go.

"You're such a waste of time, Willa."

"I don't know why I keep you around, Willa."

"You act like a child, Willa."

I went with him once. The club was dark and dirty and they didn't card for liquor. I watched two girls—barely seventeen—leave with a guy who had to be pushing thirty.

"It's not a big deal, Willa."

"Everyone does it, Willa."

"Get over it, Willa."

My mother's trust was too important to me. I didn't want to ruin it. I never stepped foot in that club again.

But now…

Now I'm not sure if I care about having her trust. I'm nineteen. I'm in college. I can do what I want. So what if I drained my savings account and jumped on a flight to New Zealand? I'm an adult! This is what adults do.

And maybe I *could* handle it if it was just her blasting my inbox with email after email, but it's everyone. All I want to do is go off the grid and hide, which would probably piss my mom off too.

Too many options.

So much chocolate.

What?

"You ate all my pancakes," Ollie gasps and frowns over at me.

I look down. There's a fork in my hand and an empty plate in front of me.

Oops.

"You didn't even save me a bite!"

"You should have stopped me!"

"I was busy!"

"Yeah, stuffing your face and getting hollandaise all over your shirt!"

Ollie's eyes go wide and he glances at the stain trickling down his white t-shirt. "Fuck."

"You're a slob," I tell him. "Go clean yourself up."

"Always paying me compliments," he mumbles, getting out of the booth. "How did I get so lucky?"

I stab my fork into a banana and eat it, living in hazelnut and chocolate bliss until a phone starts shaking against the table. The panic that twists my insides goes away as soon as I see that it's Ollie's phone. Freya is Face-Timing him. The picture on the screen is of her at Christmas kissing a bottle of whiskey beneath the mistletoe.

I'm supposed to answer it, right?

"Ollie! Is that you? When did you grow very small boobs?"

I fumble with the phone, startled by how quickly she responds. "Oh, hi, sorry! It's Willa. Ollie's in the bathroom."

"You're so pretty," she sighs wistfully. "Ollie did good."

I try to conceal my blush, but figure she can't see it. Wherever she is it's dark and her image on the screen is shaking, like she can't hold her phone still. There's so much background noise that it just sounds like static. She must be in a bar. It would explain the slur in her voice.

"Has he been good to you? He opens the door, right? Pulls out your chair? Gets you off first? Because we had very lengthy discussions about how he's meant to treat his lady friends! And if I find out he's anything less than a gentlemen, I'll kill him! We all will! Especially Emma! She made him read the *Feminine Mystique* when he was fourteen! He's well informed about things! So just tell me if he's being a little chav—"

The phone is ripped out of my hand before I can come up with a response.

I've never been more thankful for Ollie.

"Ollie Bear!" Freya cries. "We were just talking 'bout you!"

"Hey, Frey," Ollie says.

"I need to go to Antarctica!"

Ollie winces. "You've had a bit to drink, haven't you?"

"Well… yes!" she hiccups. "But I still need to go to Antarctica! They've got penguins there!"

"They've got penguins at the zoo, too."

"But they haven't got Archie at the zoo!"

"Who's Archie?" Ollie asks.

"He's in my biology course, Ollie," Freya practically sobs. "I'm in love with him and he's going to Antarctica! He wants to be with the penguins!"

Ollie scratches the top of his head, taking in his sister's dramatics. "I think you need to stop drinking so much."

"I'm not drunk!" she cries. "I'm in love!"

"You're bloody crazy is what you are."

"I'm not crazy!" she insists. "You've never been in love! You don't understand! Let me see the pretty girl again! She'll understand!"

With a heavy sigh, Ollie turns the phone to me.

"Break his heart!" Freya slurs. "And then go back to the States! He deserves to know the pain I feel!"

"Believe me, I'm trying very hard to get back there."

"Good!"

"Yeah, alright, enough from you," Ollie says, turning the phone back to him. "Get home safely, please!"

"I always do," Freya says before ending the call.

Ollie sets the phone back on the table, laughing quietly to himself. From the looks of it, this seems like a typical Freya thing to do. It must be nice to have that—a big family filled with all sorts of characters. I bet holidays are fun in their house.

"She's lost it," Ollie says after a moment.

"She seems fun."

"That's one word for it," he laughs and then looks up at me. He smiles. "And you call me a slob."

I'm confused until he leans over the table and swipes his thumb against the corner of my mouth.

"Can't take you anywhere," he says, licking the drop of Nutella off his thumb.

I force my lips into a scowl. "I don't think you have room to judge me."

"Who's judging?" he asks.

I roll my eyes.

"You ready to go back to the campsite? Or are you still leaving?"

I sigh. "Maybe. I don't know. Probably."

"Then we should get back so Daphne can talk you out of it."

* * *

DAPHNE'S HANDS, MOUTH, AND ATTENTION ARE ALL preoccupied when we arrive back at the campsite. She and Niko are making out against a tree while Emere films a close-up. I'm confused for all of three seconds before Daphne pulls away, her arms wrapped lazily around Niko's neck. She grins at her camera.

"Hope she was worth it, Xavier," she says. "He sure was."

Xavier.

The socks-and-sandal-wearing ex-boyfriend with wandering hands.

I give Daphne credit for being forward, but I also know posting that in her next vlog will be a recipe for disaster.

"Oh! Willa! Ollie!" Daphne says when she sees us,

motioning for Emere to film in our direction. "What have you two crazy kids been up to? #earlymorningrendezvous! #romanticstroll!"

"Daphne, turn the camera off," Ollie says, his hands tucked into his cut-off shorts.

"But the viewers want more of you two," she says, smiling. "You should see all the comments! They think—"

"*Daphne*," Ollie says sharply, a tone he rarely uses. "Turn the camera off."

"Who died?" she asks.

Ollie looks over at me, but I drop my eyes to the ground.

"Willa's leaving."

There's a short pause before Daphne laughs. "No, she's not."

"My mom knows I'm here."

"So she's making you leave?"

"No," I say. "Well, I don't really know. I haven't opened her emails, but she's definitely not happy I'm here."

"Yeah, so she's going off the grid," Ollie says.

"Willa's going off the grid?" Daphne laughs.

"I know, right?" he says. "She can't handle me taking a shortcut, but she's going to fly off to Australia to live like a recluse amongst the dingos."

"That's bloody ridiculous."

"*I know.*"

"Has she gone mad?" Daphne snorts.

"I mean, prob—"

"I'm literally right here," I snap.

"Have you gone mental?"

"No."

"Well, good. You're not leaving."

"Yes, I am."

"You're not leaving, Willa. You didn't come all this way to give up."

I already had this conversation with Ollie. I don't want to have it again.

"Daphne—"

"You're being ridiculous, and you're not leaving. Who cares if your mum knows you're here? It's not like she's going to fly across the world to drag you home," she says. "Now get your shit together. We have to catch the ferry to Wellington!"

Well then.

* * *

From: **Ana Loveridge-Herrera** (Willa!)
From: **Bella Karim** (Don't leave me hanging!)
From: **Felix Presto** (When's the sex tape coming out?)
From: **Martina Henrik** (Mason deserves better)
From: **Mason Stueck** (answer me willa!!)
From: **Oscar Mendez** (AHIS 120-02: Exam Review)
From: **FashionRack** (FLASH SALE! 50% OFF!)
From: **Mason Stueck** (fuck!)
From: **KiwiAir** (Book Your Next Flight!)
From: **Thad Monroe** (who's ollie?)
From: **Camilla Hernandez** (What the fuck! You're cheating on Mason!)
From: **Vincent Herrera** (Call us!!)
From: **Ana Loveridge-Herrera** (This isn't funny!)

* * *

Tosh lets out a long groan and slinks further down in his chair, his chin resting on his chest. We were warned before boarding the ferry that the waters were rough today.

Tosh has been sick since the moment he felt the boat sway beneath him. I had the option of going with Ollie while he dealt with the paperwork required to bring the campervan on board, but I ultimately decided that I'd rather feed Tosh crackers and sips of Coke.

I'm still here.

As much as I don't want to be.

Daphne was right about something. My mother's not going to fly across the world to drag me home. Sure, she sends some rather threatening emails, but she won't follow through. She has a busy job and a spawn growing inside of her. Transpacific flights are pretty much a no-go. Who wants to have morning sickness on a thirteen hour flight? Definitely not the woman who can't make it three stops on the subway before puking. I'm safe from the wrath of Ana Loveridge-Herrera.

But that doesn't mean I'm free from the persecution of my peers, who have already painted a red "A" on my chest. The emails won't stop coming. No matter how hard I wish and hope, my inbox is on fire.

Literally.

My phone is so hot that I'm pretty sure it's going to explode.

I turn it off to save myself the aggravation. After all, when in doubt, it's always best to avoid a situation entirely. If I don't see the emails, they don't exist.

Right?

Right.

"So," I say after I feed Tosh another cracker. "What's going on in the saga of Tosh and Josh?"

Tosh smiles and reaches into his pocket, pulling out his phone to show me a picture of Josh. It's of him on a field. He's a rugby player with tanned skin and a warm smile. He looks so happy and proud with the ball tucked under his arm. I only have to glance up at Tosh, who is wearing a smile that matches the picture, to see how deeply he cares for Josh. I can't wait to see their faces when they finally meet.

"Has he figured out you're coming yet?" I ask.

Tosh shakes his head.

"He's going to be so excited," I assure him. "This is very romantic. I've seen it in a thousand movies."

Tosh chuckles and opens his notes app, punching his fingers against the screen before tilting it towards me.

"*Does it work out for them?*" I read. "Every romantic comedy has a happy ending. You're an actor. You know that."

Tosh smiles and then nudges his head for another cracker, which I promptly shove into his mouth.

The ferry lurches below us. The sounds of waves crashing against the sides is muffled throughout the entire enclosed deck. The trip is only three and a half hours, but it already feels like an eternity. We've only been onboard for forty-five minutes and I'm already stir crazy. With the rough waters and the sudden onset of rain, we're stuck inside with far too many children.

They're so little. How can they make so much noise? Do they not believe in quiet time?

"I mean, look at her." Daphne's entire face is puckered in disgust when she flops into a chair opposite of me, her phone held tightly in her hand. "How can he go from *me* to *that?* And, he's such a spiteful little prat! Posting a picture of them kissing on the beach right after my video with Niko went live! Petty little bitch with a useless little dick."

My eyes widen at her outburst. I'm so distracted that I don't notice Ollie holding a paper cup out to me.

"Coffee," he clarifies, nudging it towards me. "I

thought we established that it's in my best interest to keep you happy."

I glare at him and then drop my eyes to the array of snacks he has nestled safely in the crook of his arms.

"Well," I say, taking the coffee. "If that's the case, then I hope you got me a—"

He drops a paper bag in my lap.

"—brownie."

I don't need to look up at him to know he's smiling stupidly at me, so I ignore him. He plops into the seat beside me, and takes up too much of the armrest. He has that goddamn guitar in his lap. I want to strangle him at the first strum.

"Oh my god," Daphne snaps. "She's literally half naked in all of these pictures. I mean, c'mon! Have some self respect! Keep your clothes on! What does Xavier see in her?"

"Her gigantic tits?" Niko laughs.

"And she's sharing them with the entire world! Like, why would you want to be with someone like that? I certainly wouldn't!"

I feel the heat rising up my neck and soon my entire body is on fire.

What kind of self-respecting person would take half naked pictures of herself? Who would display their body in such a provocative way? There's a word for girls like that.

I'm going to be sick.

"Where are you going?" Daphne asks when I get out of my chair.

"I need some air."

The top deck is completely empty, the soft pitter-patter of rain falling is a welcomed change from the screaming children. The sky is dark and gray, the waves crashing against the side of the ferry. I find a spot beneath an overhang and slide down to the ground, not caring that it's fairly wet.

I'm not going to cry. I already decided that. I wouldn't. I couldn't. I'm stronger than that.

At least, that's what I keep telling myself. Because if I say it enough, maybe I'll start believing it.

I'm a strong woman.

People's opinions of me don't matter.

My opinion of me matters.

But I still open my email, despite every voice in my head telling me not to.

From: **Bella Karim** (Did you see what Mason wrote on FB?)
From: **Ana Loveridge-Herrera** (Please Willa just tell me you're ok)
From: **Mason Stueck** (You're worthless)
From: **Mason Stueck** (Hope he knows what kind of slut he's with)
From: **Mason Stueck** (You blew it babe)
From: **Aaron Bates** (Has Ollie seen the infamous pictures?)
From: **Craig Dorson** (What's that saying? Once a whore always a)
From: **Mason Stueck** (I should have known)
From: **Leah Zimmerman** (Does Ollie know what you get up to? lol)
From: **Jack Barnes** (Willing Willa's still getting around I see)

I press my lips together and breathe through the threat of tears, counting down from ten. I should turn off my phone again. Toss it into the water. I could be done with it all. But I open Mason's first email and then the second and the third and the fourth. And suddenly, I've read them all.

Worthless slut.

Couldn't keep your legs closed.

How long have you known him?

I can't believe I wasted two years with you.

Should have known better.

Remember when you gave it up on the second date?

I should have known then.

Whore.

I could ruin you.

I'm only half surprised when I feel Ollie slide to the ground next to me. I try my best to hide my face with my hair, but I'm pretty sure he's already gotten an eyeful. I'm not crying. My lips aren't quivering. It's the rain—the rain is making my face wet.

"Lovely day, isn't it?" he jokes.

I don't laugh.

"Right," he coughs. "Wasn't really funny, was it?"

I don't think any of his jokes are funny. He knows that, so I figure it's rhetorical and doesn't require an answer. Even if I wanted to, I couldn't respond. I'm positive that if I open my mouth, I would choke out a sob and I really don't want to explain to Ollie that the entire world thinks I'm a whore.

So we sit in silence and listen to the water and rain as we surge towards the north island through a blanket of fog.

Ollie knocks his knee against mine seconds, minutes, maybe hours later. When I try to ignore him, he nudges my shoulder a few times until he finally gets my attention.

"What—"

He doesn't say anything.

Instead, he holds out an earbud to me, and my face softens at the gesture.

And when Alanis Morissette starts playing and when he starts singing at the top of his lungs, I laugh so hard that I start to cry.

Because he's ridiculous.

Because I'm sad.

Because I don't know what else to do.

So I cry.

And I cry.

And I cry.

10

"So, I was thinking," Daphne says, swiping a piece of her toast through a puddle of yolk on Ollie's plate. "Why don't you try contacting your mum's family? I mean, wouldn't they know where your dad is?"

I spoon more of my muesli into my mouth and watch Ollie snarl at Daphne, who soaks up every last drop of his eggs with what's left of her crusts.

"I don't know where they live," I say, reaching for my mug of coffee. "Actually, I don't know anything about them. My mom was very good at keeping her life in New Zealand in New Zealand."

"Obviously didn't do that good of a job if you're alive and kicking."

I sigh and down the rest of my drink, the fuel I need for the day after spending a sleepless night in a parking lot. Tosh had a symphony going with the crickets lurking in the bushes. I should have taken Ollie up on his offer when he asked if I wanted some of his nighttime cold medicine. He wasn't sick, but it knocked him out for a good eight hours.

Part of me is happy that I couldn't sleep. I don't want

to think about the things my subconscious would have dreamt up. The reality of my life is nightmare enough.

"I'm sure they wouldn't be hard to find," Daphne says.

"Yeah, that's what I thought about Benji."

"Still might be worth a try," Ollie adds, looking me straight in the eyes as he tries to inconspicuously steal a strawberry from my bowl. He grins when my eyes shift into a glare, juice dribbling down his chin and onto his shirt.

"Honestly, we can't take you anywhere." I say. "You're a slob."

"You flatter me, Willa."

"Yeah, well, you annoy me, Oliver."

"I love it when you call me Oliver."

"Did you hear that?" Daphne says and I look up to see her smiling at her camera. "#williebanter! #callmeoliver! #itgetshimgoing!"

"Daphne!" I snap. "What part of I don't want to be in your vlogs don't you understand?"

"I promised I wouldn't film you."

"What do you call this, then?"

"Background noise."

"Yeah, *background noise*," I scoff. "Maybe if I was like Tosh and could get all your ad revenue pulled, you'd actually listen to me."

"Well, duh," she laughs. "I'm not trying to get sued by his agencies and sponsors."

I grit my teeth and then dig around with my spoon until I finish my breakfast, protecting my bowl of fruit with my arm and fending off Ollie's wayward fingers with a fork. I'll be damned if he steals the last of my cantaloupe.

Our first full day in Wellington is just a continuation of yesterday—damp, drizzly, and gray. The weather isn't going to hold Daphne and Niko back. They already booked a bike tour that has far too many twists and turns and steep uphill climbs that would be disastrous on a warm and sunny day. It's an easy no from Tosh and an even easier no from me. We're going to find something less dangerous and more dry.

At one point the prospect of slipping, falling, and tumbling off a cliff seemed alluring, but I quickly got over that.

"How are you going to waste your day, Willa?" Daphne asks after finishing off her toast. "Are you gonna have a nap in the van? Drown yourself in coffee in this cafe?"

"Both of those sound ragingly enticing, actually," I say tightly. "But I think me and Tosh are going to visit a museum. Infuse some culture into our lives."

"As if you can't do that on a bicycle."

"Safety first."

She rolls her eyes. "You're the killjoy of my life, Willa Loveridge."

"Someone has to be, Daphne Purcell."

When she glares at me, I smile so wide that my lips lift my cheeks and my nose wrinkles. As soon as I hear the shudder of a camera, everything falls into a frown.

"What the fuck, Ollie?" I snap.

"I'm sorry." He doesn't sound sorry. "You looked like a chipmunk. I couldn't help it."

"A little something for the wank bank," Daphne coughs.

A blush instantly rises up my neck, which is nothing compared to the fact that Ollie is as red as the bottle of ketchup in front of him.

"That was so—*so* beyond inappropriate," he says, eyes widening into oceans of blue beneath the frames of his glasses.

"#williewankbank!"

I kick her so hard that her knee jerks into the underside

of the table, which causes her orange juice to spill onto Niko's lap.

"Nice going, Willa."

"#oops!"

"Can someone get me a napkin?" Niko asks.

Daphne and I are too busy trying to out glare each other, so Tosh pulls a few from a dispenser and hands them to him.

#checkplease.

* * *

Tosh and I somehow acquired an Ollie. He was supposed to be on Daphne's doomsday bicycle excursion, but decided at the last minute to come to the museum. I wouldn't be so annoyed if he didn't talk through our audio tour. I missed an entire explanation because he was giggling over something that looked like a penis.

"Honestly, Ollie, grow up."

"I can't," he laughs. "I'm a child."

"Then maybe you should go into the arts and crafts room. I think they're making hand puppets."

"That sounds like a lot of fun, actually."

"Well, no one's stopping you."

He doesn't leave.

I'm very disappointed.

But I plug my earbuds back in and do my best to ignore his existence.

I like museums. Sure, they aren't extreme like bungee jumping or speed boating, but it's nice to admire things that artists put so much time and effort into. I spend so much of my day rushing around. Sometimes I want to stop and take something in—to appreciate every little intrinsic detail. Why did the artist choose that color? What story is it telling? How did it make him feel? How does it make *me* feel? It's fascinating.

It's a conversation I would want to have with Benji. Y'know, if he didn't avoid people like the plague and if I didn't want to scream at him. I would love to talk about his art. And why he loves it more than me.

"*It looks like a monkey breastfeeding a pigeon.*"

My eyes fly open when I hear Ollie snicker. He's reading something off a notepad. I instantly backhand Tosh in the chest.

"First of all, *no,* it does *not,*" I say. "And second of all—"

Tosh holds his finger up, silencing me. Who does he think he is? I was about to deliver a speech that would have gotten me another "A" in *Public Speaking.*

"*Art is subjective,*" I read once Tosh hands me the note. I glare when I see him standing there with his arms crossed. He's smiling smugly. He definitely has been spending too much time with Daphne.

"He's right, y'know?"

"I can guarantee you that's not a monkey breastfeeding a pigeon."

"It could be," Ollie says.

"Have you ever taken an art history class?"

"No, have you?"

I failed a course in western art...

"Well, no," I say. "But I've been to plenty of museums. I've seen a lot of art!"

"So have I! And based off of your ridiculous qualifications, I'm practically an art historian!"

"You're practically a moron!"

"Only practically?"

"You know what I mean," I say. "And you've made me miss ten tracks! I'm trying to follow the guided tour!"

"Literally no one follows the guided—"

Tosh cuts Ollie off by shoving another note at him.

"*You two argue more than a married couple*," he reads. "Only because Willa has this thing where she thinks she's always right."

"I am always right!"

"No, you're right about sixty percent of the time. The other forty, you're a bloody wacko. This morning, for example! When I took that left instead of a right! You went on and on *and on* for a bloody hour about it!"

"Because I was right and you were wrong! Tell him Tosh."

Tosh quickly scribbles something and hands it to me.

"*You're both wackos.*" I read. "You're not helping."

"You're going to get us kicked out," Ollie says to me. "That security guard's been eyeing you since your first outburst."

I'm not going to dignify him with a response, so instead I walk away. If they want to giggle over breastfeeding monkeys, fine. I'm not going to take any part in it.

* * *

I DITCHED THE AUDIO TOUR.

Not because Ollie was right, but because the woman's voice got annoying and I felt like I was being rushed around.

I'm sitting in a gallery of photographs taken at various landmarks around New Zealand. The only one I'm familiar with is Milford Sound. The rest are as foreign as the life my mother left here. Things would have been so different if I grew up in this country. Maybe I would have embraced adventure and explored all of these beautiful places. Maybe I wouldn't be afraid of my own shadow, conditioned to be home before dark and to walk around with a key slotted between my fingers. Sure, there's danger everywhere, but now I'm brainwashed to expect it.

When someone sits down beside me, I shift away from them out of instinct. But then I see something blue and feathery out of the corner of my eye. I jump the second I look over.

"What the hell is wrong with you?" I ask Ollie, frowning at the puppet on his hand. It's made out of a paper bag and looks as if a five-year-old crafted it. "And what is that *thing*?"

"I thought I did a pretty good job." He shrugs. "Some little ginger bastard stole the last googly eye, but that's okay because Bill here lost his right one in an epic battle with a pelican. He thinks it's a pretty cool story to tell."

"Oh my god." I look away from him and shake my head, definitely *not* smiling. They're all crazy. I'm the only sane one in this group.

"What are you doing in here?" he asks.

"Wondering what my life would be like if I never met you."

"Boring as fuck, probably."

I laugh. "But really, just wondering what my life would have been like if my mother didn't take me away. My whole family is here and I don't even know who they are."

"I'm sure it would be easy to find them."

I scoff. "Yeah, I said the same thing about Benji… that's turned out *great*."

"Loveridge isn't really a popular name, though. I'm sure they'd be easy to track down, and they might have more information on your dad."

"And what would I say to them?" I ask. "Hi, I'm Willa, the kid you didn't want your daughter to have. Do you think you can help me find my father? I'm sure you don't like him much either, but hey, help a girl out!"

"I mean, maybe not in those words…" Ollie looks over at me and smiles. "I don't think it would hurt to try. What's the worst that could happen? They don't know where he is?"

"They could slam the door in my face."

"Highly unlikely."

I groan and then take a deep breath before standing up.

"Where are you going?"

"To steal some wifi."

"Does that mean we're investigating?" he asks, following me.

"It means *I'm* investigating."

"I don't get to help?"

"You get to bring me coffee."

"Wow, I'm such a lucky bloke."

"Bet your ass you are."

* * *

The weather clears enough for us to overstay our welcome at a pub that has an outdoor patio with a view of the harbor. Tosh and Ollie are working on their second beers. It's barely after four, but that's not too early for either of them to start drinking. I down the rest of my flat white, already feeling the effects of the four spoonfuls of sugar I added.

My eye is twitching.

My hands are shaking.

But I'm hyperaware!

Mostly of the fact that the blonde sitting at the table

next to us has been eyeing Ollie like some sort of lioness on the prowl.

Please take him away.

I could only watch him suck salt off his greasy fingers for so long before I wanted to cut them all off with dull cutlery.

I do my best to focus my attention on my computer and the blank search engine I have pulled up, but my eyes won't stop trailing to the number at the bottom of my screen. Twenty new emails.

Don't click it, Willa.

Don't click it.

Don't click it.

Don't click it.

I click it.

From: **Vincent Herrera** (Just call us!)
From: **Ana Loveridge-Herrera** (Willa please! I can't sleep)
From: **Ana Loveridge-Herrera** (Your roommate said you never went back)
From: **Vincent Herrera** (Mom's a mess!)
From: **Ana Loveridge-Herrera** (I need you to call me! I'm not mad please!)
From: **Mason Stueck** (hope he knows what a piece of trash you are)
From: **Mason Stueck** (SLUT)
From: **Mason Stueck** (SLUT)
From: **Mason Stueck** (SLUT)
From: **Mason Stueck** (SLUT)
From: **The Coffee Corner** (New! Salted Caramel Latte!)
From: **Mason Stueck** (SLUT)
From: **Mason Stueck** (SLUT)
From: **Mason Stueck** (worthless)

From: **Mason Stueck** (whore)
From: **Johnny McCay** (keep slutting it up in NZ, Willa!)
From: **Kelly Benson** (Somethings never change)
From: **Melody Stueck** (How could you!)
From: **Ticket Planet** (On Sale Now!)
From: **Bella Karim** (C'mon Willa! Spill!)

I close my eyes, clench my fist, and count down from ten.

Out of sight.

Out of mind.

"Where are we starting?" Ollie asks. He attempts to glance over at my computer screen, but I tilt it away from him. "What? I can't look?"

"You might break something."

"With what? My eyes?"

"I'm sure you have something better to do," I say, splaying my fingers over the computer keys. "Like getting me another coffee."

Ollie frowns. "Fine, but you're getting decaf. You're shaking like someone going through withdrawals."

"What's the point of decaf coffee?"

"I don't know? The flavor?"

"Ugh, just get me a Diet Coke then."

Because that has caffeine too!

"Right away, my dear."

"Extra ice and lime," I say without looking up. "And don't call me that."

"Of course, sweetheart."

He walks away before I can glare at him. Tosh, thankfully, is smiling from ear to ear, so the dirty look doesn't go to waste.

"What?" I ask.

Tosh shrugs and scribbles something on a napkin and

pushes it towards me. "*#mrandmrs,*" I read. "Honestly, Tosh, you're my favorite. Don't make me regret that decision."

He continues smiling sheepishly at me, but I turn my attention back to my computer. I figure searching my mother's name will be a good place to start.

Ana Loveridge returns 299,000 results.

Her Facebook account. Her Twitter. Her Instagram. Her Linkdin. And a handful of press releases and articles that she commented on behalf of her clients.

Model, Elle Vetrov, NOT Seeking Treatment for Eating Disorder Says Publicist, Ana Loveridge-Herrera!

Arianna Nikas, Host of New York Nightly, *Expecting First Child with NFL Player Confirms Publicist, Ana Loveridge-Herrera!*

Divorce For Actor, Brody O'Callaghan? No Comment from Publicist, Ana Loveridge-Herrera!

This is going to be harder than I thought. There are pages and pages of tabloid garbage. Why doesn't my mother have a normal job? One that doesn't include spinning stories and making up excuses for celebrities.

"Your mum knows Vivian Holiday?"

Ollie is standing above me when I look up at him, literal hearts in his eyes as he scans over the image of the lingerie model on my screen. I gag a little. Mostly because he made a trip back to the van to get his guitar. I want to tell him that her twin is sitting a few tables over and is not so subtly checking him out, but I don't want to inflate his already enormous ego.

And I definitely don't want to end up with another person in the van.

"Yes, she represents her."

"Like a manager?"

"Publicist."

"That's pretty cool."

"Not really."

Ollie plops down in the chair beside me and takes a long sip of his beer before running his hand over the neck of his guitar.

"What should I play?" he asks, strumming carelessly.

"Silence."

He looks over at me with dimples in his cheeks and I have to resist rolling my eyes. He isn't as charming as he lets on. He's a nuisance. And a pain in my ass. So when he starts playing the chorus of an Alanis Morissette song—his poison of choice as of the last twenty-four hours—like some heartbroken teenage girl, I'm not even remotely surprised.

What surprises me even less is the attention he gets. He catches a few ears and then some more, and soon all eyes are on him. He moves from his seat beside me to the oversized beer barrel next to our table, his legs dangling over the edge. He continues to belt out lyrics as the crowd cheers.

I don't understand the appeal. What's it about a quirky guy with a guitar? Is it the glasses? The perpetually messy hair he tries to *subtly* hide beneath a hoodie? The wrinkled t-shirt he's been wearing for two days? It confuses me.

But I tune him out and zero in on my computer and start to refine my searches.

Ana Loveridge New Zealand.

Ana Loveridge Queenstown.

Ana Loveridge University of Queenstown.

Ana Loveridge Benji Atkins.

Nothing.

Not even a catalogued newspaper article for winning an award at a sporting event.

Ana Loveridge might as well have never existed in New Zealand.

"Hey, did I see you on YouTube?"

My heart drops into the pit of my stomach at the question, but then I realize the voice is rather light, giggly, and very, *very* flirty.

I look up and see that the girl who has been eyeing Ollie has finally made her move. She's tiny. Ollie dwarfs her when he stands up, but I'm fairly certain girls liked that sort of thing. Cute forehead kisses. Bear hugs. Nuzzling into his chest. I wouldn't know. Most guys are my height or shorter. It's far less romantic when I could be the one giving the forehead kisses—at least, as far as fragile masculinity goes.

Tiny little pixie fairy girl has nothing to worry about.

"Uh, yeah, probably!" Ollie chuckles.

"You did the *Wonderwall* cover," she says, twirling a piece of her hair around her finger. She nibbles her lip and bats her eyes for good measure. "And you were in those vlogs…"

"Yeah, but don't let the title fool you. I'm not into reptiles or threesomes," he says as he walks over to the table, his guitar resting against his back. He reaches for my Diet Coke, chugging half of it through a straw before his lips quirk into a smile. "Well… definitely not into reptiles."

She giggles.

I gag.

I grab my drink before he can drink the rest of it, narrowing my eyes when he pouts at me. "Get your own."

He sticks his tongue out before taking his seat.

"So are you on your gap year?"

"Yeah," Ollie says, digging his hand into my basket of fries. "You?"

"Oh, no." She shakes her head. "I go to Victoria University."

"That's cool. What are you studying?"

"Early childhood education."

"You're gonna be a teacher?" He chews, swallows and reaches for another. I slap his hand away. "That's brilliant."

"I think so too," she practically sighs. "I'm Ruby."

"Ollie," he replies. He tries to steal another, but I quickly swat him away again. "And the person who can't share is Willa."

"And the person grinning like a lunatic at his phone is Tosh," I add, earning a dirty look.

"Cool," Ruby says in a way that sounds like she doesn't think it's cool at all. "Ollie, do you want to get a drink?"

"Nah, I still got half a pint."

"Oh, alright, maybe later, then?"

"Yeah, maybe!"

I'm not sure who's more confused by his response: me or Ruby. Even Tosh looks perplexed.

Did he really just…

"You realized she was coming on to you, right?"

"Who?"

I lift a brow. I'm dumbfounded by his stupidity. Tosh is too. But Ollie just shrugs and sucks the salt off his fingers.

"Did you find anything else?" he asks, turning my computer towards him.

I smack him. "Get your greasy hands off!"

"Always so violent," he mumbles, rubbing his arm. "I bruise—"

"Like a peach, we know," I cut him off. "And no, I'm

still exactly where I was before your little impromptu performance. Just with less Diet Coke and a headache."

Ollie opens his mouth to say something, but Tosh slips a note between us, silencing him.

"*Search Loveridge New Zealand*," Ollie reads and then guzzles down the rest of his beer. "Yeah, just search Loveridge New Zealand."

It's worth a shot, so I put my fingers to work, guiding them over the keys. I say a prayer as I hit enter.

And there it is.

The first result of 200,000.

Loveridge Family Farm.

Owned and run by Katarina and Jack Loveridge, Loveridge Family Farm is a New Plymouth staple! From our berry patches to our petting zoo, there's fun for all ages.

There's a picture of them at the top of the page. They're sitting on the front steps of an old farmhouse that's white with black shutters. They have a porch swing. And flower baskets on the windows.

A life like that doesn't seem real.

As much as I don't want to believe it, I can't ignore the fact that the woman looks exactly like my mother—exactly like me. The same mousy brown hair and matching brown eyes. A heart-shaped face and a dimpled left cheek. Full lips and a pert nose.

She's my grandmother.

"They own a farm."

"Close by?" Ollie asks.

"New Plymouth? I don't know where it is," I say. "I'd have to map it out, but, um, I'm gonna go get a drink. I'll be right back."

It's overwhelming. There's a tightness in my chest that's

all too familiar. *Panic*. My heart starts racing. My hands are sweating. I clench my fists. Count down from ten. Breathe.

My grandparents own a farm in New Plymouth. I have an address and their names. I can go there. I can meet them.

"What can I get you?" the bartender asks.

"A shot?"

"Of what?"

"I don't know? What do people take shots of?"

The bartender wrinkles his brow before placing a shot glass in front of me, filling it to the brim with an amber liquid. I don't ask. I throw it back. It burns the whole way down. My throat and stomach are on fire. It makes me feel worse.

"You can put it on Ollie's—"

"I need to talk to you."

Ollie's face is unwaveringly still. The grim line his lips are set in would have caused me some concern if I didn't feel the shot I'd just taken crawling back up my throat.

"What's wrong with you?" I frown when he laces his fingers with mine, tugging me away from the crowd. "Ollie! Seriously, what—"

We're stopped in front of the bathrooms when I realize he has my computer with him. He has the screen turned to me, my emails up in all their glory.

Slut.

Slut.

Slut.

Slut.

"What the hell is this, Willa? *Who* is this? Why are they harassing you? This isn't okay—"

"Why are you going through my computer?" I snap, grabbing it from him. "Seriously, Ollie!"

"I wasn't—I was trying to pull up directions and I hit

the wrong button," he explains. "But regardless, this isn't okay."

"It's none of your business," I swallow and move to walk away. "Stay out of it."

He doesn't let me get too far before grabbing my arm. "I'm not going to stay out of it. No one should be speaking to you this way. Is it because of the video? Do they think we—is Mason your boyfriend?"

"It's none of your business." I jerk my arm away from him.

"I don't care—"

"Neither do I! If it doesn't bother me, it shouldn't bother you!"

"They're *harassing* you! And if this wanker is your boyfriend—"

"He's my… he's my ex, okay? I don't… I don't have a boyfriend," I stammer. "So just let it go, Ollie. I already did."

I have more important things to figure out, like whether or not I want to go to New Plymouth to meet my grandparents.

Ollie's thoughts, opinions, and feelings will have to wait.

11

Daphne puckers her lips into the rearview, and then removes a smudge of red lipstick from her front tooth with her finger. It's ten-thirty in the morning, and she wasn't even awake five minutes ago, but now she's perched in the driver's seat, ready to take over. I'm grateful. Co-piloting with Tosh is difficult with the communication barrier.

We're outside of a gas station, and I'm pretty sure the boys have been in there for at least three hours. And while that would normally bother me, I'm just happy to have Ollie out of my hair for the time being.

We haven't spoken.

Last night, as soon as I had gotten all my things, I left the bar and went straight back to the van, giving Ollie strict instructions not to follow me. He didn't listen, which didn't surprise me. Thankfully, Daphne had beat us there. She was drunk and chatty. Ollie couldn't get a word in while she told her elaborate story about ditching Niko and his friends. Apparently, he served his purpose and she was bored of him.

"On to the next conquest!" were her exact words.

My only conquest was a decent night of sleep, so I holed myself up in the passenger's seat and haven't left since. Me, myself, and my earphones were safe from Ollie and his incessant need to bother us. He had the privilege of rubbing Daphne's back as she puked out the back door. Serves him right for being a nosey little knobhead.

I've successfully ignored him for the past two hours, but I'm not sure how much longer that will last. Being in such close quarters makes it hard to pretend someone doesn't exist. Especially when that someone has been strumming away on his guitar since the sun came up. There was a brief moment when I considered smashing it over his head, but that would mean I'm acknowledging him, which I'm not.

Ollie who?

"Where are we going?" Daphne asks, pursing her newly-coated lips at the mirror once more.

"New Plymouth."

"Where the hell is New Plymouth? And why the hell are we going there?"

"That's where my mom's family lives."

"You found them?"

"Yeah."

There's a hitch in my voice that even Daphne notices, a wavering note of hesitance. All the pieces are falling together. I have names. An address. A family that might be able to give me all the answers I need. But there's something in my gut that feels wrong—something that leaves me with a lingering doubt. Maybe this isn't the right choice. Maybe I don't need them. I have another option—Janey, the woman Arthur told me about. Maybe she can help.

"You sure about this?" Daphne asks.

"Not really."

"Are you afraid of what they're going to tell you?"

"Yes and no, I guess. I mean, they didn't support my mom having me, so it's pretty stupid of me to assume they'll welcome me with open arms."

"People can change, Willa."

"I don't know if I believe that."

"You've got to stop seeing the worst in people. You'll make yourself miserable for the rest of your life."

"I'm just trying to look out for myself."

Daphne let out a long sigh. Before she can say another word, the van shakes as Ollie and Tosh get back in. I shrink myself into my seat, hoping that my poor attempt at disguising myself will save me from Ollie and his perpetual need to aggravate me.

It doesn't.

I feel his weight on the back of my seat, and I glance up at him under hooded eyes, watching as he sets a paper cup of coffee in my holder and a sports drink in Daphne's. Whatever peace offering he thinks this is won't have me waving a white flag. I plan to ignore him for the duration of this trip.

"Look at Ollie taking care of his girls." Daphne beams at him. "Such a lovely bloke. Your mum raised you right."

"She did teach me how to treat a woman."

It feels like a jab.

It's *definitely* a jab.

Dickhead.

"Ollie Dunbar, God's gift to women," I mumble, pulling my hood over my head to conceal the automatic eye roll.

"No, not a gift," he says without missing a beat. "Just a decent person who doesn't harass people behind a computer screen, or to their face, for that matter."

"You're a regular Prince Charming."

"I'm just trying to be your friend, Willa."

"Yeah, well—"

"*Starting the day off with a little lovers spat! #willie*—"

"Daphne, turn the camera off," Ollie snaps.

"Yikes, what crawled up your arse?"

Ollie doesn't respond. Instead, he stalks off into the back with Tosh.

Finally.

"What's going on with you two?"

"Nothing, Ollie's just being Ollie," I say. "Can you drive, please?"

I don't think she believes a word I said, but twists the key in the ignition and drops the subject, leaving me to silently debate whether or not to drink the coffee Ollie got me.

On the one hand, I want to stand my ground.

On the other hand, I have a pounding headache.

Don't do it, Willa! Stay strong! He doesn't deserve the satisfaction!

I cross my arms, deciding to focus my attention out the window. The sun broke through the clouds this morning, the gray skies vanishing into a bright shade of blue. It's warm, but the van is comfortable without the air-conditioner.

"Hi, guys! I'm massively hungover, but we're heading to—"

"Daphne!" I hiss when I see her balancing her camera on the wheel. "You're not vlogging and driving!"

"I've done it, like, a million times."

"I don't care! You're gonna get us killed."

"Yeah, well, you're killing my vibe," she mumbles and tosses the camera at me. I fumble with it and turn it off. "Can you see if I have any tablets in my bag?"

"Tablets?"

"For headaches? I've got a splitting one."

I lean over my seat and pick up her purse from the floor. I mull through receipts, granola bar wrappers, and a few condoms before my fingers brush over the familiar orange bottles. I swallow when I pull one out. Oxycodone. It feels lighter than it did the last time.

I'm not feeling particularly brave, but this is an opportunity to get some answers to my questions. Why does she have this? How did she get it? What's it for? When did she start taking it? So I shake it in her direction and when she looks over at me, she laughs.

"I can't vlog, but you'd let me drive under the influence of narcotics?"

I looked down at the bottle. "Why do you have them?"

"They're from when I broke my arm," she says easily.

I dig my hand around her bag again, pulling out two more bottles. "And the Ambian?"

"I have trouble sleeping."

"And the Xanax?"

"Anxiety is the new black," she laughs. "Doesn't everyone get a prescription for it when they turn eighteen? God knows you could use it."

She's not wrong.

I frown and drop the bottles. I don't know whether or not to believe her, but I don't have anything else to go on, so I have to take her word for it.

"Is there anything else in there?"

"No, but you can have my coffee."

"You take it with too much sugar," she says. "And I prefer tea."

"Alright, well, suffer then."

"Fine, I will," she says as she comes up to a fork in the road. "Which way am I going?"

The directions are clearly mapped out on my lap. We're

supposed to stay straight on this road for fifty-five minutes and then merge onto a new highway for another two and a half hours. If everything goes as planned—and it will—we'll be in New Plymouth by two. The farm stays open till six.

But the day I met Daphne she told me that I should trust my gut.

So maybe I should start.

"Turn left at the fork."

* * *

WHEN WE PULL UP TO *THE HONEY HIVE*, A BEE SANCTUARY, all eyes are on me. Not exactly a place someone with a bee allergy should be, but alas, here we are.

"Not exactly the family farm I'd envisioned," Ollie says, shifting his eyes to me.

"That's because we're at an apiary."

"Yes, I know. I can't *beelieve* it."

"Well, no one's asking you to come," I say. "Stay in the van for all I care."

"I just don't understand why you changed your mind about meeting your mum's family."

"You don't have to understand ," I tell him as I get out of the van. "All that matters is that we're here and I'm going to see if the lady that runs this place knows where Benji is."

"And what happens if she doesn't?"

"I don't know, Ollie. I'll cross that bridge when I get there."

"Good God," Daphne mumbles as she shoves past us. "Get married already."

"I'd rather get stung by ten thousand bees and have my throat swell up and die," I say

"Well, here's your chance, sweetheart," Ollie replies.

Every fiber in my being wants to jam down on his foot, but I don't. Not because I'm the bigger person—I'm not—but because Tosh wraps his arm around my shoulders and drags me away before I can do any damage.

The Honey Hive is buzzing—both figuratively and literally. There are *swarms* of people *bumbling* about. Lines of happy customers spilling out of the small store, so eager to get their hands on a jar of honey or some weird organic beauty products or a glass of their famous Queen Bee Tea, which is simply just iced tea and lemonade sweetened with honey. They offer classes on honey harvesting. They have a museum on all things bees. For the kids, they have an arts and crafts section where they can make their very own beeswax candle.

Fun for the whole family!

There wasn't much about Janey online. Everything on her social media was geared towards *The Honey Hive*. But I did find an article about the charity benefit she hosted that mentions Benji donating a few pieces.

"Fucking wanker," Ollie hisses.

When I look over at him, he's hunched over with his hand cradling his calf.

A bee sting.

I try not to laugh.

I fail.

Miserably.

"So happy you're having a laugh, Willa," he mumbles, digging the stinger out.

I shrug. "Are you allergic?"

"No."

"Okay, then better you than me."

He snarls and shakes his leg a few times before straightening it out, gritting his teeth at the pain. "This is a terrible idea."

"Listen, I'm the one with the allergy. If I'm not complaining, neither should you."

"You've got an allergy?" Ollie's eyes go wide. "Are you bloody mad? This is dangerous."

"Please, you jumped off a bridge," I say, rolling my eyes. "And I haven't been stung in, like, ten years. In the unlikely event that it happens, I give you permission to stab me with my EpiPen. But honestly, anaphylaxis sounds a hell of a lot better than being around you right now."

"#troubleinparadise," Daphne whispers, carefully angling her camera away from us. "It's their second fight of the day."

I stomp away from them and over to the directory. There's a small map of the grounds, and next to it is a chalkboard with clearly labeled times. At two-thirty, Beatrice the Bee is holding story time for three to five year olds to discuss the importance of pollination. How To! Make Your Own Face Scrub! at three. And at three-thirty, Harvest That Honey with Janey Taylor.

"You guys can just hang at the gift shop, or something," I tell them once I turn around. "The website says they have award winning honey-lemon pound cake."

"And miss you making a fool out of yourself in a honey harvesting class?" Daphne laughs. "I don't think so. It's vlog gold!"

And that's how I find myself sitting at a picnic table, disgusted at the mere sight of Ollie sucking honey-lemon glaze off of his fingers. I need a distraction before I vomit into my lemonade. I nudge my napkin towards Tosh.

"*Does he think that's attractive?*" I write.

"*Do women not like watching men lick their fingers?*" he writes back.

"*I'd rather watch him get mauled by a cat.*" I frown. "*He has horrendous manners.*"

"*But he's a good guy,*" Tosh writes. "*He was very upset after you left the pub last night.*"

"*He shouldn't have been snooping,*" I say. "*I should call his sisters and tell them. I'm sure they know a few ways to punish him.*"

"*I think you're already punishing him.*"

"Quit being a bunch of gossips," Daphne says, leaning over Tosh to catch a peek at our note, but he hides it with his hand and sticks his tongue out at her. "God, you're turning into Willa."

"I resent that."

"You resent everything."

"I definitely resent the fact that I met you."

"Lies," she scoffs. "You'd still be stumbling around Christchurch if you hadn't met me."

"No, I'd be stumbling around Queenstown. Because I would have waited for the next flight."

"And think of all the things you wouldn't have gotten to do."

"Like almost getting married into a cult? Meeting Tweedle Dee and Tweedle Dumb?"

"And you wouldn't have gotten your YouTube debut!"

"Which has done me *so* much good! Thank you, by the way."

"You're *very* welcome."

"As much as I love listening to Willa berate someone that's not me," Ollie starts, "it's almost three-thirty."

We walk across the grounds to meet the group that has already formed. We're the youngest by decades, everyone else at least triple our ages. It seems that honey harvesting isn't popular amongst the youth of New Zealand.

"Suppose I'll call this vlog 'Field Trip From the Home'," Daphne whispers to me.

"That's not funny," I tell her. "It's rude."

Daphne shrugs. If she was going to respond, she never gets a chance. A woman quickly comes over to us with an instruction list a mile long of everything we need to know about putting our suits on.

"I feel like a Ghostbuster," Ollie laughs to himself, pulling the zipper up his neck.

"You look like one too," Daphne adds as she places her hat and veil over her head.

"Think they'd trust me with a Proton Pack?"

"Not a chance—"

"Can you two at least try to take this seriously?"

"God, Willa, don't *bee* such a *buzz*kill," Daphne says.

"Thank you for reducing me to a bad pun."

"You're *unbeelievable.*"

The veil I'm wearing hides my glare.

"We have seven hives set up," the woman says, turning to a door that leads out of the changing room. "So if you would please partner up…"

Would you please partner up…

Five words no person ever wants to hear.

"Tosh!" Daphne practically shouts. "Of course I'll be your partner! You don't have to ask me twice!"

"He didn't ask you at all!" I say.

She grins and grabs his hand. "Don't worry, Willa! Ollie's still available, but you need to act fast because the nan over there's eyeing him."

They disappear through the door and I sigh out in frustration as Ollie bumps his shoulder against mine.

"We better get going *beefore* they start without us."

"I swear to God, I'm going to kill you."

"There's my little ray of sunshine."

Outside, I'm as eager as ever to meet Janey. Her assistant said she'll be out in a few minutes, and my nerves are buzzing along with the bees. Despite it all, I have a good feeling about this. She'll know how to contact Benji. I won't have to go to New Plymouth. I won't have to meet my mother's family. I'm done. This is it. Mission complete. Someone get me a gold star.

Or a fly swatter.

There are so many bees.

"We can't avoid this forever," Ollie tells me once we're standing behind our hive.

"There is no *we*," I say. "And I'll avoid it for as long as I want to. It's mine to ignore."

"That's not the point," he insists, but I can't begin to take him seriously in these giant white suits we're wearing. He looks like a possessed marshmallow. "Willa, they're harassing—"

"Sorry I'm late!"

My heart nearly jumps out of my chest when I hear her voice. She's in protective gear from head to toe, so I can't see her face, but I assume she's Janey.

"Willa," Ollie whispers. "I don't think—"

"Shut up, Ollie," I seethe through my teeth. "I'm trying to pay attention."

"Yeah, but—"

I jam down on his foot, and he lets out a groan. His mask does little to conceal the fact that he's glaring at me.

"Welcome to Honey Harvesting 101," Janey says, patting the top of the hive in front of her. "There's just a few things we need to go over before we get started."

If I was back home in a lecture, I'd have a notebook, three pens, and a highlighter out to take notes. Today, I'll just have to use my memory, which is just as good, if I do say so myself.

Honey harvesting seems easy enough. Janey explains that the top two tiers—the supers—are where we'll be extracting our capped honey from. If we were typical harvesters, we'd have to wait a few days after placing the bee escape on top of the first super, but for class purposes, Janey has already prepared the hives. We'll each take a few frames of honey, place them inside an uncapping tub, and then bring them indoors for extraction.

It seems like a lot of work, but Janey sounds so passionate about it that it makes me want to try it.

Ollie hauls the tub inside while I swat bees away from my veil.

Don't they have better things to do?

Are there no flowers to pollinate?

No honey to make?

Surely they could *bee* much more productive than flying at my face.

Ollie sets everything on a table, and before Janey continues with the lesson, we all change out of our suits before we die of heat exhaustion in the sweltering room.

"Each frame of honey has a layer of wax over it," Janey explains. "At each of your stations you have a heated knife that we use for the uncapping. Use saw-like motions going up each frame to remove it."

The instructions are easy enough. I barely trust Ollie to operate a spoon, so I grab the knife before he can.

"Why are you smirking?" he asks me warily. "Are you thinking about stabbing me with that, love?"

"Call me *love* again and we'll find out."

"Alright, love."

My grip on the handle goes tight, and for a moment, I really consider how nice it would be to drive it straight through his stomach.

Not that I actually would.

I'm not a psychopath.

"We're studying abroad."

My ears perk at the sound of Daphne's voice, and I almost drop the knife right on Ollie's foot when I see her talking to Janey.

"Jesus Christ," he says, grabbing it from me. "I like my toes, you mad woman!"

I ignore him, eavesdropping on the conversation happening across the room.

"Really?" Janey asks as she helps Tosh uncap their frames. "Where?"

"The University of Wellington," she says. "We're all in the bio program, but I'm double majoring in early childhood education. I'd really like to show kids how fun science can be."

"That's exactly why I went into the sciences," Janey says. "Keep up the good work."

I roll my eyes and turn back to Ollie, who is diligently uncapping frames. He has his tongue parted between his lips in complete concentration.

"I'm bloody fantastic," he decides. "I should be a beekeeper."

"You're more than welcome to stay," I tell him. "We'll try not to miss you."

He narrows his eyes to me.

I smile tightly.

He goes back to work.

"How's everything going over here?"

When I hear Janey's voice, I freeze. I have no plan. Why don't I have a plan? I always have a plan!

"We're doing well!" Ollie answers. "A bit of beginner's luck, I'd say."

"It's quite fun once you get the hang of it," Janey says. "Are you enjoying your time studying abroad?"

"Uh… yeah!" he answers. "It's a beautiful country. Very chill. We've done a lot of exploring."

"What place have you enjoyed the most?"

"Queenstown," he says. "We were lucky enough to see one of Benji Atkin's pop-up galleries."

"Ah." Her eyes light up and she laughs. "Benny's something else, isn't he?"

"Really talented," Ollie says. "Someone actually mentioned he donated some pieces to an event here."

"Yeah, he's an old friend," she says. "We grew up together. Or, I guess, I grew up with his sister. We've been best friends for as long as I can remember."

"So you know Benji well?"

"Well enough, I suppose," she says. "He's quiet. I think the only person I ever saw him talk to for more than five minutes was my other best friend, Ana."

Ana.

Ana.

Ana.

"You know my mom?" It comes out of my mouth before I can fully process it.

"Willa?" she gasps.

"I'm not feeling very well," I say quietly. "I think I need to get some air."

Outside, the sun is blaring. Heat trickles over me, making it hard to breathe.

I clench my fists.

And count down from ten.

But I still feel the panic building.

Janey knows my mom, which means she's going to call her and tell her I was asking questions about my father. And what if she tells Benji that I'm looking for him? What if that drives him further away?

This was such a bad idea.

I shouldn't have come here.

I feel a tightening in my throat that usually means tears

are imminent. I don't want to cry. I don't want to give everyone the satisfaction of knowing that I'm weak.

But it's when I look down at my leg and see a giant welt that I realize the tightening in my throat probably has nothing to do with the tears. But it might have something to do with the matching welt find on my arm.

Shit.

"Willa," Ollie says.

He says something else, but I'm already in panic mode. I can't hear anything over the rushing in my ears. This isn't happening. It's some sort of nightmare. This isn't real life.

"C'mon, Willa," Daphne calls. "Come back to the class! Tosh is using the honey extractor!"

I can't move.

"So she knows your mum," Daphne says. "It's not a big deal."

I can't speak.

"Willa." There's a nervous hitch in Ollie's voice when he places his hand on my shoulder.

I don't jerk away like I usually do.

"Willa—"

"Daphne, she needs help," Ollie snaps.

"Holy shit," Daphne panics. "Did she get stung? Willa, did you get stung?"

I try to nod.

"M—my b—bag," I stammer. "I—I ne—need—"

"You're gonna be fine," Ollie says calmly.

"No, she's not!" Daphne says. "She needs her EpiPen! Jesus—help! Someone! Help! She's having an allergic reaction! Help! Someone call an ambulance!"

"Daphne, you're doing the exact opposite of helping!" Ollie hisses as a group of people—Janey included—come running from the building. "Willa, can you walk? We need to get you away from the hives."

My head is foggy and I feel dizzy. I'm not sure if it's because of the reaction, or out of fear. I'm shaking.

"Get her inside!" Janey shouts.

Since I can't remember how to walk, Ollie scoops me up in his arms and brings me inside. The venom must have already gone to my head because, for a moment, I actually feel comforted being so close to him.

The end is near.

"Set her down on the ground," Janey instructs him. "Quick! Someone grab the first aid kit. There are EpiPens in there."

"She has one in her bag," Ollie says.

Daphne is the one who tosses it at him. I watch her swallow and then place her thumbnail between her lips, gnawing it nervously.

Daphne doesn't get nervous.

God, I really am losing it.

Death is coming.

Goodbye, cruel world.

"You still with us, Willa?" Janey asks.

I nod and shift my eyes to Ollie, who has tipped my bag upside down on the floor. He rummages through receipts and tubes of lip balm with Tosh's help, eventually wrapping his hand around something.

"Brilliant, Ollie!" Daphne snaps. "Are you going to stab her with a tampon?"

"Fuck off, Daphne! I'm trying!"

I can see it out of the corner of my eye, lodged between my concealer compact and coin purse. Everyone else is so panicked that I realize the only person who's going to save me is, well, *me*. I take a deep breath, reach for my EpiPen, and rip the cap off before pressing it into my thigh for ten seconds.

I was five the first time this happened to me. I was at a

day camp in Central Park during the summer and we didn't know I was allergic to bees until I had a severe reaction that led to my first ambulance ride. Mom was more scared than I was. She was in tears when she got to the emergency room. I don't remember much from that day, but I do remember how excited I was to tell her about the ride and how the EMTs put the sirens on and that they drove faster than any taxi we'd ever been in.

I wonder if she'd have the same reaction today. I wonder if her eyes would well up with tears. I wonder if she'd smile when she realized I was okay.

Probably not.

She'd be too busy obsessing over the flutters she felt in her belly.

"How are you feeling?" Janey asks me.

"Okay," I say, sirens blaring in the distance. "I'm okay."

Ollie's whiter than a ghost when I look over at him, but Daphne and Tosh both look relieved. More so when a couple of EMTs rush in to fuss over me.

"I'm fine, really," I try to tell them, but they insist that I need to go to the hospital because I administered the shot.

"Stop trying to argue with them," Ollie mumbles after they put me on the gurney.

"I'm not arguing with them," I say. "I'm just saying, there could be another person who needs their help more than I do."

"You've just had an allergic reaction. You're going to the hospital."

I don't have the energy to roll my eyes.

"You can bring one of your friends with you," an EMT says.

"Right, I'm coming," Ollie says.

"No."

"Uh, yes?"

"No," I repeat and look away from him. "I want Daphne to come with me."

"What, Willa—"

"Let Ollie go," Daphne says.

"What? No—"

"Ollie should go with you," she insists, diverting her stare from me. "Tosh and I will follow."

"Daphne." I frown "I want you to come with me."

"I can't," she says. "I'm sorry, but I can't."

"What? Why?"

"I'm sorry," is all she can say.

I don't get it.

She'll jump off a bridge? Pop pills? Hook up with guys she just met? Display her life on the internet? But she can't come with me in an ambulance when I'm scared and alone in a foreign country?

What kind of friend is she?

"Fine," I say. "Tosh, will you come with me?"

He's taken back. He looks to Ollie as if he needs permission.

"Tosh!" I say, ignoring how upset Ollie looks. "We have to go."

He comes with me reluctantly, and the last thing I see before the EMT shuts the door is the devastating look on Ollie's face.

* * *

I'm alive.

Barely.

But still alive.

And when I see Ollie sitting in the waiting room next to Janey, I *really* wish I wasn't.

Give me a time machine. Take me back to the bees. Let them have their wicked way with me. I'd take anaphylactic shock over this conversation any day.

"They wouldn't let me come in," Ollie says when he sees me and Tosh walk into the waiting room.

"Because I told them I didn't want to see the lunatic pacing around the hospital."

"I was worried," he says. "They wouldn't tell me anything."

"I'm very happy to hear they respect doctor-patient confidentiality here," I mumble. I'm doped up on so many antihistamines that I feel like I'm walking through a haze. I need thirty-seven hours of uninterrupted sleep.

"How are you feeling?" Janey asks, adjusting her purse on her shoulder.

"I've seen better days."

I didn't realize before, but she's tiny—completely dwarfed by me, Ollie, and Tosh—but her fiery red hair commands attention. She's not the kind of woman who gets passed by. She gets the second, and the third, and the fourth glance.

She only gives me one.

And it's not very pleasant.

"It was a really reckless thing you did today, Willa," she says. "You have a severe allergy. This could have ended badly."

"I know."

"I don't think you do," she says. "Your mother is worried sick. She's been trying to get a hold of you for days."

"You called her?"

"Of course I called her! You were taken by ambulance to the hospital. She had a right to know."

Panic and rage are a dangerous combination. I'm going to pass out and explode at the same time.

"I'm an adult," I tell her, my fists clenched at my sides. "You had no right to call her."

"You are *barely* an adult," she says.

"But I'm still an adult!"

"Willa," Ollie says, a quiet warning.

"No, I'm not her responsibility anymore." *I'm not going to cry. I'm not going to cry. I'm not going to cry.* "She doesn't need to know my every step. And I certainly didn't need her permission to come here."

To prove that I'm *such* an adult, I storm away from them. Angry. Sad. And ready to cry myself to sleep.

Wow.

I'm actually a child.

Before I can get out the door, I hear Janey's voice again. Firm and commanding. I have no choice, but to stop and listen.

"You will always be her responsibility, Willa. That's the thing about mothers—you grow up and you become this wild and beautiful and headstrong woman, but you never stop being her little girl. She's going to worry about you until the day she dies."

Outside, the sun is setting. I sigh at the warmth against my skin. The hospital was too cold. I've been shivering for hours.

"I'll bring the van 'round," Ollie says. "Wait here."

"Where else would I wait?"

"It's good to know near-death hasn't softened you."

"Just as bitter as ever."

Ollie scoffs out a laugh before crossing the parking lot to get the van with Tosh. Janey goes in the opposite direction, her phone glued to her ear. She's probably calling my mom. I'm way too tired to deal with that.

"He's got it bad for you."

I jump at the sound of her voice, and when I turn my head, I see Daphne sitting on a bench. She shuts her laptop and stands up, cradling it to her chest.

"What?"

"Ollie," she says. "He's got it bad. *Real bad.* He broke at least ten speeding laws trying to get here."

Ollie? Has it bad for me? In what world? I'm about as alluring as a used tissue. Not to mention, Ollie is also about as alluring as a used tissue. All that guitar playing and incessant need to hear his own voice? No thanks.

Besides, I've sworn off men forever.

And after that scene I threw in there, Ollie has hopefully sworn me off forever, too.

"Whatever," I say, stepping closer to the curb. "I don't want to talk to you."

"Why?"

Is she serious?

"Because I'm upset that you wouldn't come with me in the ambulance," I say. "That was terrifying."

"You literally had Ollie ready to jump in the back with you. You didn't need me."

"Yeah, I did," I mutter. "But whatever. I had Tosh. And I'm alive. I guess that's all that matters."

I pull my phone from my back pocket to give myself a distraction. Even my inbox sounds more fun than talking to her does. I'd endure hours of slander if it meant I didn't have to continue this conversation.

From: **Ana Loveridge-Herrera** (I'm begging you Willa)
From: **Vincent Herrera** (Mom's ready to call the police!)
From: **Delia Sprigs** (Your mom's driving me crazy)
From: **Lyla Flores** (Your mom called! She's worried)

From: **Oscar Mendez** (7 Unexcused Absences: Automatic Failure)
From: **Ana Loveridge-Herrera** (Willa)
From: **Mason Stueck** (I told them you weren't impressive in bed either)
From: **Mason Stueck** (they weren't impressed)
From: **Mason Stueck** (showed a few more people those pictures)
From: **Trenton Fairbanks** (Were you always a skank?)
From: **The Coffee Corner** (You're Invited!)
From: **Gia Curry** (Are you some kind of groupie now)
From: **Jac Bellmont** (Willing Willa the transpacific whore)
From: **BeautyGuru** (This Season's Color!)
From: **Mason Stueck** (answer your fucking phone)

Ollie pulls up before I can start crying, and as soon as the van is fully stopped, Tosh slides the door open.

I don't remember falling asleep. I don't remember laying down or my head hitting the pillow or anything, really. I don't remember what I dreamt about, but it had to have been bad because when I wake up, I feel relieved.

I'm not sure how many hours have passed, but the sky is dark behind the flimsy curtain we use as a shade. Ollie is sitting against the wall, legs crossed and his head lolled back. He has his guitar on his lap, his hand firmly wrapped around the neck. He's not strumming. Maybe it's his version of a security blanket.

"Were you watching me sleep?" I ask. "Because that's not as romantic as the movies let on. It's kind of creepy."

"I was making sure you didn't stop breathing."

"That must have been boring."

He shrugs and sets his guitar at the end of our makeshift bed. "You make funny faces. It was quite amusing, actually."

"Glad I could be a source of entertainment," I say. "Where are we?"

"Not sure," he says. "We found an overnight car park. Daphne and Tosh went out exploring."

"Why didn't you go?"

"Someone had to make sure you didn't choke on your own saliva," he says. "I took one for the team."

I scoff and roll onto my side. My whole body aches, but I'm too tired to care.

"How are you feeling?"

"Like I got stung by two bees and had an allergic reaction." I try to laugh, but a yawn slips out instead. "I'm just tired. I could probably sleep for twenty more hours."

"You can if you want. It's not like we're in a rush."

Daphne doesn't sit still for a moment. This van would be moving by seven o'clock tomorrow morning. Bright and early. On to the next adventure, which might still include my mother's family.

Perfect.

"Look, Willa, about yesterday—"

"Ollie," I groan and bury my face in my pillow. "Please—"

"I didn't go looking for those emails. I wouldn't do that," he tells me. "You don't deserve to be spoken to that way. That twatbag should be ashamed of himself."

Mason isn't ashamed of anything. He walks through life unphased. A socialite for a mother and a senator for a father, he has everything handed to him. Not even I could tarnish his image. After all is said and done, it'll be Mason who looks like the victim.

"Can we talk about something else?" I ask.

"What?"

I don't know what I'm saying. The allergy medicine is

making my head feel funny. I should not be held responsible for anything that comes out of my mouth.

"I don't want to talk about Mason. Or my mom. Or how rude I was to Janey," I say. "Tell me about your family."

There's a pause so long that I can hear the traffic outside pass. It's late. He's probably as tired as I am. He doesn't want to talk. I don't blame him.

But then I feel the cushions shift. And when I peek an eye open, I watch Ollie lay back on the pillow beside me. After he tucks himself under the blankets, he folds his hands over his stomach.

"When I was seven, Holly tried to set me on fire."

12

Ollie and I aren't talking about the fact that he woke up with a boner.

But Tosh is.

We're in a supermarket by the lot we parked in last night, stocking up on snacks for the van while Daphne sleeps. Had she not stumbled in at five o'clock this morning—demanding a place to sleep—we may have never had to experience the most awkward moment of my life. I could have lived on blissfully unaware of Ollie's boy problems.

But no.

I'm not that lucky.

And now…

Now I have to live the rest of my life with that memory burned into my brain. The initial wake up. Ollie's face buried into my neck. His arm around my waist. My hand cupped over his. The *goddamn* boner.

"Shit, fuck," he had cursed before he thrashed his arms and legs, shaking the van as he stumbled onto his feet and away from me, hurrying to the front. Daphne was too drunk to notice, but Tosh wasn't.

He grinned like the Cheshire Cat. My cheeks flushed red. Ollie sat hunched over in the driver's seat, banging his head on the steering wheel for half an hour.

It was a great start to our day.

I'm thankful that Daphne slept through most of it. The last thing I need is for the world to catch wind of #morningglory.

"For fuck's sake, Tosh!" Ollie hisses lowly.

I turn around just in time to watch him shove an unpeeled banana straight into Tosh's mouth. My eyes widen before I turn back around, placing three more granola bars in my basket. Ollie brushes past me and disappears around the corner. A very, very, *very* small part of me feels bad that he's so embarrassed.

Tosh doesn't share my sentiments.

He knocks his shoulder against mine and waggles his eyebrows at me. I take that opportunity to jam my foot down on his.

"Listen, Mr. I'm-Sorta-Kinda-On-The-Run, if you don't want your managers to find out where you are, you'll forget about what happened this morning."

Tosh frowns, grabbing the pen he keeps tucked behind his ear. He scribbles something onto a banana.

"*Fine, but it doesn't change the fact that Ollie's in love*," I read. "We both know a boner does not signify love, Tosh."

He wages what I said and writes something else on the other side of the banana.

"*He still acts like a lost puppy around you.*"

The only reasonable response is to shove the unpeeled banana into his mouth.

* * *

Ollie banned Tosh from the front, so I'm stuck

riding shotgun. The only thing getting me through the drive (and the tension that we could cut with a knife) is the coffee that had been waiting for me in the cupholder when I got back to the van. Caffeine has a way of making everything and anyone more tolerable.

I should be jumping for joy, celebrating! Throwing a party in the small confines of our van. Ollie hasn't said one word in exactly forty-seven minutes. It's all I've ever wanted, and frankly, it's a miracle. I should be thanking my lucky stars for the silence.

But I'm not.

Because it's weird.

What am I supposed to do when I can't nag him for breathing the wrong way? Look out the window? Enjoy the scenery? Check my email? See who's calling me a whore today? None of it sounds as enticing as shooting Ollie dirty looks does.

"How much longer are we on here for?"

I choke on my coffee when I hear his voice, tie-dying my notebook with cream and sugar. When I look over at him, after wiping my mouth with the heel of my palm, his brows are raised, but not in the quizzical way they usually are. He doesn't look amused or endeared. If I'd known a wayward hard-on was all it took for him to shy away, I would have accidentally brushed against him sooner.

"It's pretty much straight the whole way," I finally say, grabbing a napkin to wipe the coffee off my leg. "Unless we need to stop for some reason. I allotted us some time in an hour and a half, so I'll just tell you when to take the turn."

"I didn't have a doubt in my mind that you wouldn't."

I can't decide how to feel about that comment. When I side-eye him moments later, he has his attention focused on the road. Not a smile in sight.

Right.

Okay.

Things are still weird.

But hopefully they won't be for long.

We're going to New Plymouth. As much as the thought of meeting my mom's family gives me stomach ulcers, they're my only hope right now. I'll get the information I need. I'll find Benji. This whole little adventure will be over. I'll never have to see Daphne, Ollie, or Tosh again.

Well.

I'll never have to see Daphne or Ollie again.

Tosh is still on my good side.

For now.

Tosh taps the back of my head and before I can swat his hand away, he passes me a note.

"*Do you think they'll know who you are? Do you think Janey or your mom contacted them?*" I read. "I mean, it's not like there's a mugshot of my face going around."

He scribbles something else. "*YouTube videos and Instagram posts?*"

And naked pictures.

But I'm trying not to think about those.

"My mom hasn't talked to her family in almost twenty years."

He writes again. "*That you know of.*"

"I highly doubt she's having secret meetings with them," I say. "She definitely wouldn't call to warn them about me."

The conversation dies, and boredom strikes forty-five minutes into the drive. As a certifiable glutton for punishment, I open my email inbox that automatically refreshed earlier when I connected to the supermarket's wifi.

From: **Ana Loveridge-Herrera** (Willa I'm worried sick!)

From: **Ana Loveridge-Herrera** (If you don't call me I swear!)
From: **Vincent Herrera** (Mom's ready to book a flight! Please call us)
From: **Mason Stueck** (slut)
From: **Oscar Mendez** (AHIS 120-02: Exam Results)
From: **Mason Stueck** (a little lovers spat!)
From: **Mason Stueck** (#troubleinparadise)
From: **The Book Warehouse** (10% Off This Week's Best Sellers!)
From: **Mason Stueck** (groupie trash)
From: **Mason Stueck** (how many songs did it take before you fucked him)
From: **Mason Stueck** (Bella just told me he's a musician)
From: **Ana Loveridge-Herrera** (Where are you!!!)
From: **Delia Sprigs** (Okay your mom's being super annoying)
From: **Zack Higgins** (getting slutty down under)

I drop my phone onto my lap with a heaping sigh. If nothing else, at least everyone is consistent.

"Oh my god, I'm so hungry!"

Daphne grabs ahold of the back of my seat, shaking it just enough to entice a groan from the back of my throat. She has been dead to the world for the last four hours. How can she wake up hungover *and* with so much energy? I can barely drag her out of bed when she's sober.

"I'm going to die of starvation if we don't stop right this second."

"We'll stop in an hour," I tell her.

"Willa, I'm going to be dead in an hour."

"You're being dramatic."

"You won't think so when you walk into the back and find that I resorted to eating Tosh's left leg."

I roll my eyes and dig around in my purse until I find a granola bar.

"This will hold you over."

"You think some weird nut and fruit bar is going to *hold me over*?" she asks. "I need twelve breakfast sandwiches and a gallon of tea."

"I don't know what else you want me to say."

"I want you to—why am I even asking you? You're not driving! You're not the boss, either," she says and moves over to her typically much weaker and easily persuaded target. "Ollie…"

He grips the wheel tighter, his knuckles turning white as he glances at her briefly. "Daphne…"

"C'mon! I know how much you love a good fry-up! Be reckless! Take your balls back from her!"

"Excuse you!" My jaw drops.

"Yeah!" Ollie agrees. "My balls are happily intact, thank you very much."

"Please," Daphne scoffs. "She blinks and you roll over and play dead."

"That's not true!" I say.

"I can answer for myself, Willa." He frowns. "That's not true."

"I'm not judging." Daphne shrugs. "Some people get off on being bossed around! It's nothing to be ashamed of."

"I'm not ashamed because it's not true! I'm my own person with my own thoughts and opinions. She doesn't control me."

"Prove it."

"What?" he practically gasps.

"Prove it."

"What? How would you like me to prove that in a moving vehicle?"

Daphne has that look on her face—the look that villains in fairy tales get right before they turn someone into a slug. She has some ridiculous plan forming in her head. I'm afraid to ask.

"Pick up that hitchhiker."

"What—"

"No!" I snap, which only makes Daphne's smile widen.

"Pick up that hitchhiker, Ollie."

On the side of the road sits a burley-looking guy with ginger hair and a ginger beard wearing a paisley button down with the sleeves cut off, no shoes, and a backwards baseball cap. He looks like a demon trying to escape Greek Row. He's one cat-call away from being every frat guy I met at college.

"Ollie, you are *not* picking him up," I say tightly as the van slowly approaches. "He could be a psychopath."

"You're your own person, Ollie," Daphne jeers. "Don't listen to Mum. *She's* a psychopath."

Ollie licks his lips and adjusts his grip on the wheel, contemplating. He glances out the window at the guy, who is leaning against his oversized backpack. We pass him at a snail's pace.

A sigh of relief, I quickly realize, is premature.

"C'mon!" Daphne cries, shaking the back of his chair. "Stop the van! Pick him up!"

"Don't you dare!" I yell. "I swear, *Oliver*!"

"For Christ's sake! Don't call him that! You're gonna give him a bone—"

Ollie slams on the brakes.

"Brilliant!" Daphne's already throwing herself out of the door before the van comes to a complete stop. I'm left to sit in my seat with my fists clenched so tightly that my nails break skin on my palms.

Count to ten.

Breathe.

Count to ten.

Breathe.

Count to ten.

Breathe.

One more person to add to our already too small van. A person who could very well be on the run from murdering his entire family. And we just invited him in with open arms.

Great.

Just great.

"If you frown any harder your face is gonna get stuck like that," Ollie tells me.

"Sorry that I can't find it in me to smile when you invite a potentially very dangerous stranger into our living space," I say, wiping the few droplets of blood on my palms onto my denim shorts.

"Once upon a time you were a potentially very dangerous stranger," he says. "And look where we are now."

"You're absolutely right." I force a smile and unbuckle my seatbelt, standing up. "Spoon him tonight."

"Maybe I will!"

I don't dignify him with response, and I walk to the back of the van just as it shakes with our new guest's heavy footsteps.

"I was starting to think no one would stop." His voice is all southern twang, and he laughs when his eyes catch mine. "I'm Gus. August if you want to be formal, but I prefer to keep it casual, so just Gus is fine."

"Just Gus," I swallow, my face puckering the way it does when I drink lemonade. This is far less sweet and entirely too sour.

"Another American." Daphne grins. "Just like our Willa!"

"I'm not from Texas," I say.

"Well, neither am I!" he laughs. "I'm from Louisiana, and you're definitely from New York."

I frown.

"How'd you know?" Daphne asks. "The permanent bitch-face? The perpetual stick up her ass?"

"Oh, no, she just sounds like my old roommate's sister," he explains. "They're from New York."

"Well, I'm a South Africa-England transplant," Daphne says. "Ollie's from Scotland and Tosh is from Japan, so it's the United Nations up in here. Welcome!"

Gus brushes by me and follows Daphne further into the back. He drops his backpack—that I'm still convinced contains a body—onto the floor before falling onto the couch beside Tosh, who bounces slightly at the force. He's way too comfortable way too fast. It reminds me of Daphne. One of her is enough to handle. I don't need her American counterpart.

"Gus is heading to the music festival in Auckland too," Daphne says, taking a seat beside him. "I told him we'd get there eventually."

"Brilliant," comes Ollie's voice from behind me. It sends a chill up my spine when he skirts around me to shake Gus's hand. "I'm Ollie. Do you like to drive? Willa's a *great* copilot."

"Can I pick the music?" Gus asks.

"Go for it."

And that's the story of how I got stuck riding shotgun while Gus auditioned for his future role in a Broadway musical.

* * *

Ollie has more blackberries on his shirt than he has in his basket. We're at *Loveridge Family Farm*, and I'm about ten seconds away from having a panic attack. I've counted to ten and then to twenty and then to three hundred, and still, I feel sick and nauseous and I just want to go home.

And by *home* I mean the van.

Definitely don't want to go back to New York.

This is a terrible idea. Really, what are my mom's parents going to tell me? Nothing probably. I bet they have a voodoo doll of me, sticking pins and needles into my arms and legs whenever they get the chance. At least that would explain my misfortune of a life.

"Would you relax?" Daphne asks, popping a blackberry into her mouth. "I can hear your mind racing.

"I can't help it," I say. "I'm nervous."

"Don't be." She shrugs. "What's the worst that could happen?"

Well…

They could slam the door in my face. Not know a thing about Benji. Maybe know something, but not tell me just to be spiteful. What if Tosh was right? What if my mom did call them? What if Janey did? What if the police are lurking around here just waiting to exile me back to America?

I'm pretty sure the worst is the only thing that could happen.

"You just gotta chill," Gus adds. "Take it as it comes. Don't worry so much."

"For someone who's only known me a few hours, I don't think you're allowed to tell me to chill."

"Well, as someone who's known you for ten days," Daphne starts, dropping her arm around my shoulder. "You need to chill out."

"I'm never gonna be chill. Okay? This is me! Crazy and irrational me! Love me or leave me! This is how I am!"

"At least you're finally admitting that you're out of your fucking mind."

I glare at Daphne, who is grinning at me as she steals a handful of berries out of Tosh's basket.

When we arrived at the farm, it took me ten minutes to undo my seatbelt. It took another five to convince myself to get out of the van. And then it took all of three seconds for me to decide I wasn't ready. It was Daphne's idea to go berry picking. She said it would help calm my nerves.

It hasn't.

If anything, I'm more nervous.

Every corner I turn, I fear I'll come face to face with my grandparents.

I try to convince myself that it's not a big deal—that the worst that could happen is that they don't know anything about Benji. But in my gut, I know it's much deeper than that. They haven't spoken to my mother in twenty years. She left them. This isn't going to be a happy reunion—a sitcom special waiting to happen. If anything, I'll end up on the eleven o'clock news when my body washes up on the beach after Gus murders me in my sleep.

Okay maybe that's an exaggeration.

He removed a spider from the van with a plastic cup.

He's probably not going to murder me.

"Did you know a serving of blueberries has twenty-five percent of the recommended daily dose of manganese?" Ollie catches a blueberry in his mouth and then grins at me.

"I don't even know what manganese is."

"I was under the impression you know everything."

I blink at him. Is this the same guy who wouldn't look

at me for the entire day? Were all those berries poisonous? Is he losing his mind? Am *I* losing *my* mind?

"They're also a great source of vitamin C," he adds.

"Great, I'm getting nutrition advice from the guy who thinks french fries are a food group."

"Might as well be." He shrugs. "There's enough variety. Waffle fries! Curly fries! Sweet potato—"

"Right." I cut him off. "What's the point of this?"

"The point is that you looked like you needed a distraction."

I swallow when he holds my stare. Because it's not like it was this morning. It's not a passing glance. Or a quick shift of his eyes. It's Ollie looking at me. Not through me. Not around me. *At me.*

And it makes me really nervous.

"If I don't do this now, I'm never gonna do it," I decide.

"Isn't that what they say in films before someone kisses someone?"

"No, I think that's what they say in films right before someone knees someone in the balls."

"That's my girl."

I try to glare at him, but my lips betray me *again* and start to flicker into a smile. Damn them for giving away my secrets.

He follows me back to the farm entrance, where crowds of people eagerly take baskets to begin their own berry picking journies. I walk through a small playground made up of hay stacks and a wooden swing set to get to the house that also doubles as a gift shop. They sell jellies and jams and blueberry donuts. I don't have much of an appetite, but Ollie is practically foaming at the mouth.

"Excuse me," I say to a woman who's stocking a shelf

with jars of strawberry preserves. "I'm looking for the owners? Katarina? Or Jack? Loveridge? Are they here?"

"They're here, but I think they're in a meeting with—"

When she looks over at me, her eyes instantly doubled in size. There's something familiar about her, but I can't place it. Have I met her before? No, that's impossible. The only person I know from here is my mom. Not even at school. New Zealand is like a completely different planet. Is anyone really from here?

But she's looking at me like she knows me, like we've met before. Have we spoken? Was it in passing? From across a street? A window of a restaurant? Was she on the plane? At the airport? Had we somehow crossed each other's path?

Oh god.

Fuck.

She saw me naked on the internet.

Or she watches Daphne's vlogs.

That's it.

That *has* to be it.

"Holy shit," is all she says before the sharp sound of a jar shattering fills the shop.

I'm still confused.

Now I'm confused with strawberry jam on my shoes.

"Mum," she screams. "Mum! Mum!"

That's when I realize why she seems so familiar. Because her eyes are my eyes, which are my mom's eyes, which are her mom's eyes. She's my aunt. My mother's sister.

I didn't even know my mother had a sister.

"Kaia, for the love of—"

Katarina Loveridge has the same look on her face that my mother did when she walked into my bedroom and found Mason in his underwear. It's a mix of shock and horror and underlying rage. She never expected this. Not in a million years. She's not prepared.

But despite her unwavering look of fury, something tells me that I won't be getting another lecture on safe sex and teen pregnancy. Perhaps if she'd had that conversation twenty years ago we wouldn't be in this position

"Look, I'm just trying to find my father." I figure someone has to start talking and it might as well be me. "I know I shouldn't have blindsided you, but I'm desperate. I've been trying to find him for two weeks. I went to his gallery. I talked to his college friends. I even, unknowingly, talked to Janey. She was mom's best friend—"

"I know," she says.

"You know? Did Janey call you?"

"Ana—your mom did," Kaia says quietly. "She's really worried, Willa."

"You should call her," Katarina replies. "All this stress isn't good for the baby."

The baby.

The baby.

The baby.

The prodigal child.

"Right," I say. "This was a bad idea."

"Willa—" Kaia says.

"Thanks for all your help."

I wait until I get into the van before I burst into tears. I'm not even sure why. I knew this would happen. Nothing has gone right since the moment I almost crash-landed into this country.

* * *

I'M LAYING ON A POOL TABLE.

For no particular reason other than I wanted to lay down and it looked like a good place to do that.

We're at an Irish pub that Daphne dubbed not very Irish at all. I didn't want to get into the semantics of what did and didn't make it Irish, but Gus did. His great grandfather was born in Belfast, after all. So despite the fact that he was born and raised in Louisiana, he was somehow an Irish scholar. And Daphne, well, her defense was that she went to Dublin once, which wasn't much of a defense at all.

Thankfully, I was drunk before they finished their rebuttals.

Everything sucks.

Everything *really* sucks.

The worst part is that I knew it was going to end this way. I felt it in my gut. My grandparents weren't going to help me find my father. They weren't going to welcome me with open arms. There wasn't going to be a TV-worthy reunion with blubbering tears and bone-shattering hugs.

This was real life.

And real life sucks.

Daphne insisted that this was just a setback—that it didn't change anything, that we still had options. She said I could try finding Benji's sister. Maybe his family had a way of contacting him.

But what's the point?

It's better this way, I just need to convince myself that. Because the sooner I realize, the sooner I'll come to terms with the fact that I have no one. And that's the scariest thing in the world—to realize I'm alone.

It's not about dependency. I know how to take care of myself. I know how to physically be alone. What gets me is the thought of waking up in the morning and knowing that I'm not on someone's mind. I won't be a first thought. Or a second thought. Or even a passing thought. I'll exist in a world that's just me.

And maybe…

Just maybe…

That bothers me.

Because there's a big difference between being alone and being lonely.

I'll have no one to talk to about that article I read. Who will I tell that joke to? Who will I go to dinner with? Sit on the couch and binge watch TV with? Sit in silence with? I'll have a phone, but it'll never ring—never chime with a new message or email. There'll be no one to catch up with.

Just me.

Willa against the world.

I need to get used to that.

But, for now, at least I have Tosh, who's holding a straw to my lips so I can suck down a shot of whiskey without having to sit up.

"Fuck, that's awful," I say, after the burning sensation in my throat settles into my stomach. "Hit me again, Tosh. Literally this time. Punch me right in the face. Knock me out. I can take it."

I brace myself for the blunt impact I anticipate feeling on my left cheek, but after moments of waiting and waiting *and waiting*, I squint an eye open. Ollie is looking down at me with his stupid dumb smirk.

"Alright, you little lunatic," he says, grabbing both off my arms to haul me forward. "Up and at 'em before these very patient blokes start using your head as a cue ball."

Dizzy, I instantly slump against Ollie, who is trying to keep me steady. That doesn't stop me from craning my neck to shoot the group of guys a dirty look, which results in them all laughing at me.

"I can take all of you!" I slur, fighting against the grip

Ollie has around me like I'm tough stuff. "Try me! I'll break your faces!"

"Yeah, alright," Ollie says, urging me towards our table. "The best you'll do is nag them to death."

"Don't test me, Oliver! I'll break your face too. I can fight dirty!"

As he forces me into a chair opposite of Daphne, I watch her grin up at him. He glares at her and slides over a basket of greasy fries and a mug of coffee.

"I don't want to be sober," I told him. "I want to be drunk forever. Why have I never done this before? Losing control is awesome. Ten-ten. I highly recommend it."

"Yeah, well, I'd rather not have to listen to you complain about a massive hangover tomorrow."

"But if I drink enough, I probably won't be alive tomorrow. Win-win for everyone!" I say, reaching over to grab what's left of Daphne's drink. I chug it. "You won't even have to notify anyone! Just toss me into the ocean! Let the waves sweep me away! No one will care!"

"And you call me dramatic," he scoffs.

"Oh, go write a song about it," I mutter.

"I will," he says. "And I'll call it *You Smell Like The Floor Of A Pub*."

"How original."

"Only the best for you," he says. "Eat the damn chips and drink the bloody coffee."

"I don't like being told what to do. I like to tell people what to do."

"Yeah, I've noticed, Boss Lady."

"#williebanter! #hewroteherasong! #willasasloppydrunk!"

I glare at Daphne and shove a fry into my mouth. "Don't make me fight you too."

"You're both ridiculous," Ollie decides before walking

away from us. He has his guitar slung around his back, his sights set on the abandoned mic.

Great.

Now I'm not just a sad drunk who wants to fight.

I'm a sad drunk who wants to fight *and* smash Ollie's guitar over his head.

I drop my head to the table and groan when he taps his finger to the mic.

"Is she always like this?" Gus asks.

"Drunk? No, never," Daphne says. "Dramatic? Yes."

If I wasn't too busy slamming my head against the table, I would have defended myself. I have every right to be dramatic after the day I had. Just like I have every right to get drunk off my ass and feel sorry for myself. I was dealt a shitty hand. I want to wallow in it.

"I don't know why you're acting like this is the end of the world," Daphne says, digging her hand into my fries. "Because if I were you, I'd just use this as fuel to find Benji. Fuck them! Prove them wrong! Come out on top! Be the Willa I know you can be!"

I blink at her. "Have you taken up motivational speaking?"

"I like to keep my options open."

I roll my eyes and push myself from my chair. It takes me a moment to get my bearings, but I eventually slump over to the bar, passing the group of girls eyeing Ollie. I don't understand what it is about a guitar that makes him alluring. I'm sure if they knew he has been wearing the same pair of socks for the past four days, they'd be running for the hills.

"I would like something that will make me feel like I got hit by a train in the morning," I tell the bartender. "Bonus points if it actually kills me."

He holds my stare long enough for it to be awkward,

and then he shrugs, accepting the challenge. While he mixes my drink, I contemplate writing my will on a paper napkin that is stained with red wine.

"Hey, you're friends with the singer, right?"

I look over when I hear the voice—soft yet sultry with just enough command for me to know she means business. She has a good few inches on the chick from Wellington who wanted to bone Ollie. She also has at least three cup sizes on me, which I'm beyond envious of.

"Friends is a strong word," I say. "He's more of a nuisance."

"Right, so is he single?"

"Painfully."

"Perfect."

I watch her walk back over to the stage where Ollie is finishing up his second cover of a song that is nearly as old as him. I turn my attention to the drink the bartender slides over to me and I take a long gulp. It tastes like battery acid.

Excellent.

I quickly learn that Drunk Willa is just as much a glutton for punishment as Sober Willa. While some people would take this opportunity to text an ex to confess some unrequited feelings, I dive straight into my inbox. Might as well kick myself while I'm down.

From: **Ana Loveridge-Herrera** (YOU WERE AT THE FARM? KAIA CALLED!)
From: **Ana Loveridge-Herrera** (Willa this is getting ridiculous!)
From: **Ana Loveridge-Herrera** (This stress isn't good for the baby!)
From: **Ana Loveridge-Herrera** (YOU WERE IN THE HOSPITAL)

From: **Mason Stueck** (call me!)
From: **Mason Stueck** (I want to talk!)
From: **ShoeShack** (Boots and Booties GALORE!)
From: **Mason Stueck** (and just so he knows what a fuckin easy slut you are)
From: **Mason Stueck** (just so he knows I was there first)
From: **Mason Stueck** (I should send your boytoy those pictures)
From: **Mason Stueck** (you're a pathetic whore)

"Didn't we talk about this?" Ollie grabs my drink away from me, and before I can reach for it, he's already chugging it down.

"Excuse you!" I frown. "There's a girl over there undressing you with her eyes. Why aren't you shoving your tongue down her throat?"

Ollie glances over his shoulder at Ms. Soft and Sultry and then turns back to me, shrugging. "She's not my type."

"She has a pulse and a great rack. What more do you want?"

Ollie scoffs and shakes his head before flagging down the bartender to order another basket of fries.

"We should head back to the hostel soon," he says.

"Why? It's not like we have plans for tomorrow."

"You're just going to give up on finding Benji?"

"I don't have much to go on," I say. "It's a waste of time. I'm over it."

"You're not over it, Willa."

"Yeah, I am," I tell him. "I'm tired of being disappointed."

"Willa—"

"We'll find something else to do." I shrug. "I'm sure Daphne wants to jump out of a plane or wrestle an alligator or something."

He opens his mouth to say something, but nothing comes out. The bartender drops the fries onto the counter next to him and the conversation ends. I have the luxury of watching Ollie suck ketchup and salt off of his fingers. When a glob spills onto his shirt, he lifts his collar like some sort of barbarian and attempts to lick it off.

"What's wrong with you?" I cringe. "Your mother would be appalled!"

"What?" he asks as if he hasn't done anything wrong.

"You're a slob," I say and grab his hand.

He frowns. "You're holding this slob's hand."

"Shut up, Ollie," I say, dragging him through a crowd of people until we break free into an empty hallway that smells like spilled beer and urine.

"Okay, but that still doesn't change the fact that you're holding my hand."

I ignore him and push open the ladies' room door with my shoulder. There's a woman reapplying her lipstick at the sink, and she shoots me a crooked smile before capping the tube and walking back into the bar.

"I don't think I'm supposed to be here," he says as I push him up against the sink that is completely graffitied with permanent marker. Erin loves Jean-Paul. Leah is a bitch. 1D 4 Ever!

"Well, if you didn't eat like some sort of ravenous animal, we wouldn't have to be in here," I say, turning the sink on. "But, alas, you're a man-child who has yet to grasp hand to mouth coordination."

"There you go flattering me again."

I roll my eyes as I wet a paper towel, pumping what little soap is left in the dispenser onto it. I hook my finger into his collar to pull him closer, and then I scrub the stain with the fury of a thousand burning suns. I'm not even sure why I'm trying. It's not going to come out. He's better off just tossing it in the trash and cutting his losses.

"You were wrong, y'know?"

"That's highly unlikely," I say. "About what?"

"No one caring if you were gone," he says. "I'd care."

I look up and catch his stare. His eyes are heavy and his lids are drooping, black bags lining them. But he's still alert. He still demands my attention, taking it hostage and holding it for ransom.

"You'd be happy to see me gone," I try.

"No, I wouldn't," he says. "You never fail to make things interesting."

"Please," I scoff. "You'd be the first one to throw a map burning ceremony. Guitar jam session included."

His eyes narrow. I don't think I'll ever get used to Ollie being serious. There's something off about it—something so cosmically wrong that it makes me nervous.

"Don't worry, Gus'll keep you warm at night," I say, attempting to lighten the mood. "He looks like a cuddler."

"You don't have to put on this act with me."

"I'm not putting on an act."

"You're so afraid to feel something that you pretend that you don't feel anything at all. And you don't have to do that. Not with me. You're hurt. It's okay to be sad and upset and angry."

I break free from his stare and toss the wadded up paper towel into the trash. I don't have to feel anything if I don't want to. If I want to keep everything bottled up, I can do that. I'm allowed.

"Willa—"

"You don't get it, Ollie. You have this family that's so full of love. You don't get what it's like to have no one, to be *alone*, to be replaced, and rejected—"

"Don't… just don't assume that everything in my life is perfect. Because it's not."

"Yeah, well, at least you have a place to go home to and a family that loves you," I tell him. "I don't have anyone."

"You have me."

Five vowels.

Four consonants.

Three words.

Maybe it's because I'm drunk. Or maybe it's because I'm tired of feeling lonely. Maybe I don't have a reason at all. Or maybe I do. I'm not sure. My head is too foggy for me to even begin to comprehend why I do it.

I kiss him.

He has surprisingly soft lips that are sweet and salty from the orange juice that laced my drink and the fries he just shoved in his face. If he's surprised, he hides it well. His arms snake around my waist and he pulls me closer. He's kissing me back with the same desperation I reek of, our mouths fighting for control. I refuse to give it up. There are very few things in my life that I have control over right now. My body is the one thing I can do what I please with. I'm in charge.

"Willa," Ollie breathes against my mouth.

I shut him up with another kiss—a deep one that leaves me pressing my entire body into his. When I hear that quiet groan trickle from the back of his throat, I know I have him exactly where I want him. I need this. I need him. I need to not feel anything. I need to forget.

So I go for his belt.

And he grabs my wrists.

"No," he says, his lips still hot against mine. "Willa, fuck, I can't… we can't…"

"What?" I laugh and press my mouth to his, swallowing his moan. "Am I not your type either?"

"Fuck," he says when I go for the buckle again. "Willa, you're not—"

"C'mon, Ollie, you don't have to pretend. I'm easy. I'm a slut, remember? I'm everyone's type."

"Willa—"

"Isn't this what guys like?" I ask. "I don't need you to be a gentleman. I don't want romance. It's just casual, no-strings-attached sex with a girl who doesn't expect you to stick around long enough for her to put her pants back on. Isn't that the dream?"

"No," is all he manages to say before pushing himself away from me. He walks out of the bathroom without giving me a second glance. And I'm left to face the reflection in the mirror.

I don't know who that girl is.

She's certainly not me.

13

Gus has a banana smoothie in one hand and a breakfast burrito in the other, a strange medley for someone who is sitting in a barber's chair. I'm not sure why he decided eight-thirty on a Friday morning was a good time to get a haircut, but I would have taken any excuse to get out of our room at the hostel. Hungover and completely mortified weren't a winning combination, so my only option was to get as far away from Ollie as possible.

I kissed him.

I.

Kissed.

Ollie.

Ollie Dunbar.

I.

Kissed.

Him.

Worst of all, I was ready and willing to do a whole lot more, and I would have had he not stopped me.

I want to crawl into a hole and die. It's one thing to get drunk and embarrass myself completely, but it's another thing to get rejected. I shouldn't be surprised. Guys want a girl with self-respect. They don't want someone with naked pictures on the internet. It's not like I even *want* Ollie to want me, but the principle of the matter's still there. I'm damaged goods. The bottom of the barrel. The desperate times call for desperate measures girl. The last resort.

I slump over in my chair and groan into my green juice.

"Shoulda got the burrito." Gus glances at my reflection in the mirror, an I-Told-You-So smile flickering over his lips.

"I can't stomach the thought of chewing anything," I tell him. "I also can't stomach the thought of drinking ever again."

"Jameson'll do that to you."

My stomach churns at the memory.

"I should have gotten coffee."

"We can stop on the way back to the hostel."

I groan again. "I'd rather walk into the ocean with ankle weights."

Gus lifts a brow. "You have quite the flare for dramatics."

"No, just a flare for doing stupid things."

Gus chuckles and drops his chin to his chest as the barber taking the buzzer to his neck. We're there for ten more minutes before Gus is clean shaven and much more put-together than he was before. He has a pep in his step —a new lease on life—as we exit the shop into the cool New Plymouth morning.

His phone dings from his back pocket and he removes it without a moment of hesitation. I wonder what that's like—to not panic every time the phone rings or buzzes with a new message. He even looks amused as he scrolls through the screen. Clearly he doesn't have a world of people out to get him. I wonder what that's like too.

"My parent's love to check up on me," he laughs. "I don't remember them being this concerned with my older brother when he went away to college."

"Do they know you're here?" I ask.

He looks at me with a sly smile. "Well… sort of."

"Sort of?"

"They think I'm studying abroad," he admits.

"Aren't you afraid they'll find out? Does anyone know? A friend? Girlfriend?"

Gus sucks down the rest of his smoothie. "I mean… I didn't lie to them. *Technically.* I went to the first day of classes. I decided it wasn't for me, and figured I'd get more out of backpacking. I'm thinking about starting a vlog. Daphne offered me some pointers."

"Oh." That has bad news written all over it.

"And I broke up with my boyfriend before leaving, so I don't have to worry about that. The whole long distance thing… we figured it was for the best. It's not like we were serious."

"Oh," I swallow, my cheeks flushing at the assumption I made. "I'm… sorry. I shouldn't have—"

"No, it's fine," he laughs. "I have ex-girlfriends too. My last partner just happened to be a dude."

"He's not going to tell your parents?"

"He doesn't know," he says. "He's studying in Amsterdam for the semester, and he never met my parents, so nothing to worry about there."

"Just beware of Daphne's vlog," I say. "It's very public and she has an extremely wide audience."

"She mentioned you ran into a few problems."

"A few is one way to put it."

"#williebanter."

I glare at him.

"Don't give me that look." He nudges my shoulder, which really nudges my whole body, and I almost stumble into the window of a shop we're passing by. "I've only just met you two, but I can tell there's a spark."

I frown. "The only spark between us is the one I'm gonna use to set him on fire."

"Romantic."

Gus babbles on for the rest of our walk back to the hostel. I try to keep myself distracted, listening to him talk about the bed and breakfast his parents run in New Orleans and how his brother recently got drafted to the Astros. But I can't stop thinking about this so-called spark Ollie and I have.

There isn't one.

Right?

Right.

He wears socks to bed. He always smells like spearmint. He has an annoying laugh. He thinks his own jokes are funny. He doesn't take sugar in his coffee.

And, yeah, okay, he's an *alright* kisser. He's not sloppy. He doesn't slobber. He has well-controlled *and* soft lips, and he didn't try to shove his tongue down my throat. He clearly knows what he's doing. My knees *may* have gone weak, but I was also hammered. Liquor was surely to blame.

After all, he wears *socks* to *bed.*

That's enough to fizzle any spark.

Not that I have to worry because nothing between us is sparking.

I'm sure of it.

Especially after he turned me down in the bathroom.

* * *

All of the van's doors are wide open when we get back to the hostel. Daphne is lounging carelessly out of the back, her legs crossed and extended in front of her. Her brows are raised above the frames of her sunglasses, and she's eating cereal out of a paper cup. Tosh is in the back on the couch. He's frowning down at his phone, looking more aggravated than I ever thought he was capable of.

I begin to wonder where Ollie is, but then I smell the rich scent of freshly brewed coffee. He's standing next to me, and out of the corner of my eye, I see a paper cup.

He looks just as tired as I feel, like he hasn't slept at all. There's a thin-set frown on his lips where a smile naturally rests. He doesn't give me a second glance as he nudges the cup into my hand.

"Thanks," is all I manage to say before he gets into the driver's side of the van. I watch him buckle his seatbelt and then sit back with his hands resting on the wheel, ready to go.

"It's about time," Daphne says when she stands up. "We thought you two ran off and got married. I was ready to #williebreakup! #willagetsslutt—"

"Enough, Daphne," Ollie snaps.

"Oi! What crawled up your arse?"

"Nothing," he says softer. "I want to leave. We'll hit traffic if we don't go soon."

"When have you ever worried about traffic?" Daphne asks. "I think you've been spending too much time with Willa. #willieneedsabreak."

"What I need is for you to get in the bloody van."

"Geesh," she mumbles. "Sound a little more like Willa…"

I ignore the grin on her face and breeze by her to get into the van. With Gus in the passenger's seat, I collapse onto the couch in the back next to Tosh with a sigh of relief. I have no idea where we're going, and normally it would bother me to not have a detailed itinerary or complete control, but right now I'm just happy I don't have to sit next to Ollie.

"Where are we going?" I ask, taking a sip of my coffee.

"Hot Water Beach for some R&R," Daphne says. "Catch some rays. Lounge in some hot springs. Maybe a bit of zip-lining. River rafting. The usual."

"What's relaxing about zip-lining?"

"Well, nothing when you break your arm, but I'm hoping not to do that again."

"Was that not enough to scar you for life?"

"Literally, yes." She lifts her left arm to show me the gash that curves upward around her elbow. "Figuratively, no."

"I think you should quit while you're ahead." I already have visions of her flying through the air and breaking her good arm. That's a mess I don't want to clean up.

"I don't let things scare me away from living."

"Yeah, you've made that painfully clear." I roll my eyes. "Let's hope you don't get yourself killed in the process."

"At least it would be by my own accord."

"What?" I look over at her.

"Nothing," she says. "Can you pass me my earbuds before Gus turns this van into the Richard Rodger's theater?"

I don't want to give them to her. I want her to explain what she meant by that comment. *At least it would be by my own accord.* What does that even mean?

But before I can say anything, Tosh tosses the wires straight at her face, earning a nasty glare in the process. He shrugs it off and scribbles something down in his notebook. He shoves it at me.

"*What happened with you and Ollie last night?*"

I looked up to find him smiling dumbly at me.

"*Nothing?*" I write.

"*He walked out of the women's restroom looking rather disheveled,*" Tosh writes back. "*You walked out three minutes and fourteen seconds later.*"

"*Do you not have anything better to do than time my trips to the bathroom?*" I ask.

"*Not when they involve Ollie.*"

"*I helped him remove a stain from his shirt.*"

"*With your lips?*"

"*I don't like what you're insinuating, Toshiro,*" I write. "*The fact that you think I'd put my lips anywhere near Ollie's is repulsive. I might throw up.*"

"*You're very dramatic.*"

"*And you're incredibly nosy.*"

"*I'm not the one getting defensive,*" he writes.

"*Of course I'm getting defensive. You're accusing me of hooking up with Ollie Dunbar in the bathroom of a bar.*"

"*You say that like thousands of girls wouldn't kill to be in that position with him.*"

"*They can have him,*" I write. "*He's a slob who eats like a toddler with no hand to mouth coordination.*"

"*How's his mouth to mouth coordination?*"

"*I don't know, Tosh. Why don't you go hook-up with him and find out?*

"*He's not my type,*" he writes.

"*Then I guess his mouth to mouth coordination will remain a mystery.*"

"*As mysterious as your little bathroom tryst.*"

I throw the pen at his face, and a scowl forms over his lips that mirrors mine. We have a stare off.

"I'm very hungover, and you're annoying me," I tell him.

He quickly writes something down in the notebook.

"*My face is insured for more money than you'll ever see in your lifetime,*" I read. "Then I'd worry more about those frown lines. We wouldn't want you to get all wrinkly before you meet Josh. "

Tosh doesn't waste a second whipping the pen back at my forehead.

I'M SITTING IN A HOT SPRING WITH DAPHNE, TOSH, GUS, and Dorris, a woman in her early seventies who wears a bikini better than me. To say I'm uncomfortable is an understatement. But it could be worse. I could have stayed at the van and spent the rest of the afternoon being ignored by Ollie. I'd much rather be sitting in this muddy sand pond having a weird warm water orgy with people I barely know.

"Why's Ollie being such a sour apple?" Gus asks.

"Probably because of his perpetual state of Willa-induced blue balls," Daphne says. "They're both so cranky. You think they'd just—"

"I'm literally right here," I snap.

"See," Daphne says lowly. "Cranky."

"I'm not cranky. I'm annoyed that you talk about me when I'm sitting right next to you."

"I talk about you when you're not next to me too," she says. "You and Ollie shagging is probably the only thing I talk about."

"That's weird."

"I'm just concerned," she says. "And I watch a lot of films, so I know where this goes. The playful banter. The bickering. The back and forth. You're everyone's favorite trope."

"I'm not a trope. I'm a person. And my life is not a romantic comedy."

"The little Scottish boy that follows you around with a guitar says otherwise."

"I fantasize about smashing that guitar over his head," I tell her.

"I mean, whatever gets you off, Willa."

I fist some wet sand into my hand and throw it straight at her chest. The splatting sound stings my ears.

"You bitch!"

"Vlog about it."

The whole #willie thing needs to end. It was mildly annoying at first. I tolerated it. But now it's caused nothing but trouble. And after our kiss, the only hashtag I want next to my name is one announcing my departure from this hell trip.

#bonvoyagewilla

#ihopewenevermeetagainwilla

#thiswassuchawasteoftimewilla

"Feet," Dorris says after a few moments. "That's what got my first husband off."

"Is that why he was your *first* husband?" Gus asks.

"No, he was my first husband because he couldn't get *me* off." A grin lifts her lips. "Don't settle, girls."

"I would never," Daphne says, tilting her head back just enough for the sun to reflect off her sunglasses.

"Well, from a male's perspective—"

"We didn't ask for a male's perspective." Dorris cuts Gus off.

"Yeah, you're right," he says. "I'm sorry. I took a women's studies class. I get feminism."

Once Gus launches into a story about a rally he went to with his ex-boyfriend, I tune him out. Not because I'm not interested, but because I'm more interested in the look on Tosh's face when the word boyfriend leaves Gus's mouth.

Is that a spark in his eye?

A dose of shock and awe?

A dash of sudden interest?

All of which are a perfect recipe for payback.

* * *

My first mistake of the day was not reapplying sunblock.

My second was getting into a taxi when Daphne suggested food.

I walk for an hour and a half back to the van after realizing her invitation to dinner was actually an invitation to a bar. I had no desire to drink ever again, so Tosh bought me a dodgy sandwich and a bottle of aloe from a gas station, and I ventured back to the twenty-four hour spot we were parked at by the beach.

I'm exhausted—physically, mentally, emotionally. I want to fall asleep before everyone gets back. I can only hope that Ollie has taken a heavy dose of his nighttime cold medicine. Being alone with him while he's sleeping is one thing, but the thought of being awake and in silence makes my palms sweaty.

God.

He's not supposed to have this effect on me.

So when I get to the van and realize he's not here, I should be jumping for joy. Instead, I have a small (but noticeable) flair of concern twist in my stomach that I *really* want to blame on early onset food poisoning.

Me? Worried about Ollie's wellbeing? In what world?

We spent most of the day at the beach. I haven't seen him since we left at two. It's almost eight now. Daphne sent him a message before we left to get *dinner*. I should have known something was wrong when he didn't answer.

God.

What's this headline going to be?

Swan Song: Guitar-wielding YouTube Sensation Found Floating in Pacific Ocean

There will be exclusive interviews. I'll be called in for questioning. How many times does one have to threaten someone's life before they become the prime suspect? I'm screwed.

#TheNakedTruth: Willa Loveridge—Yes, That Willa Loveridge—Who Took Her Top Off For The Internet Found Guilty Of Murdering Ollie Dunbar—Yes, That Ollie Dunbar—Whose Only Crime Was Playing His Guitar

I could tear the van apart. Put all those crime TV reruns to good use. After all, I'm practically a private investigator. A bad one, but still. Clear my name before it's slandered all over the internet. *Again*. It's an easy fix.

But Daphne vlogged the entire time we were at the hot springs. As much as it annoyed me, at least I have a #alibi.

I still have to find him.

Mostly because I don't want to explain to his mother and three thousand sisters that he's missing.

Unless he took off on foot—which is doubtful considering he spent the better part of the drive here complaining of a hangover—he couldn't have gone far. The only option is the beach.

Or, well, he could be holed up in any one of the vans parked around us.

Serenading a hot girl.

In a bikini.

But I'm choosing not to think about that option.

The short path down to the beach is graveled and rocky and overgrown with beachgrass, a weathered fence inviting me to the shore. Once I hit the sand, I peel off my sandals and dig my toes into the warmth. I take a deep breath, drinking in the salty ocean air and letting it out slowly.

It does nothing for me.

The sun. The sand. The tranquil lapping of waves against the shore.

None of it is comforting.

It definitely isn't relaxing.

But it's not like I'm here for fun in the sun. I came for a reason. I need to make sure Ollie isn't in the process of becoming fish food.

He's not.

I find him a quarter of a mile down the beach sitting in the sand, his arms draped over his knees as he looks out at the water. The sun is setting. The sky is bright pink and orange and beautiful.

This is the first time I've gotten a good look at him since last night. My stomach is still in knots. Not because I'm embarrassed—*I am*—but because I'm nervous. I'm not good at apologizing. I'd rather gnaw my own arm off than admit I was wrong. But I was. Last night, I was out of line. I shouldn't have kissed him. And he deserves an apology.

He doesn't look over when I sit down next to him. I don't blame him. I wouldn't want to look at me either. In fact, I've been avoiding mirrors all day for that very reason. If I can't face my own reflection, how can I expect anyone else to?

"About last night," I say, deciding it's always better to rip off the bandaid. "I'm sorry. I… I shouldn't have kissed you. I was out of line. And really drunk. Not that that's an excuse, but it kind of fucked with my judgement."

He rolls his lips together. I think that's his attempt to muffle the laugh he eventually scoffs out.

"You think I'm upset that you kissed me?" he asks, finally pulling his attention from the waves that are rolling onto the sand. He looks at me. For the first time since last night. *Finally*. "Willa, I'm upset that you think so low of me. I'm more upset that you think so low of yourself."

I shy away from him, my eyes falling to my knees. Shame washes over me the same way the water washes over the sand.

"You're a person," he tells me. "And you spoke about yourself like you're an object—like the only thing you could possibly offer someone is sex. And you're… you're so much more than that."

"I'm not, though." My heart is in my throat. I'm hot all over.

Count down from ten.

Breathe.

"Yes, you are."

"Would you think so highly of me if you knew I took naked pictures of myself?"

If he's shocked, he hides it well. The still look on his face doesn't waver.

"Yes, I would," he says. "Your body. Your choice. Doesn't make you any less worthy of being treated like a person."

I scoff. "Maybe you should tell that to Mason."

"What?"

"My ex," I say. "He sent the pictures to all of his friends."

That's all it takes for a flare of anger to spark in his

eyes. "All those emails? Calling you all those awful names? It's because of that?"

"Yeah," I say. "It's true. I mean, I took those pictures. I can't really be upset."

"Yes, you can be upset," he tells me. "And you should be. Because you sent those pictures to someone you trusted and he violated that."

"I didn't really trust him that much," I whisper. "That should have been my first red flag. Honestly, a relationship built on someone pressuring me into doing things I wasn't comfortable with probably wasn't very healthy. Probably wasn't very smart either."

Admitting that out loud is like lifting a weight off of my chest. I've been carrying it around for so long that it didn't just feel like part of me—it felt like all of me.

Like it defined me.

Now I know that it doesn't.

I'm more than a picture.

I'm more than a body.

I'm a person.

"You're shivering," Ollie says.

I'm so used to feeling numb that the chill from the breeze doesn't phase me. But that doesn't stop Ollie from unzipping his hoodie and dropping it carefully around my shoulders. It smells like spearmint and coffee and him.

Comforting.

I can finally breathe.

14

"WILLA, UNLOCK THE DOOR."

"No."

"Willa, unlock *the door.*"

"No."

"Willa—"

"No."

Daphne vastly underestimates my tolerance for listening to her bang on the window of the van. She can scream and shout all she wants. I'm not getting on a zipline. I may talk candidly about dramatic ways I could end my life, but I'm not stupid enough to actually try them.

Especially not on a wire.

In the middle of the forest.

With bugs.

It sounds painful.

And dumb.

"Willa—"

"No means no, Daphne!"

"I'm not some chav trying to get into your knickers!

I'm your friend trying to open you up to new life experiences."

"The only life experience I want is a nap in this van."

Through the passenger's side window, I watch Daphne ball her fists as her lips flaring into a snarl.

"Ollie!" she snaps. "Talk some sense into your girlfriend!"

In what world am I Ollie Dunbar's girlfriend? Definitely not this one. Not even in some alternate one. Our intimacy doesn't stretch past him buying me coffee. And some occasional spooning. And a brief restroom rendezvous.

I'm not his girlfriend.

I'm just the girl who sits in the passenger's seat and tells him how to drive.

"Willa."

When I look over, Ollie has his eyes narrowed beneath his sunglasses, giving me a look that thousands of girls would drop their panties for. I roll my eyes, cross my arms, and nuzzle my shoulders into the seat. I'm not going anywhere.

But then I hear the click, and then I feel the soft breeze, and when I turn my head, Ollie has the door propped open with his hand.

"What… how—"

"Magic," he says with a grin, dangling the keychain between his index finger and thumb. "Let's go, love."

"Don't call me that, you baboon."

"What did I do to deserve you?" he asks.

Before I can answer, he's already nudging his head.

"I'll haul you over my shoulder if I have to."

"I'll kick you in the balls if *I* have to."

"That's my girl," he says. "*Let's go*."

"I'm not your girl! I'm my own person and I make my own choices and—Ollie! Put me down! No means no!"

He somehow manages to get my seatbelt off before I come to my senses and he scoops me up in his arms. I can't stop him. I kick and flail until he sets me on the ground.

"Alright, you mad woman!" he cries. "There! Are you happy?"

"No, I'm absolutely *not* happy!"

"Well, tough luck. You've got no choice."

"Oh, I've got choices, you—"

"Baboon? Yeah, yeah, I know. We haven't got time for this."

"Oh, we've got time—Gus! Put me down! I'm not some rag doll, you yeti! This is unethical!I'm calling the police! *Help*!"

I'm upside down, over his shoulder, and not one person cares.

* * *

ANY WALK THAT REQUIRES ME TO WEAR A HELMET AND A harness was a walk I didn't want to take. Any walk that requires me to sign a *waiver* was definitely a walk I didn't want to take.

Yet here I am. Sandwiched between Thing One and Thing Two—Ollie and Gus—while our guides, Vlad and Hana, give us a safety briefing and a quick history of the reservation we're on. Our *excursion* (aka our 150 dollar Dance With Death) is three hours long, and doesn't just include ziplines, but also swing bridges.

Fun for the whole family!

"I can assure you that this time I won't end up in an emergency room in Costa Rica," Daphne says to her vlog. "I might end up in a pub drunk off my arse, though."

I roll my eyes at the thought of having to pick her up off the floor of a bar.

"It wouldn't kill you to smile," Ollie whispers to me.

"It might," I hiss. "I'm being forced here against my will. It's practically a hostage situation."

"You're absolutely mental."

"I know."

He cracks a smile, which is so *stupid* and *dopey* and not *charming* at all. I roll my eyes again, and he bumps his shoulder against mine as a soft laugh whistles past his lips.

"Now if you'll follow me," Vlad says once he finishes his speech, "we'll walk a short trail before we get to our first bridge."

I groan loudly when everyone starts to move, my feet firmly planted on the ground. I can't—I *won't*—do this.

"And there's Willa clearly being a team player," Daphne says to her camera. "The look on her face! You'd think we were forcing her to be here."

"You are!" I cry.

Daphne shakes her head and continues on. "We're not going to let our little black cloud rain on our parade."

Our little black cloud.

More like a realistic ray of reason.

This is a stupid idea.

I can't be the only one who realizes that.

"One foot in front of the other." Ollie presses his hand to the small of my back and urges me forward until I stumble.

"I'll break your hand if you touch me again."

"You mean the hand you're always keen to hold?"

I glare at him. "I hope your zipline snaps."

He merely chuckles in response. I ignore him—because I can't take him seriously with one of Daphne's cameras strapped to his helmet—and I trudge along to catch up with our friends, every step inching me closer to my impending death. If anything, it'll make for a good write up. Maybe it'll make the morning news. Maybe my mom will see it when she's flipping through the channels.

"*Willa*," she'll think. "*Why does that name sound so familiar? Vinny? Do we know a Willa?*"

"*Willa? Who's Willa?*" my stepfather will reply. "*We don't know any Willas.*"

Maybe Benji will see it. I bet he'll be really upset that he paid a dead girl's college tuition. Or maybe he won't be upset at all. Maybe I'm just another girl to him. Another life lost to a completely stupid and reckless *adventure*. Nothing more than a passing thought.

I guess it's better this way. Because once I fly into oblivion, that'll be it. I'll be gone. Sure, my boobs are on the internet and the whole world thinks I'm a slut, but it could always be worse.

Right?

Right.

At least I have an excuse to haunt the hell out of Mason.

I can't wait to see the smear campaign he'll write about the dead.

"It's so green." Daphne is twirling around, making sure her camera catches every angle of the reserve. "Can you believe how *green* it is? I've never seen so many trees before. They're *everywhere*!"

"Of course they're everywhere! We're in the forest!"

"I'm sure you've all learned to ignore Willa by now," she says to her camera. "Well, accept for Ollie. Because judging by the angle of his head, all of his GoPro footage will be of her bum."

"Daphne!" his voice squeaks.

"#hesnotsubtle! #shedoesntevenhaveabum!"

"I hate you both," I say, picking up my pace so that neither of them can see my cheeks flame red. "Keep your eyes and cameras to yourselves!"

Tosh is laughing when I catch up to him, and before I can properly glare at him, he's reaching into his pocket for a pen. He scribbles a few words onto the palm of his hand.

"*Eye to bum coordination is on point.*" I narrow my eyes to his. "You better hope your harness to zipline coordination is on point. We wouldn't want Japan's most prized possession to get hurt."

He holds up one finger and reaches into his pocket, pulling out a receipt to write on.

"*We wouldn't want Ollie's most prized possession to get hurt either.*" The second the words leave my lips, I crinkle the paper in my hand. "Good thing he left his guitar in the van. Not that I'd be complaining if it did get hurt. That would actually make me very happy."

"What would make you very happy?" Ollie asks when he comes up behind me.

"If your guitar suffered a tragic death."

"What did my guitar ever do to you?"

"There aren't enough fingers and toes in the world for me to list off everything I hate about it."

Of all the things I've said to him, I don't think Ollie has ever looked so offended. It's as if I spoke ill of his family or his slightly crooked nose or the fact that he's a weirdo who wears socks to bed. No, his precious guitar is kept so near and dear to his heart that one bad word about it sends a frown line a mile down his face.

"Are you gonna cry?" I ask him.

"I might," he says.

I roll my eyes and take a step towards Tosh, who is listening to Vlad explain a few safety procedures that I should be paying more attention to. It's not every day you sign your life away. I'd at least like to know how this is all going to end.

"Once you're clipped to the line," he explains, "you walk down the steps as far as you can and then the line will take you. When you reach the landing, extend your legs to help stable yourself."

How am I supposed to remember any of that? I'm pretty sure I'll be too busy trying to figure out how not to die.

"Who's the first victim?" Hana asks, rubbing her hands together.

To my surprise, there's nearly a brawl between Gus and Daphne, both ready and willing to, well, *die.* I put my money on Daphne. She's scrappy. All Gus has on her are a few inches and a hundred pounds, which are all moot when she threatens to chop his dick off with a plastic fork. He cowers back like a child and Daphne clips onto that zipline in all of her glory.

She's in her element. Bold. Wild. Reckless. She pulls it off so well, exuding a type of carefree spirit that I never could. She's always ready and willing and thinking of the next adventure. Nothing holds her back. Not danger. Not fear. Not herself.

Maybe I've had her wrong this whole time. Maybe she isn't trying to die. Maybe she's just trying to live.

In fifty years, she'll look back on this with no regrets. Can I say the same? Because Daphne lives each day like she's not going to get another. I live each day in fear of… *everything*. What Mason will say. What my mother will think. I need a plan or a map or a list. I need to know what's going to happen before it happens.

And sure, my brain chemistry has a mind of its own and it's almost impossible for me to not obsess over things.

But still.

That's not living.

It's existing.

It's being controlled.

And I don't want to live like that anymore.

"You look like you've just had an epiphany," Ollie whispers into my ear. "I hope it's not about all the ways you plan on breaking my guitar."

I elbow him in the ribs.

"Christ," he huffs. "Perhaps it was about all the ways you plan on puncturing my lungs."

"Perhaps it was about all the ways I can puncture your lungs with the neck of your guitar."

"You… you're absolutely mental."

"I'm surprised it's taken you this long to realize."

He laughs that stupid little laugh that makes his nose crinkle, and I blame the flutter in my stomach on the dodgy coffee I had earlier this morning.

"Ladies first," he says, nudging his head towards the zipline.

"And die before I get the chance to witness your death? I don't think so, Ollie. I've been waiting my entire life for this moment."

"We've known each other for two weeks."

"I've been waiting an entire two weeks for this moment."

"Okay," he says with a slow nod. "But I'm pretty you're just using that as an excuse to make a run for it."

"I can assure you watching you die a gruesome death is right at the top of my bucket list."

"Like the very top?"

"I mean, I'd like to see Buckingham Palace and the Eiffel Tower, but your death is a solid number three."

Ollie purses his lips like he's in deep thought. "Y'know… I live in London."

"You sleep on your sister's couch in London."

"It's pretty close to Buckingham Palace."

I blink. "Are you offering to take me?"

"Depends if you want me to be offering."

I hum and look over at Vlad, who is not-so-patiently waiting for one of us. "You're about to die, so I guess we'll never know."

Ollie smiles and brushes by me. That's when I realize my palms are sweaty and my heart is racing.

What was that?

Nothing, obviously.

Ollie didn't sort-of kind-of ask me on a date.

Right?

Right.

Jesus.

I'm so distracted by the fact that the wind got knocked out of me—*because of a stupid conversation with a stupid boy*—that I completely miss Ollie making a safe landing at the other end of the zipline.

Damn.

He was supposed to die.

This ruins everything.

"It's now or never, Willa!" Daphne screams, her camera pointed straight at me.

Good.

At least my death will be documented.

I'll probably go viral.

Again.

With my clothes on this time.

There's a complete disconnect from my brain and feet

as I make my way over to Vlad. I should be running in the other direction—back to the van, back to the airport, back to the US, where I'd be safe and sound and not attached to a stainless steel cable that could snap at any given moment.

But I stand there with my heart hammering in my chest and my stomach lodged in my throat. Vlad tells me to relax. He says that a focal point helps some people, so I take his advice and I look straight ahead and I see Daphne and Tosh and Gus and Ollie. And he's smiling that stupid, stupid, *stupid* smile and I'm feeling so many things at once—an overwhelming rush of adrenaline, sheer terror, and nerves that leave chills zipping down my spine.

I'm screaming.

The sound echoes off of every leaf in the reserve, breezing through the trees like a gust of wind.

I scream.

And scream.

And scream.

But I feel free.

And I'm out of control, but have never felt more in control.

I'm alive.

My feet hit the landing and I'm still screaming, but I stumble into Ollie and he wraps his arms around me and I feel lighter.

I *am* lighter.

* * *

THE SALTY PICKLE IS BEST KNOWN FOR, *WELL*, THEIR pickles, but I think that's blasphemous, because their dessert waffle is the best thing I've ever put in my mouth. It's bigger than my face and slathered in peanut butter, Nutella, and chocolate ice cream. I'm supposed to be sharing it with Gus, but he only manages to sneak a bite before I build a fortress around it.

Ziplining works up quite an appetite.

Also the adrenaline.

I feel wired.

And now I'm living in peanut butter bliss. Nothing can ruin my night. Mason could show up with my naked pictures plastered on a banner and I'd still be in my Nutella coma. Nothing can hurt me. I'm practically a new woman.

"You were supposed to share that with me." Gus frowns at the nearly empty plate.

"I don't remember agreeing to that," I say.

"I do," he says. "You looked at the menu and said, 'who wants to split the dessert waffle with me?' and I said, 'I will!'"

"Are you sure?" I ask, spooning the last bite of ice cream into my mouth. "That doesn't sound like something I'd agree to."

"You don't play fair."

"Never said I did." I lick some Nutella off my spoon and grin at him.

Gus rolls his eyes and digs his hand into the basket of fried pickles Ollie ordered and then neglected when the mic stand became available. "So does Tosh have a significant other?"

I kink a brow, scrapping some peanut butter off my plate. "Why?"

He shrugs. "He's always on his phone."

"He's a celebrity. They're surgically attached to their phones."

"He's a celebrity on the run," Gus says. "You'd think he would have ditched his phone in a trashcan."

I'm not sure what angle Gus is playing. I might be a

changed woman, but I'm still skeptical. For all I know, he's an undercover journalist trying to out Tosh on national television.

"He likes to do crosswords," I say, unsure if that's even true. "Helps him with his English. He's very insecure about it."

"Oh, that's understandable," he decides. "So no girlfriend? Boyfriend?"

"Why? Are you interested? You've only known him for, like, three days."

"You've known Ollie for two weeks and you're practically married with three kids and a mortgage."

"Excuse you! We're divorced, no kids, and I get alimony." I glare at him. "But yes, Tosh has an internet boyfriend."

"An internet boyfriend?"

"It's the twenty-first century. It's a thing. He's very secretive about it, but he's meeting him in Auckland."

"Okay," Gus says.

I'm not sure if he's really okay with it, but he pops another fried pickle into his mouth and turns around to watch the crowd of girls drool over Ollie's cover of a One Direction song. I roll my eyes so hard that they almost get stuck in the back of my head. He eats up the attention like some sort of starving artist. He has over a million views on YouTube. Isn't that enough?

Certainly not when he has dozens of pretty girls throwing themselves at him.

I sigh and grab the basket of fried pickles from Gus, shoving a few in my mouth as Daphne stumbles towards the table. She isn't drunk, which is the most surprising thing ever, but something seemed off ever since we left the reserve. She's slower. Slightly off kilter. She looks tired, like today really knocked it out of her.

"You okay?" I ask her when she sits down.

She places her glass of water next to my Diet Coke and nods. "Yeah, I think the zipline just messed with my equilibrium."

I don't believe her. It's a gut feeling that I can't shake. She's keeping something from us. I'm not sure what, but it definitely has something to do with the pill she popped when she thought I wasn't looking.

I would have spent the whole night speculating (and probably rummaging through her purse whenever she left it unattended), but when Tosh pushes through the crowd with someone in tow, my priorities shift.

All the Nutella in the world couldn't save this night from being ruined.

Because for some unknown reason, Kaia Loveridge is following Tosh to our table, and I need twelve shots before we have another family reunion.

Tosh clears his throat and hands me a napkin. "*Someone's here to see you.*"

"I gathered that, Tosh," I say tightly, shifting my eyes to her.

Kaia is a mirror of my mother. Only the mirror is ten years younger and has a half-sleeve of tattoos—cherry blossoms entwined with vines—and a nose ring. She clearly had a rebellious phase. I don't blame her. At least she didn't get knocked up. She didn't run off to another country. Tattoos seem pretty tame in comparison to what my mother did.

"I don't make a habit of stalking people," she says.

"You're stalking me?"

"Is it really stalking when Daphne posts your every location on social media?"

"I think so?"

"Oh, well, I wasn't doing it for any weird reasons."

"So you don't want Ollie's autograph?"

Why are you trying to make jokes, Willa?

Shut up.

"I needed to talk to you."

I pick up my drink to distract myself. "If you can't tell me anything about Benji, I really don't think we have much to talk about it."

I swirl the straw around a few ice cubes and the wedge of lime that's floating along side of them. I glance over to the bar where Tosh is ordering another drink. I look over at Ollie as he gets off the stage. I see Gus shooting pool. I look everywhere but at Kaia.

"Benji doesn't really like being kept track of. He's all over the place. He goes where the inspiration is. I think. I don't know. He's an artist. I've never tried to understand why he does what he does," she says. "I haven't seen him in years."

My eyes snap to her. "So you know him?"

"Not well. Not at all, really. I was a lot younger than him and Ana. They didn't want to hang around with a kid," she swallows. "He has a sister. Angela. And a nephew. Matty. He's your age. I think he goes to the University of Waikato. I'm not sure."

I went from having no information to an influx in a matter of seconds.

"Do you have a phone number? An address?"

"No, I'm sorry," she says. "That's not why I came here."

"What?"

"What happened the other day," she starts. "I don't think we handled it the right way. Things were really bad when Ana left, and then she called to tell us that you were here, and—"

"Listen, I'm not looking for a family reunion or for you

guys to welcome me with open arms... I just have some things I need to talk to Benji about. My mom never—"

"She's here," Kaia cuts me off. "Ana—*your mum*—she's here. She's in New Zealand."

Well.

Fuck.

15

DAPHNE IS on a social media blackout, which means I have to listen to her complain about all the ad revenue I'm costing her by forcing her to go off the grid. In just a few hours I'm already in debt two million dollars and I'll have to hand over my first born child upon birth. It's a pretty steep price, but I'm willing to pay it to ensure that my mother doesn't find me.

Because she's in New Zealand.

My mother.

Ana Loveridge-Herrera.

The anti of all antis.

Is.

In.

New.

Zealand.

After exiling herself from the country, I'm surprised they even let her back in.

"I think you're being ridiculous." Ollie is sitting on the floor of *Suds & Bubbles*, the self-service laundromat we're at, wearing a pair of mismatched socks, a rather small pair of boxer-briefs, and one of Daphne's hand-made I ❤ Ollie Dunbar t-shirts, because he dribbled chocolate milk on his last clean outfit. Somehow, I'm the ridiculous one.

"I think I'm being completely rational."

"You're wearing a hood and sunglasses." He blinks at me and then strums his guitar. "It's highly unlikely that your mum is lurking around a launderette in fucking Rotorua."

"I thought it was highly unlikely that she'd come to *fucking* New Zealand, so I wouldn't put anything past her right now."

"She's your mum, Willa," Daphne says from her seat on top of a folding table. "Of course she was going to come after you if she was worried."

"Please," I scoff. "This isn't her being worried. This is her trying to control every aspect of my life, like I'm one of her clients!"

"Keep telling yourself that, babe," she says and hops onto the floor. She's unsteady on her feet, knocking her hip against the corner of the washer. I watch her shake it off, regaining her composure as she slings the strap of her purse over her shoulder. She pretends it didn't happen. "Let's go, Tosh. I need ice cream."

"It's nine in the morning," I tell her.

"I didn't realize there were rules for when I can and cannot eat ice, *Mum*."

I snarl at her. "I hope you get brain freeze."

"I hope you get laid," she says. "Maybe you'll be a bit more bearable."

"Sex isn't always the solution, Daphne."

"Yeah, well…" She shrugs, propping the door open with her foot. "Ollie's already in his pants, so it would be a waste not to take advantage."

Ollie blushes and diverts his stare to the cracks in the floor.

"I'd rather take advantage of a machete."

"That sounds wildly painful." Daphne cringes, holding the door open for Tosh and Gus. "Hope you're up for the challenge, Oliver."

"Yeah, I'm very uncomfortable right now," he says.

"Good," she says. "We'll be around! I'm not sure where. I'd say check my Twitter, but I'm not allowed to use that, so… send a carrier pigeon if there's an emergency."

The door to the laundromat closes behind them, and I'm left to bask in the humming of three dryers and a washing machine while Ollie tunes his guitar. It's a recipe for a splitting headache.

Kaia's words are still ringing in my ears. I replayed the conversation over and over again, trying to figure out why she bothered finding me at all. Did she really think we were going to have some blissful reunion? Three generations of Loveridge women under the same roof! After twenty years of not speaking, it's highly unlikely that we'll be making plans for Christmas.

Unless Mom has turned a new leaf, and has decided that her new spawn is worthy of meeting her family. After all, it won't be born out of wedlock. It won't be a bastard like me. This is my mother's chance to have her perfect life—to do it right. Six-figure job. Quirky husband. Cute little love goblin. They'll spend Christmas in Mexico with Vincent's family and then jet here for the New Year. Her Facebook feed will be all dorky Christmas tree pictures with a drooling baby and a husband who wears a funny little hat made of mistletoe.

I'm going to throw up.

Kaia did, however, bring some promising information that could help me find Benji. Angela and Matty. I'll have to put on my private investigator hat again, and hope my mother doesn't get to them first.

I pick up my phone to start another search. I'm ready to hit the button for my internet browser, but get momentarily distracted by the number of unread emails I have.

I groan.

From: **BeautyGuru** (10 Lipstick Musts!)
From: **Ana Loveridge-Herrera** (Harbor View Hotel)
From: **Ana Loveridge-Herrera** (Willa! I'm not going to chase you around!)
From: **Ana Loveridge-Herrera** (Willa! I did not fly for 2 days to be ignored!)
From: **Mason Stueck** (no one wants a girl like that)
From: **Mason Stueck** (he'll realize all your good at is being on your back)
From: **Mason Stueck** (he'll get bored)
From: **Mason Stueck** (you don't have anything else going for you)
From: **Mason Stueck** (because you'll send him tit pics)
From: **Mason Stueck** (he's only into you because you're easy)
From: **Mason Stueck** (worthless willa)
From: **The Coffee Corner** (Caramel Delight!)
From: **Mason Stueck** (just like I did)
From: **Mason Stueck** (he'll forget about you when he finds a hotter piece of ass)
From: **ShoeShack** (25% Off! Time's Running Out!)
From: **Mason Stueck** (groupie slut)
From: **Vincent Herrera** (We're here!)
From: **Mason Stueck** (shitty little whiny musicians?)
From: **Mason Stueck** (Is that what you're into now?)
From: **Mason Stueck** (He's a fucking joke just like you)
From: **Ana Loveridge-Herrera** (I'm here!!!)

"You good?"

I drop my phone when Ollie speaks.

"Yeah," I say, picking it up. I ignore the skeptical look he shoots me. "I'm fine."

"Please don't use that line on me," he laughs. "I'm not daft."

"I'm fine."

"I have five sisters."

"Yes, I'm well aware of your PhD in Women's Studies, Oliver."

He bites his lip.

Not that I'm watching his lips, or anything.

"What's wrong?" he asks, this time much more shyly, but still just as sincere.

I sigh. "Mason."

"What did he say?"

"Nothing worth repeating… or rereading."

Ollie sits up and sets his guitar on the floor. "Can I see?"

"No, it's nothing. It's fine. I'm already over it. Like I said before, I'm numb to it at this point."

"But you shouldn't be," he says. "It should have never gotten to this point."

"Look, I made this mess. I could have said no. I didn't. It is what it is."

Thinking about it. Talking about it. Reliving every little detail of how I obsessed over angles and poses and lighting makes me feel dirty. And I hate that. I hate him. I hate myself.

"Willa." Ollie's thumb brushes over my hand, his touch sending a ripple of chills down my spine. His eyes are soft against mine. He's looking at me, like I'm a person and not a picture on the internet. "Can I see your phone?"

I don't know why I give it to him, but there's something

about Ollie that makes me believe that not all men are complete assholes. He could easily be playing me, and maybe I'll be eating my words in a few days, but I trust him for some god awful reason.

"This is complete rubbish," he says, his lips twisted into a snarl. "Shitty little whiny musician? As if! I've got over a million views on YouTube! I'm bloody brilliant."

It feels good to smile. It feels even better to laugh. It feels normal. Whatever that is.

"He's a piece of shit."

"I know."

"And it's not true—everything he said, it's not true."

"I know."

I don't.

But I hoped, eventually, that I would.

"I mean it, Willa," Ollie says. "It's not true."

The conversation feels too intimate, like something has shifted between us, something that runs much deeper than some occasional spooning and a drunken make-out session.

I'm not sure how I feel about it, but I'm ragingly uncomfortable with the way he's staring into my soul.

"Teach me how to play guitar."

"What?" Ollie looks offended. "You hate my guitar."

"I know," I say, sliding onto the floor next to him. "Teach me to play it."

"Why? So you can snap the neck when I'm not looking?"

"Give me a little more credit," I scoff. "The inevitable smashing will be much more dramatic. This laundromat isn't worthy of it."

"Right," he says, eyeing me skeptically as he picks up his guitar. "I feel like I'm handing my child over to the wolves."

"Don't be ridiculous." I grab it, which causes him to wince.

"Jesus, woman! You don't have to be so rough!"

"It's a guitar, Ollie. Not a piece of glass. It was made to sustain wear and tear."

"Yeah, well, you're going to wear and tear it into oblivion with the death grip you have around it," he says, his hand skimming mine. "Relax."

I loosen my grip.

"Okay, there are six strings—E, A, D—"

"I don't want to know them. I just want to play them."

"How do you expect to play them if you don't know them?"

"I'm not looking to start a band, Ollie. I just want to play a chord."

"You sound ridiculous, but okay, put your index finger on the second fret—"

"What's a fret?"

"Something we would have gone over had you let me give you a proper lesson."

"Someone who's such a *professional* should be able to give me the abridged version."

"I have too much respect for the instrument."

"Please, you spilled beer all over it last night. Where was your respect then?"

Ollie narrows his eyes into a glare, grabbing my hand and jamming my index finger onto a string.

"Ow! *You* don't have to be so rough." I pull my hand back to examine the string shaped mark that was surely seared onto my finger. I'm going to file a complaint with the Scottish embassy. He's a hazard to my wellbeing.

"What happened to your hand?"

"What?" *Shit.* I try to cover it quickly by gripping the

neck, but Ollie brushes his fingers over my wrist, forcing me to turn my palm to him. "It's nothing."

"Those don't look like nothing, Willa."

He stares at the half-moons tattooed into my palms, and then shifts his eyes to mine. My mouth goes dry.

"It's just… a nervous habit," I say.

"You clench your fists?"

"I have control issues."

His chuckle is soft and breathy. "*I know.*"

"No, I have *control issues*," I admit. "Like I have a therapist and I take medication. Or I'm supposed to be taking medication, but I forgot it and that's probably why I've been more irritable than usual."

"Willa," he whispers. "I'm sorry. I had—"

"It's fine," I say.

"No, it's not. We always give you a hard time—"

"Because I always give you guys a hard time," I laugh, trying to lighten the mood. "It's not like I go around broadcasting it."

He nods. "So you clench your fists when you… lose control?"

"Yeah." I nod. "Usually counting to ten helps. Sometimes it doesn't. My medication usually makes me feel less stressed out about things."

"Is it like OCD?"

"I have OCPD. Obsessive Compulsive Personality Disorder," I tell him. "I get really rigid about routines and doing things a certain way and when things don't go as planned, I panic."

"Like when I don't follow directions or when Daphne changes the plans?"

"Ollie—"

"I wish you would have told me sooner," he says. "I would have been more mindful."

"I appreciate that," I say. "But I understand that things won't always go my way and I'm usually a lot better at handling when they don't. And everything with Benji and my mom and Mason, it's just been hard to control what I'm feeling."

After that verbal diarrhea, I'm left feeling more vulnerable and exposed than I did in my naked pictures. Since when am I so comfortable with Ollie? I need to lay down.

"Okay, show me the chords now."

"Ring finger on B," he says quietly. "Middle finger high E."

I place my fingers where he tells me. "Can I play it now?"

"Sure."

He hands me his pick and I grab it with so much enthusiasm that I mess up my finger placement. When I strum that first note, it sounds like a fork in a garbage disposal.

"Yeah, don't go quitting your day job," he laughs.

"It's not funny." I frown. "And it's not my fault. You didn't teach me properly. You can't expect me to play it right when you didn't give me the complete instructions. Seriously, Ollie, it's like you wanted me to fail—"

"For Christ's sake," he laughs.

"It's not—"

"Funny, I know," he says, sitting up on his knees. He scoots behind me, his chest flush with my back. He snakes one arm over my shoulder, cupping my hand that's holding the pick. And with his other hand, he cradles mine softly around the neck of the guitar. "Index finger on G, ring finger on B, and middle finger on high E," he says quietly into my ear, his fingers pressing mine like they're piano keys.

He could have said something more. Maybe spoken

French. Or recited the Declaration of Independence. I don't know. Because all I can focus on is how smooth his hands are and how careful his touch is and how I'm shivering despite how warm he is.

God.

"And then," he whispers, slowly guiding me into a strum. "*Music.*"

It's so basic and simple, but still so beautiful.

I look up at him and he's smiling and I'm smiling and I forget how to breathe. Because when someone looks at you like that—like they're proud of you, like you've done something so much more than what you've actually done, like you've just cured cancer or solved world hunger—how could it not take your breath away? How could I not want to kiss him?

God.

I want to kiss him.

And I want him to kiss me.

And I think maybe he's going to.

But.

The dryer buzzes.

* * *

For the second time in my life—and for the second time in the past two days—I'm taking a long walk with a helmet. The only difference is that this time I'm wearing a life vest instead of a harness and I'm holding a paddle.

Daphne and I have two very different definitions of going off the grid.

"Willa's not complaining," Daphne says to her camera. "We must have knocked the adventure into her yesterday. Or, perhaps, Ollie knocked something into her this morning."

"I'm literally going to strangle you."

"As opposed to figuratively strangling me?" She beams.

"I hate you."

"I know," she says. "That's what makes this fun."

I trudge along behind her, carefully trying to keep myself out of camera view. Just because she's on a social media cleanse now doesn't mean she can't make future vlogs. Her words, not mine. I don't care as long as they're not getting posted in the immediate future. My mom is already on my trail. I got a handful of new emails this morning letting me know that she's on her way to Rotorua. The joke's on her because we're leaving after this little excursion. I'm almost tempted to have Daphne post something with the wrong location, but I figure purposely sending my pregnant mother on a wild goose chase around the country would be in bad taste.

Besides, if luck is on her side, which it always seems to be, she'll be hearing about my death on the local news tonight.

We're going whitewater rafting. While ziplining had opened my mind to the prospect of adventure and I liked that rush of adrenaline, that doesn't mean I'm not nervous.

And believe me, I am.

"You'll be fine." Gus throws his arm around my shoulders and gives me a tight squeeze.

"I know," I lie.

"Then why do you look like you swallowed a bug?"

"Because I probably did. We're in the jungle."

"Honestly, Willa, where did we find you?" Daphne shouts over her shoulder.

"Civilization."

"Talk about Westernization," she mumbles.

"I'm just not cut out for this. Museums thrill me. Itineraries! A good guided tour!"

"What do you call this?"

"A crazy person with a video camera."

Daphne hums, shooting me a sly smirk.

This is my own fault. I should have minded my own business at the airport. I should have stayed seated like I was told to. I would have already been in Auckland. I probably would have found Benji by now. All of this could have been avoided.

"Okay," Addie, our guide, says when we reach the dock. "Remember what I told you—brace yourself. Keep your front foot tucked under the tube in front of you. Stay seated on the outer rim unless I tell you otherwise. And your paddle is going to help you brace yourself when we hit the rapids. *Always* be ready to swim."

"More importantly," Daphne adds, "make sure your GoPros are on! I need good footage. Preferably not of Willa's arse, Ollie."

"If you fall off the raft, don't expect me to give you a paddle to grab onto," he tells her.

"You'd never let me drown, Ollie." Daphne grins at him, and pinches his cheek for good measure.

"But I might," I say, knocking my shoulder into hers.

"We both know that's not true," she says. "You wouldn't have followed me out of the airport if you weren't keen to save my life."

I groan when she brushes into me. "Someone has to look out for you."

"Lucky me," she says, placing a sloppy kiss on my cheek. "#waphne! #watchoutollie! #chicksbeforedicks!"

I nudge her again. This time with enough force to send her stumbling into Tosh.

Thankfully, Addie is already ushering us into the raft, so I don't have to dignify Daphne with a response. Gus takes the front. Daphne and Tosh are behind him, and Ollie and I are behind them. Addie is at the back.

"Are we ready?" she asks.

"Not even a little," I say.

"That sucks," she laughs, and then pushes us into the river.

It's nice.

At first.

The water is still and calm—*tranquil.* I can hear birds chirping. The trees are bright and green. I would have taken my phone out to snap a picture if I had it with me. Maybe I was wrong. Maybe this *will* be enjoyable.

But then we hit the first rapid, and my stomach lurches into my throat. I'm practically on my feet. Water sloshes into the raft. I'm soaked.

"No!" I scream.

"Yes!" Daphne screams back.

I'm going to be sick. My heart is racing. This is so not fun.

Okay.

It's kind of fun.

But I'm still wet and about to lose my breakfast.

"I hate this," I yell.

"No, you don't!" Ollie laughs.

I look over at him just in time to catch that stupid smile.

My stomach flops.

In a good way.

"Paddle!" Gus shouts.

We hit another rapid, and I brace one foot beneath the tube in front of me, paddling hard until my arms burn. A wave hits me in the face, and I swallow a mouthful of water as the raft floats into a calmer stream.

"How you doing, Willa?" Daphne looks back at me, droplets of water dripping down her face.

"I don't know."

"You're smiling."

"Shut up."

It's nice to not play it safe. To not hold myself back. To be a little reckless. To lose control. To actually be part of the adventure. It feels like I'm on a high.

Just not high enough to jump off a bridge.

"We're about to hit the falls," Addie shouts. "Get ready."

The falls.

I look ahead to where the river disappears. My throat goes tight. I try to stay calm. I paddle the way Addie tells us to. I can do it. It's all part of the adventure. I don't need to be scared.

"Stop paddling!" Addie shouts.

I know what that means.

It's time.

You can do this, Willa.

It's a slow motion moment. I feel the raft tip. I feel my heart racing. I feel the seat below me. I feel Ollie's hand wrapped around my wrist.

And then I don't.

I'm floating, gasping for air as I gulp down white foamy water. It's pulling me under. Waves hit me with a force I've never felt before.

Am I drowning?

Panic.

"Willa!"

He sounds so far away. Or maybe it's me. Maybe I'm already slipping under. Maybe I'm already gone. Maybe I've finally gotten what I've been wishing for. This is my out. This is what I wanted.

"*Willa!*"

But I can still hear him. He sounds just as scared—as panicked and as desperate—as I feel.

God, I'm never going to get to kiss him again.

"Ollie!"

Daphne. That's Daphne.

"Ollie! Willa!"

This is it.

Everything is going hazy. I'm too tired—too weak—to keep fighting, to keep swimming.

But then I feel it.

I feel him.

Because even when I'm blacking out and ready to drown, I know what Ollie's hand feels like.

The water is still rough and I'm still struggling, but he has his arm braced around me, keeping me afloat.

"You're fine," he gasps. "Willa, you're fine."

I can't speak. I try to. I open my mouth, but nothing comes out. I'm caught in a limbo, so close to death, yet still so alive. I cling to him.

"Willa," he says, his lips parted as he struggles to breathe. "You're okay. You're okay."

I think he's saying it more for himself—to calm his own nerves. Because I know I'm okay. I know I'm alive. He's the one that still needs convincing.

"Ollie," Daphne shouts as a rope splashed into the water.

He grabs it without tearing his eyes from mine, and as our friends pull us in, we knew that something changed.

We knew that there's no turning back from this.

16

"*Angela Atkins is a ballet teacher.*"

The note Tosh drops on my lap is written on a greasy napkin. Before I can ask any further questions, he hands over his laptop. He found an article.

CAMBRIDGE'S SHINING YOUNG STAR ACCEPTS FULL SCHOLARSHIP TO THE UNIVERSITY OF WAIKATO

Don't be surprised when you see Matty McGregerson's name in lights. He's been a staple in the Children's Theater since age five when his mother, Angela Atkins, convinced him to try out for the annual production of A Christmas Carol. *The McGregerson-Atkins family are no strangers to the stage. Angela, a former teacher for the Royal Ballet, and Matty's father, Calvin McGregerson, was a Sydney-based director before his death in 2009. McGregerson credits his love for the theater to his parents, and was quoted saying that he just wants to make his late father proud.*

—Samaira Srivas, The Cambridge Enquirer

"Oh my god?"

"What?" Daphne has pizza crust hanging out of her mouth.

"Angela," I say, sitting up. "She's a ballet teacher."

"Who's Angela again?"

"Benji's sister," I say. "Her son goes to the University of Waikato."

"Cool," she says, grabbing another slice. "We won't stick out so much when we lurk around there."

I laugh, resting back against a pillow on the couch. We're in the van, working on the last of our fourth pizza, and I'm trying very hard not to think about the fact that I have my feet in Ollie's lap.

Or how he's mindlessly tracing circles over my ankle.

I'm *definitely* not thinking about that.

We got back from our rafting adventure a few hours ago. All the hostels in the area are booked, so we're stuck at a campground in a cramped van that now smells like a whole variety of pizza toppings.

But it's nice to just chill for a while. We're always on the go, and after nearly drowning, I need a night to veg out.

"If I started walking right now, I could probably get two more pizzas before it gets really dark out," Gus says.

"Ice cream would be better," Daphne says, glancing up from her laptop.

"It would melt."

"True." She shrugs, and Tosh drops another note written on a napkin onto her keyboard. "Tosh would like a falafel."

Gus thinks for a moment. "I could always go for a falafel."

"I had a dodgy falafel in Brighton once," Daphne says. "I got sick in bin in front of a primary school."

"Were you drunk?" I ask.

"It was one in the afternoon, Willa." She smiles. "Yes, I was drunk."

I roll my eyes, and looked over at Ollie, whose lips are set in an unusually grim frown. He looks angry at whatever is on his phone, his fingers flying across the screen. I don't want to pry.

"God, this is so unfair!" Daphne throws herself back against a pillow in a fit of dramatics. "I can't retweet this! And I can't call this guy a twat! Willa, you're ruining my life."

"You'll survive."

"Literally, what's the point of being alive in 2019 if I can't blast a fuckboy into Mars on a public forum?"

"You can always do humanitarian work."

"That *is* humanitarian work."

It's best not to indulge her, so I return my attention to Tosh's computer. Angela owns Cambridge Dance Academy. The address was easy enough to find, and it's only a few hours away. We *could* go tomorrow. But there's a very high chance Mom already got to her.

Matty is my best bet. What are the chances that he knows about his uncle's estranged daughter? And even if he does, Daphne's a good liar. I'm sure she could come up with an elaborate scheme to get information out of him.

Either way, I'm hopeful.

Which is a very strange emotion for me to feel.

"*Ollie.*" Daphne's face is a sort of serious that I've never seen before.

"*Daphne*," he bites back.

"You need to stop," she says lowly. "Think about what you're doing."

"I know what I'm doing."

"Then think about who you're hurting."

I lift a brow as I look between them. "What the hell are you two talking about?"

"Ollie made a bad move in this game we're playing."

"What game?"

"Words with *Friends*."

"Oh," I say. "I didn't realize either of you could spell correctly."

Daphne whips a pillow at my head.

* * *

THE UNIVERSITY OF WAIKATO IS A GHOST TOWN.

Daphne makes it a point to tell us that it's summer here, so most classes aren't in session. I make it a point to tell her that we aren't idiots. I'm the one that did a Google search. I know exactly what's going on at the good ol' U of W.

Absolutely nothing.

Except the theater department is having rehearsals for their upcoming production of *Les Mis*, and the public can view it at a discounted price. Gus is thrilled. He pretended he was auditioning for the role of Jean Valjean the whole drive here. Ollie was the only person who indulged him.

I'm going to find Matty.

I considered going straight to Angela for all of five seconds. I couldn't exactly mosey into a dance studio and be coy.

Not that I'm a pro at moseying or being coy.

But it'll be easier to play a role here. Matty won't know who I am. Not unless he watches Daphne's videos, which I highly doubt he does. I'll blend in with all the other students. I'll be just another girl to him.

Or Daphne will be another girl to him.

I can't be the one to ask him all the nitty-gritty questions. He'll for sure think I'm coming onto him, and I'm definitely not desperate enough to flirt with my cousin. Daphne, however, will flirt with a doorknob if it means she'll get laid. Not that she's going to sleep with my cousin. That's definitely a thing that won't be happening.

I'm going to make sure of it.

For now, I'm soaking up the few rays of sunshine that this very overcast day has to offer. We're laying in the grass on the quad. Tosh is using me as a human pillow while I rest my head on Ollie's balled-up flannel. He's typing on his computer with all the vigor in the world. It's giving me a headache. Daphne and Gus need to hurry up and get back with my water so I can take something.

To make matters worse, Tosh crumples up a brochure and tosses it up at me, hitting me square in the forehead.

"Rude," I hiss, lifting my sunglasses to glare at him before I unravel the note.

"*Stop breathing,*" he writes. "*It's making me nauseous.*"

I frown. "*Maybe it's the midnight falafel run that's making you nauseous. You have a boyfriend, remember? Should you be going on Middle Eastern rendezvous with Gus?*" I write.

"*It was a falafel, Willa.*"

"*Did you share a pita?*"

"My English isn't very good," he writes. "*This 'share' you speak of… was that what you and Ollie were doing with a blanket last night? Because if it is, then no, we didn't share a pita. We also didn't share a spoon.*"

"Your English is fine, asshole." I ball the brochure up and throw it at him.

Ollie stares down at me with a lifted brow.

"Was I talking to you?"

"No, but you're being awfully mean to Tosh."

"I'm not mean. I'm the nicest person in the world."

They both scoff.

"You're both assholes."

"That's my girl."

I glare at him as Tosh stands up and dusts off his pants.

"Off to have a midday falafel tryst?"

He flips me off.

"I'm going to call the tabloids and sell them a story about how rude you are to your fans!" I shout at him as he walks towards the cafeteria. "You'll no longer be Tokyo's sweetheart!"

Once he escapes inside the building, I settle back against my makeshift pillow.

"He wasn't lying," Ollie says and I can tell by the tone of his voice that he's smirking. "We were sharing a blanket."

I glare up at him. "It's rude to read over someone's shoulder, *Nosey*."

"It's rude to hog all the covers, *Greedy*."

"No one said you had to sleep next to me."

"Says the girl who fell asleep *on* me."

"I had a very traumatizing day yesterday. I was physically and mentally exhausted. I didn't know what I was doing. I can't be held accountable for my actions."

"Okay, if that's what you're going with."

I sit up on my elbows. "Are you insinuating that I *wanted* to sleep next to *you*, a certifiable sock-wearing weirdo?"

"Yes."

"Well, I didn't."

I totally did.

"Mhm," he hums. "I didn't want to sleep next to you either."

"Good," I say. "At least we're on the same page."

"Same page. Same couch. Same blanket."

I whip his flannel at him, but I have bad aim and he dodges it with ease.

"Asshole."

"You wound me, Willa Loveridge."

"I'd *really* like to, Oliver Dunbar."

He has that wildly mischievous glint in his eyes. What is he going to do? Slam his laptop shut? Tackle me? Will we roll around in the grass like two loved-up teenagers in a romantic comedy? Will there be eye-roll-worthy PDA? Will people gag when they see us? Will they shout for us to get a room?

God.

As if I'd ever let that happen.

That is literally the last thing I need.

The world already thinks I'm a slut.

I don't need to add another notch to my belt.

Thankfully, the moment is ruined when Ollie's computer starts ringing. He tears his eyes from mine, settling them on the screen. His lips lift into something magical.

"Ollie!" The voice is soft and tiny, catching me by surprise. The women in Ollie's life—at least the ones I've come to know—all sound strong and demanding. This voice—this voice belongs to a child.

"There's my favorite girl," he says with an adoring smile. "It's way past your bedtime, Aggie."

Aggie.

His youngest sister.

"Freya's home for the weekend," she explains. "She just got in and woke me up. Callum had to carry her up to bed. She's crying about Archie and penguins again."

"She's absolutely mad. What are we going to do with her?"

Aggie laughs. "Are you upset I called?"

"Absolutely not," he says. "I miss you the most. You're always sleeping when the girls call."

"They say you have a girlfriend and that she's really pretty and that she's American."

I look down at the grass to conceal my bright red cheeks.

"I… uh…. I have a friend," Ollie says. "Her name's Willa."

"Have you snogged her?"

"Aggie, I don't kiss and tell," he laughs "And I think you've been spending too much time with Emma and Holly."

"They said that if you say that, it means you have kissed her."

I pick at the blades of grass to distract myself, refusing to look anywhere near Ollie.

"Right, anyway, how's life in Year Four? Learning anything fun?"

"Just about paragraphs and decimals."

"Brilliant. What els—"

"Is Willa with you?"

"Uh… yes."

"Can I see her?"

Ollie sucks in a deep breath. I have a hunch—judging by the pained expression on his face—that he has a hard time saying no to her. I understand why once he turns the screen towards me. Aggie is adorable—strawberry blonde hair, freckles splattered across the bridge of her nose, and a gapped-tooth smile that leaves dimples in her cheeks. The Dunbars are going to be the death of me.

"Have you and Ollie snogged?"

A 'hello' would have been nice, but she went straight for the kill, which catches me off guard and leaves my cheeks burning a brighter shade of red.

"You're blushing!" she squeals. "You've *so* kissed! Where did he take you on your first date? One time a boy took my sister Eva to McDonalds on a date and she cried for, like, three hours. I hope you didn't take her to McDonalds, Ollie. Mum will be so cross with you—"

"Alright, Agatha, Mum will be very cross with *you* if I tell her you're up at half-two in the morning on a school night."

"Fine," she says with an exasperated sigh. "Be nice to her, Ollie. She's pretty."

"Goodnight, Aggie,"

"Goodnight, Ollie."

Ollie shuts his computer and tosses it onto the empty grass beside him before he lays down in the space next to me, nudging my shoulder until I offer up some space on the flannel.

"Aggie's adorable," I tell him.

"She's turning into a mini Holly."

"Better than a mini Freya?"

"The world couldn't handle another Freya," he laughs. "But yeah, Aggie's great. She… uh, she had to go into therapy last year when Eva told her that our dad left after she was born. She thought it was her fault. She's just started to get back to her old self."

"I can't even imagine," I say, looking over at him. He has his eyes set on the gray clouds, his hands folded and resting on his stomach. He looks peaceful. "To be that young and to carry that kind of burden…"

"It's fucking unfair is what it is," he says. "He left because that's what he does—it's what he's done my whole life. He was in and out. Always had bigger and better things to do. His family was never his top priority. I'm almost glad he stopped coming 'round. It's better than being disappointed all the time, right?"

"Right."

* * *

MATTY IS KIND OF A BIG DEAL.

The worst part is that he knows it. I'm surprised we make it out of the theater alive—with his ego being so massive and all. It was suffocating. Three standing ovations? For a rehearsal? *Please.* Save it for the Tonys.

Luckily, massive egos attract massive egos, and Daphne got us into an after party at the residence halls.

"Do you know what you're going to say?" I ask Daphne as we walk through a cloud of smoke leading to the door of the dorm. I might be a little high.

"Of course not." She shrugs and smiles at Tosh, who opens the door for us. "What fun would that be?"

"It's not supposed to be fun."

"Everything's supposed to be fun, Willa. Once you realize that, life is so glorious."

Glorious.

"Just find out information about Benji, Daphne."

"God, you're so bossy," she says and turns to Ollie. "She's so bossy. How do you deal with her?"

"It's part of her charm."

"Yeah, she's charming alright."

Daphne stalks off before I get the chance to defend myself, which is probably a blessing in disguise. I am bossy, but I always have good intentions.

Which is more than I can say for the guy pouring a handle of vodka into a girl's cup. He isn't well-intentioned at all. I'm going to keep an eye on him. Actually, I'm going to keep two eyes on him. He just made an enemy and he doesn't even know it.

"That little scowl of yours is never a good sign," Ollie whispers into my ear. "Should I be worried?"

"You should always be worried."

"Trust me, I am."

The party is tame in comparison to the things I've witnessed at school. There's a pool table that people are actually using to play pool and not...y'know, *to hook up on.* The music is loud, but not deafeningly so. There's a rousing game of strip poker going on, but… to each their own.

"I can actually hear my own thoughts," Gus says. "This never happens back home."

"Right?" I laugh. "It's truly a different world here."

"They still got the goods, though," he says when we stop in front of the drink table, which could be classified as a liquor store with the assortment that's spread out. "Pick your poison."

"Diet Coke," I say easily. "I'm on a mission, remember? Plus, I have to make sure Daphne stays on course."

"You've got a better shot at seeing God," Ollie says, nudging himself between me and Gus. He grabs a bottle of water and a handful of pretzels.

"Thanks for the optimism, Oliver."

"It's what I'm here for, babe."

"Don't call me that."

"Sure thing, sweetheart." He winks at me before returning to the party.

I ignore the fact that my stomach betrays me and flutters.

"It's sickening," Gus says, sipping his drink. "But, like, in a way that makes me really jealous."

"What?"

"How into you Ollie is." He clarifies.

"Please," I scoff.

"Oh, come on! The kid looks at you like you're the center of the universe."

"I think you need glasses."

"I think *you* need glasses."

"I don't have time for this," I say and turn my back to him. "I'm on a mission, and my target has been out of sight for far too long. She's probably up to no good."

She is *definitely* up to no good.

After getting an eyeful of two girls when I peek into the wrong room, I find Daphne in the last room at the end of the hall with the door cracked open. Matty is sitting on the bed with her, and she's laughing a flirty little laugh that suggests she's much more interested in nailing him than finding out the whereabouts of Benji. Why I thought using her as the pawn would be a good idea, I'll never know. I have half a brain to storm in and demand the answers to the questions Daphne is neglecting.

But I don't.

Because out of the corner of my eye, I watch the girl from earlier—who is verging on alcohol poisoning—stumble into a wall, barely conscious and definitely not consenting to the prick sucking on her neck,

"Hey!" I shout. "Are you okay?"

"Mm," she slurs. "M—m'room's on fl—oor four."

"We're fine," the guy says over his shoulder. "We're going to my room, right, baby?"

"No," she says. "M'sleepy."

"We're gonna sleep in my room, remember?"

"No—no," she says and tries to push him away, but he's a foot taller and built like a linebacker.

"She said no," I say, grabbing her arm.

"Who the fuck are you?"

"Who the fuck are *you*?" I snap. "She said no."

"She doesn't know what she's saying."

"Exactly," I say, struggling to hold her up as she collapses against me. "Do you make a habit of taking advantage of girls?"

"Please, she's been all over me."

"She's drunk."

"She still wants it."

"You're a piece of—"

"Willa?"

Gus throws his cup into a trash bag wrapped around a doorknob, his eyes fixed on the guy next to me. Tosh follows closely behind.

"Is everything okay?" he asks.

"No," I say and push the girl toward him. "Can you two take her up to her room? She lives on the fourth floor. She's really drunk and needs to sleep."

"Yeah, sure," he says, eyeing the guy once more. "I'll be right back."

"Thanks."

Once I watch Gus and Tosh get her into the elevator, I turn to leave. I need something stronger than Diet Coke—something to take the edge off, something to calm me down.

"You know…" I feel the grip around my arm before I hear his voice—dark and dangerous, but not enough to scare me. "You're a bitch."

"Yeah, I am," I say, ripping my arm from his hand. "And you're a scumbag."

I'm shaking once I get back to the common room. My sights are set on a bottle of rum. I consider guzzling straight from the bottle when I spot Ollie in the corner getting awfully cozy with a redhead, but that would mean I'm jealous and I'm definitely not. Not even a little bit. He can talk to whoever he wants, and I'll just stand here trying to breathe through the fact that I want to scream.

Not because Ollie is talking—flirting, *laughing*—with someone else, but because guys like the one in the hall exist. Guys like Mason. Guys that think they're entitled to something because a girl is drunk or weak or intimidated. It makes my blood boil.

"I swear to God, Sasha," someone whispers into a phone as they pass by. "It was Toshiro. I know it was him. And he's with that YouTuber! Daphneby—whatever. They're here. They're at the residence hall. I'm completely serious. You need to get here now."

I down my drink so fast that I start coughing.

Shit.

We need to leave.

Like ten minutes ago.

We need to be gone.

"Someone just asked for my autograph?"

I look over at Ollie when he reaches for another handful of pretzels. "Don't get an ego, Rockstar."

"Keep calling me Rockstar and I just might." He grins.

My eyes roll on cue.

"Hey, are you okay?" Gus says after he practically barrels into me. I stumble into the table and almost knock over an uncapped bottle of whiskey.

"I'm fine. We really need to leave, though."

"What happened?" Ollie asks.

"Nothing—"

"Some prick was trying to get with a drunk chick," Gus explains. "Willa got involved."

"Jesus Christ." Ollie pinches the bridge of his nose. "Are you okay?"

"What? Of course I'm okay. And she's sleeping peacefully in her own bed, and we need to leave. People know who you are. People know who Daphne is. People know *Tosh.*"

Tosh squeaks.

"Yeah," I say. "I'm gonna get Daphne. You're gonna get the van. And we're leaving."

I don't know where the burst of adrenaline comes from, but I'm going with it. Perhaps it's rage. Maybe it's fear. Let's be real, it's probably the drink I just finished. But whatever it is, it has me storming through the halls like a girl on a mission. I don't even knock when I burst into Matty's room.

"Tell me what you know about Benji Atkins."

Daphne and Matty are mid-kiss and his hands are not-so-shyly up her shirt.

Awesome.

"Willa!" Daphne shrieks. "We're in the middle of something."

I don't care.

"Benji Atkins," I snap as Matty scrambles away from her. "He's my father. Where is he?"

Math equations are forming in Matty's eyes, numbers and variables flashing like sparks in the sky. It's all coming together. One thing is added to another. It clicks.

"Oh my God," he says. "I saw my cousin's tits."

"What?"

"Holy shit," he says and stumbles over to his computer. His fingers fly across the keyboard to unlock it. He pulls up the internet browser and there it is.

All over Twitter.

My face.

My *tits.*

My picture.

Mason.

Ollie.

@mason_stu: some days I wake up and think, "wow thank god that slut's out of my life. Really dodged a bullet there."

@olliedunbar: @mason_stu some days I wake up and

think, "wow thank god I'm not a manipulative twat bag. Really dodged a bullet there."
@mason_stu: @olliedunbar says the wannabe rockstar banging the groupie slut.
@olliedunbar: @mason_stu so tell me was she a slut when you were begging her to take the pictures?
@olliedunbar: @mason_stu or was she a slut when you manipulated her into taking them?
@olliedunbar: @mason_stu was she still a slut when she trusted you with them?
@olliedunbar: @mason_stu let me guess: she was also a slut when you showed them to your friends? that was her fault, right?
@olliedunbar: @mason_stu or maybe she's not a slut and you're just playing the pissbaby victim because she realized what a fucking asshole you are.
@olliedunbar: Creating a smear campaign about a girl who YOU asked for pictures from because you're a ragingly jealous dickhead? Sounds legit.
@olliedunbar: Harassing her via email because you can't stand the fact that she MAYBE moved on with someone else? That's logical.
@olliedunbar: I might be a shitty whiney musician, but at least I was raised with enough sense to respect people.
@olliedunbar: which is more than I can say for human trash bag **@mason_stu**

I can't breathe.
I can't think.
I can't speak.
This is a new kind of rage—the paralyzing kind.
I'm going to pass out.
Because there's more than just an exchange.
There's a screenshot of my picture.

My naked picture.

I'm covered in emojis with a little thought bubble by my head that reads *#willie*.

I'm going to throw up.

Count down from ten.

Breathe.

Count down from ten.

Breathe.

Count down from ten.

Breathe.

"Willa…"

Ollie is standing in the doorway and he knows before I say anything. He sees the look on my face. He knows I saw what he didn't want me to see—what he did so publicly. Because why? He thought it was romantic? Or because he thought I needed saving? That I needed him to fight my battles? Because he couldn't just, I don't know, leave it alone?

"Willa, I—"

"I told you to stay out of it."

"I couldn't."

"Yes, you could have!"

"He's harassing you! It's not okay!"

"And what you did is? My picture is *everywhere*. I'm a fucking meme!"

"Willa, I was trying—"

"Trying to what? Trying to help? Trying to be my knight in shining armor? Newsflash! I don't need to be saved!"

"Willa—"

"Fuck you, Ollie."

17

"You slept with my cousin."

The optimistic part of me thinks that if I keep repeating it, it will somehow not be true. But after the 308th time, Daphne still slept with Matty. If I wasn't already sufficiently disgusted by that thought, the fact that Daphne is puking in the bathroom stall next to me would have definitely sealed the deal.

We're at some dodgy diner that I've taken up residence at after storming out of the party last night. I refused to go back to the van. The thought of being anywhere near Ollie made me sick, so I parked myself in a corner booth and Tosh started me a coffee tab. I had a pot delivered to me every hour on the hour.

I'm wired.

My right arm has also developed a twitch, but I'm not sure if that is related to my current caffeine high.

The thing about not sleeping is that I had plenty of time to think and reflect on the fact that Mason is the epitome of scum and there is now a picture—censored and uncensored—with an eggplant emoji dangerously close to my mouth. I'm so angry. If I imagine it enough, I think I might actually be able to strangle him telepathically. I can only hope he's suffocating on the floor of his dorm right now, gasping for air the same way I did when I saw those pictures.

"I feel like hell," Daphne says when she stumbles out of the stall. I'm sitting on the lip of the sink, and she immediately nudges me off so she can rinse out her mouth.

"Alcohol will do that to you," I tell her. "So will sleeping with my cousin."

"Enough," she shushes me before gargling water. "It's not a big deal."

"Of course it's a big deal! You were more interested in hooking up than you were about my wellbeing!"

"I figured Ollie had it under control."

"The only place I want Ollie is under a bus."

"You really need to tone down the dramatics. It's too early."

"I'm a fucking meme, Daphne."

"Look, I get it," she says, cranking the lever of the paper towel dispenser. "And yeah, Ollie should have left it alone, but Mason's a dickhead and this only proves what a petty little bitch he is. #masonthehumantrashbag was trending this morning."

"And yet I'm still naked on the internet. Which is worse?"

"Are you a minor in those pictures? Because he can probably get in trouble. Send his ass to jail."

"I don't think you understand how the law works in America because it's definitely not in the victim's favor."

"You should still think about getting your mum involved," she says. "He can't keep harassing you. He's taken it too far this time."

"Okay, Ollie."

"Look, he's a boy. He's dumb. It's, like, encoded into their DNA, but he's a good guy and he really cares about you. And I get that you don't need to be saved or have someone defend your honor, but it's nice to have someone in your corner willing to fight alongside of you."

What alternate universe did five pots of coffee send me to? Daphne? Being logical? I need to lay down.

"Your silence suggests something I said resonated with you."

"I had a momentary blackout."

"Sure."

The restaurant is crowded when we walk out of the bathroom, the sound of grease cracking and splattering guides us back to my booth. A woman by the door shoots me the evil eye. Little does she know, I'm practically paying rent here.

Well.

I have Tosh's credit card, so he's paying rent.

"I have a splitting headache." Daphne slumps into the bench opposite of me, and immediately drops her bag on the table. She pulls out a handful of receipts, half of a candy bar, a tampon, and finally, an orange pill bottle. She twists the cap, pours one white pill into her palm, and pops it into her mouth, chasing it with lukewarm coffee.

"Are those for headaches?" I ask, watching her shove everything back into her bag.

She shrugs. "They get rid of headaches."

"That wasn't the question."

"I don't have a drug problem, Willa."

"I've watched you—"

"Have fun," she says. "I like to have fun. I don't have a problem. But I *do* have a headache and a dire need for a breakfast burrito, so please plant those judgy eyes of yours on the menu. I'm sure they have a bowl of boring muesli for you."

"Muesli isn't boring. It's very customizable. And healthy."

"Yeah, well, breakfast burritos are good for my mental health."

"I can't argue with that."

Daphne gets her burrito. I get my muesli. And we get an unexpected visitor. Well, unexpected to me. I have a hunch Daphne knew he was coming.

Matty walks into the diner wearing sunglasses and a baseball cap, like some sort of celebrity hiding from the paparazzi. I wonder if the local papers realize they created a monster by feeding his ego.

"Morning, ladies," he says, falling into the space next to Daphne. "You almost ready?"

"For what?" I ask.

"To meet my mum."

* * *

A HOARD OF GIGGLING SIX-YEAR-OLDS IN FLUFFY PINK tutus come barreling out of the front door of Angela Lawson's Dance Academy, which could mean one of two things: the world is ending, or intermediate ballet class has just finished. Either are completely plausible.

"Does she know I'm coming?" I ask Matty as we climb the stairs. "Because if she does there's a good chance my mom's here, and I'm not mentally prepared to deal with that."

"She has back to back classes, so I don't think she's expecting anyone."

So we're going for the surprise attack—my method of choice the past three weeks. It's probably better this way.

She won't have time to make up an elaborate story, or send out an SOS signal to my mom.

"C'mon," Matty says, nudging his head. "Her next class starts in fifteen minutes. We don't have much time."

The girls for the next session are already lined up against a plain white wall in the hall of the studio. They're a few years older than the previous class, dressed in simple black leotards, and the moment they see Matty, their eyes shift into hearts.

I swear one almost faints.

I'm smart enough not to point this out to him. His ego would go into overdrive and his head would probably explode and no one has time to scrub brains off the floor.

Matt turns into a studio and motions for me and Daphne to follow. There's a woman by the window fiddling with a set of speakers, cursing quietly under her breath.

"Hey, Mum!" Matty practically shouts.

"Oh, Matty, I haven't got the time," she says, not bothering to turn around.

"Someone wants to meet you."

Angela twirls around, straightening up quickly as she blows her auburn bangs out of her eyes. She looks frazzled one moment and then surprised the next. Her eyes double in size.

"Hi, I'm—"

"Willa," she breathes. "Your mum is going crazy. You know that, right?"

"Look, I just want to talk to Benji."

"I think you need to talk to your mum first." Angela pulls her phone from a cubby by the speakers.

"No!" I say quickly. "I've had nineteen years of talking to her. I just want five minutes with Benji."

"I think that's something—"

"It's something I decided a long time ago." One? Two?

Three weeks? Who's keeping track? "I deserve five minutes of his time."

"I'm not saying you don't," she says. "But your mum is a mess and this stress isn't—"

"Good for the baby, yeah, I know." I shake my head. "Thanks for the help."

"Willa," she calls after me, but I'm already out of the studio. I ignore the whispers coming from the gossiping ballerinas, and I break free into the morning air.

Count down from ten.

Breathe.

Count down from ten.

Breathe.

Count down from ten.

Breathe.

Every turn is a dead end—an endless loop, a constant cycle. No one wants to hear me. No one cares. No one understands why this is so important to me. Maybe I'm not even sure why this is important to me. I mean, Benji had the opportunity to see me. He was in California. He was at my school. But he chose to drop a load of cash and leave before I knew what was happening.

And yet here I am.

Across the world.

Trying to track down someone who clearly doesn't care enough to be found.

I'm not going to cry.

I won't.

I refuse to.

"326 Prince Street," Matty says once he catches up to me.

"What?"

"It's his address" he says. "326 Prince Street. Auckland. Apartment 1101. That's where Benji lives."

"You know where he lives?" I ask.

Matty nods. "I don't have his phone number, but my mum does. I was hoping if I brought you here… I don't know. Maybe she'd call him, or something. Obviously I was wrong."

326 Prince Street.

Auckland.

Apartment 1101.

I thought I'd feel something. Maybe relief. Or nerves. Even a rush of excitement. I have an address—something much more solid than two college friends, a beekeeper, and an unhelpful sister. But I don't feel anything other than irrational anger when I see Ollie leaning against the van in the parking lot. Hands in his pocket. Sunglasses on. Head tilted to the sky.

What a fucking buzzkill.

"Why is he here?" I shoot Daphne a grim look out of the corner of my eyes.

"How do you expect us to get to Auckland?"

"I'd rather walk," I say. "In fact, I'd rather take my chances with Truth and the gang than be anywhere near Ollie right now."

"You can't avoid him forever, Willa."

"Watch me."

"That's mature."

As if she has room to judge my maturity.

From what I remember from the car ride here—which is everything because I have an exceptional memory—the dance studio isn't too far from the diner. It'll take me an hour to walk back. If Tosh's card is still on tab, I'll get another pot of coffee and figure out a plan to get to Auckland. It's 2019 after all. I have options.

Limited options.

But still options.

Options that definitely don't include sitting in a van with Ollie Dunbar.

"Willa, we need to talk."

Is that a bird? A plane? A mysterious buzzing sound indigenous to New Zealand? Hm, not sure. I continue stomping towards the main road.

"You can't just ignore me!" Ollie grabs my arm, and I instantly rip it away from him, spinning around so fast that I nearly lose my balance. "Sorry—I'm sorry, I shouldn't have done that."

"No, you shouldn't have," I snap. "And yes, I can ignore you."

"Will you at least here me out?"

"No, I was dealing with it!"

"You weren't, Willa," he says, cradling his hand around the back of his neck, clearly frustrated. "He was harassing you. That's not okay."

"And what you did was? Ollie, you don't know me! You don't know Mason. You don't know the situation. You had no right to get involved."

"I don't know you?" His face falls. "That's what you're going with?"

"It's been three weeks, Ollie. We had a drunken kiss and we shared a blanket. That doesn't exactly constitute as falling in love. Who are you trying to fool?"

"Obviously not you," he scoffs. "Don't worry. I won't interfere anymore."

"Awesome."

"Have a nice walk."

"I will."

I get a blister half a mile down the road, and sit on a rock until Matty pulls over and offers me a ride.

* * *

MATTY DRAGS A FRENCH FRY THROUGH A GLOB OF MAYO, and I have to choke back my sip of coffee. We're back at the diner and back in my booth after having to wait twenty minutes for five tweens to take their gossip hour elsewhere.

"So… what's he like?" I ask.

"Who? Benji?"

"Yeah," I say. "It's kind of hard to find any information about him. He's really vague in interviews, and most articles written about him are just about his art, or who he's suing, or what charity he donated to."

Most recently, I'm his charity of choice.

Matty finishes chewing, wiping the salt from his fingers onto a napkin before balling it and dropping it onto the empty plate. "I guess he's just a typical uncle? I really only see him on major holidays and birthdays. Our family isn't all that close, but we see each other when we can. He took me to Ho Chi Minh City a few years ago, and I got to sit in on a photoshoot he was doing. It was pretty cool."

I try not to let my mind go there—to the place where Benji would have taken me to Ho Chi Minh City or Shanghai or Dubai for a photoshoot. To the place where we would have bonded over art and music and our favorite authors. To the place where he actually acknowledged that I'm his daughter.

"I don't understand… any of it, really. I mean, why would he set up a scholarship for me? It doesn't make sense."

"Fuck if I know," he laughs. "I didn't even know you existed until yesterday."

"No one ever talked about me?"

"No," he says. "I mean, my mum used to talk about her friend that moved to America, but she never mentioned that friend also had Benji's kid."

"Nice."

"But I think that's the way your mum wanted it? At least, that's the impression I'm getting from my mum. She would talk about her friend in New York and the amazing life she had there, but it was always very vague."

An *amazing* life.

My mom really has everyone fooled.

"Do you know his schedule?"

"Benji? Pretty sure he's always working."

"So there's a chance he won't even be at his apartment? Or in Auckland at all?"

"I mean, I guess, yeah," he says. "But it's not like you're rolling in options right now, so…"

He's not wrong.

What's one more dead end to round out this terrible trip?

* * *

THREE GIRLS ARE FIGHTING OVER WHO GETS TO POWDER Matty's nose. I roll my eyes and I slump further into my chair. I have no desire to watch another one of my cousin's rousing performances, but he promised to drive me to Auckland after. Beggars can't be choosers, and I am definitely choosing to stay as far away from Ollie as possible.

Which isn't very far because they're keeping the van parked in the visitor's lot on campus.

Going to see Angela was the second worst idea I've had today. The first—by far—is opening my email when I know I shouldn't.

From: **Ana Loveridge-Herrera** (I'm coming there!)
From: **Ana Loveridge-Herrera** (You went to see Angela?)
From: **Delia Sprigs** (your shit is in the way)

From: **Delia Sprigs** (but seriously are you coming back to school?)
From: **Lyla Flores** (I'm so worried, Willa!)
From: **Delia Sprigs** (why is your ex such a dickhead?)
From: **Delia Sprigs** (wtf is going on?)
From: **Mason Stueck** (baby you wanted it)
From: **Mason Stueck** (I manipulated you?)
From: **Mason Stueck** (slut)
From: **Bella Karim** (What gives Willa? I need details!)
From: **Mason Stueck** (you deserve everything that happens to you)
From: **Mason Stueck** (pathetic little shit)
From: **Mason Stueck** (your boyfriend thinks he's tough)
From: **Ana Loveridge-Herrera** (Where are you?)
From: **Ana Loveridge-Herrera** (Did you suddenly fall off the face of the earth?)

I send the entire inbox into the trash, and drop my phone onto my lap. I'm not sure about a lot of things, but I know I need to get far away from this university before my mother tries to drag me back home kicking and screaming. I think she's forgetting that I'm an adult. It's not like she can tell me what to do. If I want to meet Benji, I can.

And I fully intend to.

Once Matty finishes rehearsals.

He does have a flare about him. I'll never tell him that, but there's something there. Charisma. Charm. He was made for the stage—for fame, fortune, and whatever else those lucky few are destined for. If my five minutes in the limelight have shown me anything, it's that I'm not cut out for it. I don't have the spine or the confidence or the guts it takes to put myself out there—to open myself up to public scrutiny and bored journalists with nothing better to do than pick apart my every flaw. I'm not meant to be a celebrity—an internet one or otherwise—but Matty is.

He has it.

Whatever *it* is.

Daphne has it.

Tosh has it.

Ollie has it.

I don't, but I'm okay with that.

Because there are people who are born for center stage, and then there are people who are born for backstage.

I'm okay with being the latter.

The latter means I get to tell them what to do.

A playbill falls onto my lap, and I merely lift a brow when I see Tosh collapse into the seat next to me.

"*I can't deal with Broody Ollie much longer*," he writes.

"*So do us all a favor and run him over with the van.*"

"Or you two could just be adults and talk about your issues," he writes.

"*I'd rather surgically remove half of my liver without anesthesia.*"

Tosh elbows my arm. "*Can you not be dramatic for five seconds? He cares about you. Maybe he shouldn't have talked to Mason so publicly, but he was doing it because he couldn't stand to see him tear you apart.*"

"I'm tired of the Ollie Defense Squad," I write. "*Where's the Willa Defense Squad?*"

Tosh looks over at me, lifting both brows.

"Shut up," I mutter. "I meant in this situation."

Tosh slides the playbill over to me. "*He's not going to get it right every time. He's going to make mistakes. You both are. But he means well.*"

"It's too early for you to be philosophical," I say.

He nudges the playbill at me. "*It's 6:00 PM.*"

"Honestly, Tosh," I mumble and crumple the paper in

my hand. "You're giving me a headache. Don't you have a boyfriend to text?"

He grins, and digs into his pocket until he pulls out a receipt. He scribbles something quickly, and then passes it to me. "*Perhaps the headache is because your personal coffee delivery service is out of commission.*"

"I'm going to strangle you," I say. "Or drag you back to the dorms in hopes someone else will recognize you, and then it'll be your picture on the internet that everyone's talking about."

He glares at me.

"Where's Daphne?" I ask.

Tosh nudges his head to the stage.

"Of course," I sigh. "Now she's going to distract him. We're supposed to be driving to Auckland after the performance."

Tosh sits up abruptly, his eyes widening.

"Don't give me that look," I say. "Auckland was always the final destination. Just because I'm not getting back in that van doesn't mean I'm not going."

Tosh's jaw drops, and for a second I think maybe he's going to say something. He closes it seconds later, eyes still wide with… what? Worry? Before he gets a chance to grab a pen and something to write on, the lights dim in the music starts.

* * *

MATTY GETS STOPPED FOUR TIMES FOR AUTOGRAPHS ON OUR way to his car. For now, he eats up the attention. On the off chance he breaks free of his small town celebrity status and makes it to the big leagues, I know his views will change. Everyone loves the taste of fame until it turns sour. At least, that's the vibe I get from my mom's clients. The novelty of being stopped in the street for a selfie wears off fast, and those paid club appearances aren't as fun once you get caught stumbling out of them one too many times. Because pictures lead to articles and articles lead to headlines and suddenly you have a drinking problem and a one-way ticket to rehab and—

"Willa?"

I look over at Matty. "Yeah?"

"So you're down?"

"For what?"

"Grabbing a pint," he says. "Everyone's over at *The Black Balloon*."

No, I'm definitely not down for grabbing a *pint*. That's not part of the plan.

"What about driving to Auckland?"

"Auckland will still be there tomorrow."

"But my mom's going to be here *today*," I tell him. "I need to leave before she sniffs me out! She's like a bloodhound these days. The pregnancy has everything heightened. When I was home for Christmas, she knew the bagel shop three blocks away had garlic and herb back in stock as soon as she stepped off our stoop."

Matty blinks. "Is that a no? Because it's kind of a *thing*. The whole cast is going, and I can't really miss it. I'm the lead, after all. That would be like missing my own birthday party. I'm practically the guest of honor."

He can't—*won't*—be swayed. It's Matty's way or no way. I have *no* idea where he gets it from. It's *definitely* not a gene we share. How *insufferable*.

"Yeah, whatever," I sigh heavily.

Matty drives for five minutes in dead silence. This, apparently, is his post-show ritual. He is *meditating* while *operating* a vehicle, which is as dangerous as it sounds. He blows through a stop sign because the color red is too brash for his aura.

"Dead is too brash for *my* aura," I scream at him.

"Chill with the negative energy, Willa. You're killing my vibe."

"Says the guy who almost just killed us."

"Can you just—*shh*."

Oh, I'll *shh* alright.

I *shh* the rest of the drive to *the Black Balloon*, and when he pulls up to the curb in front of the bar, I *shh* right through the front door.

The first thing I notice—way before I notice Ollie sitting on a stool with his guitar and a brunette next to him twirling a curl around her finger as she laughs at whatever he's saying—is the fact that Daphne is drinking tea. The only time I see her with a mug in hand is in the morning when she's complaining of a headache. What's the occasion? Why'd she suddenly switch from vodka tonics to a more herbal blend? More importantly, how long did it take Ollie to make a new friend?

Not that I care.

Because I don't.

"Well, this is a surprise." Daphne takes a long sip of her tea. "Willa Loveridge in a ten foot radius of Ollie Dunbar? The boy she never wants to see or speak to again? Were your jealous girlfriend senses tingling?"

"I'm not his girlfriend, and I'm not jealous. I'm not even here because I want to be," I tell her. "I'm supposed to be on my way to Auckland."

"I can't believe you'd actually go to Auckland without us," she scoffs into her mug. "After all we've been through… you'd ditch us for a pretty boy with a God complex?"

"He's my cousin." I blink. "Who better to take me to my father than his nephew?"

"I don't know." She shrugs. "Maybe your group of misfit toys who've been here since the beginning? Honestly, Willa, I'm offended."

"Of course you are." I roll my eyes. "Why aren't you drunk?"

"You say that as if I'm always plastered."

"Because you usually are when you're at a bar?"

She shrugs. "I don't feel well."

"Then why are you here?"

"Because I'm the president of Ollie Dunbar's fan club, and it's my civic responsibility to make sure he doesn't hook-up with a girl who looks like she has gonorrhea."

"Daphne! That's rude."

"I'm just looking out for you."

"Well, don't. I don't care who he sleeps with. He could fall off a bridge, and I probably wouldn't go out of my way to make it to his funeral."

"You're so unnecessarily dramatic," Daphne says, crossing her arms as she sits back in her chair. "And you're both acting like wankers."

"Excuse me?"

"You're shutting Ollie out because you're mad he put your twatbag of an ex in his place. And he's reacting to your reaction the only way boys know how to."

"By hooking up with a girl who looks like a model?"

"With gonorrhea."

"Daphne!"

"He's hurt, Willa! Do you realize how much he likes you?"

"Obviously not enough to keep it in his pants."

"He's a boy—"

"He's a boy. He's a boy. He's a boy. *He's a boy.* That's

not an excuse! He's an adult. He knows right from wrong! And he was wrong. He shouldn't have encouraged Mason. I'm the one who's naked on the internet. I'm the one who's a meme. He still gets to be the cute dopey boy with a guitar. No one's calling him a slut on social media. He's a hero and I'm the whore who should have kept her clothes on. So stop telling me 'he's a boy.' I'm fucking tired of men not being held accountable for their actions because society thinks they don't know how to use their brains."

"Okay."

"Okay?" I'm still heated from my rant. Give me a podium. I'm about to announce my candidacy for president.

"Okay." She nods. "But you also have to be willing to let him apologize. Or, at the very least, hear him out. You don't have to forgive him. You don't have to forget, but you can't hold this grudge against him when he's willing to admit he was wrong. You push people away, Willa. And I get it. I get that you've been burned by so many people, but you have to let the good ones in. And Ollie's… he's a good one. He's probably the best one."

It's so easy—pushing people away, keeping myself at a distance. It means I won't get hurt. Because I refuse. I refuse to ever let someone treat me the way Mason did. Deep down I know that Ollie isn't like him, but the fear of letting someone else get that close to me is crippling. I don't want to get hurt again.

And seeing Ollie with another girl hurts in ways I never thought something could hurt. Because he's charming and she's laughing and together they make it look so easy—so natural.

Maybe their hands would touch. She'd brush a piece of hair away from his face. He'd buy her a drink. They'd fall in love. Get married. Have kids. I've seen it in movies.

I've seen it at parties. I've seen it every single day of my life.

I know exactly what she's whispering into his ear. I know exactly what she wants when she laces their fingers together. I know that subtle head nudge. I know that smirk. I know where this is going.

"Oh, for fuck's sake." Daphne downs her tea, slamming the mug onto the table, and then gets out of her seat. She has that sort of electric pull that forces everyone out of her way. Drunk or sober, she owns the room, dripping confidence with every step. She doesn't care about the damage she leaves in her wake.

Which is why I'm not surprised when I watch her throw her arms around Ollie with enough force to knock him back against the wall.

"Oh my god, you're Ollie Dunbar!" she giggles and slurs. "I'm, like, your biggest fan! Can I have your autograph?"

"Daphne, what—"

"Who's this girl? She looks like a massive minger," she says. "And don't you have a #girlfriend? And gonorrhea?"

"What the hell is wrong with you?" Ollie pushes Daphne away, but his conquest is already taking off towards the other side of the bar. "Seriously, Daphne? What the fuck?"

"Oops?"

"Fuck off with that," he says, shaking his head.

When his eyes catch mine, I drop my gaze to the table. Maybe I didn't cause the scene, but I feel responsible. Daphne wouldn't have done it if it wasn't for me—if she wasn't trying to save something that she thinks is worth fighting for. But judging by how Ollie's face is boiling with anger, I know we're long past saving.

Whatever we were, it's over.

Dead and buried.

It's fine.

I don't care.

"You're welcome." Daphne grins.

"For what?"

"For saving your relationship," she says. "This is the point in the film where you run after him and have a massive argument before you confess all your feelings and kiss dramatically in the middle of the street."

I look up at her and scoff. "*For fuck's sake.*"

"A thank you would suffice."

When I stand up and brush past her, I have no plans to fulfill her romantic comedy dreams. I just want to leave—to get as far away from everyone as possible. I'll walk to a train station if I have to. Maybe I'll go to the airport. Jump on a plane. And go completely off the grid.

Or maybe I'll just call my mom and let her drag me home.

But then I see Ollie standing in the middle of the sidewalk with his guitar slung around his back and his hands fisted into his hair. I want to cry. I don't, but I want to. Especially when he turns around and looks through me. Like I'm nothing. Like I'm no one.

"What do you want from me, Willa?"

"I don't want anything from you."

His laugh is sinister. "You don't get to have Daphne pull stunts like that."

"You don't get to tell me what to do, or not to do! And for the record, I didn't! Just because—"

"Because what?" He cuts me off. "You were jealous? That for the first time in *weeks* I wasn't chasing after you? Because I took your fucking hint?"

"You took my fucking hint? Yeah, you took it straight to the internet for everyone in the world to see! God, Ollie,

I don't need you to fight my battles! I just needed you to be there for me."

"And I was there for you," he snaps back. "I've *been* there for you. And I'm sorry, okay? I shouldn't have went at it with Mason. I'm sorry that he's a fucking asshole. I'm sorry that I've caused you more pain. I shouldn't have done it. But you don't get to jerk me around either, and you certainly don't get to be jealous. Because I couldn't have been more obvious, Willa. It's been you. It's always been you. From the moment I met you, it was *you*. But I'm done. I'm not playing your games anymore. I'm tired of losing."

"You're tired of losing?"

He shakes his head. "I'm done, Willa. I can't do it anymore."

When he turns away from me, I feel it all at once. Shaking with anger and bordering on tears, I'm floundering in the middle of the street. There's no grand-romantic kiss. Or happily-ever-after. Violins don't play. He doesn't pick me up. Or spin me around.

There are no whispered I-love-yous.

There's just us.

Two broken hearts.

Saying goodbye for the last time.

"Walk away," I scream after him, half-expecting him to stop and turn around.

He doesn't.

"I should have never gotten in that stupid van with you!" I yell. "I never wanted to be in that stupid van!"

I don't realize we have an audience until I turn around and see three faces that look as heartbroken as I feel.

18

Matty bangs on the hood of his car and startles me awake. When I open my eyes, I'm blinded by the sun. I feel hungover despite not having had a drink last night. Someone should put me out of my misery and run me over.

"Where are we?" I ask, sliding up in my seat, squinting. I pull the visor down to shield the glare from the sun.

"Just outside of Huntly," he says, shoving the gas nozzle into the car. "We still have about an hour left before we hit Auckland. You should use the toilet if you have to."

I don't have to, but Matty's car was not made for humans with long limbs, so I get out to stretch my legs. There aren't any other cars around. Huntly is a ghost town. It's just me and Matty and the clerk I see through the window pocketing scratch cards.

Nice.

"Have you thought about what you're gonna do if he's not there?" Matty asks.

I lean against the trunk and yawn. "I'm kinda just

taking it one step at a time. But I don't know. I'll probably sit in front of his door until he shows up."

"What if he doesn't show up for, like, three months?"

"Then I guess I'll die on his welcome mat."

I'm out of options. If he's not there, I'll wave my white flag. New Zealand isn't that big of a country. He's probably not even here. Mom will catch up to me eventually, and this whole trip will be nothing but a very expensive conversation with my therapist.

"...and how did you feel about that?" she'd ask.

"Not that great, to be honest!"

"But for real," Matty says, glancing at the meter on the gas pump. "What's the plan after today?"

"I'm sure your mom has a tracking device on your car, so my mom will probably be waiting to haul me back home."

"How do you feel about that?"

Awesome, I'm getting free unsolicited therapy.

"I don't know." I shrug. "After everything that happened, I think I'm ready to leave."

"Everything with Benji? Or everything with your friends?"

"Both, I guess," I say. "It's not like I came here to make friends. It kind of just happened."

"Do you regret how you left things?"

Ingrained in my head is the image of how hurt Tosh looked after I told Ollie I never wanted to be in the van. Shoulders slumped. Lips parted. Completely defeated. Gus looked upset. Daphne looked angry. We weren't the same people who had eaten four pizzas in the back of the van a few nights before. We weren't the people who laughed until three in the morning—the people who spent hours taking quizzes to find out what pasta shape they were or which celebrity would murder them.

Am I allowed to be sad about something I barely had? I've had longer relationships with zits than I had with them. Three weeks. That's not long enough to bond with someone—to make a lasting impression on their lives.

Right?

"Willa?"

"Yeah, of course I regret how I left things," I say. "I was upset. I let my emotions get to me. I shouldn't have taken it out on them."

"What would you say if they were here?"

I sigh, toeing my sandal into the ground. "I don't know. I'm sorry I'm such a moody bitch all the time? Thanks for putting up with me. I didn't deserve any of you."

"I'd work on your delivery," he says.

The sound of gravel under tires tears my attention from Matty.

Gus is behind the wheel, the van coming to a squeaking stop in the middle of the gas station. Tosh is sitting shotgun. I don't see Daphne or Ollie until the side door slides open. Judging by the look on his face, he's been blindsided too.

"What's going on?" I hiss at Matty. "This wasn't part of the plan."

He shrugs. "They needed directions."

"So give them a map."

"Do maps still exist?" he asks.

"Yes," I say. "And they have cell phones with navigation!"

"They said they'd be more comfortable following someone."

What an absolute lie.

I push my body off the car. "I'm going to the bathroom."

I cross the parking lot in long strides. Ollie is a few

steps in front of me, and when he reaches the convenience store, he doesn't bother holding the door open for me.

Nice.

I skirt around the aisles, avoiding Ollie at all costs, and lock myself in the women's restroom that has not been cleaned since 1997. There's toilet paper lining the floor, a ghost town of tampon applicators, and a negative pregnancy test. I don't touch anything. I walk over to the mirror stare at my reflection through the cesspool of smudged fingerprints and dried hairspray.

Whoever the person staring back is, I don't like her. I don't know her. She's not me. Three weeks is such a short amount of time, but I somehow managed to lose myself completely.

I want to cry.

But I don't.

Count down from ten.

Breathe.

Count down from ten.

Breathe.

Count down from ten.

Breathe.

"Willa?" It's Gus.

"Yeah?

"We're leaving."

"Okay."

I give myself another minute before using my t-shirt to open the door. That's when I realize it's not my t-shirt I'm wearing. It's Ollie's. And my belt is Tosh's. And my sandals are Daphne's. Mementos from a trip I'm not sure is worth remembering.

Ollie is comparing candy bars when I start my walk of shame out of the store. He doesn't even look in my direction. I steal a long enough glance to know he's wearing the same clothes he had on last night, only his hoodie is wrinkled and his hair looks like it has been pulled in every direction.

Was he running his fingers through it?

Or was someone else?

Don't go there, Willa.

So instead I go outside. I bask in the warmth. I smile at the sun. I count the clouds in the sky. And I watch Daphne, Tosh, and Gus pile into Matty's car.

"What are you doing?" I ask, panicking.

Daphne rolls down her window. "We figured that you started this journey together, so you should probably finish it together.

"I started this journey with *you*."

"Yeah, well, you're not in love with me."

Matty throws up a peace sign, smiles at me, and speeds off with Daphne hanging out the window.

Count down from ten.

Breathe.

Count down from ten.

Breathe.

Count down from ten.

Breathe.

"Fuck's sake," Ollie sighs. "Of course she'd do this."

"Daphne does what Daphne wants," I say.

Ollie doesn't respond. He trudges over to the van. It's still running. The driver's side door is open. He can make a quick getaway, leaving nothing but a dust cloud in his wake. For the second time in twelve hours, I'll have to watch him walk away.

"Let's go," he says, not bothering to look back. "I'm exhausted and really not in the mood for you to go into your dramatics, so save us both the headache and get in the van."

"That's a really lazy kidnapping technique."

He doesn't laugh or respond or acknowledge that I said anything. He gets in the van, places both hands on the wheel and waits.

In the distance, I hear wheels on gravel again. A taxi? A bus? An elusive Uber in the middle of nowhere ready and willing to drive me to Auckland?

It's none of those things.

As soon as I see Truth turn into the gas station, I jump into the van at a speed I didn't realize I could move.

It's strange sitting in the passenger's seat again—eerie, even. Maybe it knows I've been talking ill about it. I've offended it. It's going to swallow me whole. Strangle me with its seatbelt.

I sound ridiculous, but I need the distraction. Partly because of the Truth sighting, but mostly because I see the empty cup holder next to Ollie's coffee, and I want to cry.

"What are the directions?" Ollie asks.

"You never follow my directions," I say.

He glances over at me. It's so brief that I barely catch it. "What are the directions, Willa?"

He doesn't call me *babe* or *sweetheart* or *Boss Lady*. He calls me Willa. It's strange.

"Right at the lights and then straight until you hit State Highway 1."

Silence is a strange sound when Ollie Dunbar typically talks just to hear his own voice.

I turn the radio on and scan through the stations until I hear a song I'm familiar with.

London Eyes by The Filthy Doorknobs.

Ollie turns it off before I can hear the chorus.

"Okay," I sigh. "Silence it is."

"Figured you'd appreciate that."

"Right," I say. "It's all I've ever wanted."

I distract myself with the landscape outside. There's a run down farm in the distance, and a man is driving a rusted tractor. A few stray cows graze on the grass. Others simply enjoy the sun. I bet it's nice being a cow. What's there to worry about?

Other than, y'know, being slaughtered.

Or milked to death.

Maybe being a cow isn't that great.

"I wasn't going to sleep with her."

I look over at Ollie. "You don't have to explain yourself to me."

"Yeah, I do," he says, gripping the wheel tighter. "It was… it was just an in the moment thing. I was upset and angry and I thought… I don't know what I thought. But I wasn't going to sleep with her. You're not that easy to get over."

I don't get a chance to say anything. Ollie turns the radio back on. We listen to a Thursday morning sermon for the rest of the drive to Auckland.

* * *

THE ELEVATOR CRAWLS TO THE TOP FLOOR OF HARBOR View Residences. Each floor passes like seconds on a clock. I barely have time to comprehend what's happening. The doors part on the eleventh floor. There's only one apartment—the penthouse.

It's now or never.

After spending the last three weeks insisting that this is something I needed to do on my own, actually being here alone is terrifying.

I drag my feet along the black floor planks. Everything is cold, gray, and industrial. Minimalist. Emotionless. I get chills.

There's a very small—okay there's a very big—part of me that wishes Ollie would have offered to come with me. But when we pulled up to the building, it was silence. I got out and told him not to wait around and he left.

And here I am.

Standing in front of my father's door.

It's now or never.

Put on your big girl pants, Willa.

My hands are shaking, but I somehow manage to knock.

Silence.

I knock again.

And again,

And again.

Silence.

Of course. This is *so* typical. He's not here. Why would he be? It's a Thursday morning. There are much better places to be. A coffee shop! The grocery store! The dentist! The hospital getting a super invasive colonoscopy! Any place is better than your apartment.

Count down from ten.

Breathe.

I'm not going to cry. I'm tired of crying, so I decide to knock once more before walking away—from the apartment, from New Zealand, from my father. I'm done. It's over.

I lift my arm and…

"Oh, sorry!" The door swings open and it's an older woman with rosy cheeks and gray hair who greets me. She has a pair of headphones around her neck. "I can't hear a thing with these on. My daughter says I listen to my music too loud, but the only way to listen to Rod Stewart is loud. Gotta keep my heart pumping so my FitBit knows I'm alive! Anyway, hi! How can I help you?"

I blink. "I… um, is Benji home?"

"Oh, no, Mr. Atkins hasn't been home in a few weeks. I'm Leslie, his housekeeper," she says, giving me a once and then a twice over, stalling at my face. "Are you Willa?"

"How do you know my name?"

"Your dad told me," she laughs. "You've grown so much since the pictures I've seen."

"The pictures?"

She laughs. "Yeah, the pictures. You had to be nine or ten in them. You were at the beach eating candy floss and wearing flower-shaped sunnies. You were adorable. Would you like to come in? I can show you. He keeps the photo on his nightstand"

I don't need to see it. I know the picture she's talking about. We were up in the Hamptons. It was the Fourth of July. I ate so many s'mores that I got sick before the fireworks. How did Benji get that picture?

"I don't think that's a good idea," I whisper. "Thank you. Sorry for interrupting your work."

I make a run for the elevator, jamming the button until it lights up and dings. When I'm inside, I bang my head against the wall.

Why does he have a picture of me?

Who gave him a picture of me?

None of it makes sense. I mean, he doesn't even know me, but he keeps a picture of me and sets up a scholarship? Why? Because he wants to be reminded of his mistake? Because he feels guilty? It's so screwed up.

Outside, it's Tosh that's waiting for me. He's leaning against the window of a yarn shop, deep in thought as he reads something off a piece of paper. I cross the busy street to join him, completely defeated.

"He wasn't there," I tell him. "Not that I was expecting

him to be, but y'know. It's a nice way to bookend this hell trip."

Tosh waits until I finish before thrusting the paper at me.

"What's this—"

BENJI ATKINS EXHIBIT
THURSDAY, 31 JANUARY 2019
AUCKLAND PUBLIC LIBRARY
6:00 PM TO 10:00 PM

"No," I say. "I'm done chasing him. I'm tired of getting my hopes up. It's not worth it. I just have to accept it and move on."

Tosh sighs. "Okay."

"I'm sorry, what?" My ears are malfunctioning.

"Okay," he says again. "You tried. That's what matters."

I can list a million things that went wrong today, but none of them matter when I hear Tosh's voice. Confident. Clear as day. His beautiful voice that someone tried to silence. Today he took it back.

I link my arm with his and we walk down the road, both a little lighter, no longer bearing the weight of our pasts.

"I'm really glad I met you, Tosh.

"I'm really glad I met you too, Willa."

Tosh directs us down a side street, past a pharmacy and a fish and chips shop, to the hostel they're staying at for the duration of the Rhythm & Sound Festival. The party must have already started because as soon as we get close enough, I see a police car and an ambulance with flashing lights.

And on the sidewalk is a wave of turquoise blue hair.

"Daphne," her names comes out in a barely-there whisper and I run until I feel my legs burn. "*Daphne.*"

Ollie stops me, his arm slipping around my waist, pulling me back before I can topple over onto the ground. "Willa."

"Ollie, let me go." I'm fighting him, but he doesn't budge. He pulls me closer. "What happened? What's going on? Why is she on the ground?"

"Willa, Willa, hey." His hand brushes my cheek, forcing my eyes to his. He looks at me. Not through me. *At me.* "Hey, listen to me, she's going to be fine."

A tear splashes down my cheek, and I look down at Daphne, who's strapped to a stretcher, and looks, decidedly, not fine.

"Willa, look at me."

I focus on his eyes and then the freckle on his bottom lip and then the sad excuse for scruff lining his jaw.

Count down from ten.

Breathe.

Count down from ten.

Breathe.

Count down from ten.

Breathe.

"She's going to be fine, love."

I want so badly to believe him.

I want so badly for her to jump up and tell me this was some sort of sick, elaborate joke.

But she doesn't.

The ambulance doors close, and all we can do is stand in the devastation that Daphne left.

And as I slump into Ollie's arms, the only thing I know for sure is that I need my mom.

19

Ollie traces his thumb over the dips in my fingers, strumming them like strings of a silent guitar. We don't speak. We sit. And we wait.

And we wait.

And we wait.

Time stopped moving the second we piled into Matty's car. We followed the sirens bleeding through the streets of Auckland until we arrived at the hospital. Minutes. Seconds. Maybe even hours passed. We were told to sit and wait.

And wait.

And wait.

And wait.

Patience has never been my strong suit.

"I still don't understand," I say, leaning back in my chair until my head hits the wall. "Can you walk me through it again?"

"She was complaining about being tired this morning," Ollie says. "I got to the hostel and we were unloading the van. She said she felt lightheaded and the next thing I know she's on the ground."

"And you told the EMTs the medications she had?" I ask.

"Yes, we went through her purse—showed them everything," he says, squeezing my hand. "She was conscious, Willa. She's going to be okay."

"It's taking too long." I shake my head. "It's never good news when it takes this long. I watch *Grey's Anatomy*. I know these things."

"Right," he laughs and it sounds so so *so* good. "Willa Loveridge, MD."

"I'm scared, Ollie."

"I know," he says. "I am too."

Next to me, Tosh rests his head on my shoulder and I lean into him—onto him.

Because that's what friends are for—to be there for you when it's good and when it's bad and when it's just fucking awful. Whether you've known them for twenty years or twenty minutes. Friendship isn't defined by time. It's the people who rally behind you—the ones who stand with you and defend you, the ones who will tell you when you're right and love you when you're wrong. Time… time has nothing to do with it.

"*Willa.*"

Ana Loveridge is standing in the waiting room looking like a sigh of relief feels. Her whole body slumps when she sees me, and the second she starts crying, I start crying too. We meet somewhere in the middle and I run into her arms, clinging to her like my life depends on it.

Because it does.

She's my mother and I'm her daughter and nothing will change that. Not a new husband. Or a new baby. Or the twenty thousand mistakes I've made along the way.

"You're grounded for the rest of your life."

"I know."

She kisses the top of my head and my forehead and my cheek, pulling me as close as her bump will allow. She's suffocating me, but after everything I put her through, I deserve it.

"Willa Loveridge?" A nurse calls.

I pull away from Mom, wiping a tear with the heel of my palm. "Yeah?"

"Daphne's asking for you.'

"Can I see her?"

"Of course," she says. "Follow me."

It's a quick walk down a long, brightly lit hallway. Babies scream. Machines beep. All the noises blend into one giant headache. I feel dizzy.

We turn into a room that's fitted with a row of curtains, and the nurse shows me into the fourth one on the right.

Daphne is laying on a gurney, fiddling with the tube delivering oxygen through her nasal cannula. She has her tongue out. Peace sign in hand. She's taking a selfie.

"*God*, Daphne." I start crying again.

"Relax, Willa," she laughs weakly. "It's not like I'm dying, or anything."

"*Daphne!*"

"Sorry," she says, shrinking back. "I probably shouldn't joke like that."

"No, you shouldn't."

"This'll have to be quick, girls," the nurse tells us. "Daphne needs her rest."

I nod and the nurse leaves to give us a few moments alone.

"Did you and Ollie make up?" Daphne asks "He was a broody little wanker all morning."

"That's what you want to talk about right now?"

"Of course," she laughs. "We're getting to the best part—the happy ending. It's exciting."

I roll my eyes. "We haven't talked about it."

"What are you waiting for?" she asks.

"Uh, we've had more important matters to tend to." I nudge my head towards her and the bed and this whole hospital room. "What the hell happened, Daphne?"

She sighs, looking away from me. "I was being stupid."

"I mean, yes, but can you elaborate?"

A small smile flickers over her lips. "I was sick a few years back. It was pretty bad—*really* bad, actually. I had ALL—acute lymphocytic leukemia. I did chemo and it was rough for a while. Just being in the hospital… anywhere near a hospital, really… it brings back all the memories.

"But after the bone marrow transplant, I got better. I've been in remission, but the past few weeks I've been feeling tired and achy and weak. And that's how I started to feel before I got diagnosed, so I started to panic that the cancer came back. I've been taking my anxiety and sleeping medications, but I haven't been keeping track of how much and when I was taking them and I think I took too much today."

"Daphne," I whisper, reaching for her hand. I offer her a soft squeeze, and in return, she smiles. "You're not invincible. And I get it now… I get why you have this thirst for adventure and life and living to your fullest, but you're human and you need to take care of yourself. Because this world is not ready to be without you—*I'm* not ready to be without you."

"Does that mean you don't regret getting in the van?"

"I think getting in the van was the best decision I've made in a very long time."

"Yeah, it was."

"Ms. Percell?" the doctor interrupts us. "We got your blood work back."

This conversation has been played out in thousands of movies, and yet I never thought I'd be in the room when it actually happens. It's life changing—life altering. Good. Or bad. It's hard to prepare for the unknown. All the hopes and dreams you once had could be gone in an instant.

Daphne grabs my hand and she's not letting go without a fight.

Whatever the doctor says, we're in it together.

"Everything looks fine." She smiles. "Your blood counts are great. I don't see any reason to be nervous. You just need to be more careful about mixing medications. You got lucky today."

"I know." Daphne nods.

"We're going to keep you overnight for some observations," she explains. "And if all goes well, you can go home tomorrow."

"And I'll be good to go to Rhythm & Sound?" Daphne asks hopefully.

"As long as you promise me you'll take it easy," she says. "Lay off the drinking and the… *whatever else,* and just enjoy the music."

"I can do that," Daphne say.

"No, she can't," I laugh. "But I'll be there to make sure she follows the rules."

Daphne gives my hand another squeeze, a gentle reminder that I'm stuck with her.

Probably forever.

And I'm good with that.

* * *

MOM IS ALTERNATING BETWEEN A CHOCOLATE PEANUT

butter milkshake and a slice of banana toffee pie. A bag of fries—or I guess, *chips*—and half of a grilled cheese sits between us for good measure. I wipe salt from my fingers with a paper napkin.

We're sharing a bench down by the harbor, the water in front of us rippling as boats bob along the dock. The night is cool. The air is still. I breathe.

"Did I ever tell you how I found out I was pregnant?" Mom has her free hand resting on her bump, and my lifted brow causes her to laugh. "With you."

"Oh, no."

"I started having very vivid dreams about pineapples," she says, placing the straw of her milkshake between her lips. She takes a sip. "Like they were so strange. Pineapples chasing me. Pineapples in my bed. Flying pineapples. My professor was a pineapple. Weird, right? And I'd wake up, and I'd need pineapple. Sometimes I'd wake up at three in the morning, and I'd have to go to the store and get pineapple. Fresh pineapple. Frozen pineapple. Dried pineapple. I needed it all. I never even liked pineapple all that much."

"Some people just take a test," I laugh, grabbing a fry.

"I did, eventually," she says. "I was in Angela's dorm room. I told her about all the pineapple and how I'd been nauseous… and we went to the pharmacy, and I took the test in the men's bathroom because the women's was out of service."

"Classy," I scoff. "I'm sure you have a better memory this time around."

"Not better," she says. "Just different."

"C'mon, Mom." I grab her fork and steal a bite of her pie. "You can't tell me that you don't think of this as a second chance to do it right."

"Willa, you can be financially stable and in a

committed relationship having a planned pregnancy and still not do everything right."

"But you don't have to struggle, and this baby isn't going to hold you back. It didn't ruin your life."

"Willa, you did not ruin my life." She sets her cup on the arm of the bench and turns to me, grabbing my chin between her thumb and her index finger, forcing my attention to her. "Everything I've done with my life, I've done it for you. *Because of you.* I loved you the moment I saw those two lines—before I saw that grainy little picture and heard your heartbeat, you were mine and I loved you with every fiber in my being. It didn't matter what your dad thought or that my family didn't think I was ready to be a mother, I already was. You were so real to me. And I promised myself that I was going to give you the best life I could. Because you deserved everything. And I never wanted you to go a day in your life where you felt unloved or unwanted. Because I always wanted you, Willa. I was eighteen and I was scared, but I was your mother and I was going to be the best one I could be. And I'm sorry that I failed you. I'm sorry that I made you feel unloved or unwanted for even one second. I'm sorry that you felt like you had to come here—that you felt like you were missing a part of yourself. I'm sorry—"

"Mom." I wrap my arms around her, burying my face in the crook of her neck. The jasmine and freesia of her perfume smells like home. "You didn't fail me. I may have failed you as a daughter, though."

"Oh, Willa," she laughs as she pulls away. She brushes a strand of hair from my eyes, and smiles. "You're the best daughter."

"No, I'm not. You're pregnant and I didn't tell you where I was going and I made you worry—"

"You did all of those things, but that doesn't mean

you're a bad daughter," she says. "It means you're a teenager."

"I shouldn't have come here," I tell her. "I understand why you didn't want me to meet him."

"It's not that I don't want you to meet him," she says. "That's never been it. I love Benji. He's extraordinarily talented, and he gave me the best gift I could ever ask for. And I don't know, maybe it's not my story to tell, but being a parent didn't come as easy for him. But his reasonings, they aren't mine to try to explain to you."

"Apparently, they aren't his either," I sigh. "He's very hard to track down."

"You certainly thought of everyone."

"It's been an experience," I say. "Are you mad at me?"

She gives me *The Look*—the mom look she's been perfecting for years—and she sucks in a sharp breath as she reaches for her pie.

I know what's coming.

The lecture.

I'm not mad. I'm disappointed in you, Willa.

"I'm not mad," she says. "Okay, I'm very mad. I'm mad that you didn't use the frequent flyer miles and I'm mad that you sent me on a transpacific wild goose chase. Mostly, I'm mad that you didn't feel like you could come to me when Mason started harassing you. The things he's been posting—the things he's saying about you—that's not okay, Willa. And it's not something you should be dealing with on your own."

"No one really wants to talk about their naked pictures with their mom."

"Most people's moms don't deal with celebrity scandals on the daily. I've shut down sex tapes and prostitution allegations in a matter of minutes. A senator's dickhead son? I can handle him with my eyes closed. I can also make sure his father doesn't get reelected next year. I'm going to rip the Stuecks apart, Willa. Every single one of them."

I forgot how terrifying she can be.

"But I'm not mad that you came here," she finishes. "I'm not mad that you wanted to meet your dad. I'm sorry it hasn't gone as planned."

I shrug back against the bench. "It's okay. Who needs a dad when you have a great mom? And a stepfather who puts up with his bratty stepdaughter."

"He loves you so much."

"I know," I say. "I don't think I tell him that enough."

"It's not too late to start."

I nod and she wraps her arms around my shoulders, pulling me close enough to splash kisses over the top of my head.

"God, *Mom*."

"Don't *Mom* me! After all the stress you caused me, you're never allowed to complain about me being overbearing again," she says. "I'm never letting you out of my sight."

"*Great.*"

When she laughs, I feel a soft thump against my side. It's her belly. The baby.

"I'm never letting *either* of my girls out of my sight."

I pull away, staring down at the bump bulging from her white shirt. "It's a girl?"

"We found out last week," she says with a smile. "You're gonna have a little sister, Willa"

A sister.

That doesn't sound so scary.

"There's a cafe by the Auckland Public Library," Mom starts, "I thought maybe we could grab breakfast there tomorrow."

"Yeah, I'd like that."

"Your Aunt Kaia will be there," she says. "And your grandparents… it seems like you've inspired a family reunion."

"Funny how your past has a way of catching up with you."

Mom laughs. "And I think you forgot these at home." She pulls an orange bottle out of her purse. "How've you been doing without them?"

"I've been a little moody," I laugh. "Probably because I stopped completely without weaning. I might see how I do without them for a while."

"Well you have them if you need them," she says. "You can talk to your therapist about it too."

We spend the next hour playing catch up and fighting over who gets the last fry.

Mom does.

She pulls the pregnancy card.

* * *

Tosh stops me before I can get into the room at the hostel. Before I can ask why he's smiling like a certifiable weirdo, he *discreetly* places something in my hand.

"We'll be back by eleven," he says.

I frown at the condom in my hand. "Shouldn't you save this for your boyfriend?" I ask.

"That would require him to answer his phone," Gus hums.

Tosh glares at him.

"Anyway," Gus says. "We're off to sneak Daphne in a contraband burger."

"Visiting hours ended at eight."

"Hence the sneaking."

Gus grabs Tosh by the arm and drags him over to the

stairwell, Matty following closely behind. I roll my eyes as I walk into the room.

Ollie has his feet kicked up on the small table in the center of the room. He's tuning his guitar, plucking at the strings with an intense focus that leaves his tongue lolling out of his mouth.

"Did you have a nice talk with your mum?" he asks, looking up at me briefly. "You were gone a while."

"Yeah, we had a lot to talk about."

"I can imagine," he says. "What's in your hand?"

I groan and look down at my clenched fist, a metallic corner poking out from between my knuckles. "Tosh was just…" I open my hand to show him. "…being a dickhead. I just came to get my things. I'm sure you don't want me here."

"Of course I want you here, Willa," he says. "Do *you* want to be here?"

I know what he's asking. And yesterday, my answer probably would have been different. But just like so much can change in three weeks, even more can change in twenty-four hours.

"I owe you an apology."

"Willa—"

"And a thank you," I say. "I never thanked you for defending me. I've been fighting this battle on my own for so long that I forgot what it's like to have a friend stick up for me."

"Just a friend?"

"You know it's more than that, Ollie."

"How much more?"

"I don't know," I say. "Why don't you put that guitar down, and come over here and find out."

He moves slowly. Patiently. He sets his guitar on the

floor. Gently. Takes a deep breath. And then takes careful steps the long way around the table.

"You're such a—"

His lips are on mine before I can comprehend what's happening. Soft and slow, drinking my breath away. He slips his arms around my waist, pulling my body flush against his.

"I'm such a what?" He smiles into me.

"Such a pest," I sigh into his mouth. "Someone should exterminate you."

"That's my girl." He nips my bottom lip, a silent plea for more access. I give in. Because I have absolutely no self control.

"You're a really good kisser." I can't believe I say it out loud.

He grins. "I'm sorry, I didn't quite hear that. Can you repeat it?"

"Absolutely not," I say. "Stop talking."

"So bossy. Is kissing you all I'm good for?" He nips over my jaw and the corner of my mouth before landing on my lips. "I'm feeling a bit used, Willa Loveridge."

"I can leave if you want."

"We've established I want you here."

"I might need a little more convincing."

"I think I'm up for the challenge."

"I'm not easily persuaded."

He drags his lips down my neck, settling on the spot just below my ear. My knees buckle and I see stars and constellations and the suns from thirteen different universes. I'm pretty sure I blackout.

Ollie Dunbar might be the death of me.

20

Mom's late.

I've been sitting in front of the Auckland Public Library for twenty-seven minutes. The bus comes and goes three times. A man in a suit talks loudly on his cell phone. He's wearing one navy shoe and one black shoe. His wife of ten years is cheating on him with their nanny. He's verging on tears when he gets in his cab.

I guess it's been a rough start to the year for everyone.

Thankfully, my year is starting to look up. I woke up this morning without that nagging sense of guilt in my stomach. Everything in my life is still a work in progress, but it's nice to feel content. It may have taken me a while to realize, but I'm very lucky to have the people I do in my life.

I'm even luckier that they stuck around when I didn't give them any reason to.

I glance at my phone. It's nine-thirty. Ollie and I are meeting at the festival at eleven. When I told him I wasn't sure if I'd be able to get a ticket, he told me not to worry—that he'd get me on the list.

The list.

I really hope his list doesn't involve me sneaking in under a fence. Because I've done enough reckless things in the past week to last me a lifetime. Going to jail really isn't high on *my* list.

The bus comes again, and I'm half paying attention to my phone when a man sits down next to me. He's wearing jeans, scuffed-up checkered slip-ons, and a pink button-up with the sleeves rolled-up. He extends a cup of coffee to me, and the first thing I notice is the dried blue and green paint on his nails.

"Heard you take it with milk and a shit ton of sugar," he says. "Also heard you've been looking for me."

Benji Atkins has a scruffy face and messy black hair. I already knew this. He's a public figure. As much as he hates it. His picture is everywhere. Still, I never imagined what it would be like to be this close to him.

"You're not easy to track down."

"Your mum has my phone number."

"And who's to say you would have answered?" I say. "You came to my university and bailed on your appearance."

"The chair of the art department is a twat."

He has a point.

It's strange. I spent three weeks chasing dead ends trying to find him, and now I'm sitting next to him and I can't think of anything to say. I wrote him off—closed this chapter—and now here he is. Next to me on a bench. Watching the slow traffic of a Friday morning. Basking in the not too hot and not too cold weather.

Nineteen years of questions—all of them could be answered if I just… remembered… how… to… speak.

"Willa," he says, sitting back. "I didn't want to be a dad. I can't make excuses. I can't make myself seem better than I was. I was a dick. And I was selfish, so I let your mum take it on because I couldn't be the parent you needed me to be. Do I regret it? Sure, now I do. But I was a dickhead kid then. I wasn't interested in being responsible for anything let alone another human. It wasn't anything other than selfishness and after that it was just me being a fucking coward."

"Was there ever a time…"

"The twenty-fourth of July 2006," he says. "It was a Monday. You were wearing a yellow dress and your hair was in two plaits. You were terrible at the hula-hoop."

"This is bordering on *To Catch A Predator*."

He laughs and takes a sip of his coffee. "You were at camp in Central Park. I was watching with your mum. I was planning to move to the city. We were figuring out how to introduce you to the idea of me. But then I got a call from a museum curator in London and you got stung by a bee and I didn't know how to react, but your mum… she was your mum. She knew exactly what she needed to do and where she needed to go and if she was panicked, she didn't show it.

"She called me later that night and I was already at the airport, and she said to me, 'I love you, Benji, but I love her more. She will always be my first priority. And I'd rather her not know you than have her ask me why her dad's only around when it's convenient for him.' And she was right. You deserved a parent who would be there constantly, and I couldn't be that parent. And by the time I stopped being a self-centered dick, it was too late. You had already grown into this person who was thriving without me. Or maybe I wanted to think you were thriving. I'm sure it affected you—I'm sure you had questions your mum wished she didn't have to answer. So I convinced myself you were better off without me. And since I couldn't be there physically or emotionally, I could at least do something financially. But judging by the fact that we're sitting here, I fucked up big time."

I laugh quietly at his honesty. "I never wanted your money."

"I know," he says. "It was a pretty shitty thing for me to do."

I take a deep breath and try to gather my thoughts, but my head is like gridlock traffic in Manhattan and every driver is laying on the horn.

"I was really angry when I came here," I tell him. "Like I don't think I've ever been that angry in my life. You set up this scholarship. You came to my school. And you didn't even try to see me? It's such a shitty feeling, especially after spending most of my life wondering what I did wrong—what made it so hard to love me? To just be a dad, y'know?"

"You didn't do anything wrong, Willa."

"I know that now," I say. "But when you're a kid and you see happy families everywhere… you wonder. But I get it now—I understand why you couldn't be there. Not everyone's ready to be a parent when it happens. And I think… I think Mom was smart to keep you out of my life."

"She's a smart woman."

"I know," I say. "I don't give her enough credit."

We sit in silence for a few minutes. The bus comes again. An elderly woman hobbles off with a cane. She smiles at us before disappearing into the library.

"You keep a picture of me at your apartment," I say, my eyes focused on the holistic health shop across the road. The chalkboard sign advertises a sale on elderberry syrup.

"Angela gave it to me," he says. "She wanted to make

sure I knew what I was missing out on. And turns out I missed out on a pretty great woman."

I scoff. "I've been kind of bratty lately."

"But having enough self-awareness to admit that is pretty mature."

"I guess," I say. "This whole being an adult thing… not all it's cracked up to be."

"Tell me about it."

There's another beat of silence. A cyclist blows a red light and almost gets nailed by a minivan. A gust of wind breezes through a tree. A few leaves scatter to the ground near my feet.

"Willa," he says. "I know I don't deserve the time of day, and I will walk away right now and never look back if that's what you want, but I would love to get to know you."

I didn't come here looking for a relationship. I just wanted to yell at him—to rant and rave and scream about a scholarship that didn't make up for nineteen years of neglect.

But I'm tired of carrying around so much anger. Being upset all the time? It's exhausting. Imagine all the things I could do if I wasn't sitting around stewing in a temper-tantrum. I could learn to knit! Or join a club! I could be *president* of the *knitting club*. I could learn to make pie! Start a business! I could—*maybe*—sleep at night! The options are endless.

"Can we take it a day at a time?" I ask.

"Whatever you want."

"Maybe we can get dinner before I leave," I say. "Mom's here."

"I know," he laughs. "She refused to leave my gallery last night until I came and talked to her."

"Ana Loveridge-Herrera," I laugh. "She gets shit done."

"The woman is terrifying," he says. "Can I get you a car to take you somewhere? Where are you staying?"

"At a hostel by the ferry terminal," I say. "But I'm going to meet my friends at the Rhythm & Sound festival."

* * *

DAPHNE WAS RELEASED FROM THE HOSPITAL WITH STRICT orders to take it easy. Naturally—in her strange little mind—that translated into her getting the all-clear to dance in a muddy field with no shoes on. She's not drinking, and she looks happy, so I bite my tongue and let her be.

Which is more than I can say when it comes to Ollie, who literally will not shut up.

"We've been best friends for three weeks, Tosh." He sits next to me with his arms crossed like a petulant child. "And the fact that you've spoken to everyone but me… it hurts."

"For the love of God, Ollie, let it go," I groan.

"I won't!"

"We know," I say. "You haven't stopped going on about it for the last three hours."

"Because it's a complete blasphemy!" he says, turning to Tosh. "And to think I was going to thank you in the credits of my first album. You can forget about that now. The world will never know a Toshiro!"

"The dude is famous as fuck," Gus laughs. "You'd probably get sued for even mentioning his name."

Tosh nods.

"This is what I get." Ollie throws his hands up and falls back into the grass, the sun glaring off of his wayfarers. "This is my punishment for helping the kid trying to read a map upside down. What's the opposite of good karma? Because this is it."

"Bad karma?" I blink.

"Yes, that. This is bad karma."

"I'm pretty sure that's not how karma actually works."

"Just let me be miserable, Willa."

"Alright, you weirdo."

"Weirdo is an understatement."

Ollie shoots up so fast that I'm pretty sure he makes himself dizzy. He's on his feet with his jaw hanging open, completely in awe of what he heard.

"You just—he just." He looks from me to Gus to Tosh. "Did you hear that?"

"Must have missed it," I hum. "Did you hear that, Gus?"

"Don't think I did," he chuckles. "What about you, Tosh?"

"Can't say that I did."

"You all suck," Ollie says, falling back to his spot next to me. He takes a long swig from his bottle of beer.

"You'd be lost without us," I tell him. "Literally. You'd be lost. You'd probably still be driving in the wrong direction down in Lake Pukaki if it wasn't for me."

"You're always so full of compliments, sweetheart."

"Don't call me that."

"Whatever you say, babe."

I whack him in the chest, and just to be dramatic, he clutches his heart and falls backwards.

"Idiot," I mumble.

"But I'm your idiot."

"For now."

"For now?" He rips off his sunglasses to glare at me.

I shrug. "I might be interested in seeing what kind of break-up songs you'd write about me."

"Surely you'd rather hear the romantic ballads I've written about you."

I wrinkle my nose, disgusted. "Do you have romantic ballads written about me?"

"No," he laughs. "Not yet. But I did write a song about how much you drool in your sleep."

"I do not!"

"I honestly don't know how you haven't drown yet."

"I honestly don't know how I haven't murdered you yet."

"*God*," Gus groans. "You're making us sick."

"I can assure you no one is as nauseous as I am," I tell them.

"I might be," Tosh says. "You two really—Joshua?"

Tosh's entire face drops and I watch him scramble onto his feet. There's a group five deep walking towards us, one more familiar than the rest. Tosh has shown us pictures of his boyfriend, and there's no mistaking that it's him.

There's also no mistaking the redhead who has an arm around him.

"Toshiro?" Josh tries to save face by smiling, but there's no denying that he got caught—literally—red handed. "What are you doing here? I—I thought you were filming."

"I wanted to surprise you." Tosh frowns at Josh's redheaded friend. "Obviously I did."

"It's not—"

"Please, don't lie to me."

"I… I didn't think we'd ever meet. You're always so—"

"Bro, quit making excuses for being a lying, cheating dick," Gus says.

"Tosh," Josh starts.

"No." Tosh shakes his head. "I hope he makes you happy."

And then he walks away.

With his head held high.

And he shotguns a beer with Gus.

And dances in the mud with Daphne.

And maybe this wasn't the happy ending he had in mind, but it's a happy one, nonetheless.

* * *

Our weird little group of misfits fuses into one giant group of misfits when we meet up with both Ollie's and Daphne's groups of friends. And as nice as it is to see everyone reunited, I'm selfishly happy when Ollie insists we sneak away.

"So what's the plan?" he asks, our hands swinging together as we walk through the field of mud and matted down grass, flattened water bottles crinkling beneath our feet. I almost slip on an empty potato chip bag.

"I thought we were going to watch some bands?"

"I meant the plan with us," he laughs, fiddling with the strap of his guitar. "When are you leaving?"

"Oh," I swallow. "My mom has a flight out the day after tomorrow."

"Are you going with her?"

"I'm supposed to be," I say. "But I don't know if I am. You're going to Sydney, right?"

"Yeah." He nods. "My mate knows a guy who's gonna let me open a couple club shows for him."

"You must be so excited."

"I am." He smiles. "I think Daphne and Gus are gonna come over with me. Tosh has to go back to Tokyo to deal with the mess he made. And you're…"

"And I'm…"

We knew this wasn't going to be easy. He lives in London. I live in New York. Talk about long distance.

"For what it's worth," he starts, "I'd like you to be on the plane to Sydney with me."

"For what it's worth," I say, looking up at him, "I want the window seat."

Ollie's eyes crinkle when he smiles at me, and I don't hesitate before I kiss him. Quick and innocent. Just enough to leave him wanting more. I may have failed my *Foundations of Western Art* class, but I have *Teasing Ollie Dunbar* down to a science.

"Where are we off to?" I ask.

"Main Stage," he says, tugging my hand. "This way."

We weave between crowds of people, slinking through the matted grass and stepping over the graveyard of missing shoes. Ollie squeezes my hand, pulling me until we break free of the cloud of smoke suffocating us.

First secondhand high of the day? Check.

"We're going over here," he says, nudging his head towards a fence guarded by security.

The laminate around my neck says ALL ACCESS, but I have my reservations about what that actually means.

"How much smoke did you inhale?" I ask him. "We can't go backstage."

"Sure we can," he says, flashing his laminate at me. "Says so right here."

"Ollie," I whine. "I don't want to get in trouble."

"We're not going to get in trouble."

When we get to the security guard, I brace myself to get turned away. But, to my surprise, he waves us through. We're backstage… with all the press and bands and artists.

Like? What?

More importantly: why?

"I know you have a million views on YouTube," I say, "but I don't think that qualifies you to storm the stage."

Ollie laughs. "I'm not storming the stage."

"Then what are we doing?"

He starts to say something, but the first guitar chord vibrates through the speakers. It's *loud*. Every drum beat goes straight through me. The crowd cheers. The beat drops. And it literally feels like the music is inside of me.

But I can't help feeling confused. We're standing side-stage for The Filthy Doorknobs. The chorus of *London Eyes* fills the whole festival. I've been under the impression that Ollie hates this band.

"I didn't think you liked them," I scream over the music.

"I don't," he says, frowning. "I hate them."

Now I'm frowning as I look back to the stage. The guitarist is pulling a cord from an amp. He has a pick between his teeth and he slings an acoustic guitar around his back before walking to the mic stand.

"That's my dad."

My heart sinks. "What?"

He doesn't respond. He watches his father sing and engage with the crowd, an unwavering look of disappointment clearly painted on his face. This kind of anger is not a look I wish to see on his face ever again. No wonder he changed the station whenever one of their songs came on.

But the crowd would never know that behind their favorite band is an absentee father, who walked away after his youngest daughter was born. They continue to scream and cheer, pushing as far as the barrier allowed them. As far as they're concerned, this is the best day of their lives.

I squeeze Ollie's hand as the band says their final thank-you. The music stops. And the crowd gives one last applause before leaving. Ollie drops my hand when his father walks over.

"Ollie, my boy!" His dad is all smiles, oblivious to how

upset his son is. He goes in for a hug, but Ollie steps away. "Ollie, c'mon—"

"I just came to return this." Ollie pulls his guitar over his shoulder and holds it out to his dad. "I don't need it anymore."

"Ollie—"

"Take it."

And he does.

The defeated look on his face is the last thing I see before Ollie pulls me back through the security entrance. He never looks back.

"Ollie," I say once he stops sprinting. "Are you okay?"

"Never been better." He smiles and kisses me. "I've been waiting a long time to give that back to him."

"But how are you going to play?"

"I have some cash," he says. "I'll pick up a new one, so don't start your celebration yet."

"Damn it," I laugh. "But really, I feel like an asshole. I was so mean to that guitar. And obviously it was more than just an instrument to you."

"You are an asshole," he says, smiling. "But for a million other reasons.

"I hate you."

"Yeah, I hate you too, sweetheart."

We walk back to our group hand in hand. With every step I try my best not to think about tomorrow, or Sydney, or where I'll be next week. I'm never going to get today back, so it's best to enjoy it for what it is—a music festival with my friends.

Daphne is arguing with her socks-with-sandals-wearing ex-boyfriend. Matty is vlogging it. Tosh and Gus are passing each other notes written on the backs of stolen tour posters. They kiss quickly—*shyly*. Someone lets Ollie borrow a guitar.

And I…

I'm taking it all in.

I'm learning to stay in the moment.

And to not dwell in the past.

Or worry about the future.

I want to appreciate the now.

And continue to remind myself that sometimes life is about losing control.

EPILOGUE

A DROP of coffee dribbles onto my desk, bleeding through the corner of my *Social Psychology* syllabus. *Boss Lady* is scribbled on the side. I look up and glare at Ollie, who looks far too happy for someone who was half-dead thirty-five minutes ago.

"It wouldn't be a Monday morning if I didn't start it with your beautiful snarl," he says, falling into the desk beside me. "How's my girl?"

"She's been better," I mumble. "Daphne was up filming a video until four, and I just fell asleep when an ambulance came barreling down the street outside my window."

"How rude of that person in need of emergency medical attention."

"I know," I say. "So selfish. Don't they know I need my beauty rest?"

"Clearly they haven't been informed. I'll be sure to put up some posters around your flat to make sure everyone is aware."

I roll my eyes. "You realize you're technically not

allowed to be here unless you're registered for the course, right?"

"What kind of boyfriend would I be if I didn't bring my girlfriend coffee on her first day at her new university?"

"A terrible one."

He leans over his desk, kisses my forehead quickly, and stands up. "Meet me over at the park when you're done. I'll let you buy me breakfast."

"Lucky me." I shoot him a coy smile, watching him closely as he ducks out of the room.

Class drags by. The first day is notoriously a giant suck-fest. It doesn't help when you get stuck with a group that actually enjoys the icebreakers. I'm in hell.

Cold, English hell.

My decision to study abroad was the easiest one I've ever made. I wasn't happy in California. I learned to be happy in New York, but something—*a couple of someones*—was missing. Mom was surprisingly supportive, but I think that was just because me studying in London meant I wasn't backpacking through Australia and getting bit by poisonous spiders.

Not the kind of news you wanted to break to your very pregnant mother.

As much as I enjoyed my adventures, I did like staying in one place for a while. Ollie came to New York in May. I showed him the ins and outs of the city. It was our own little staycation before he flew back to London. We ate bagels every morning and laughed over the news headlines.

Constitution? More Like Prostitution: Former Senator Godfrey Stueck's Torrid Past.

Like Father Like Son: Actual Disgusting Human Being, Mason Stueck, Expelled from University

Absolutely No One Is Surprised: Olympic Track Hopeful, Melody Stueck, Caught Doping.

Now that's what I called karma.

Not that I was dwelling in the misfortunes of others.

I was too busy rolling my eyes at my sudden popularity with the likes of New York's *finest.*

Everyone wanted to be your friend when you were dating the next big thing.

Those weren't my words

They were Ollie's.

And the countless music blogs who were already charmed by him.

If he wasn't so cute, his ego would be insufferable.

"Please start reviewing the material from lesson one," the professor says once time runs out. "We'll begin our discussion on social cognition during our Wednesday meeting."

Everyone makes a mad dash to the door, making it rather obvious that we all have far better things to do on this cool September morning. I sling my bag over my shoulder, and push my way through two girls who think the middle of the hall is a great place to start a conversation. I break free through a side door.

My walk to the park is short, the familiar sounds of passing traffic cutting through the music pumping through my earbuds. The weather in California was nice, but there's something about London that vibed well with my New York upbringing. It feels like home—cold and crowded yet quiet in all the right places. No one looks you in the eyes. Cyclists have a death wish. And there's some sort of unwritten rule that you don't wait for crossing signals.

I've nearly died three times following Daphne across a street. I survived bee stings and spider bites. I'm not about to be taken down by an asshole on a rented bike.

But I love it here.

Really.

Truly.

I'm happy.

My phone buzzes in my pocket as I walk through the gates of the park. I pull up the new email and smile.

From: **Ana Loveridge-Herrera** (Someone misses you!)

Never in a million years did I think a picture of a sticky little five-month-old goblin would make me smile so wide.

"What are you smiling at?" Ollie asks. "Pictures of your sexy boyfriend?"

I roll my eyes. "My mom sent me a picture of Lily."

"How's my favorite little munchkin?"

"Covered in avocado." I show him the picture.

"Thatta girl," he laughs. "I can't wait until she's eighteen and you have to deal with her crying to you about boys. You'll finally understand my pain."

"Oh, God. Freya?"

"Yes, she just FaceTimed me from Selfridges," he says. "She was crying in the dressing room because all the coats make her look fat and she'll never get Archie to love her if she looks like an abominable snowman."

"She's really going to make the most of her semester abroad, isn't she?"

"She's going to step off that plane, burst into tears, and come running home."

I smile. "She's gotta make mistakes."

"Listen to you."

"I'm a changed woman."

"Really? You're going with that?"

"Fuck off." I glare at him. "I won't let you crash in my bed anymore if you continue to be mean to me."

"I think we both can agree that I'm anything but mean to you in that bed."

He gets a swift kick in the knee.

"Jesus, woman!" he cries. "Is that what I get for being a generous lover—"

"So did you talk to Tosh?" I change the subject.

"Yes, everything's arranged for the movie premiere. We're flying in with Daphne, and Gus is flying in from Jakarta," he says, rubbing his shin. "But I'm rethinking sharing a room with a violent wanker like you. You might try to suffocate me in my sleep."

"If I haven't done it yet, I think you're safe."

"You're so sweet to me. How'd I get so lucky?"

"Beats me." I shrug

He rolls his eyes at me and gets off the bench, extending his hand out to me. "C'mon, you're supposed to buy me breakfast, remember?"

"How could I forget?" I ask, lacing my fingers with his.

"I am pretty unforgettable."

I nudge him in the ribs.

"Ow!"

"Idiot."

We walk silently through the park, crunching over fallen leaves. Autumn is alive and well, and I, for one, am enjoying the chill in the air.

"My dad's in town next week," I tell him. "He has a pop-up in Hackney. I told him we'd get dinner after."

"Sounds good," he says. "You're still coming home with me for Aggie's birthday, right?"

"Wouldn't miss your mom's roast dinner for the world."

Ollie smiles at me and I smile at him and it's so sickeningly sweet, but it feels so damn good to be happy.

"Alright," he says when we cross through the park gates. "Which way?"

I think for a moment.

"You decide."

THE END

THANK YOU

I'm gonna be honest, I never thought I'd get to the point where I'd have to write a THANK YOU section at the end of a novel.

Especially Willa Loveridge's novel.

We've had a very rocky—maybe even unhealthy—relationship for the past four years. Somedays I wondered why we were together at all. It wasn't working for a very long time. But I loved—*still love*—Willa fiercely. And her story deserved to be told. So to anyone who feels like they've lost themselves and to anyone who feels like they don't belong, this is for you. I hope you find your group of misfit toys who love you the way Daphne, Tosh, and Ollie loved Willa.

Sam, this book would've never been finished if you weren't standing behind me. Thank you for being Willa's biggest cheerleader. Thank you for loving her when I couldn't see anything to love. Thank you for constantly encouraging every crazy book idea that my weird imagination comes up with.

Sonya, thank you for putting up with my constant

crying and complaining. You always know what to say and when to say it. This novel wouldn't be what it is without you.

To my beta readers: Nicole, Kitty, Bridget, Stephanie, Nadine, and Katelyn, thank you for all your wonderful feedback!

To my copy editor: Riley, thank you for your suggestions! I appreciate you taking the time to go over this for me!

To my cover designer: Jasmina, I could look at the cover art for this book all day long. Thank you so much for creating exactly what I had imagined in my head!

And to all my readers—new and old—thank you for taking a chance on me and Willa!

If you'd like a preview of the next adventure I'm taking you on, keep reading!

ALSO BY ASHLEY SHEPHERD

Faking Under the Mistletoe

(preview)

FAKING UNDER THE MISTLETOE

To: *Loveridge & McGowan Employee Network*
Cc: *Ana Loveridge-Herrera, River McGowan*
From: *Olivia Langley*
Subject: *12 Days of Holiday Cheer!*

Twas the night before Thanksgiving when all through the office, not a person was stirring, not even Alba from Human Resources trying to get in the last of her ten thousand steps. The stockings were hung by the water cooler with care, in hopes that St. Nicholas soon would be there—in 33 days!

If the peppermint hot chocolate on tap in the break room and the absurd lines at Macy's (and just about every other store in this city) weren't obvious enough, it's THE MOST WONDERFUL TIME OF THE YEAR! But as far as I'm concerned, it's been Christmas since November 1st and I would like to personally thank all of you for humoring my playlists—even that one person who turned it off on

November 11th at 1:49 PM when they thought I left the building. I'm not upset. Anymore. Asher.

In the spirit of all things holly and jolly, I've taken it upon myself to plan a few events to get everyone in the holiday spirit!

November 27th: Christmas Kickoff!

Enjoy drinks and appetizers after work while we select Secret Santas.

November 29th: Oh, Christmas Tree!

Bring your family to our special viewing of the Rockefeller Center tree lighting ceremony!

December 1st: Lace Up Those Skates!

Bring your family back to Rockefeller center for a night of ice skating! Hot chocolate, cookies, and skates will be provided!

December 4th: Holiday Trivia!

Join us down at the Rose Tavern for holiday-themed trivia! Winner gets a paid day off for holiday shopping!

December 6th: It's a Pajama Party!

Wear your pajamas to work and enjoy a rooftop viewing of your favorite Christmas movies! Blankets, popcorn, and heating lamps provided!

December 8th: The Christmas Crawl!

Drink around the city! Uber reimbursement will be provided for a safe sleigh ride home!

December 12th: Ugly Sweater Day!

Wear your ugliest holiday sweater to work! Prizes will be

awarded to the most hideous! And don't forget to stay for our menorah lighting ceremony!

December 15th: Cookie Exchange!

Bring in your favorite holiday dessert and a box to take home some extra goodies! Prizes will be awarded to the most delicious!

December 16th: An Afternoon of Giving!

Volunteer your time at the New York Children's Hospital's Christmas Extravaganza!

December 18th: Winter Wonderland Gala!

Enjoy a night at the Metropolitan Museum of Art for our annual holiday soirée! Mingle with coworkers, clients, and history's finest!

December 22nd: Secret Santa Swap!

Enjoy drinks and appetizers after work while we swap gifts!

December 31st: Ring in the New Year!

Say goodbye to 2019 and hello to 2020 at the Gansevoort rooftop park! Open bar and appetizers provided!

The global calendar has been updated with each event! For everyone's convenience! And so that you can't say you forgot! E-mail reminders will also be sent a business day in advance!

I wish you all a safe and happy Thanksgiving! Enjoy your extra long weekend and I look forward to Christmas Kickoff on Monday!

Yours truly,
O. Langley
Social Media Intern & Santa's Executive Helper

Loveridge & McGowan International
98 W 52nd St, New York, NY 10019
olivialangley@lmi.com

***

Levi Booker is ten thousand times hotter when he's standing underneath the mistletoe holding my hand. I am also ten thousand times hotter when Levi Booker is standing underneath the mistletoe holding my hand. I'm dizzy and lightheaded. I think I might pass out.

"You, my dear, are a breath of Christmas cheer." He presses his lips to the whites of my knuckles and I want to bottle up this moment in a snow globe and keep it on my mantel forever.

Me and Levi Booker. Underneath the mistletoe. Like that movie he starred in last year. I'm his leading lady. We're in love. He's going to propose. We'll have a June wedding. And three children. With his dreamy blue eyes and my blonde hair. A house in Connecticut. With a white picket fence. And a Range Rover.

Our Christmas cards will be legendary.

"Olivia? My bagel?"

My eyes don't leave Levi. I throw the white paper bag at Asher. My lack of hand-eye coordination leaves it landing at his feet. I feel him scowl.

"It better be cinnamon raisin."

"It is."

"Double toasted?"

"Of course."

"Extra cream cheese?

"A whole tub."

Levi Booker is still holding my hand. Underneath the mistletoe. Like a freaking romantic comedy. Where is my Oscar for Best Outstanding Actress in a Dream Role?

"From the place—"

"Asher, she's an intern. Not a waitress."

Levi drops my hand and looks over my shoulder at Asher. I feel empty, like a box that was carelessly opened on Christmas morning and cannot be used again. I'm ruined. *Destroyed.* Throw me in a recycling bin.

"I'm aware," Asher snaps. "But if you offer to get my breakfast, I don't expect it to be *thrown* at me and I'd prefer it to be delivered before I *die* of starvation."

"I see someone's brushed up on their acting skills since middle school drama club."

The whole office laughs. Asher doesn't. He slams his door shut and the wreath I hung this morning falls to the floor. What a Grinch.

"I guess some things never change," Levi laughs and glances back at River McGowan, the co-CEO and Asher's father, who is also laughing.

"Let's go to my office," he says.

For one last time, Levi looks down at me and winks. "It was a pleasure standing under the mistletoe with you."

The only thing I can think to say is, "thank you."

He walks away and I don't move for at least forty-five seconds. I keep waiting for him to come back. To get down on one knee. And confess his love.

He doesn't.

I sigh wistfully as I search blindly behind me for the doorknob and stumble back-first into Asher's office.

"I hope you're here to apologize for assaulting me with a bagel that is neither double toasted nor slathered in cream cheese."

"Sorry."

"Yeah, you sound it."

Levi Booker held my hand. Underneath the mistletoe. If I had a blog—*which I definitely don't, especially not one about extraterrestrial conspiracy theories that the government might be interested in*—I'd never stop writing about this moment. For the rest of my life. It's all I'm ever going to talk about. I have officially peaked.

"Levi Booker is a fucking toad."

I take a deep breath and count to three, which is how I start every conversation with Asher.

"There's a prince charming inside every frog."

"No, he's just a fucking toad," Asher says and he has cream cheese smeared over his lips. "But he sure did charm the panties right off of you."

"That's rude."

He shrugs. "I wouldn't feel too special, though. He did the same thing to Harriet from accounting and she's, like, sixty-eight."

"Stop trying to ruin my moment."

Asher rolls his eyes. "You're gonna meet a lot of Levi Bookers in this industry and the sooner you realize he's already forgotten your name, the sooner we can move on to more important matters, like this exceptionally *wrong* bagel and the press releases I needed on my desk thirteen minutes ago."

"I was just getting them."

"Were you? Because I think you were drooling over a troll."

"That is so—"

"Time is money, Olivia." Asher clicks his pen and tucks it behind his ear. "And while you were making a fool out of yourself with one *client*, another just gave birth to Nashville's next little country starlet. Ava Mae Rutland. Born at 4:45 AM on November 27th at Vanderbilt University Medical Center. Nine pounds. Six ounces. Twenty-one inches long. Mother and daughter are both happy and healthy. Dad and big sister, Maisie Lane, are smitten with the family's latest addition—why aren't you taking notes?"

"Oh, you want me to write the press release?"

"Yes, Olivia! I'm a busy man. You think you can pull yourself away from the North Pole long enough to get some actual work done?"

I take a deep breath and count to three again. "You'll never get off the Naughty List with that attitude."

"That's not really my top priority."

"Well, it should be," I say before grabbing a stack of manilla folders from his desk, and then I leave him alone to eat his *normally toasted* bagel in brooding silence.

***

Darius throws back a nip of tequila and chases it with a gingerbread cookie. He smiles at me and shrugs, "tis the season!"

The break space at Loveridge & McGowan International is shaking to the beat of a Mariah Carey song. I want to start belting out the lyrics, but I bite my tongue. It's too early in the evening for a choreographed performance. I need everyone to be significantly less sober. Not that I'm shy, or anything. But for the sake of my co-workers, my dramatic rendition of *Christmas (Baby Please Come Home)* must be viewed with vodka-colored glasses. They would thank me later.

"Olivia, you've put together such a lovely evening." Ana Loveridge-Herrera is standing next to me and she's glowing like a Christmas tree that's fitted with thousands of tiny, bright white lights. If I hadn't walked into the bathroom at the same time her pregnancy test returned a faint positive sign, I would assume her glow was holiday-related.

Turns out she likes Christmas a normal amount and is just hyped up on all those blissful baby pheromones.

"Thank you for humoring me," I say, replenishing a tray of peppermint hot chocolate cupcakes. "I know it's a lot, but I just really love this time of year."

"You don't need to thank me," she laughs. "It's about time someone got this office into the holiday spirit. Keep up this enthusiasm and after your internship is over, we might have ourselves a permanent holiday coordinator."

"Really?"

"Really," she says. "I'll have my assistant email you about getting involved with the winter gala. I think you deserve a spot on that team."

I wait until Ana walks away before I squeal. It's not every day that you practically get a job offer from the most *badass* publicist in New York City. She once stormed onto a set of a live morning talk show because the host asked a question they weren't supposed to. It was the most streamed video on YouTube for three months.

"Are you having a seizure? Should I call an ambulance?"

Asher blinks at me before his eyes shift into a glare. He lives in a perpetual bad mood, which I think is a shame. Life is too short to be unhappy all the time. And he's too cute for frown lines.

Also, he has a penthouse loft in SoHo and his girlfriend is a freaking Rockette. He hit the life lottery.

"Of course I'm not having a seizure," I say. "And I would hope you'd have a bit more urgency if I was."

"There's fifty other people here," he says. "I'm sure someone knows how to dial 911."

"Wow, you're definitely the person I'd want to be around during an emergency."

"Speaking of," he says as he reaches for a cupcake. He

takes a bite and puckers his face in disgust. I'm offended. "I need you to moderate a book signing tomorrow in Union Square."

"You consider that an emergency?"

"Not really, but I was tired of the small talk and it was the reason I came over here, so… be at Barnes & Noble at four o'clock. It's for Emmy Raynard. Her book is about nail polish, so it'll be a bunch of tween girls asking for makeup tips. You'll fit right in."

"I'm sorry, Asher, but I can't."

"You can't?" Now he looks offended, like I just insulted his very expensive Gucci boots or ran over his grandmother's dog.

"When I got the internship, I told HR that I couldn't do late nights on Tuesdays, Thursdays, and Fridays. They said it wouldn't be an issue."

"Of course it's an issue," he huffs and takes another bite of a peppermint hot chocolate cupcake. His face puckers again. "Because if you don't do it, then I have to do it, and I would much rather get my wisdom teeth extracted without anesthesia than moderate a book reading about nail polish."

"I'm really sorry."

"You don't sound really sorry," he says. "What could you be doing that's more important than this? Are you singing Christmas carols to homeless people in Central Park?"

"No, that's not until December 10th."

"Of course." He rolls his eyes. "I'm very upset."

"You look very upset. Especially with all that chocolate all over your mouth."

His face turns a funny shade of red as he reaches for a napkin to wipe his mouth.

I feel bad because, well, I always feel bad when I disappoint people, which is why I try very hard not to do it. But I can't skip a shift at the restaurant. I make more in tips in one night than I make here in a week. I don't have a trust fund or a wealthy great aunt to fall back on. I have rent and student loans that aren't going to pay themselves.

"Will it be over by seven?"

"I would hope so," he says. "How long can teen girls talk about makeup?"

"Hours. Days. Months, really."

"Then it'll probably go all night."

I sigh. "I can stay till seven."

I'd only be a half hour late for my shift. I could make it up after hours. Staying at the restaurant until one in the morning won't be fun, especially when I have to get up at five o'clock to make it here by eight, but I knew this wasn't going to be easy and I'm prepared to lose sleep in order to achieve my goals.

And there is a light at the end of the tunnel. Ana said that if I continue to do a good job, they'd take me on permanently. It's probably not in my best interest to blow off this book signing.

"Fine," he says. "Seven it is. I'm sure her manager can *manage* after that."

"Perfect."

I'm daydreaming about the four creme brûlée lattes I'm going to need to drink tomorrow when the Secret Santa hat comes round to me and Asher. He snarls at it like the Ebenezer Scrooge he is.

"I'm not participating," he says.

"Yes, you are," I tell him. "Your name is in there. You have to."

"I didn't put it in there."

"I did."

"That's forgery. It's illegal."

"As if I could forge your terrible penmanship," I say. "Please stop trying to ruin the spirit of this. Pick a name and then buy a twenty-five dollar present. But not a gift card! That's thoughtless and impersonal. And I think everyone deserves a little time and effort and not something that's bought ten minutes before the party at Duane Reade."

He glares at me as he shoves his hand into the Santa hat that Alba from HR is holding. When he reads the name written on the tiny piece of folded paper, his face stiffens.

"Wow, someone's gonna be *real* happy when they find out you got them."

He crumples the paper in his hand before he stomps off towards his office. I sigh and pick a name.

Eleanor McMannis.

A copywriter on a visa from Ireland.

She just became the luckiest person in the office.

Preorder Now!

ABOUT THE AUTHOR

Ashley Shepherd lives in Boston where she is a full-time French toast bagel connoisseur. When she's not writing or daydreaming about being in Disney World, she's baking (mostly cupcakes), watching TV reruns (mostly Friends), and shopping (mostly at Target). Her debut novel, The Fine Art of Losing Control, will be published on October 7, 2019.

Made in the
USA
Middletown, DE